WHERE JASMINE BLOOMS

**Center Point
Large Print**

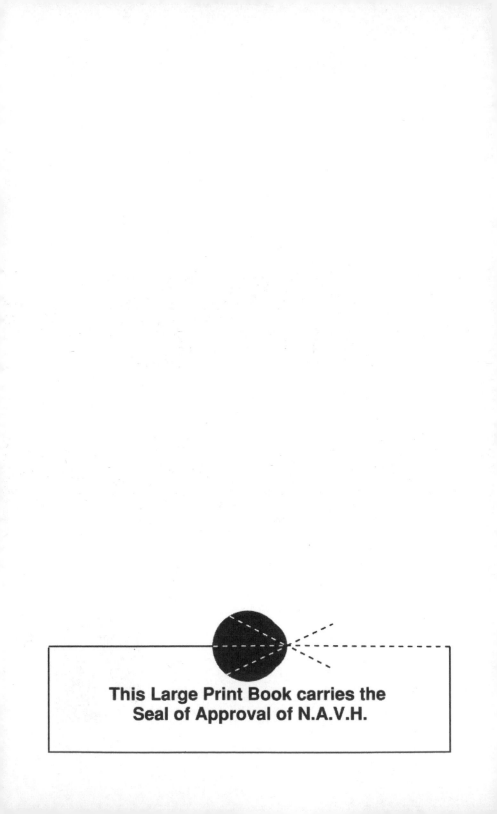

**This Large Print Book carries the
Seal of Approval of N.A.V.H.**

WHERE JASMINE BLOOMS

Holly S. Warah

CENTER POINT LARGE PRINT
THORNDIKE, MAINE

The text of this Large Print edition is unabridged.
In other aspects, this book may vary
from the original edition.
Printed in the United States of America
on permanent paper.
Set in 16-point Times New Roman type.

ISBN: 978-1-68324-411-0

Library of Congress Cataloging-in-Publication Data

Names: Warah, Holly S., author.
Title: Where Jasmine blooms / Holly S. Warah.
Description: Large print edition. | Thorndike, Maine : Center Point
Large Print, 2017.
Identifiers: LCCN 2017008792 | ISBN 9781683244110
   (hardcover : alk. paper)
Subjects: LCSH: Arab American families—Fiction. | Acculturation—
United States—Fiction. | Arab Americans—Cultural assimilation—
Fiction. | Large type books.
Classification: LCC PR9570.U543 W373 2017b | DDC 823/.92—dc23
LC record available at https://lccn.loc.gov/2017008792

To Sami

# Chapter 1

Seattle Suburbs
May 2004

The mood in Margaret's living room reminded her of when Ahmed's father died. Dressed in their good clothes, the family sat checking their watches and waiting. The only sounds came from Ahmed's mother. She was the worst, sighing and muttering under her breath, fidgeting with her prayer beads. The mother wore a white headscarf and her best *thob*, a floor-length caftan of black velvet with red cross-stitch embroidery across the front, up the sleeves, and down the sides. Her festive dress contrasted with the pained look on her face. This latest pain was triggered by Khalid, her second son, who had just announced—only three days before—his plans to marry.

What the mother considered a misfortune, however, was good news to Margaret. Finally, an ally in the family. That's what came to mind when she first heard of Khalid's plans to marry an American girl. Now as Margaret waited at the edge of the room, at the edge of the family, she imagined the conversations she and her new sister-in-law would have while the family was going on and on in Arabic. Margaret had much to tell her—survival strategies mostly.

The family had been fretting for some time about Ahmed's younger brother, Khalid. It had started three years before, when the mother first brought out those photographs. The mother, on a visit from Jordan, her white scarf pinned under her chin, sat on the couch between her sons, Ahmed and Khalid. Margaret had just served tea. Everyone was quiet and watching the steam rise from their tiny tea glasses when the mother pulled out the stack of photos. She slid closer to Khalid and described the girls one by one, pointing to the photos with her thick hands. He resisted at first, turning away to prove his disinterest. Eventually he looked more closely and even held one of the photos in his hand. This got the mother to the edge of the couch, gesturing and talking louder. "She'll finish high school next month!"

This scene repeated itself for the next three summers as the mother carried the photos, worn from too much handling, from Amman to Seattle in an old envelope tucked in the pocket of her black *thob*. The girls were cousins and neighbors, Muslim girls from good families in Jordan and the West Bank. Each year the increasingly thick deck of photos was updated and dealt anew to Khalid. It took all of Margaret's self-control not to laugh at the girls in the photos, their lavender eye shadow and humorless expressions.

But now those years of matchmaking were over,

as the mother and the family waited awkwardly in Margaret's living room to meet Khalid's bride of choice. When his car turned into the cul-de-sac, the family members rose from their places and moved to the front window, each trying to get a good look. Khalid stepped out of the car first, then walked around to the passenger side. The family held their breath in unison as he reached for the handle and opened the door. Out she stepped, revealing a spiky heel and boot-cut slacks. Then she appeared, her total form, blond and American.

That morning had begun with a phone call to Liz. From her bedroom armchair, Margaret gave her friend an account of the latest developments.

"So, how's your mother-in-law taking it?" Liz asked.

"She's been sitting around with her arms crossed, staring at nothing."

"Doesn't she do that anyway?"

"Yeah." It was true, especially since Ahmed's father had died four months before.

"What do you know about this girl?"

"Not much," Margaret said. "Just that she's American with some Arab blood."

"I wonder if she knows what she's getting into."

"Did either of us?" Margaret sighed and ran a hand through her long red hair. As Liz chattered on, Margaret realized she had been married to

Ahmed for nearly half her life. Had it been that long? Their teenage daughter Jenin's developing body—not to mention her developing political views—told her yes, it had.

Margaret noticed the time. "I've got to go. We've still got to cook."

In the calm before their guests arrived, Margaret and Ahmed prepared the meal side by side. Being in the restaurant business meant that Ahmed treated the meal as a small catering event. He stood at the stove, frying cauliflower, the white florets bobbing in the hot oil. She stood next to him chopping cucumbers. They smiled and brushed against each other, and, for a moment, it was like old times.

Three-year-old Leena streaked into the kitchen, half-naked. Her older brother Tariq raced in behind her, reaching for her bare shoulder.

"Kids, *shway shway*," Ahmed said. "Take it easy."

Margaret turned to Tariq. "Stop chasing Leena." Their son had his father's dark curly hair and brown eyes. In fact, all three of their children had Ahmed's splendid eyes and lush eyelashes.

She knelt down next to Leena and brushed a curl off the face of her youngest child. "Where's your shirt, sweetheart? Go find something to wear." Margaret guided both children out of the kitchen, then returned to her chopping.

"It'll be nice to have a new sister-in-law," she

told Ahmed as she slid the tiny cucumber cubes into the bowl of yogurt. "Khalid will finally be responsible for someone."

A look of agreement came into Ahmed's eyes. Then a question occurred to Margaret; she knew better than to bring it up, but she couldn't help herself.

"Who's gonna pay for the wedding?" She began to chop more vigorously.

Ahmed's tone shifted. "Can we talk about this later?"

"I need to know if we have to use Jenin's college savings."

Confusion filled Ahmed's face. "We don't have any college savings."

"Exactly!" Margaret gestured with the knife.

"I don't know what Khalid's planning. Maybe he has some money."

"Oh, sure." Margaret rolled her eyes. She stirred the yogurt salad and inhaled the mint. "I hope she's not expecting a pile of gold jewelry."

Margaret stopped talking when the mother walked in, a deep frown drawing across her face. She was a small woman but had a full-size presence, her short height balanced by her ample middle. Her black velvet *thob* skimmed the floor, and her white headscarf fell past her shoulders.

She released a burst of Arabic. Ahmed and Margaret turned to listen, although Margaret only caught a few words. The mother shook her head mournfully from side to side, uttering the word *amrikia*. When finished, she stood with her arms crossed, lips pressed together. Ahmed patted her shoulder and led her to the living room couch. He spoke a few words, reached for her prayer beads, and pressed them into her hand.

When they were alone again in the kitchen, Margaret asked him, "What now?"

He hesitated. "She said her two worst nightmares came true this year." He spoke in low tones, even though his mother couldn't understand English. "Her husband died and her other son decided to marry an American."

The meaning behind the words struck Margaret. "You shouldn't have translated that."

Ahmed gestured for her to keep her voice down.

"Is it such a nightmare to have another American in the family?" She stared at him. "Have I been such a nightmare?"

"Honey, it's not about you." Ahmed turned back to the large pot he was layering with chicken and fried cauliflower. "She wanted Khalid to marry a girl from the family. He chose someone unknown, who's not Muslim, not Palestinian." He measured out some rice in a drinking glass. "He didn't even ask her permission. He just told her." Ahmed looked at Margaret. "Just try to under-stand her."

"I understand. I really do." Margaret attempted a casual tone. "Well, I want you to know one of *my* nightmares came true this year."

Ahmed's face clouded. "Don't say it."

Suddenly sorry, Margaret wished she hadn't brought up this problem—a problem sitting in the living room with no sign of leaving. "Fine," she said flatly. "I won't."

The *maqluba* simmered on the stove; the *kufta* meatballs were in the oven, bubbling in their juices.

Ahmed's voice came from the living room. "My sister's here."

These were not the guests Margaret was waiting for. Still, she went to the window. Mona was marching up the driveway, past the jasmine plant, followed by her husband and four sons. As always, Mona's headscarf coordinated with her handbag and heels, this time the same shade of deep red.

With the usual commotion, Mona and her family entered the front door, which—like all other split-level homes in the cul-de-sac—opened to two sets of stairs, one going up and the other going down. They kicked off their shoes in the tiny entry and came up the stairs single file. Mona gave Margaret a firm handshake and an authoritative kiss on each cheek.

Margaret couldn't follow the Arabic murmurs

in the living room, but she could feel the tension. The mother held her lips in a tight line. Mona sat next to her, patting her leg, trying to soothe her. Someone turned on the television, and muted scenes of US soldiers in Iraq popped up on the screen, which transfixed the family. Or were they Israeli soldiers in the West Bank? In Margaret's mind, the invasions and occupations in the Middle East ran into one another—one tangled mess.

Next, Ahmed's cousins appeared, Ibrahim and Salim, both tall and slim. They were community college students who dressed in black and smelled of cigarettes. They installed themselves in the living room, now filled with family members waiting in uneasy silence.

At last, Khalid and his girlfriend arrived. When they entered the front door, Margaret tried to get a closer look at the girl, but the family crowded tightly and formed a bottleneck of traffic at the stairs. It was a poor house design—thoughtless really.

Khalid entered the living room first. He was like a younger version of Ahmed, but leaner and, Margaret had to admit, slightly more attractive. He was carefully groomed, clean-shaven, and sleek, almost smug.

Margaret smiled at him. "You're on time."

"It's Alison—she doesn't like to be late." He said this as she entered the room. The family parted, and everyone stared at her without speaking. Her slim body, smooth hairstyle, and trendy clothing could be summed up in one word: *young*.

Khalid began the introductions. Mona, who had worked her way to the front, stuck her hand out. Alison flawlessly performed the classic exchange: handshake, three kisses, and formal greetings in Arabic.

He moved around the circle of family. "And this is Ahmed."

Alison gave him a kiss on each cheek. "You're good-looking like your brother."

Margaret glanced away. She would have some things to explain to Alison. *Rule number one: in this family, you kiss the women on the cheek. Not the men.*

Khalid led his fiancée over to his cousins. "You already know these guys." Alison tilted her head and smiled. Was she flirting with them?

Next it was Margaret's turn. Renewed optimism fluttered up as her eyes swept over Alison's youthful skin and uniform teeth. "Great to meet you," Margaret said.

"Nice to meet you," Alison replied, adding nothing more.

Next, Khalid came to his mother. "*Yama,*" he said, "this is Alison."

Alison extended her hand, and the mother leaned forward to kiss her in the Arab manner. As the family stood gaping, Alison looked into the mother's eyes and said something in Arabic, something rehearsed. Despite her accent, she appeared versed in the basics of Arabic *salaams*. The mother nodded and seemed to understand. Margaret wondered if Khalid had prepared Alison or if she had arrived with this know-how.

The family arranged themselves back in the living room, where Alison replaced the television as the object of their attention. The mother's eyes roved over her, from the tip of Alison's pointy shoes all the way to her layered blond hair and back down again.

Khalid, his arm around Alison, explained how they had met. It was in a coffee shop near the university, where he'd noticed her studying Arabic. "What a surprise to see this girl with an Arabic textbook." He gave Alison a squeeze, and her face glowed with affection.

As Khalid spoke, Ahmed translated his brother's words to their mother, who looked pale and stricken.

"And guess what?" Khalid said. "She's Arab— from Syria!"

At this, the room pulled back in disbelief— except for the mother, who turned to Ahmed for further translation.

"Well, not *me,*" Alison said. "My grandparents. I've never been to Syria."

"And not only that." Khalid paused until he had

everyone's complete attention. "Her grandfather was Muslim." He nodded slowly while the room took this in.

"It's true," she said, her chin held high. "And the rest of my family is Greek Orthodox."

Margaret met Alison's eyes, and she nodded in a way she hoped would convey an easy acceptance because Margaret knew that no matter what traces were in this girl's background, what ancestral branch she claimed, whatever Arabic greetings she mastered—it would never be enough.

But then Alison revealed more: her father's parents had arrived in Chicago from Syria in the 1940s. Her mother's side went further back, with relatives fleeing Syria in the late 1920s. Alison's parents didn't speak Arabic—only a few phrases—but they could understand.

Margaret excused herself and went to the kitchen to get the meal on the table. Right behind her came Mona, her heels clicking sharply. She poked around like a restaurant inspector. Steam rose when she lifted the lid to a pot on the stove. She arched an eyebrow. "Just *maqluba* and *kufta*? I would have made—"

"We did some side dishes, too." Margaret had a flash of relief that soon Mona would have another sister-in-law to pick on.

Mona tapped her wristwatch. "What about *asr*? We need to pray *asr*."

The afternoon prayer. Margaret had forgotten. "Of course."

She left the food and went to gather the prayer carpets. *Damn.* Why hadn't she thought of this? She searched her bedroom for the carpets and her prayer covering.

In her bathroom, she turned on the faucet and began her *wudu*, the ritual cleansing before the prayer. To herself she whispered, *"Bismillah." In the name of God.* She washed each hand, rinsed her mouth, and splashed water on her face—each action performed three times. Over her clothes, she pulled on her long white prayer skirt and smoothed out its wrinkles. She slid the matching scarf over her red hair as she had done countless times. Checking herself in the mirror, she leaned toward her reflection. The deepening lines around her eyes stood out more than ever. *Damn again.*

By the time she returned to the living room, the men had pushed back the furniture to make room for the prayer. Alison was lounging on the couch, smiling as if she were about to witness something entertaining. Margaret handed the carpets to Salim, who positioned them across the floor. The men and boys lined up shoulder to shoulder, and behind them, the women did the same. The family waited until the mother emerged from the hall-way bathroom and took her place in line, water still dripping from her chin.

Ahmed led the prayer. He raised his hands to the sides of his head. *"Allahu Akbar."* *God is great.* Margaret closed her eyes. She tried to focus on the meaning behind the words. She tried to feel submission toward God, but all she felt were Alison's eyes on her as she moved through her prostrations.

When the prayer was complete, Margaret scrambled up, snatched off her prayer covering, and gathered up the prayer carpets. In the kitchen, Ahmed was already drizzling olive oil over the side dishes. He placed a perfect sprig of mint on the yogurt salad. She knew he couldn't be rushed as he carved a small rosette out of a cucumber as the final garnish for the *babaganouj.* Together, they flipped over the big pot of *maqluba* onto their largest platter. They fluffed the rice and arranged the chicken. Ahmed sprinkled roasted pine nuts over the steaming mound and a dash of chopped fresh parsley. For him, taste and appearance were one and the same.

The dining room was not designed for a sprawling Arab family. Ibrahim and Salim would eat in the living room and Mona's older boys at the breakfast bar while the rest would squeeze in at the table, where the platter of *maqluba* sat heavily in the center. As soon as the side dishes were placed down, the sixteen family members stood around the table in a frenzy of self-service.

Margaret nudged her way in and filled a plate for Leena and another for the mother, who looked up when presented with it.

"God bless your hands," she said.

"And your hands, too," Margaret answered in Arabic.

She was the last to sit down. She surveyed the table: Ahmed sat at the head next to his mother, who was still frowning. Jenin was wearing her "I love Jerusalem" T-shirt. Khalid and Alison were glued together like Siamese twins. Mona was unusually quiet, perhaps giving Alison a grace period.

Margaret took another look at Alison. She was complimenting the food while Khalid relished his role as cultural ambassador. "This is *maqluba*," he said. "It means 'upside down' in Arabic." He gestured flipping a pot upside down.

"Yes, I know, babe," she said. "My grandmother used to make it, too."

Margaret was about to ask about Syrian cuisine, but Alison opened a topic of her own.

"Another assassination in Gaza. Can you believe it?"

The table gave a collective groan of disgust over the news.

Jenin gasped. "No way. Not again?"

Ahmed translated to his mother, who said, "Curse their fathers."

"Oh really?" Margaret asked. "Another one?"

"A missile dropped on a car," Alison said. "Three deaths. You didn't hear about it?"

"Well," Margaret said. "I didn't have time to read the paper today."

"It was yesterday. You don't follow Middle East news?"

"I try to. It's just with three kids . . ." Margaret wanted to explain that she didn't need to follow the daily news to know what was going on. Her life was colored by what was going on. Margaret couldn't follow the news from Palestine without the images invading her thoughts. Children getting shot, houses demolished, suicide bombers. She felt helpless about the occupation, and Ahmed worried about his sisters in the refugee camps. Even fifteen-year-old Jenin was obsessed, fixated on Israeli human rights violations and illegal settlements.

"We need to know what's happening," Alison said, "if we want to do something."

Margaret's chest tightened. "It looks like Khalid's gotten you involved in politics."

"Oh, it's not Khalid. I'm getting a bachelor's in Near Eastern studies at UW."

Margaret swallowed the bite in her mouth. "Khalid didn't tell us."

"Really?" Alison nudged Khalid, who was engrossed in his chicken leg.

"So, I guess that makes you a Middle East

expert." Margaret stopped herself there, already saying too much.

"A person would really need their master's degree to be a true expert." Alison spoke in an affected manner—or perhaps it was her natural way of speaking. "I plan to get my master's, though. I'm graduating this spring with Khalid."

Margaret looked at him, eyes widened. "You're graduating?" How many times had she heard this before? He had been expected to graduate the year before. And the year before that.

"*Inshallah*," he said. *God willing*.

The meal ended and the family retired to the living room, leaving behind a disarray of dirty plates and chicken bones. Rather than following the conversation into the other room, Margaret began the tedious duties of cleanup. Fortunately, Mona was by her side, taking brisk charge of scraping food off plates.

Voices came from the other room. They were discussing when Khalid and Alison were getting married. Margaret hurried to the living room, her apron still on.

"Did I hear right?" she asked, looking at the couple on the couch—Alison's arm around Khalid in a gesture of ownership. "Are you getting married tomorrow?"

Alison smiled broadly. "Khalid made an appointment at the mosque."

Margaret pictured the large mosque, the one

Ahmed and Tariq attended for Friday prayers, the one where she had taken her first *Qur'an* class.

"*Mabruuk.* Congratulations," she said to Alison. To herself, she thought, *God help her*.

The kitchen was finally in order, the dishwasher making its gentle sounds. Margaret took out her aluminum teapot, added five spoonfuls of sugar, fresh mint leaves, and three tea bags. In the living room, she offered tea to Alison first. All eyes were on Alison, waiting for her to take the tea.

"No, thanks. I'm not a tea drinker."

The brass tray felt heavy in Margaret's hands. She lowered her voice and said to Alison, "You should take it anyway."

"I'm fine," Alison replied. Then recognition passed into her eyes. "Yes, of course," she said and reached for a glass.

Margaret served everyone else, then took a tea for herself. She stared at the empty tray. It seemed Alison didn't understand the significance of accepting tea at this time—when meeting the family for the first time. Didn't she know any-thing of Arab culture? This was so basic.

Margaret excused herself from the gathering, which was winding down, and gestured for Alison to follow her into the kitchen, where the two sat at the breakfast bar. "Seeing you and Khalid reminds me of when Ahmed and I met."

Margaret tilted her head and sighed. "We're having our twentieth anniversary soon."

"Wow!" Alison looked stunned. "How old were you when you got married?"

"Twenty-one."

"So young."

"How old are you?"

"Twenty-three."

"I see." Margaret took a sip of tea. "You know, we also met while studying at the U."

"Just like us," Alison said. "What was your major?"

"Anthropology, but I didn't finish."

Again, Alison had that stunned look. "Why not?"

"We got married." Margaret swirled the tea in her glass. "Ahmed graduated. I stopped studying just before we opened the first restaurant. I always thought I'd go back. Then I had Jenin, then Tariq, then Leena."

Alison shook her head. "That's so sad."

"Not that sad." Margaret crossed her arms. "What would I have done with a degree in anthropology?"

Ahmed called from the living room, "Can you start the coffee?"

Margaret slid down from her stool and gathered the coffee paraphernalia.

"So, you speak Arabic?" Alison asked from across the counter.

"I get by." Actually, Margaret knew more of the language than she let on. It was easier that way, checking in and out of the conversation as she pleased.

"I should be fluent by the time I've been married twenty years."

Margaret considered mentioning how tricky Arabic was with its various dialects and impossible pronunciation. Actually, she hadn't lost interest in improving her Arabic. The truth was, she'd lost interest in what the family was saying.

Margaret stirred the Turkish coffee pot on the stove, and the smell of cardamom filled the kitchen. She wondered if Alison knew coffee was the last thing served and a sign for guests to leave. Margaret handed a cup to Alison.

"No thanks," Alison said.

Margaret set the cup down and looked at Alison. "This is a coffee-and-tea drinking family. You might as well get used to it."

Alison explained she only drank decaf cappuccinos.

Margaret wondered how this girl would fit into this caffeine-addicted family. She went to the living room to serve the final round.

When Margaret returned, Alison asked, "Can you do me a favor? I need to borrow a scarf. I need to wear one at the mosque."

"Sure, I got a closet full of 'em. Come with me."

When they entered the bedroom, Margaret noticed Alison's eyes fall on her sitting corner, furnished with an armchair, television, small table, and lamp. As they passed the space, Margaret stroked her big tabby cat, asleep on the chair. "This is where I escape from the kids." The half-truth slid easily out of her mouth. Well, it *was* a place of escape; that part was true.

Margaret went to her closet and brought out a mountain of colors, textures, and patterns.

Alison's mouth fell open. "Why do you have so many scarves?"

Margaret gazed down at the memories spilled across the bed. "I used to wear *hijab*, then I stopped." The thought of covering her head with a scarf prompted Margaret to touch her hair. She had covered her long thick red hair for more than a decade, but during those last few years, her attitude toward hijab had gradually changed until finally she'd tormented herself over what to do. Drop it or trudge on?

"Why did you stop?"

Margaret gave her standard explanation. "After 9/11, I didn't feel safe wearing *hijab*. I just felt too visible and exposed." She studied Alison's face, and like most people, Alison seemed to accept this answer. This wasn't the true story. Margaret could pinpoint the exact moment she had decided to give it up.

It had been the year before. She had been

shopping with Jenin in a department store crowded with mirrors and mannequins. In a side mirror, Margaret had caught a glimpse of a middle-aged Muslim woman in a familiar dark-colored scarf, hunched over a clothing rack. Margaret turned to the older woman, but she was gone. Nowhere to be seen.

Margaret had turned again, momentarily disoriented, and then saw her own reflection. It had been a glimpse of herself that she had seen—not someone else. Herself. Prematurely aged in her navy blue scarf, pinned under her chin. Barely forty and already looking old.

Alison picked up a scarf. "I think a white one would be good."

"You can keep it." For a moment Margaret considered showing her how to fold and pin it and the various hijab-wearing styles, but decided to let the Middle East expert figure it out on her own.

❧ Chapter 2 ❧

Alison started the day skimming the *Seattle Times* world news and opinion pages, her cappuccino and yellow highlighter by her side. There was a brief article about an Israeli threat on Yasser Arafat's life, which Israel denied and Arafat had brushed off. Typical. She didn't linger over this article; it was old news. However, she did find an intriguing editorial piece. George Bush's "Roadmap to Peace," it argued, favored Israel and would jeopardize the Palestinian right of return.

As she sat at her tiny breakfast nook and took in the key points from the article, Alison was distracted by the white scarf across the room. The scarf made her think of Margaret. Images of her sister-in-law-to-be in that outdated kitchen—her red hair and apron—filled Alison's head as she tried to concentrate on the issue of the Palestinian right of return, one of her pet topics. Her mind drifted to where her life would be when she was as old as Margaret. Alison would be well established in her career by then; maybe she and Khalid would be living overseas. A dead-end street in the suburbs? She'd rather die.

The scarf sat folded neatly on the bookcase, which displayed evidence of her studies: textbooks on Islamic civilization, Arabic literature in translation, and books on Islamic architecture, colonialism, and Middle Eastern film. Another shelf held her three years of Arabic language study: textbooks, grammar guides, and her *Hans Wehr* dictionary.

The white scarf taunted Alison, reminding her she still needed to figure out what to wear. Of course, exchanging vows at the mosque wouldn't be their true wedding—that would come later—

but rather a request to fulfill, a showing of love that would please Khalid. It would be a field trip of sorts, getting married there.

The clothing decision was difficult: dressy yet modest. Alison laid out the choices on her bed. Her favorite dress was made of clingy fabric with slits up the sides. Out of the question. She settled on a light-gray suit, fitted and flattering, but the pants were wide and the jacket long. The modesty requirement was crucial. She didn't want to be kicked out of the mosque on her first visit.

Now she was ready to confront the scarf. She had hoped to wear it draped gently around her face in the style of Queen Noor, but it wasn't the right scarf for that look. Her new plan was to pin it on her head when she arrived at the mosque. Standing at her bathroom sink, Alison did a test run. She struggled with the safety pin and rebellious hairs popping out. She repeatedly shoved hair under the scarf, sliding the thing back and forth, seeking the best placement. By the time she got it in place, she had started to perspire and felt the onset of unexpected tears. All at once, Alison was filled with a longing—a yearning to see her Teytey Miriam, her late grandmother, and ask her for guidance.

Nearly all of what Alison knew of her Syrian background she had learned from her two grand-mothers, Teytey Miriam and Grandma Helen, both from Damascus, both immigrants to Chicago.

Grandma Helen, her mother's mother, was Alison's only surviving grandparent—still alive and living on Chicago's northwest side, still attending her Orthodox church in Oak Park and maintaining her identity as a doctor's wife.

But it was her Teytey Miriam, her father's mother, whom Alison longed to see. A Greek Orthodox woman who had married a Muslim man, Teytey Miriam had been disowned by nearly all her family.

Foremost in Alison's memories were their trips to the Middle Eastern grocery store off Michigan Avenue—the two of them admiring the imported items and their labels, and Teytey Miriam chat-ting with the shopkeeper in Arabic. The spoils of these excursions would be spread out on Teytey Miriam's kitchen table—bottles of rose water and pomegranate molasses, jars of tahini and grape leaves, bags of Turkish coffee, *zataar*, and sumac, as well as trays of spinach pies and shortbread cookies.

Now, three years after her death, Alison fell back onto her memories of Teytey Miriam. Details that had once seemed merely quaint now played in Alison's mind as clues that might help bring her own choices into focus, like how to slip on and off a Muslim scarf—surely her Teytey Miriam would have known this. And how to finally tell her parents about Khalid. Teytey Miriam could have helped there, too.

A recent email from her mother flashed through Alison's mind. It was the usual anti-Islam slander, something about Muslim extremism and the niqab —her mother's attempt to inform and correct. There was no use explaining things; her mother's views ran long and deep.

While Alison's father described himself as "Arabian"—which always made Alison think of horses—her mother never admitted to understanding Arabic, nor referred to herself as Arab, preferring instead "Mediterranean ancestry" or "Greek Orthodox" to explain her background.

Staring at her reflection, Alison tucked the last strand of hair inside the scarf and realized she would just have to wear the thing to the mosque. In her tiny living room, she sat on the couch, making sure not to disturb her throw pillows. She touched the scarf on her head and waited for Khalid.

It wasn't a long car ride from Alison's Capitol Hill apartment to the mosque on the north end. With its minaret and dome, the mosque was a unique sight in the city. As a student, Alison had toured mosques in Jerusalem and Cairo, but none in the States—and never as a bride.

The steady spring rain had slowed to a drizzle, and the view from I-5 was gray. Alison looked at Khalid's hand on the steering wheel and admired his profile. He turned to her with his brown eyes, long-lashed and brilliant. He put a hand on her thigh. She laced her fingers through his and told herself how lucky she was, how happy she would be.

The whole thing was moving on fast-forward. But in reality, it was last fall when Alison first noticed Khalid. He was sitting in a coffee shop near campus with a group of friends squeezed around a table. They'd laughed loudly and spoken in a mix of Arabic and English. Of the five, it was Khalid who caught her eye. Not only was he the most handsome—his dark curly hair falling over his forehead, his face begging to be looked at—but he had an aura about him, which drew his friends in and held their attention.

She saw him there again and again, her heart rate speeding up each time. She would sip her cappuccino while keeping one eye on her Arabic homework and the other on him. He drank Americanos and was always with his friends, two of whom she later learned were cousins. Alison caught his gaze several times and bits of their conversation—mostly exchanges on events in Palestine. After a month of observing him, Alison had arranged her textbook in a way for him to notice it as he passed by.

The bait had worked. He glanced down at her books and then up at her. "Do you know Arabic?" Those were his first words to her.

"I'm studying it." She tilted her head and took

in his presence: his steady eye contact, parted lips, and his cologne, which hung in the air and mixed with the scent of coffee beans.

He raised an eyebrow. "Say something in Arabic."

"*Ana ahib al lughat al arabia.*" *I love the Arabic language*. She flashed a smile.

"Can I sit?' he asked, gesturing to the empty chair. He didn't wait for an answer but placed himself across from her. With a sense of ease, he leaned toward her. "So, why Arabic?"

When she told him her major, he nodded with approval. He didn't ask why she had chosen Near Eastern studies, a question posed by nearly everyone.

After that, she'd trekked to the coffee shop daily, her palms always sweaty, her breath caught in her throat. He approached her again and again and flirted in the same breezy manner, his demeanor suggesting adventure and mystery. For weeks she could hardly focus on anything else, her mind continually turning back to him. He was an IT student, a green card holder, and a senior ready to graduate. Soon he was helping her with Arabic and teaching phrases from his dialect.

It wasn't just his looks—although he certainly was gorgeous. In the end, it was their long talks that had captivated her, the way he considered her views, listening as though her opinions mattered. He followed her every word with his attentive eyes. No one had ever listened to her like that. Their discussions began with Palestine and went to other places: Syria, Lebanon, Iraq, Egypt—and back to Palestine. Everything came back to Palestine. Their favorite talking point was the plight of Palestinian refugees. Khalid outlined all his family had endured since 1948, captivating her with their history: a story of land lost, a refugee camp, another war, and continued displacement. She was moved by this and even more by the fact that he, after spending the night for the first time, told her that he loved her.

Love? she had wondered.

Weeks later at the coffee shop, during a discussion on the assimilation of Arab-Americans, Khalid had speculated on the motives of Alison's own grandparents—their desire to pass as white —a motivation even she had failed to see. She smiled at his insight, rested her chin on one hand and regarded him: the perfectness of his face, the intensity of his eyes, the single curl that had fallen down onto his forehead.

And Alison realized: *Yes, love.*

It wasn't long before he mentioned marriage— not as part of a romantic proposal the way a girl would expect, but rather as an inevitable progression of their relationship: sex, then love, then marriage. "Why don't we just get married?" he had asked.

Out of all the smart and beautiful girls on

campus, he had picked her. She gazed at him driving for another moment, then turned toward the window. She was startled by her reflection— her head covered in the scarf. She had forgotten she was masquerading as a Muslim woman. A pang of concern rose up: what if someone she knew saw her? What would her American classmates say? The unspoken attitude in her circle was that you studied Islam and Muslims, you didn't *become* them.

Before Khalid, her social life had revolved around those friends. But from the day Alison started seeing him, she'd began to drift away, meeting only occasionally to discuss assignments and the war in Iraq. Who had time to socialize? Dating Khalid was all-consuming. He gave her purpose and energy, bringing to life everything she was studying. She cultivated new insider views, and her world immediately expanded. Before him, she had moved in a tiny orbit, attending only to the motions of study, work, and home.

She glanced at the traffic on the freeway. It was a Sunday morning, not many cars on the road. No one would recognize her in hijab—she barely recognized herself.

"You told your parents, didn't you?" Khalid asked.

"Don't worry, babe."

"So, you told them?"

"Like I'm gonna ruin our wedding day."

"You said you were going to call them."

"I wanted to call them, I really did." Of course, Alison was simply delaying the inevitable. No amount of justifying could change the facts about Khalid: the wrong faith, the wrong class, the wrong background. A Palestinian refugee, and Muslim, too.

"Now they'll be upset for sure," he said. "I should've called them myself."

"That's all I need—my mother freaking out." Alison's head felt pinched by the scarf.

He looked at her sideways. "Your parents, they'll never respect me."

"I can't tell them over the phone anyway." She tried to sound positive. "It's better if they meet you in person. When they come out from Chicago, we'll tell them. Besides, for my parents, it's the big wedding that counts."

Khalid drove on without speaking, his jaw set.

Were they arguing? They rarely argued, not even about politics. She caressed his hand, but he remained quiet.

As the scenery changed from the boats on Lake Union to the urban sprawl of north Seattle, Alison began picturing herself walking into the mosque, passing through the elaborate entrance. "So, you made an appointment?"

"Yeah, I saw the *imam* and gave him the papers." Khalid took the exit off the freeway. "And I invited my cousins."

She blinked. "Ibrahim and Salim?"

"We need witnesses. Two male witnesses."

"Why those two?" She imagined them making fun of her scarf. "You should've told me."

"I'm telling you now," Khalid said as he pulled into the parking lot. "We need to wait for them."

Alison stared out the car window and up the brick building, its dome and minaret rising into the gray sky. How horrified her mother would be if she knew her youngest child was getting married in a mosque. Alison's older sisters had married men named Alex and Stephen and had obediently declared their wedding vows in their mother's church.

Alison flipped down the sun visor and looked in the small mirror. The scarf made her face appear angular and gaunt.

Khalid stroked her arm. "You get to see the mosque." Then he looked at her more closely. "Your face is white."

"It's the scarf. Makes me look washed out."

"You look beautiful."

Alison touched the scarf. "Please don't get used to it." She heard voices from outside and turned to see Ibrahim and Salim walking toward them, putting out cigarettes. Khalid got out of the car first, and the men exchanged their Arabic hellos. At last, she stepped into the wet parking lot, and Ibrahim greeted her.

"Today, it's your big day."

She braced for one of them to make a joke about her scarf, but they didn't.

As the group moved toward the mosque, Khalid pointed to a side door. "You go in that entrance."

Alison stopped and stared at the plain white door, dirty with scuff marks. The women's entrance. *Of course.* "How will I know where to go?"

"Don't worry." He put a hand on the small of her back. "I can't get married without you." His touch was warm and reassuring. Then he pulled away, smiled, and waved. With his cousins, he disappeared around the corner without looking back.

Alone in the parking lot, she paused. The men would be opening the heavy doors of the main entrance and strolling under the calligraphy inscription. Feeling a slight wave of nausea, she reached for the doorknob. Inside, cheap plastic sandals were scattered about. She removed her strappy high heels and slipped them into the low shelves. To her right was a stairwell, where Khalid stood at the top.

She went up to him and followed him down a hallway and into a room lined with books. A man sitting at the table stood and nodded to Khalid. "*As-salaam alaikum.*" *Peace be upon you.* To Alison, he said, "I'm Daud, an *imam* for this *masjid.*" He wore a button-down shirt and little wire frame glasses, his beard closely trimmed.

Alison extended her hand. He made a slight bow and touched his chest.

"He doesn't shake women's hands," Khalid whispered.

"I just forgot," she whispered back.

The imam sat and gestured for them to sit across from him. Ibrahim and Salim were already sitting off to the side. Beside them, a gray-haired man sat clutching a string of prayer beads.

"This is Mr. Barakat, an extra witness for today," the imam said.

Alison nodded to the man; then her gaze turned to the papers on the table. She recognized their marriage license and the application she had hastily signed the week before.

The imam looked up. "So, you're not Muslim?"

"I'm not." She crossed and uncrossed her arms.

"I see that you're Christian," he said, reading off the form.

Alison's face grew warm. "I was raised Greek Orthodox." What else could she say? The truth was the last time she had stepped into the church was for her sister's wedding. Her sharpest memories of church were the corrections dished out by her Grandma Helen: *Sit still. Be quiet.* To this day, whenever Grandma Helen was around, Alison held her breath, waiting for a scolding.

Khalid leaned in. "Actually, her grandfather was Muslim."

"*Masha'Allah*," the imam replied. *What God wills*. He looked at Alison.

"My father's father," she said, growing more flushed, though this fact that Khalid celebrated was a detail that no one in her family spoke of. Her grandfather, who had arrived from Syria to Chicago in 1945, changed his first name from Issam to Sam, and his last name from Thayer to Taylor. He'd married a Christian woman and hardly practiced Islam at all. It wasn't until he was elderly, Alison still in grade school, that proof of his faith had surfaced. It appeared on his bedside table: a *Qur'an*, its sheer pages lined with Arabic script—so alien and mysterious. Just like her grandfather.

"Have you had any premarital counseling?" The imam spoke with an American accent.

"Do we need it?" Khalid asked.

"It's not required," the imam said. "Though I'd like you to know what you're getting into."

Alison had a good idea. She had studied the language, culture, history, and religion. Between her studies and her family background, she knew more than most American girls marrying Muslim guys—that was for sure. Then she noticed the imam tilt his head and gaze at Khalid like a concerned parent. It was Khalid, not her, the imam was worried about.

"How long have you known each other?" the imam asked.

"Almost a year," Alison said. "We met at the U, actually, at a coffee shop."

The imam held up his hand, signaling that it was not part of his job to hear these details. He looked at her. "Do you plan to work?"

"After I get my bachelor's degree, I'd also like to get my master's. I'll work after that." She felt her tension dissolve as she talked about her plans.

"You two have discussed this?" The imam looked at Khalid.

"It's okay with me."

"What about children?" The imam glanced down at his notes and back up again.

"*Inshallah*," Khalid answered.

"If you have children, who'll take care of them when she's working?"

"She will," Khalid said.

The imam turned to Alison.

"It's hard to say." She shifted in her seat.

At this, Khalid shot her a look.

"It's kinda far off," she said. "God only knows, right?" They couldn't argue with that.

"But what are your intentions?" the imam asked pointedly.

Alison kept her gaze away from Khalid; she could already imagine the look of irritation on his face. She became aware of the imam tapping his pen and the perspiration on her upper lip.

"Do you intend to take care of your children?" the imam repeated.

41

"Yes . . . *Inshallah*," she mumbled.

"Would you like to make *shahadda* today?" He peered over his wire frame glasses. "That is, do you wish to declare your faith in Islam?"

Alison shook her head. "No."

The imam took off his glasses to look at her. "There is no compulsion in religion, but I do encourage you to seek knowledge." He shuffled his papers. "We're ready to start."

Alison took a deep breath and tried to focus. Her heart pounded and sweat spread below her clothing. The imam continued with questions about their names and dates of birth. Her eyes darted around the room from Khalid, to the prayer beads in Mr. Barakat's hand, to the bookshelves lining the walls. Her eyes passed over the shelves, which held a jumble of books and row after row of the *Qur'an*.

Once Alison had suggested buying a *Qur'an* for Khalid's mother as a gift. They were in the Pakistani shop that sold a mix of *halal* foods and Muslim clothing. Amongst a pile of Islamic literature, Alison had found a small gold-trimmed *Qur'an*. She asked Khalid if his mother would like it. Without glancing up, he said, "She can't read." He said this as though it were a normal thing, the way one might say: *She can't cook.*

The imam continued with his questions. "And who will be the bride's *wakeel*? Her representative?"

"He will." Khalid pointed to Ibrahim, and anxiety fluttered inside Alison.

Pen poised to write, the imam asked, "May I have your name please?"

As Ibrahim spelled his name, Alison stared at the gangly young man. He was younger than she and not as smart. She knew this from their discussions at the coffee shop.

The imam glanced at Alison. "Do you accept this man as your *wakeel*?"

"Yes," she said. What else could she do?

The imam peered at her. "Has someone explained your marriage rights?"

She had studied this in her Human Rights in Islam course. But when she tried to think of what she knew, all that came to mind were vague, theoretical notions. Alison cleared her throat. "Could you tell me?"

"You have the right to *mahr*, money paid by the husband to the wife at the time of marriage. You have the right to a marriage contract, in which you can outline your own conditions. Do you have a marriage contract?"

"Do I need one?" Her head swelled with regrets. Why hadn't she thought of this? She had allowed herself to be swept up into these Muslim vows without any preparation at all.

"It's a personal choice. Some women have conditions."

Alison nodded. The conditions were protection

for needy women. She lifted her chin. She didn't need that type of security.

"About the *mahr*, what have you agreed on?"

Everyone turned to Khalid, who said, "I was thinking of . . . I don't know if this is okay. I wrote . . ."

Alison held her breath. She felt suffocated by the scarf and wanted to speak up. She didn't need any money. She wasn't Muslim, and this wasn't her custom.

"I wrote one dollar," Khalid said.

A trickle of sweat rolled down Alison's back.

"Is that what you two agreed on?" the imam asked.

"We haven't talked about it," Khalid said.

The imam switched his gaze to Ibrahim.

"It's fine with me," Ibrahim said. Alison stared at him, her mouth agape.

The imam looked at her. "Are you okay with that amount?"

She thought for a moment and reminded herself this wasn't her practice. "It's fine." She shrugged. Everyone was acting so official about a silly dollar.

"Should I give it to her now?" Khalid asked.

The imam gestured for Khalid to hand it over. He took out his wallet and opened it. Alison saw the edge of a ten and a twenty. "I don't have any ones." He looked to his cousins.

"Let me check." Salim reached for his wallet

and drew out a dollar bill, crisp and new, and passed it to Khalid, who handed it to Alison, the way a man would tip a waitress.

The imam fixed his eyes on her. "Do you freely choose to marry this man, Khalid Mansour?"

"I do."

"Khalid, do you freely choose to marry this woman, Alison Taylor?"

"Yes."

As Alison watched Khalid sign his name on the certificate, she smiled. At last, relief, a giddy breathlessness that rose up in her chest. That was it. They were married.

"As a final note," the imam said, "I'd like to read from *Surah An-Nisa*." He reached for the *Qur'an* in front of him and began to recite in Arabic. Alison caught some of the words, but none of the ideas. Three years of studying Arabic, deciphering its three-letter roots, including a spring quarter in Cairo, and all she could comprehend were bits and pieces.

The imam finished, closed the *Qur'an*, and handed it to Alison. "For you."

She took the book, heavy in her hands, and everyone rose from their seats. The men shook hands all around, and the cousins kissed Khalid multiple times on each cheek. As Alison stood by, she had a sudden impulse to kiss Khalid, but knew this was out of the question inside the mosque. Meanwhile, Ibrahim performed a small bow for her, and Salim said, *"Alf mabruuk." A thousand congratulations.*

Out in the parking lot, it had stopped raining and the air was fresh. Alison stood by the car while the men laughed and patted one another on the back. The brick mosque loomed over them; she wouldn't be going in there again. One day, she and Khalid would visit the famous mosques of Damascus and Jerusalem. She would wear her scarf Queen Noor-style next time.

"Yalla," she said. *Hurry up.* Khalid waved good-bye and then was next to her, sliding a hand around her waist and kissing her cheek. As they drove away with the mosque behind them, tears of relief welled up behind her eyes, and she released the breath she had been holding.

Alison reached behind her and placed the *Qur'an* on the backseat. She stared down at the marriage certificate in her hand, examining her signature, tidy and consistent, written with deliberate style. Next to it was Khalid's, in his child-like script. She still had the dollar bill pressed in her palm. She stared at the bill, no longer crisp and new, but crumpled in her hand.

# Chapter 3

The alarm clock went off at 3:20 a.m. Zainab reached for it, and although she knew better, she glanced to see if her husband Abed was next to her. Alone, she slowly got up and shuffled down the hall to the bathroom, passing the room where her son Ahmed and his wife slept. Zainab, still half asleep, splashed water up her arms, preparing for the morning prayer. Back in her room, she stood at the edge of her carpet and adjusted herself in the right direction. Covered in white, she began the prescribed movements, bending, prostrating, and mentally reciting her prayers.

Afterward, she remained kneeling for her supplications. With palms up, eyes closed, she whispered, *"Allahu Akbar." God is great.* "Thank you for the blessings you've bestowed upon my family." She carried out her regular formula of praising, thanking, and asking for guidance. "Grant health to my body, my blood pressure, and my sugar levels. Don't let me get sick in this disbelieving country."

Her prayers then shifted to specific family members. "Guard and protect my mother, my brother Waleed, and my sister Anysa. Ease their suffering." Eyes still closed, she could see her family in the refugee camps of the West Bank.

She made a special *du'a*—a prayer inspired by guilt—for her youngest daughter Nadia, bless her, left behind in Jordan. *Poor girl.*

Zainab progressed to immediate matters. "Praise be to you that my son finished university." For a moment, she got a tingle of delight thinking of Khalid graduating later that very day. "*Ya Allah*, please guide Khalid's new bride—what's her name? Guide her to be a good wife. Lead them both down the right path. If that is your will."

Zainab exhaled. "And Ahmed. Protect and guide him. Help him get a job in an Arab country. Let their children learn Arabic and be good Muslims. Have Margaret wear *hijab* again." She whispered, "*Ya Allah*, there is nothing easy except what you make easy."

When Zainab was certain she had mentioned each of her two sons, five daughters, and twenty-five grandchildren, she took a deep breath and moved to her final and most important *du'a*: "*Ya Allah*, have mercy on Abed's soul." Her hands trembled at the thought of her late husband. "Remove from him the punishment of the grave. Reward him with paradise. There is no deity but you." A vision of Abed flickered in her mind. She reached for her prayer beads and recited *subhan'Allah* at each bead. *Glory be to Allah.* After squeezing each of the thirty-three beads, she put them back in their place, removed her prayer garments, dropped back into bed, and fell asleep.

Zainab hoisted herself into the front seat of the minivan, next to Ahmed. For this day, she wore her best white scarf and best embroidered *thob*. Margaret and the three kids settled in the back. They pulled out of the cul-de-sac, and Zainab, as usual, surveyed the neighborhood as they passed. The wooden houses seemed temporary compared to the sturdy stone homes in Palestine—those were homes you could live in for generations.

Her grandchildren Tariq and Leena bickered in the backseat. "Be good," she said in Arabic, and then remembered: they couldn't understand her.

Zainab wished Mona and her family were coming. Ahmed had said there weren't enough tickets, and Mona had no one to watch the boys. What a shame, Khalid's own sister not attending his graduation.

Zainab's thoughts moved to Khalid, a graduate at last—a surprise even to her. Even though he had smarts—*masha'Allah*—he was lazy and undisciplined. No self-control. But now Zainab could hold her head up when visiting her sister Anysa, whose words always intruded Zainab's thoughts.

"Eight years?" Anysa had said, "Whoever heard of someone taking eight years to finish university?" Then she added, "*Inshallah* he'll finish. Maybe."

When Zainab admitted to her sister over a long-distance phone call that Khalid had married a foreign girl—more American than Arab—Zainab had to endure Anysa's questions about the girl's background and religion. What started as congratulations had twisted into condolences.

Zainab thought of Khalid's bride, that skinny girl with the tight clothing. Any Arab blood pumping in those veins had to be weak, diluted from living in America. Truth be told, it was hard to grasp why Khalid was drawn to her. Could she give him what he needed? Could she help him overcome his faults? Could the girl even cook?

Zainab turned to Ahmed. "Is Khalid's bride going to be there?"

"Alison. Her name's Alison. I told you, *Yama*, she's graduating, too."

Ah, yes. Zainab remembered. "*Masha'Allah*." *By the grace of God.*

"Alison's parents will be there, as well," Ahmed said.

Zainab clicked her tongue. She didn't like this arrangement and preferred to receive them at home, where she could inspect the bride's parents at her ease and show them her eldest son Ahmed owned his own house.

From the freeway, all Zainab could see were the towering evergreens, not the houses or streets behind them. She felt swallowed up. In

Palestine, there were trees, yes, but she could still see the stone walls and hillsides. Zainab sighed. She pulled out her string of blue prayer beads, which were smooth to the touch, their tassel soft and worn. The beads were from Jerusalem and had passed through her fingertips for years.

By the time Ahmed parked, the sky was completely gray. Zainab's joints were stiff as her feet hit the pavement. They joined a crowd, all walking in the same direction.

Ahmed took her arm. "This is the university, *Yama*. Khalid and I studied here. Margaret and Alison, too."

The university was like its own city, orderly and contained. Ahmed guided Zainab through a rose garden and into a large stadium. He stayed by her side as she pulled herself up the cement steps, feeling the eyes of others upon her. Each time she turned to face an observer, the person looked away. Perhaps they were admiring the hand embroidery on her *thob*, which was indeed beautiful, its stitches compact and uniform. Any Palestinian woman of her generation would recognize the motif as a pattern from Bethlehem.

Zainab sat between her son and Jenin. The stadium was a daunting place, immense and wide open. She missed the company of Mona and tugged at Ahmed's sleeve. "Why didn't you tell me this was outside?"

He didn't answer; he was busy talking to his

wife. Zainab felt alone and glanced at Jenin next to her. She had the body of a woman but the face of a girl. *May Allah bless her,* Zainab thought.

Still, Zainab would have rather sat next to Abed. The only person happier about Khalid finally graduating would have been his father, who had been intent on sending his sons to study abroad. If Abed were here, she would lean on him, and he would pat her hand and chuckle at her jokes. She could almost feel his hand on hers. How could Abed be gone five months now when she felt his presence so clearly?

He had died in the morning—a heart attack over breakfast. There had been no warning, no illness, no hospital stay, no sickbed vigil. He was buried the same afternoon. *To Allah we belong and to him we return.*

Zainab rubbed her eyes, looked at the sky, and noted the position of the sun behind the clouds. She turned to Ahmed. "I'm going to miss the noon prayer."

"You can make it up when we get to the restaurant," he said.

Zainab considered this. It would upset the order of her day, which was organized according to prayer times.

Ahmed placed a booklet in Zainab's lap. "See that? It's Khalid's name." Zainab squinted at the tiny row of letters, lined up like cross-stitch.

Then Ahmed flipped through the pages. "There, Alison's name." Zainab glanced at the page and smiled at her son to make him happy.

When music started and the graduates poured into the stadium, Ahmed patted his mother's arm. "*Yama*, there's Khalid!" Zainab craned her neck, but there was no way she could distinguish him among the sea of black gowns. Ahmed startled her again. "There's Alison!" Zainab made a partial attempt to locate her but soon gave up.

Next was an endless string of speeches. Zainab passed the time surveying the people around her. Her eyes roved in an arc and landed on a young couple. The man wore sandals with woolen socks, which made no sense. The woman wore a childish necklace with a tiny charm. It was clear foreigners didn't appreciate gold. The couple shifted in their seats, and Zainab looked away.

At last, the speeches ended, and the graduates approached the stage in two lines. A sequence then repeated itself over and over: a student stepped onto the stage and shook hands with a large man in a robe. Then the next student would do the same.

As she waited to hear Khalid's name, a drop of water hit her head, and a gentle rain began to fall. Surprisingly, no one got up. Zainab considered moving, but she didn't want to miss Khalid. She adjusted her scarf and crossed her arms.

Ahmed tapped her leg. "Khalid's next."

Zainab sat upright and recognized the profile of her last-born son as he stepped onto the stage. Excitement rose inside her, a feeling that momentarily erased all worries and heartaches. As Khalid stepped off the stage, she clapped fervently and smiled through the misty rain.

What followed was a great wave of relief. She would no longer have to worry about him finishing university, wasting all of his brother's money and bringing shame to himself. Eight years was a long time to worry about the same matter. Even Zainab had her limits.

At last, the rain stopped, the gray receded, and the sun appeared. Ahmed tapped her arm. "*Yama*, Alison's next."

Zainab caught sight of the blond girl, her figure stepping onto the stage. In that second, Zainab realized this girl would now be woven into her life, just as Margaret was. This girl could give birth to more foreign-speaking grandchildren. What's more, this girl could be called upon to take care of her poor mother-in-law when she was old. Would the girl do that?

Zainab told herself to stop this indulgence, this self-worry. There was a more urgent matter: her youngest daughter Nadia, who was staying at her sister's home in Amman. With her father gone, *Allah yarhamhu—God bless his soul—*and Zainab in America, Nadia was practically abandoned! This thought gave Zainab a shudder.

Why hadn't the American Embassy given Nadia a visa? Curse their fathers.

Nadia was nineteen and Zainab's last child to marry; she had just completed her two-year certificate in English translation at a college in Jordan. Zainab had worried about Nadia before, but it was a minor worry compared to so many others such as Khalid not graduating, Khalid marrying a foreigner, and Zainab's fear of what would happen to her in old age. Finding a husband for Nadia would now be her top concern into which she would pour all of her hope and anxiety.

Zainab engrossed herself in making plans for Nadia, her mind clicking away, pausing at images of nephews and neighbors, creating a mental catalogue of potential husbands.

When the ceremony was over, Zainab finally rose out of her seat, her knees sore and achy. She eased down the steps with Margaret next to her, and they followed Ahmed outside the stadium, where he stopped by the entrance to the parking lot.

"This is where we're meeting Khalid and Alison," he said.

Zainab saw Khalid moving toward her in his black gown, his face radiant with joy. He reached her and embraced her with both arms. Zainab squeezed him back and then held his handsome face between her hands.

"May God protect you and keep you safe!" she told him.

She stepped back to admire her two sons. Bless them, both university graduates. *Masha'Allah*. It was no surprise foreign girls would want to marry them.

A camera appeared and Margaret began directing the family for photos. In the first arrangement Zainab stood between her sons. As always, Margaret demanded that her subjects smile. Zainab lifted her chin, lips closed, a small act of defiance. Margaret continued to snap photos until Zainab felt weak from holding her head up and suppressing her smile.

There was a tap on her shoulder. It was Khalid's bride, also in a black gown. "*As-salaam alaikum*," she said. "How are you?" Zainab nodded, and the girl continued in her stilted Arabic. "This is my mother and father." She gestured to her parents next to her.

"*Salaam*," they mumbled.

Zainab's eyes scanned the girl's mother, skinny like her daughter and wearing chin-length hair, small dots for earrings, and slim-fitting clothing. Clearly American.

The father was a male version of his wife—the same startled expression and silvery gray hair. Could he truly be Syrian? The son of a Muslim? If so, this country had transformed him, just as she feared it would alter her sons.

Zainab offered them tiny handshakes and an even tinier smile. Greetings floated in her head, but she stayed silent. Would she even mean them?

The girl said something, but Zainab wasn't in the mood to understand. She wasn't in the mood to contemplate this bride of Khalid's. Nor was she in the mood to stand on the concrete any longer. How did Zainab get into this situation? She felt trapped by the parking lot and by circumstances beyond her control. She turned to Ahmed and told him it was time to leave.

Ahmed guided her again through the rose garden, now full of people foolishly posing for photos. Margaret stopped to take more pictures. How many photos did a person need? Zainab found herself positioned next to Khalid's bride, who put her arm around her. Zainab stiffened as Margaret held up the camera. There would now be a photo to record this moment—a moment Zainab would prefer to forget. She adjusted her scarf and stared straight ahead.

At the restaurant owned by her son, they were joined by Mona and her family. A flush of relief rose up in Zainab at the sight of her daughter and her grandsons. Then Zainab crept down to the basement office where Ahmed had left a prayer carpet for her. She prayed the afternoon prayer and made up for the noon prayer she had missed. She recited long sections from the

Qur'an and offered lengthy supplications thanking God for Khalid's graduation. She asked for guidance on how to cope with the foreign parents sitting in the dining room upstairs.

Zainab sat on the floor with her palms up. Her mind wandered to the West Bank and to a string of faces, to those Palestinian girls Khalid could have married. She thought of a neighbor girl who would have been perfect. Zainab had known her parents as far back as she could remember. She knew the whole family, everything about them, the good and the bad. What did she know of this Alison? Or her parents? Nothing. Khalid was marrying into strangers. Foreign strangers.

When Ahmed spoke of marrying Margaret so many years ago, Zainab had heard the news from Palestine.

"This is the price you pay for sending your son to America," her sister Anysa had said.

Ahmed had reassured his mother that he wouldn't marry Margaret without her approval. Of course, Zainab couldn't say no to Ahmed, her eldest and most successful son. By the time he brought Margaret to Palestine, Zainab had gradually accepted the idea of a foreign wife for him.

This time was different. One afternoon Khalid had announced his plans. Next, Zainab found herself hiding away in a basement, prolonging her prayer.

She raised her arms and shook her fists. "*Ya Allah*, why did you do this to me?" Her arms dropped, and she rocked back and forth. She would not go through this with Nadia, she vowed. *Thanks be to God.* Nadia would marry someone close to the family, maybe a cousin, inshallah.

"*Yama.*" It was Mona in the doorway. "The food is served."

Zainab stood, feeling the ache in her legs. She took her time folding the prayer carpet and moving to the dining room, where the meal had indeed been served. The table was spread with an adequate sampler of Middle Eastern foods: lamb kebabs stacked neatly, steaming rice pilaf, fried cauliflower, *fattoush* salad, and more. Unfortu-nately, the plate of grape leaves was meager, but it was too late to do anything about that. Zainab sat next to Ahmed, who said, "*Yama*, Alison's parents want to know what you think of America."

"What do I think of America?" she repeated.

The table was quiet and everyone was leaning in, looking at her, waiting for her answer. She spoke quietly and leaned toward Ahmed, who translated her reply. "America is good."

Everyone laughed high and loud; Zainab wondered if they were making fun of her. The conversation continued on without her, noisy talking in English. She tapped Ahmed's arm. "What are you saying?"

"I was telling Alison's parents," he said, gesturing to the couple, their faces finally softening, "I was telling them how much Khalid and I enjoyed studying here, how much we have benefited, how much we appreciate America."

Zainab grunted and pulled back from the table. Perhaps she should have said the truth: America was full of disbelievers, and the country was pulling her sons away from her.

❧ Chapter 4 ❧

The house was steeped in Arabic discussion. Family members filled the living room, all attempting to raise their voices above the others. Margaret had escaped to the armchair in her bedroom by telling them she was tired—the only acceptable excuse for leaving the throes of family interaction.

The mother had moved in with her and Ahmed soon after her husband had died, turning their home into the center of familial activity. The blessing of having the largest home in the family had turned into a cruel trick. Mona dropped by to see her mother nearly every day with her entourage of boys. Khalid came for rolled grape leaves, stuffed zucchini, or whatever else the mother was preparing. More distant family members popped in, as well. Once, Margaret had tried to determine the link to Ibrahim and Salim, who increasingly showed up for meals and conversation, but any uncertain relation was simply referred to as a "cousin."

"We're all from the same village," Ahmed said with a shrug. "That makes us related." He was referring to the family village in Palestine that no longer existed and only the mother had seen. "The point is," he said, "if we have a conflict outside the family, they'd stand with us."

So there it was. The possibility of tribal warfare earned them free meals. These explanations used to fascinate Margaret. Now she rolled her eyes.

The strident Arabic reached the bedroom, where Margaret sat in her armchair. Her cat rubbed against her leg. "Are you hiding, too?" she asked her.

Margaret looked at her watch. It was almost time to leave. The noise from the living room had increased. Were they arguing? Had another relative arrived? Soon none of this would matter.

Her daughter Leena appeared in the doorway, and her eyes fixed on the large zippered tote bag on the floor. "Mama, are you going?" At three, Leena knew the bag was a signal that her mother was going out. Margaret reached for her daughter and held her in her lap. Smelling Leena's hair, Margaret explained, as she did every week, that she was going to meet other mothers from the cul-de-sac.

"I wanna come."

She picked up her bag and walked down the hallway, with Leena following behind. In the living room, the mother was engrossed in an exchange with Ahmed, the cousins, Mona, and her husband—all of them sitting in a circle of overlapping speech and gestures. In their hands were tiny cups of Turkish coffee on the verge of spilling. The tone had turned serious—the topic politics, most likely. Margaret predicted the gathering would go late into the evening, no one willing to be the first to say good-bye.

She made eye contact with Ahmed. "Honey, you need to take Leena." He got up and detached their child from Margaret's leg. She said good-bye to her children, announced her salaams to the rest of the family, and gave Ahmed a wink in lieu of a kiss. On the porch she paused, her eyes fluttering closed as she inhaled. She walked down the driveway, past the jasmine plant with only a single white bloom.

Stepping into the cul-de-sac, Margaret entered a world of nuclear families, tidy lawns, and normalcy. She wasn't going far—just across the street.

It was seven o'clock and still light out. The neighborhood was showing early signs of summer: a couple strolling hand in hand, the man next door trimming his hedge. He looked up at Margaret passing by. "Running away from home?" he called out.

Were her feelings that obvious? Then she remembered her tote bag, which looked more like an overnight bag. "Not today!" she called back.

Margaret reached Jan's house, where the impatiens along the walkway spilled onto the bricks. It reminded Margaret how far behind she was with her own gardening. Jan answered the door with a perky, "Hello!" Scented candles flickered in the entry, and soft music played. Margaret followed Jan into the dining room, where Jackie and Josephine had already spread out their photos and albums. They called their weekly group "Three J's and an M."

"You look fabulous," Josephine said.

Margaret touched her red hair. "Thanks." Ever since she had stopped wearing the headscarf, the women repeatedly complimented her. Jackie had even declared Margaret "liberated." It had been a year, but she still felt self-conscious, though never as much as on that first day when she had stepped out of the house without a scarf. She had felt so exposed and imagined the cul-de-sac would split open and swallow her up. After all, Margaret had worn hijab for nearly ten years, adopting it the year after she had converted to Islam.

Jan turned to Margaret. "That's such a cute outfit on you."

She smiled and looked down at her fitted

blouse. It wasn't just the hijab; she had also dropped her shapeless clothing. It was all part of her midlife makeover—her "midlife hijab crisis" as her friend Liz had called it. Yet it wasn't so much a crisis as it had been a fresh start. It was only after the scarf came off that Margaret realized how withdrawn she had been in hijab, how she had allowed it to become a barrier, an excuse.

She sat down and took out her scrapbook. The room filled with cheerful talk of plans for the Fourth of July and day camp for kids. All three J's appeared fresh, at ease, and well adjusted—not one of them worn down by situations beyond their control.

Margaret opened her scrapbook. It was their family album, displaying photos of events such as birthdays and the *Eid* holidays. She felt a surge of inspiration as she visualized the pages she would create.

Jan set a dish of artichoke dip and four wine glasses on the table. She poured white wine in three glasses, stylishly twisting her wrist at the last drop. Each glass displayed a different charm attached to its base for identification purposes, although Margaret's glass didn't need one. For her, Jan brought out a jug of orange juice.

The other women sipped their wine and explained what pages they were working on.

"I'm doing Khalid's graduation," Margaret

said, eyes fixed on the bright juice in her stemmed glass.

Jan looked up. "He graduated?"

"Yes, and I got some great photos at the rose garden."

Jackie tilted her head and smiled. "And how's the family?"

This was Margaret's cue to amaze and entertain. "The graduation was lovely," she began, not wanting to disappoint, "although Ahmed's mother didn't think so. She was bothered by something." Margaret looked at a photo of the mother, her face devoid of expression as she stood next to Khalid, smiling broadly, his arm around her. "Look at this." Margaret slid the photo across the table.

"She doesn't look too happy," Jackie said.

"I thought she'd be thrilled—Khalid finally graduating." Margaret took a sip of juice. "He just married this young woman, Alison. She graduated, as well."

"Same graduation?" Josephine asked.

"Yes, and her parents came out from Chicago." The women worked quietly, cropping, arranging, and adhering as Margaret spoke. "It was strange because the mother barely said a word to them." Margaret examined a photo of Alison with her parents at her side. They had attempted smiles, yet there were no arms around the shoulders in this photo. Alison's mother gripped the strap of her purse while her father stood awkwardly. "I wanted to pat this woman's hand and say it'd be okay, Khalid's a great guy."

"Why didn't you?" Jackie asked.

Margaret studied a photo of the young couple in their caps and gowns. Alison's smile accentuated her high cheekbones and revealed her perfect row of teeth. "I'm not sure it's true."

The women looked up, eyebrows raised. Margaret passed the photo to Jan.

"She's pretty."

"Her background's Syrian American."

"Syrian? But she's blonde."

"There are blonde Syrians. Have you see that anchor woman on CNN?"

"They make a nice couple." Jackie was holding the photo now. "You don't think he'll be a good husband?"

"He's a bit irresponsible." Margaret tried not to sound bitter. "He gets away with it because Ahmed basically supports him." She looked at the image of Khalid. Granted, he was charming with his dark eyes and good looks. "For Palestinian families, it's natural for the older brother to do everything for the younger."

"Honestly, Margaret." Jackie shook her head. "I don't know how you do it."

"Don't get me started," Margaret said, but she already had.

"You're a saint," Jan said.

"I wouldn't say that." Margaret strained to keep her smile as her thoughts flashed with arguments she had had with Ahmed over Khalid. Their father had sacrificed and saved for Ahmed's university with the understanding that Ahmed would do the same for his younger brother. It had seemed fair in the beginning. In fact, Margaret had found Ahmed's devotion to his family endearing. She had not understood until years later what these obligations truly meant.

"How long is Ahmed's mother staying with you?" Josephine asked.

Margaret held up her hands. "Who knows?"

"My mother-in-law comes for three days," Jackie said. "I want to slit my wrists."

"Now that Ahmed's father has died, we don't know where his mother will live." Margaret mindlessly slid her photographs around on the page. "Traditionally she'd live with her oldest son—that's Ahmed—but we just don't know where she'll end up."

"Why don't you ask her?" Jan said.

Margaret lined up the best graduation photos in front of her. "Once we bring up the subject, we need to invite her to stay permanently. It will no longer be just a visit." She began trimming them one by one, cropping away parts of each photo that weren't necessary. Too much brick wall. A stranger that made his way into the photo. The grumpy mother. Margaret wished she could trim the mother right out of her life.

"It's true," Josephine said, "You're a saint." That word again.

"There's also the issue," Margaret explained, "of Nadia. The mother can't exactly leave Jordan for good until Nadia gets married." Margaret leaned forward until she had everyone's attention. "My plan is to have the mother live with Khalid and Alison."

Jackie raised an eyebrow. "Sounds like you don't like Alison."

"She's a bit of a know-it-all. I mean, she's only been married five minutes. A marriage like that takes work."

"You'd know." Jan stood and topped off the wine glasses. "Hasn't it been twenty years, you and Ahmed?"

"Twenty years next month." Margaret pondered the length of two decades. So much had happened, from the good times of the early years, to running the restaurants and raising three children, to the never-ending demands of Ahmed's family —all culminating with the mother moving in with them. What could Margaret do? She couldn't turn away Ahmed's mother, newly widowed and still in mourning, could she?

"How are you going to celebrate?" Josephine asked.

"We're staying in a hotel downtown. Going

out to dinner, window shopping. No kids, just us." The women expressed their approval, and Margaret continued, "But before we can enjoy that, there's one more family event we have to attend—Khalid and Alison's wedding."

Jackie looked up. "I thought they were already married."

"They did the marriage license at the mosque, but there wasn't any celebration." Margaret fingered her long beaded necklace. "Now they're having a wedding, more like a reception. The fabulous thing is that her parents are paying for it."

"Isn't that the tradition?" Josephine asked.

"Not in Palestinian families," Margaret said. "I was worried Ahmed and I would be the ones to pay."

"You'd pay for *their* wedding?" Jackie asked.

"That's what Arab brothers do. It's their system. They help each other out." Margaret stopped herself. How could she explain the very social customs that made her crazy?

"What are you going to wear?" Jan said.

"Not sure yet." Margaret had flicked through the dress racks at the mall, surveying the strapless and backless gowns—all too revealing. So instead, she had channeled her energy into getting a dress for Jenin, whose breasts seemed to have grown one cup size since the last time Margaret took her shopping.

Thankfully, the topic shifted to Jan's two-page spread of a St. Patrick's Day party. In one photo, people wore green hats and held up pints of beer.

Jan stroked the base of her wine glass. "It was a great party. I got a lot of good pictures." She held up a photo. "See this? Totally staged. The first shot was a dud, so I refilled their glasses and made them do the toast all over again."

"Living the lie," Jackie said in a voice full of cheer.

Josephine held up a photo of a child blowing out candles. "Mine, too. Completely faked. We had him blow out the candles three times."

"Living the lie," Jackie repeated.

Margaret looked down at her scrapbook. The entire thing was a lie, a highly abridged version of their life, edited as she wished it to be. Page after page denied the sprawling chaos just outside the viewfinder.

The day of the wedding arrived quickly. In the driveway, their household all piled into the minivan. Margaret took her seat behind the mother and stared at the back of the woman's head, covered in a white scarf. It was one thing for Margaret to give up her seat for a week, but this arrangement was going on month after month. Today especially she wanted to arrive at the wedding like a normal family.

The reception was held at a hotel on the Seattle

waterfront. Margaret and Ahmed entered just as Mona cruised in with her husband and boys. The lobby was inviting and cozy with its stone fireplace. Even the children were subdued.

"No new dress?" Mona raised her eyebrows.

Margaret blinked. "What?"

"You wore that to the last wedding."

Margaret glanced down. She had settled on a dress she'd worn to a previous wedding—not particularly flattering but suitably modest. Granted, the fabric and cut were a bit out of style. Meanwhile, Mona wore a never-before-seen dress—floor-length and glittery with a fitted jacket.

"No, Mona, no new dress," she said. "But yours is beautiful—so shiny!"

Margaret retreated to the ballroom, where a quartet played jazzy Arab music near the dance floor. Each table was draped in white and topped with white roses. Beyond the tables were floor-to-ceiling windows with a panoramic view of Puget Sound, where a ferry passed by.

Margaret, Ahmed, and their children chose seats by the dance floor. As the ballroom gradually filled, Mona's boys darted between the dinner tables. Margaret scanned the room for Mona; of course, she was nowhere to be seen. It would be yet another event with those boys running around.

Margaret sighed, and Ahmed reached for her

hand and held it between his. It was a tender moment, one of unspoken affection—a feeling that had become increasingly rare between them. With the mother constantly around, Margaret and Ahmed hardly had a private moment together—and when they did, any conversation inevitably turned back to the mother.

Servers circulated offering ginger ale and sparkling juice: the Muslim bar selection. The wedding cake was wheeled in—four tiers garnished in real flowers, a culinary detail Ahmed would surely take interest in, as he favored unusual garnishes for cakes at his restaurant.

The appetizer buffet opened, offering Arab *mezze*, hummus, and *babaganouj* artistically arranged as a gourmet spread, not as the simple fare it really was. Margaret began filling her plate when something caught her eye across the room. Two of Mona's boys were giggling behind the wedding cake. Margaret set her plate down and hurried over. Sure enough, the two were dipping into the white frosting and licking it off their fingers.

"Stop that!" she said. "Get away from there!"

The boys scattered, and Alison's mother approached, her eyes surveying the damage. Her cropped silver hair matched her metallic sheath of a dress. "What's wrong with these children? Don't they know any better?"

Right behind her was Alison's grandmother, grimacing and clicking her tongue sharply, dressed in a beaded cardigan and calf-length skirt.

Margaret found herself defending the children. "They're just excited."

Alison's mother leaned in and asked in a confidential tone, "Is this typical of these people?"

A shiver passed through Margaret. She couldn't think of anything to say except "Well, it depends," then quickly excused herself and returned to Ahmed's side, trying to erase what she had heard. *These people.*

Margaret fixed her eyes on Ahmed's mother making her way across the ballroom, shaking hands with the Arab guests. The mother was in her special-occasion regalia, her black velvet floor-length *thob* embellished with colorful embroidery. The mother was smiling, but her wrinkled face looked much older than her sixty-something years. It was an odd juxta-position, the weary mother next to Alison's mother, trim inher silver cocktail dress. Margaret considered the new family relation-ships forming. How would Alison fit into the Mansour family?

At that moment, Alison's grandmother came into view—standing directly across from Ahmed's mother. Though both were Arab women of a similar age, they were worlds apart: Ahmed's mother in her white headscarf and *thob*, and Alison's grandmother in her prim clothing, handbag and heels, her hair stiff and coiffed. The two old women said not a word to each other but simply stared, scanning the other from head to toe.

Margaret's observations were interrupted by loud drumming. Making their entrance, Khalid and Alison walked in holding hands and beaming like they had just stepped out of the cover of *Arab American Wedding*. Alison's slim-fitting white gown had tiny cap sleeves and an open back— way too sexy for this family but gorgeous nonetheless. They headed for the dance floor, where they raised their arms. Arab music started up, and Khalid's shoulders took on the rhythm while Alison's slim arms undulated. The guests clapped as the couple performed their own version of an Arab wedding dance.

When their dance ended, the dinner buffet opened. Margaret led Leena to the food and scanned the dishes: seasonal greens, wild rice pilaf, northwest salmon, roasted lamb.

Leena looked up at Margaret. "I want a kid's meal."

"They don't have that here, honey. How about rice and fish?"

Leena made a face and crossed her arms, and Margaret took her hand. "Okay, let's see what we can find." After some negotiation, they walked back to their table with Leena carrying only one item on her plate: breadsticks.

They sat and took their first bites. Mona walked by, her eyes on Leena's plate. She touched Margaret's shoulder. "If my child ate like that, I'd kill myself."

Margaret sighed once more. She was again called upon to offer Mona a response, pointed but not too sharp. Margaret looked up and smiled. "Lucky for you, your boys are big eaters."

After the meal, servers placed fluted glasses of sparkling white grape juice in front of each guest. Alison's father stood and clinked a spoon against his glass.

He addressed the room, his face upturned and smiling. "Almost sixty years ago, a couple in Chicago married. A young Christian woman and a Muslim man, both new immigrants from Syria, defying the cultural norms of the time." He paused and nodded. "Those were my parents." At this, the crowd murmured. "And today my daughter Alison continues the tradition."

Margaret looked at Khalid, who appeared pleased with himself. She recalled the tiny photo Ahmed had shown her when they first met. "This is my brother," he had said. Khalid was six years old in the photo. A first grader. When he came to the States, he was barely eighteen.

Her gaze moved to Ahmed, dressed in his suit with his arm around Leena. He looked up and smiled at Margaret, his eyes warm and loving. Margaret responded with a tender look. Despite everything he had put her through, he was a good husband and father. And after twenty years, she was still happy to be by his side.

Alison's father finished speaking and raised his glass to the couple, gesturing widely. "I'd like to make a toast. To my beautiful daughter Alison and her husband Khalid. May they find love always."

Ahmed held up his glass and turned to Margaret, who knew what he was about to say.

"Next year, Jerusalem." It was a private joke between them, Ahmed's toast. If Jews could yearn to return to the holy city, Ahmed reasoned, then so could he. After all, he still held residency there, something he said he would never give up—all part of his bittersweet fantasy of one day returning to Palestine. Whenever he made this toast, Margaret smiled and played along. Of course, she had no intention of moving to Palestine —or anywhere.

They clinked glasses, and he leaned in to whisper something.

"Honey, I've been thinking," he said. "I don't think our cash gift is enough. We should buy Khalid some furniture, too."

Margaret stiffened. "What?" Her voice was high-pitched. "We've done enough for your brother."

"Lower your voice."

"He's an adult now. He needs to take care of his own things."

"Okay." Ahmed patted her hand.

"No one bought furniture for us." Margaret leaned back and rubbed her forehead. *Damn.* Why did they keep going over these same things? She pictured their split-level house at the end of the cul-de-sac and their unruly life there: the mother, the relatives, the shoes piled by the door, the tea glasses scattered about, the television continuously projecting news in Arabic, the needy brother, and Ahmed—who could never say no.

In her mind flashed another image, her life separate from all that. She allowed herself a brief daydream, running through the usual considerations: where she would live, how she would support herself, how she would manage as a single mother. The snag in this scenario was always the same: would she willingly choose a life without Ahmed?

The band was playing a traditional Arab song, and on the dance floor, guests danced for the newlyweds. This was their ritual to honor the couple and celebrate their happiness. The mother was there, too, her hips twitching, arms raised. Her weathered face held an open smile. It was the first time Margaret had seen her show any joy since her husband died. She was surely missing him, yet there she was, dancing for her son and his American bride—the one she didn't want.

Margaret felt a nudge and turned around. Ahmed flicked his head toward the dance floor. It was their turn. She knew some Arab dance moves; she had been through this before. There was no point in resisting. Ahmed would simply remind her that it would be impolite to refuse. The only choice was to do some shimmies and shoulder shakes.

❧ Chapter 5 ❧

"There's no room for all this." Alison gestured toward the stack of Khalid's boxes and his shoes piled by the door. He sat nearby on the sofa, pressing buttons on his cell phone. She fixed her eyes on him until he looked up and smiled at her. He set down the phone and patted the seat next him. Alison sat, and he wrapped his arm around her shoulders.

"We can't stay here any longer," she said. "You've been here a month already."

He brushed a strand of hair from her eyes. "We'll look this weekend."

She leaned against him. He smelled of coffee and aftershave and was wearing his black crew-neck that she liked.

"This studio is designed for one person," she said, "Not a married couple." She did like to think of herself as part of a married couple. Even more so, she loved being a college graduate—finally ready to step into adulthood.

Khalid's cell phone beeped. She waited until he read his text message, then gently pried the phone from his hand and set it out of reach.

She turned back to him. "We've got to move out of here." They did agree on one thing: moving off of Capitol Hill. For Alison, its flamboyant counterculture, its tattooed and pierced residents, had already served their function of shocking her mother.

"There's a place up by my brother's."

"I'm not living out there, babe. You know that."

He stroked her hair. "We'll be close to my family."

"Your family? I moved out here to be away from my own."

"Don't say that."

"If I hadn't moved," she said, "I never would've met you."

"So, you don't like my family?"

Alison flicked her gaze upward. "It's not that . . ." How could she explain? Families had a way of encroaching, judging, and messing things up. "Hey, what about living in Greenwood?"

He reached for his cell phone. "Just look for something we can afford."

"What can we afford?" Her voice rose a little, and she stopped herself. She wouldn't spoil the moment by bringing up their dismal financial situation.

Khalid snapped his cell phone shut and stood. "I'm going out."

"Where?"

"The coffee shop."

Her mind jumped to an image of its interior brick walls and the hissing sound of the espresso machine. She and Khalid could read the newspaper there while sipping cappuccinos from heavy cups. Just inside its alleyway entrance was where she'd seen Khalid for the first time.

She stood. "Give me ten minutes to get ready."

"I'm meeting the guys."

"So?" she said. "I like talking with your friends." Actually, it was more than a casual pleasure; the discussions on Middle East politics energized her.

"Sorry, babe, I'm going by myself." Khalid moved to the door.

"You're going alone?" She pushed herself out of her seat. "Is it because of what I said about your family?" She stepped toward him. "Is it because I don't want to live in the suburbs?"

Khalid fingered his car keys. "You shouldn't be sitting around with my friends anymore."

"So, I'm supposed to sit at home while you go out?"

"You're my wife now."

"I don't see how—"

"They're waiting for me." He held up his hand. "That's it. I'm done. *Salaam*."

Alison's thoughts froze as she stared at the closed door. Her heart pounded. She hadn't even finished what she was going to say. She ran to the door and opened it, but he was already gone. She had an urge to run after him. Could she make him change his mind?

The moment had passed. She closed the door, stood there, and reviewed what had just happened. *I'm going out. That's it. I'm done.*

She refused to cry. Instead, she turned and went to the kitchen. Her hands reached for the first breakable item she saw, a serving platter from the night before, resting innocently in the drying rack. Alison smashed it against the corner of the kitchen counter. She turned away and collapsed on the sofa.

In her mind's eye, she traced the way to the coffee shop where their relationship had begun. It was off the Ave in the U District, a few minutes' walk from Denny Hall, where many of her classes had been held. Soon after she and Khalid hooked up, Alison joined in with his friends and their coffee shop debates, which burned with intense political views—discussions she had assumed would continue.

Alison sighed. She got off the sofa and went to the kitchen, where she knelt down and picked up the pieces of her favorite platter.

• • •

The next morning, neither Alison nor Khalid brought up the matter of his visit to the coffee shop. They sat at their small kitchen table, which was stacked with graduate school printouts. The ones on top were from the Department of Near Eastern Languages and Civilization and the Jackson School of International Studies. The others were from similar programs in other states. Next to this was a pile of loose papers, which was Alison's primary concern at that moment.

"Here, sign this." She handed a cover letter to Khalid, who signed it without reading. "I adjusted your résumé slightly to suit this particular job." She took the letter and handed him another printout, this one from online classifieds, with a particular IT job highlighted. "What do you think of this one? It relates to your field."

Khalid smiled sheepishly. "Can we do this later?"

"Fine." Alison's shoulders dropped. "I have an idea. Let's look at apartments." She passed him another printout of classifieds. "I found a couple places closer to your family."

"Wallingford? That's not close to my family."

"It's ten minutes closer. Besides, it's close to my work."

"Your work? How long are you going to keep that campus job?"

"As long as I need it!" Alison stopped herself

from reminding him that her job at the International Programs Office was their only income. Granted it wasn't ideal, but it was something. "Let's just look."

"Okay, but let's see the place I was telling you about."

"Fine," she said. "But we'll see mine first."

"Are you going to wear that?" Khalid pointed at her neckline. "It's a little low."

She looked down. "I wear this all the time."

"We're going to my brother's."

She looked at him closely, his solemn face and eyes. Was her blouse really worth the conflict? She remembered their day ahead and the apartments she wanted to see. "Give me a minute to change."

The first apartment, in the ideal neighborhood of Wallingford, was old but classic. Khalid held Alison's hand as they entered. She followed him into the living room and regarded the hardwood floors. Bright summer sunlight streamed in through the window, and she pictured her sofa there. As they admired the built-in china cabinet, a stale smell reached her nose. Everything about the apartment satisfied her, except the musty smell.

"We'll think about it," she told the manager outside. Alison was relieved to be breathing fresh air again.

The next place was near Green Lake. Alison

liked the idea of being able to jog around the lake or hang out in the grassy areas, then walk to one of the local coffee houses. But the unit was in a fourplex built during an unfashionable decade; its boxlike structure held zero interesting features. They thanked the property manager and walked down the sidewalk.

"What do you think?" Khalid asked. "The price is better."

Alison stopped in her tracks. "How could you even consider living there?"

"You chose the place. Now let me show you something."

They headed north on I-5. By the time they exited, they were well into the suburbs, which held none of the charm of the previous neighborhoods. They drove into a large apartment complex, passing a wooden sign that read PINE VIEW.

Khalid parked in front of the office. "Let me see if someone's here."

Alison remained in the car. All around were identical, blandly oppressive buildings, all with the same generic landscape, each building marked with a different capital letter, bold and ugly.

Khalid returned. "They have a two-bedroom available. The guy will show it to us now."

Alison got out, regretting this waste of everyone's time.

They entered a second-floor apartment in Building F. The place was new and bright. One living room window looked out onto parking spaces and the other onto some old pine trees. Alison admitted to herself that the place had a clean appeal to it, but could she see herself living there? She turned to the manager. "We'll think about it," she said, and signaled to Khalid that she had seen enough.

"So what's wrong with it?" He asked as they drove away.

"I can't live in a complex." She turned to the window. "I hate this area. Okay?"

"Just think about it," he said. "Now let's go see my brother."

As they entered the cul-de-sac, Alison felt a vague sense of unease at the sight of the split-level houses all lined up, announcing a repetition similar to that of the apartment complex. They parked in front of Ahmed and Margaret's house. Alison reconfirmed to herself that she would never live in a house like that, either.

Margaret welcomed them in. It was only the second time Alison had entered that living room, which smelled of cardamom and cooking odors. Palestinian plates decorated the walls, and embroidered pillows lined the couch; in the hallway were framed photographs of Jerusalem: the Dome of the Rock and Damascus Gate.

Sitting on the sofa was Khalid's mother, who

rose to greet them. Alison promptly brought to mind some Arabic phrases and approached her mother-in-law, whose kisses were wet on her cheeks. At that moment, Leena ran in with her brother Tariq right behind. They shook Khalid's hand and kissed him, and to Alison's amusement, they did the same for her.

Alison sat next to her mother-in-law and said in her basic Arabic, "We saw houses." Khalid jumped in to explain to his mother that they were looking for a new place in order to be closer to her. Alison felt a ripple of nausea and realized the idea of the suburbs simply made her sick.

Margaret invited Alison to the kitchen and gestured for her to sit at the breakfast bar. Alison recalled the last time she had sat in that spot, more than two months ago. So many things had happened since then: the vows at the mosque, the graduation, the wedding. The mix of events swirled through her mind, landing on the unsettling memory of having to tell her mother about Khalid.

The tea kettle whistled, and Margaret asked, "How's married life?"

"It's great." Alison smiled like a newlywed. "We're job searching and apartment hunting."

Margaret spooned loose tea into the teapot and added a handful of mint leaves. "How's that going?"

"Khalid has another interview this week." Then

Alison thought of something. "I want to thank you and Ahmed for the gift. The money's really helpful. The thank-you note is coming."

"No need for a note," Margaret said and pulled out the same brass tray as last time.

But Alison was thankful. She had insisted they save all of the wedding money for a deposit on an apartment, as well as first and last months' rent.

"There's something I wanted to ask you." Margaret spoke as she poured tea into the glasses arranged on the tray. "Why did you choose Middle East studies?"

Before Alison could answer, Margaret picked up the tray and said, "Excuse me, I'll be right back." She disappeared and left Alison to prepare her answer. Of course, the truth of it would sound crazy.

Margaret returned and sat. "Here." She slid a tea glass to Alison.

"Thanks." Alison had been making so much tea for Khalid lately that she had gotten used to its sweet taste. She cradled the steaming hot glass and began. "When I was a freshman at the U, I did a study abroad program. One quarter in Jordan and Israel—I mean, Palestine. It was spring of 2000, before the Second Intifada started." She sipped the tea, and its minty flavor along with the photos in the hallway conjured memories of her trip to Jerusalem, a trip her parents had paid for but sent her mother reeling with worry. "It was a good time to be there," Alison said. "I studied the history, the culture, the language . . . Basically, I was hooked." Alison smiled, content with her explanation, which was general enough to be true.

When Alison had first announced her major, her mother had asked, "What on Earth would you do with a degree like that?" Alison had explained the various career options—researcher, journalist, diplomat, scholar—but her mother couldn't com-prehend, couldn't even listen, and replied simply, "You're obsessed with the Middle East."

Later, when Alison announced her engagement to Khalid, her mother had said it again: "You're obsessed!" No, Alison had explained, she wasn't obsessed; she was in love. And no, he wasn't religious or traditional—Americanized, in fact, with a college degree and a bright future ahead. Her mother's face had showed she wasn't convinced. "Probably just wants a green card."

"He has one!" Alison had screamed back.

Her father—thank God—had been under-standing and reasonable. "I'm happy for you," he said, and at last her mother went grudgingly along.

"What made you go there in the first place?" Margaret asked.

"Curiosity about my background mainly. I've

always been drawn to that part of the world. Plus, my job in International Studies. I wanted to do a study abroad trip. Later, in my junior year, I went to Cairo for intensive Arabic."

"Have you ever thought about visiting Syria?" Margaret asked.

"Oh, many times," Alison said, explaining that her grandparents had praised the food, landscape, and culture of Syria, but by the end of their lives, they had not been back to the motherland in decades. "I asked my grandmother why she stopped going."

"What did she say?"

"Damascus is not how she remembers it. According to her, everyone she knew has either left or died."

"How sad."

"I know." Alison looked down at her empty tea glass. Her grandparents were of that generation of immigrants who had assimilated and tried to drop all traces of the old country. "It's easier to fit in than to stand out," Grandma Helen liked to say.

"We looked at apartments today," Alison said, changing the topic.

Margaret brightened. "Pine View?"

"Yes."

"What did you think?"

"Not for me. I don't like the suburbs."

"I felt the same before I had kids. Now I love it

here." Contentment spread over Margaret's face. "I know my neighbors. We feel rooted here. It's our home."

"We saw a nice place in Wallingford," Alison said. "Great location, hardwood floors . . . except it had a smell."

"How so?"

"It was sort of a mildew scent, even though the place seemed clean."

Margaret set down her glass. "Weird."

"Khalid couldn't smell it, just me."

A quizzical look appeared on Margaret's face and then a sudden sureness. Nodding her head, she reached out and touched Alison's hand. "I wonder if you're pregnant."

"No," Alison said a bit too loudly. "That's not possible."

"It's not?" Margaret raised her eyebrows.

"We use protection. There's no way." Alison twisted the wedding ring on her finger. Accidental pregnancies were for careless people, not her. Besides, she had plans. Grand plans, which didn't include babies—not for a decade at least.

"When's your period due?" A little smile played on Margaret's lips.

"I don't know. I had my period . . . It was light." Alison felt flustered and didn't know why she was even answering.

"Light? How?"

"It only lasted a day or two."

90

"I bet you're pregnant." Margaret sat back, clearly pleased with herself. The sound of her voice annoyed Alison, who had an abrupt urge to flee.

Margaret snapped her fingers in the air. "You know what?" She pointed at Alison. "I've got a pregnancy test." Margaret jumped off her stool. "I had a scare a while back," she said and rushed out of the kitchen. Alison crossed her arms; she didn't want someone's old pregnancy test.

Margaret returned, tapping the label on the box. "The expiration date is still okay." She set it in front of Alison, who stared at the box sitting shamelessly on the counter.

"It's fine. Really." Alison slid the box back. "I can get my own."

"Take it." Margaret put it back in front of Alison. "*Inshallah*, I'm through with these."

Alison slid it back. "I don't think I'm pregnant."

"Just take it!"

Alison could no longer argue and didn't want to see the box another second. She slipped it in her purse, got off the stool, and walked to the living room. "*Yalla*, Khalid, let's go."

In the car as they drove back to Capitol Hill, Khalid talked about his upcoming job interview. "I have a good feeling about this one. The job's perfect for me."

Alison turned to him. "Do you love me?"

"What a question." He put his hand over hers. "Of course I love you."

He unlocked the door to their tiny apartment. They squeezed past the boxes piled by the door. He sat down on the sofa and took out his cell phone. Alison went to the bedroom and slid the pregnancy test under the foot of the mattress.

That night, she slept fitfully as she pushed away thoughts of the item under her feet. She dreamt she gave birth to a dark-haired baby boy who cried incessantly and looked like Khalid.

In the morning, Alison awoke with a weary, restless feeling. She busied herself in the kitchen, waiting impatiently for Khalid to leave the house. She made cappuccinos with her stovetop espresso maker. The newspaper editorials were of no interest, and her cappuccino tasted gross. For the first time, she suggested Khalid go to the coffee shop and meet a friend.

"I'd rather have coffee with you." He smiled at her from their breakfast nook.

Alison got up and poured the remainder of her coffee down the kitchen drain. "That's sweet, but I have some things to do. Don't you want to see one of the guys?"

At this, he began his text messaging, the familiar rapid pressing of keys. It didn't take long for a reply to arrive; he always had friends readily available, as though on standby. Khalid gave Alison a kiss, and the door clicked behind him. She went to the bedroom and retrieved the box. In the bathroom, she locked the door, sat on the toilet, and took a deep breath. After staring at the box for a long time, she took out the directions and finally performed the humiliating procedure.

Alison sat on the bathroom floor and leaned against the wall, waiting for the five minutes to pass. She thought about the life she had planned for herself: graduate school, travels around the Middle East with Khalid, and an international career. She wondered why five minutes was taking so long. When it was time, she picked up the test strip and looked at it.

"Shit."

 Chapter 6

The morning rain had given way to a deep blue summer sky. Zainab ventured out and walked from Ahmed's house at one end of the street to the other. She had given up the idea of leaving the street on her own. Each time she reached the four-lane main road, she watched the cars whiz past. Would they stop for her? Was it like in Amman, where she could trust they wouldn't run her down? *Allahu alim. God only knew.*

Zainab followed the cars with her eyes, toward the direction of the supermarket. She needed to buy eggplant and oil for the day's cooking. Unfortunately, she had to rely on Margaret for that. What Zainab needed was a small *dukan* on the street, where she could buy yogurt, bread, and vegetables. That would be simpler than asking Margaret to drive her. If Abed were alive, Zainab would have complained to him about this, and he would have understood.

Back in front of her son's house, she looked at her watch. Another hour before the noon prayer. From the garage, she retrieved a large flattened box. She looked around for a sunny patch of grass, spread her cardboard, and sat. She eased her string of prayer beads from the pocket of her long *dishdasha* and gently passed them through her fingers while staring at the houses across the street. Zainab's eyes fell on their sameness: each one made of wood, two stories, and a two-car garage dominating the front. All the grass lawns ran together into one.

A woman walked by with a dog on a leash. As she passed, she waved.

Zainab replied, "*Sabah al-khair.*" *Morning of Goodness*. She went on to praise God that the rain had stopped. The woman smiled and shrugged.

Ah, yes. These foreigners didn't understand Arabic. Zainab gave the woman a nod and looked away. She realized what was missing—if her son's front yard had a wall around it, she could truly relax, even remove her scarf. With her face toward the sun, she closed her eyes and sighed deeply. The air was warming up and finally felt like summer.

Her peaceful moment ended when the front door closed with a thud, and Margaret was coming toward her. What was wrong now? Margaret reached her, stopped, and put a hand on one hip. "I'm sorry, but you're in the neighbor's yard," she said in her broken Arabic.

Zainab glanced from her son's house to the neighbor's. She paused and slowly stood. Then she picked up her cardboard and ambled past Margaret. How in God's name was she supposed to know where one yard ended and the next began?

Inside the house, Zainab chased the cat out of her room, closed the door, and opened the top drawer of her dresser. Her hands reached for a bundle, Abed's black-and-white checked *kufiyah*. She gently lifted it out and brought it to her bed. With a tender hand, she unfurled the scarf he had worn over his shoulders. First, she only looked— a wristwatch with a black leather band, a pair of wire frame eyeglasses, a tarnished cigarette lighter, and a string of prayer beads—all Abed's. She regarded them lovingly for a few moments, and then one by one, she held each item in her hands. His prayer beads carried the most memories—the thirty-three little amber-colored balls, their tassel long gone. She could picture them in Abed's fingers so clearly. Zainab held the beads against her chest until she couldn't bear it any longer. Then all at once, she rolled up the items and put them back in her drawer.

In the living room, she paced. She looked at the time, a constant gesture, as there was no call to prayer in America. Every evening she asked Ahmed the times of the five prayers for the following day. They changed slightly with each dawn, and Zainab preferred to pray at precisely the correct time. Ahmed consulted a list of prayer times in Seattle for the seventh month, July, which had just begun. The problem was Zainab couldn't read it.

She had no memory of her brief schooling as a young girl. Anysa occasionally mentioned their short-lived attendance at the village *madrassa*. Anysa was older, and to this day, she spoke of the sheikh who had taught *Qur'an* recitation and stories of the prophets. When the *nakba*—the catastrophe of 1948—struck, the family had fled their home in the village, and Zainab's main job became hauling water to the family's tent. She had been a young girl at the time, but almighty God, Zainab still recalled the heaviness of the canister and the ache in her shoulders.

From that sole memory, the whole refugee camp arose in her mind—those first years when the camp had been row after row of tents, and the muddy pathways between. That was when Zainab's *Qur'an* studies had ended. She'd forgotten the numbers and letters she had learned, a loss among so many others, too many to count or contemplate. Somehow Anysa remembered how to read numbers, but she'd never taught Zainab. So typical.

Zainab tried to focus on her prayer. Had she done one *rak'ah* or two? May God forgive her for any missed sets. She had been distracted by thoughts of her sister ever since the phone call. Zainab had called Anysa and confided her hope that a good man would ask for Nadia. Zainab had brought up this topic in such a way so as not to make Anysa suspect they were desperate. There were others Zainab called: her brother Waleed, still in the same refugee camp, and her daughters: Huda, also in the camp, and Fatma in Jordan. Zainab revealed her hope to all of them.

After completing the prescribed prayer, Zainab moved on to her supplications. "Praise be to God for the baby that Khalid's wife carries." This had been particularly surprising news. And so soon! A wedding night baby perhaps? Foreign wives generally took their time getting pregnant and usually had only two or three babies. It had been a joy to hear Khalid announce this news at his last visit. Now all Zainab needed was for him to get a job and for Nadia to marry. Inshallah.

Zainab pulled her mind back to her prayers, to something she had been asking for all week. "*Ya Allah*," she whispered. "Let Ahmed move his family to an Arab country. He has worked so hard, let them have this chance. If that is your will." She rocked back and forth and reached for her prayer beads. Her son had spent more than twenty years in America. Enough was enough. It was time to return, time to be near her and the rest of the family.

Finally, Zainab made her prayer for Abed. As she asked God to have mercy on the soul of her dead husband, her mind wandered back to Anysa, who professed to know everything about widow-hood, having been one herself for more than ten years. The pain of missing Abed would lessen in time, Anysa had predicted.

Wrong.

It had been nearly six months, yet Zainab still grieved for him. The shape and patterns of her life had been forever altered. Each new family event—the graduation, wedding, and now the pregnancy—all made Abed's absence more acute. She needed him now more than ever. How could she alone decide who would be the best match for Nadia? It took a man to judge another man.

"*Ya Allah*, I seek your guidance," she whispered. "You are the knower of hidden things." Zainab concluded by asking for protection for all of her blood relatives and for everyone suffering in Palestine.

At last, she stood up, exhausted.

"*Yama*, wake up."

Zainab opened her eyes. Ahmed stood over her with the telephone in his hand. "It's Aunt

Anysa." He gave her the phone and left the room.

Sitting up in bed, Zainab oriented herself. There was still another hour before the morning prayer.

The two sisters greeted each other, asked if there was any news, and inquired about each other's health. To each question, the answer was the same: *Alhamdulillah. Praise be to God.*

They got down to business. "My son Mohammed is interested in Nadia," Anysa said, "but he hasn't seen her since the funeral." The mention of Abed's funeral produced a slight tremor in Zainab. Anysa continued, "He wants to travel to Amman to sit with Nadia, to talk to her. Then he will decide."

Zainab wanted to say that it wasn't only for Mohammed to decide. Nadia needed to give her opinion, as well. Maybe she didn't want her aunt's son, divorced and with a child. Maybe she didn't want the first man who approached her.

But Zainab didn't say this. Instead, she laughed and said, "*Inshallah*, our children will marry. *Inshallah*, we'll be grandmothers together. It's in God's hands."

Anysa echoed the sentiment. "God is the best of planners!" Her voice was so piercing, Zainab had to hold the phone away from her ear.

They said their salaams and Zainab hung up. Her prayers were already taking effect.

Just after the noon prayer the following day, Mona's car pulled up in the driveway. When the doorbell sounded and the four boys darted up the stairs, Zainab's heart rose up and the fatigue of the day lifted.

After greetings and kisses, the boys ran to the backyard, and Mona said, "I'll make tea."

"Not yet," Zainab replied. "I have news." They settled next to each other on the couch, and she recounted the events of the past day—the phone calls, the requests, the prayers, and the immediate reply.

"Anysa was just so sure Nadia would accept him," Zainab said. "So sure!"

"Mohammed's a nice man, *masha'Allah*," Mona said. "I can't say a bad word against him, but his wife—he'll always be attached to her."

Zainab shook her head. "I know, I know."

Mona slid closer to Zainab and squeezed her hand. "Whatever God has planned for Nadia, will be. *Inshallah*, she'll find a good man."

Mona got up to prepare tea, but Margaret appeared and insisted on doing it herself. When she returned to the living room with the tea tray, she set it on the coffee table, poured, and served. Nearby, Leena played on the floor with her own aluminum teapot. The child wore only a pair of shorts and no shirt.

"*Habibti*," Zainab said. "Go get dressed."

The child looked up and ran to her mother sitting nearby. It was then that Zainab noticed Margaret sitting, looking expectantly at her and

Mona. It seemed Margaret had news to share, as well. Oh, what a struggle understanding her. Zainab turned to her daughter as Margaret began speaking in her mix of English and muddy Arabic.

"What's she saying?"

Mona lifted a finger. "It's about her and Ahmed's anniversary."

"Ah." Zainab nodded to Margaret.

"Something about a hotel," Mona explained. "She and Ahmed will go to a hotel."

Zainab said to Mona, "What made her think of such a thing? Why do they need a hotel? They have their own bed in their own house."

Mona gave Zainab a piercing gaze. "*Yama*, be nice."

"Just like a bride and groom!"

As if Margaret was the first person to be married for twenty years. Zainab had been married for as long. Longer. Yet she had never celebrated an anniversary. She wondered how many years she and Abed had been married. Forty? Fifty? Truth be told, she didn't know the year of her wedding—or even the year of her birth.

Zainab turned to Margaret. It had been a while since she had regarded her daughter-in-law closely, but now she brought her into focus: her long red hair spilling down her shoulders onto her plain shirt, the neckline a bit too low. She took in Margaret's serious face, the freckles dotting her cheeks, wrinkles beginning to form. Both familiar and foreign, her son's wife had a hopeful manner about her, the way she sat upright at the tea tray, gazing back in anticipation, as though waiting for approval. Zainab had to admit, Margaret was faithful in marriage, diligent, and dependable, as both wife and mother. A twinge of affection crept over Zainab, and she gave Margaret a gentle nod.

"*Mabruuk, habibti*," Zainab said. *Congratulations, my love.*

Margaret smiled back, and they sipped their tea in silence. Zainab glanced at the telephone on the side table. She recalled Anysa's words: "I'll call you. Don't call me." As if Zainab were going to call and beg for Anysa's divorced son. Divorced with a child.

Maybe instead Khalid would call. Bless him. He was finally showing some promise. Better yet, maybe he would come and see her; his last visit had been so short. Soon Mona and her boys would say good-bye, and again Zainab would feel lonely and restless in the house at the end of the road that went nowhere, talking only to Margaret who could say just a few sentences in Arabic. Inshallah, Khalid and his wife would move to this neighborhood. Maybe then, Zainab could walk to his house and see her new grandchild after he was born.

Leena was watering the houseplant with her

teapot. Margaret followed her, trying to slip a dress on her.

Zainab pulled out her prayer beads and ran them through her fingers. She was unsure whether she would still be living in Ahmed's house when Khalid's baby was born. Where to live? It was a problem. She could not go back to live with her daughters, who were each living in the homes of their husbands, taking care of their husbands' families. She could not live alone in a house without Abed. She would die from boredom living in Ahmed's house watching Egyptian soap operas and the bad news on *Al Jazeera*. Perhaps there was another solution she hadn't thought of. As Abed used to say, "God may create that which you do not know." This thought calmed her for a moment until her mind came back to the matter of Nadia.

What about Nadia? Poor Nadia, left abandoned in Amman. "*Astaghfirullah*," Zainab said. *May God forgive me.*

❧ Chapter 7 ☙

To get to the coffeemaker, Margaret would have to step past the mother, who was firmly planted in the center of the kitchen. Margaret couldn't trust herself not to sigh or roll her eyes. It was always about pretending—this time, pretending not to be bothered by the insult of a shared kitchen.

Margaret had missed an hour of sleep. It wasn't due to something normal like a dog barking or a child with a fever. It was a phone call in the middle of the night, which began with the mother's loud, "*Allo? Allo?*"

All middle-of-the-night calls originated from the Middle East, where the family seemed unaware of the ten-hour time difference between Seattle and the West Bank. As if the phone call weren't bad enough, the mother had come looking for Ahmed and gotten him out of bed, too. Afterward, he immediately fell back to sleep, his soft snoring filling the room. But Margaret flipped back and forth under the covers, her exasperation keeping her awake.

Now she sat at the counter, hunched over her coffee and newspaper. When the mother spoke, Margaret pretended not to hear.

The front page displayed news about the war in Iraq. Margaret could only cope with skimming the headlines. The international page was no better, with its news of violence from the West Bank. A subhead caught her eye. *Nine-year-old Palestinian boy shot by Israeli soldiers.* The same age as Tariq. Relieved they didn't live anywhere near there, Margaret imagined the victim: a boy with black hair, wearing his school backpack. She turned the page before she could discover any more details that would stay lodged in her mind.

The mother asked for something and pointed to a shelf. Margaret got off her stool, reached to the top of the cupboard, and handed a bag of dried *meramia* leaves to the mother, who was talking about Nadia. Margaret comprehended little and suspected that even if she and the mother shared the same language, they still wouldn't understand each other. The mother put a large pinch of *meramia* into her pot of tea, and the kitchen filled with the smell of the dried herb. Why couldn't the mother just stop talking?

Ahmed strolled into the kitchen, refreshed and content from sleeping in. "*Sabah al-khair*," he said to his mother. *Morning of goodness*.

"*Sabah al-noor*," she replied. *Morning of light*.

Margaret rolled her eyes to such flowery greetings. So overly elaborate! She looked at Ahmed. "Who the hell called last night?" she asked. The fact that the mother didn't understand English had its benefits.

Ahmed smiled. "Good morning to you, too."

"And what's she saying about Nadia?" Margaret glanced at the mother, who was arranging a tray for herself—tea, *zataar*, olive oil, bread, and yogurt—a reproduction of her breakfast back home.

Ahmed poured himself a cup of coffee. "Nadia's getting married."

The last time Margaret had seen Nadia, she'd been wearing a blue-and-white school uniform. "Isn't she still a kid?"

"She's nineteen." Ahmed sat down as his mother slipped out of the kitchen with her breakfast tray. "She's completed her certificate in English translation."

Margaret nodded. "Who's she marrying?"

"Mohammed, the son of Aunt Anysa."

Margaret closed her eyes and pinched the bridge of her nose. First cousins. If she hadn't married Ahmed, would he have chosen a cousin? Margaret tried to blink away that image. "Isn't Anysa's son already married?" she asked.

"Separated, planning to divorce," Ahmed said. "That's why they called—to make sure my mother and I agreed."

"You?"

"I *am* Nadia's oldest brother." Ahmed crossed his arms. "I think he'll be a good husband. Besides, it's what she wants."

Margaret hoped he was right. Nadia's choice of a husband would be the most critical decision of her life. Of Ahmed's five sisters, only Yasmine had married outside the family, and she lived an impoverished life in a refugee camp in the West Bank.

Ahmed continued, "The engagement will be official next month."

Margaret conjured an image of the engagement party ahead: Nadia in a frilly dress, posing for photos and showing off her new gold jewelry.

Ahmed took a sip of coffee. "We're all going."

"What?" Margaret set her cup down and stared at him.

"I told them already."

"We never went to Yasmine's engagement party."

"Things are different. I have to be there because my father can't. *Allah yarhamhu.*"

"But you didn't ask me."

"Honey, we need to go. Last time I was there, everyone wanted to see the kids. They haven't even met Leena yet."

Margaret brought her hand to her cheek. "This is going to be expensive. Five of us, plus your mother."

"We'll manage."

"I think it's a bad idea."

"I've already decided."

The new family patriarch had spoken. He had made up his mind in the middle of the night with his mother. Then Margaret remembered the summer vacation they had planned for the next month. She had negotiated with Ahmed through all of the details, and they had settled on renting a cottage for ten days on San Juan Island—not an easy feat for August. There was even space for the mother. "And our trip to the islands?"

Ahmed leaned back and clasped his hands behind his head. "We'll do it later."

Margaret stood up without saying anything.

He reached out to her. "She's my sister."

Margaret flinched and pulled away. She left the kitchen and went to her bedroom, closed the door, and sat in her armchair. In her head, she could hear the voices of her neighbors: *I don't know how you do it. You're a saint.*

Damn! She tried to grasp what bothered her most. Was it the cancelled trip to the islands? The fact that he hadn't consulted her? How he did anything to please his family?

Then she remembered someone else's words, those of Aisha from her *Qur'an* study group. "You'll receive blessings for all you've done for your husband's family." Margaret wondered just when she'd be able to cash in on these blessings. Would she get double points for having the mother move in?

She was aware, of course, that it was wrong to feel this way, so bitter and resentful, wallowing in self-pity. She was aware, too, of their anniversary the next day—twenty years. Yes, twenty years and three children and three restaurants and seven trips to Jordan.

There was a tap at the door. Ahmed stood in the doorway and Margaret turned away. He sat on the bed. "I'm sorry. I know it's not easy going to Jordan." He looked down and ran his hand along the bedspread. "I'll make it up to you."

More promises. What could she do? She didn't want to ruin their anniversary. Twenty years celebrated by not speaking to each other. Or worse.

"I'll go to Jordan—under one condition." As if she had any leverage. "I want to stay in a hotel. Not at your sister's."

"Fine. We'll stay in a hotel."

Some of the pressure left Margaret's chest. At least they wouldn't sleep on floor mats at Fatma's house. "I can't believe Nadia's getting engaged," she said.

"I know." He shook his head. "She wasn't even born when we got married."

The next day, Margaret packed her sexy nightgown in her suitcase and tried to push away the troubles with Ahmed from the day before. Check-in time at the hotel was two o'clock. Then, for twenty-four hours, there would be no meals to prepare, no housework, no children, no yard work, and, most important, no mother-in-law. It would be just the two of them, a normal couple. And when was the last time she had felt that way? With that, Margaret turned to her closet and to the soft waves of memory.

Fall of 1983, the annual Culture Fest on the UW campus. Margaret had gone to watch the folk dancers as part of her anthropology research on the rituals of dance in daily life. Between performances, she went to the ethnic food booths run by students selling specialties from their countries. She decided on Middle Eastern food and took in the cheerful young man taking her order: his black curly hair, strong arms, and white apron tied across his fit body. He smiled at her as he placed two perfectly formed falafels onto the bread. He added tomatoes, pickles, and sauce and presented the sandwich with a flourish. She paid him, and he took his time with the change, the two of them lingering over the transaction.

Later that afternoon, she went to the Middle Eastern dance performances, sat in the front row, and took notes. There was a voice behind her. "Do you mind if I sit here?"

She turned and saw him, no longer wearing his apron, a backpack slung over his shoulder. Behind him was row after row of empty chairs.

She gestured to the seat next to her. "Please." She lifted her chin toward the stage. "Do you know anything about this folk dance?" Somehow she sensed that he would.

He looked at the dancers, four women of uncertain origin, twisting their bare midriffs and swirling their wrists. "This is not really a folk dance."

Thus began their first conversation, an interview on Arab dance customs. Margaret was amazed that any man could know so much about women's dancing. She pulled out her camera and took photos of the dancers, who, according to Ahmed, were performing a variation of Egyptian cabaret. When he wasn't looking, she snapped a photo of him, too.

They met again over tea, for the purpose of Margaret's research, as Ahmed explained the role of *dabke* dancing at Palestinian weddings. He was an international student, a Business Administration major, working his way through university. Margaret took careless notes and focused more on Ahmed's hands as he spoke and on his eyes—holding her gaze until she blushed.

At the end of their meeting, he invited her to dinner at a Lebanese restaurant in the U District. He ordered a generous sampler of his favorite Arab foods—he wanted her to try them all. A few days later, he came to her apartment and cooked *maqluba*. She was transfixed by the sight of him in her kitchen, arranging the platter of rice, chicken, and fried cauliflower. As he moved about her tiny space, he had a familiar, carefree way about himself.

The two of them sat on the floor and ate together at the coffee table in Margaret's living room, which was decorated with foreign film posters and Iranian tablecloths. She noticed the way he garnished the food, set the table, and arranged it all. She felt taken care of, and at that moment she found herself falling in love with him.

They saw each other twice a week, then daily. They met quickly on campus, stealing moments together before dashing off to class or their part-time jobs. On his days off, Ahmed would prepare complex Arab meals for Margaret and describe in great detail the restaurant he planned to open. He struck her as sincere and hard-working, spon-taneous and fun. Her love for him grew steadily, and she said yes without hesitation when he proposed to her one evening over a candlelit meal of savory lamb kabobs and fragrant rice pilaf.

Margaret's parents, impressed by Ahmed's respectful manner and earnest work ethic, accepted him right away. A year after meeting each other, the pair exchanged vows at the Seattle mosque. A month later, under the July sun, Ahmed and Margaret were married in a small ceremony in her parents' rhododendron-filled backyard on Whidbey Island. Their university friends attended, as well as Margaret's two brothers, who flew in from the East Coast.

In order to meet Ahmed's parents, however, Margaret needed to get a passport and they had to save up for airline tickets. When they eventually traveled to the West Bank six months later, she took pleasure in getting to know his family and seeing their simple way of life. His mother gave Margaret three gold bangles, which surprised and touched her.

But at the same time, she was secretly overwhelmed by Ahmed's family, by their noise level and sheer numbers. Granted, they were warm and welcoming, but the small house overflowed with people and chaos. So many siblings! Five already, and a sixth on the way. Margaret remained patient throughout the monthlong visit, reminding herself that she and Ahmed would be back in Seattle soon, just the two of them.

Meanwhile, Ahmed showed her the most historic sites in his country: Bethlehem, Jericho, Yaffa, and Jerusalem. It was years before the political problems of the intifada, and they were able to travel around freely. The high point was Jerusalem. Walking together through the covered alleyways of the Old City, they held hands, and she fell in love with him all over again. Margaret believed that she would love him all her life.

Two decades later, the memories from those early years swept through Margaret as she packed the small suitcase for their anniversary getaway. She thought back to that younger version of herself, so optimistic and full of confidence. What began as tiny adjustments to accommodate Ahmed's culture had expanded over the years into a life that her younger self could never have imagined—the endless family obligations, savings sent overseas, the long trail of visitors and houseguests, the mother moving in—the main requirements of which were tolerance and flexibility of an extreme variety.

Ahmed walked into the bedroom. He put his arm around her waist and pulled her toward him. "Honey, let's get out of here."

"*Yalla*, let's go." Margaret closed the suitcase

and handed it to him. She checked herself in the mirror and smoothed her long red hair. They went to the living room and kissed their three children good-bye. She gave Leena a tight hug. Margaret nodded good-bye to the mother. "*Ma'a salama.*"

While Ahmed was offering a lengthy good-bye to his mother, Margaret gave final instructions to Jenin. "Sweetheart, let your grandmother do the cooking. Keep Tariq from chasing Leena. Don't call unless there's an emergency. Make sure Leena keeps her clothes on." She blew a last kiss to Leena and followed Ahmed out the front door. He turned and looked back at her expectantly, then grabbed her hand and led her to their waiting car. She felt a rush of anticipation, yet one ques-tion continued to disturb her.

Could she ever have a normal life with Ahmed?

❧ Chapter 8 ❧

Dark clouds hung over the skyline as Margaret and Ahmed drove toward downtown Seattle. He reached over and placed his hand on hers.

"Thanks for understanding about the trip to Jordan."

"You're going to make it up to me. Remember?"

He flashed a smile, a genuine one, and Margaret willed herself into a better mood. After all, it was the first time they'd been alone in months—the undeniable consequence of the mother living with them. *Stop!* Margaret told herself. There would be no more thoughts of the mother. Margaret intended to enjoy herself and make the most of their little anniversary getaway.

The hotel room that Ahmed had booked was a spacious suite with a love seat in the corner. Margaret stretched out on the king-size bed; she was relaxed yet excited at the same time. Ahmed joined her. He kissed her and something stirred inside her, a flicker of their old passion.

Their lovemaking was that of a couple who understood each other's bodies, preferences, and rhythms. It was the usual sequence, slightly prolonged in honor of their anniversary. Afterward, they curled up together and caught their breath. Ahmed caressed her shoulder. "That was the warm-up." He brushed her hair aside and kissed her neck. "Wait till tonight."

Margaret smiled to herself and then realized the time. "Honey, we need to get going for the afternoon tea."

Ahmed held her closer. "Do we have to?"

Margaret sat up. "That's why we chose this hotel."

The Victorian Room was aptly named. Chandeliers hung from the ceiling, curtains flowed from the arched windows, and the chairs flaunted a brocade motif. The hostess led them to their table, where they relaxed into their chairs, and Margaret touched the thick linen tablecloth. After having worked at their Capitol Hill restaurant for so many years, she relished being in an establishment run by other people. She looked at Ahmed and fixed him with an affectionate gaze.

"What?" he asked.

She glanced down at her tasseled menu. "I'm just happy."

When the tea server arrived, Margaret ordered the Imperial Afternoon Tea for two. The server brought two gold-rimmed teapots with matching cups and saucers. The food arrived next, a three-tiered silver tray, delicately arranged with tiny sandwiches, petit fours, and scones.

As they admired the food and took their first sips, Margaret savored the moment—the same glow she had felt before during other special times she and Ahmed had shared, times she deeply missed.

She waved to the server. "Could you take our picture?" Margaret handed over the anniversary gift that Ahmed had presented her with that morning: a Canon Rebel, her first SLR digital camera. She liked the name. *Rebel*.

Ahmed reached for her hand. Margaret turned toward the lens and smiled big. With an opening and closing of the shutter, their perfect moment was documented. They weren't living the lie this time.

They left the Victorian Room satisfied and in high spirits. Next, they explored the rest of the hotel, then walked the streets of downtown Seattle, cozily sharing an umbrella under the drizzle. Back in their room, Margaret was content and relaxed as she prepared for their eight o'clock dinner reservation. She did her hair and makeup with care and put on a new wraparound dress and long beaded gemstone necklace, a gift that Ahmed had given her the year before. Meanwhile, he looked striking in his crisp white dress shirt and dark slacks.

The candlelit dining room was just as spectacular as the tea room. After serious consideration, they selected their starter and main courses. Over a smoked black cod appetizer, Ahmed looked at her and caressed her arm. Margaret loved how their life still revolved around food, whether they were preparing it together or enjoying a meal out. And Ahmed was still so charming when he focused all his attention on her, rather than on his family—or worse, his mother. Margaret pushed this thought aside as he reached for her hand and held it between his own. Then he lifted it and gently kissed her fingers. This was how a twentieth anniversary was supposed to feel.

The main course arrived, and Ahmed raised his glass. "Next year, Jerusalem." Margaret met his gaze and raised her glass, too. They took in the presentation of the food, the unique garnishes and flavor combinations. They tasted each other's dishes and agreed that their choices were excellent.

Ahmed laid down his fork. "Honey, there's something I want to discuss."

Margaret bit into a grilled prawn dipped in a buttery sauce.

"There's an opportunity . . ." he began. "Something I've been thinking about, something I really want to do."

She swallowed and held her breath.

His eyes met hers. "I have a job opportunity in the Gulf."

She blew out a breath of air. It wasn't the first time Ahmed had brought up vague plans of returning to the Middle East. In fact, he had been mentioning it more often lately. Fortunately, Margaret had always found a way to dissuade him.

"An opportunity?" she asked.

"There's a hiring director in the United Arab Emirates. He's seen my restaurants. He wants me to manage a chain of coffee shops there."

She raised her eyebrows, speechless for a moment. There was something about his tone and the look in his dark eyes that unnerved her. "You can't be serious."

"The UAE is a small Gulf country." He spoke as though he were already convinced. "It's located next to—"

"I know where the hell the UAE is."

Ahmed cleared his throat and looked away.

Margaret sat back in her chair. "You know how I feel about this."

"And you know how I feel."

"There's no way," she said, shaking her head. "Why are you bringing this up now?"

"We never have any time alone."

She rolled her eyes. "You know why that is."

"I need a change. Do you know what it's like being an Arab in this country? The prejudice we face?"

"Oh, please, not this again." She closed her eyes for a moment.

"It's growing, this discrimination against Arabs and Muslims."

"I know it's unfair," she said, "but has it affected you personally? No, it hasn't."

"Am I supposed to wait until it does?"

She pushed away her plate. "Have you lost your mind?" She leaned in. "It's not enough your mother's living with us?"

"Leave my mother out of it."

"You want to drag us around the world, as well?" Margaret's chest tightened and squeezed in on her. "We're not leaving our house."

"You hate that house."

"Three successful restaurants." She touched her breastbone to relieve the pressure. "You're willing to start all over? And with someone else's business?"

"We can have a good life there. The kids can learn Arabic, experience the culture."

"Our kids are settled in school."

"They'd be better off there."

"How can you say that?" Margaret's voice was shrill. "They were born here."

"Jenin's going to be *sixteen*." He said the word like it was a disease.

"So?"

"You know what happens to teenage girls here."

"That's ridiculous," she hissed.

The waiter approached their table, then took a step back and disappeared.

"It was your dream to have those restaurants," she said.

"That was never my dream."

"All of sudden it's your dream to live there?"

Ahmed crossed his arms. "I've been living here for twenty-four years. I've done more than enough. It's *my* turn now."

"Are you saying you've stayed here for me?"

He grimaced. "Keep it down."

Margaret became aware of the gentle sounds of silverware clanking and the conversations coming from nearby tables. She lowered her voice. "You were educated here." She counted on her fingers. "You started your business here, you send money to your family."

"Leave my family out of it."

"Plus!" Margaret's voice became agitated

again. "You got your brother educated, got green cards for your parents." She tapped the table for emphasis.

"Yes, I appreciate all of that. But we've been living here a long time."

"Who's this guy offering you a job? How can you trust him?" Margaret thought of their restaurants, which had started out as one small café on Capitol Hill. She and Ahmed had transformed it into something unique, offering meticulously prepared Mediterranean meals and gourmet desserts displayed in a glass case. With sweat and sacrifice, they'd opened two more—one in Fremont and another in Greenwood. They had received a string of good reviews—and even a local award. Could he really give it all up?

"Do you honestly think it would be better?"

"I'm tired of working here." Ahmed dropped his shoulders. "I just don't feel I belong anymore —and it's exhausting the hell out of me."

"You think it'd be perfect over there? It wouldn't be." She tried to picture this faraway country but couldn't. Instead, memories of their trips to Jordan filled her head: the garbage on the side of the road, the clumsy stone houses, people pushing to be first in line. "How would we live?" She covered her face with her hands.

"Calm down," Ahmed whispered. "You're entertaining the entire restaurant."

She looked around. People turned away when

they saw her. Ahmed signed the bill as her mind swirled with thoughts of her mother, Lois, and how she adored her time with her grandchildren. Her twice-monthly visits were always planned in advance—such a contrast to the disorder of Ahmed's family. Jenin, Tariq, and Leena were Lois's only grandchildren living in the same state. Margaret's brothers and their families had settled on the East Coast, five and six hours away by plane. Lois complained bitterly that she saw those children only once or twice a year. Margaret could never move so far away.

When they were alone in the elevator heading back to their room, Margaret turned to Ahmed. "Isn't our life already Arab enough?" She waited for him to say something. When he didn't, she went further. "We constantly have a houseful of your family. It's like we're already living in the Middle East!"

Again, Ahmed said nothing. Once behind their door, he slumped into the love seat.

Margaret paced the room, which now seemed cramped. "What about your mother?"

"My mother goes where I go."

"Great." Her voice was dripping with contempt, but she didn't care.

"I'd be a jerk if I didn't take care of my mother." He paused for a moment. "Maybe we should stop talking before we say something we shouldn't."

He was right on both counts, but Margaret couldn't stop. "If we lived over there, you wouldn't need me. You'd be in one room with your mother and your family, and I'd be in another, by myself, wishing for our home to just be *our* home." She realized that she had just described their current life. "It'd be like now—only worse."

"Is your life with me so bad?"

"Everything has to be your way." Margaret sat on the bed and felt her energy dissolving. "This is my life, too."

"I'm ready to leave this country."

She balled her hands into fists. "Please don't say anything else, not another word."

They went to sleep without speaking, each at opposite sides of the king-size bed. She dreamt Ahmed's family was socializing noisily in a crowded living room, while she ran back and forth from a kitchen, carrying an enormous tray of tea glasses. She opened her eyes in the morning, not knowing where the dream had taken place, in Seattle or over there. Margaret sat up and looked at Ahmed while he slept. Her chest filled with post-argument remorse. Could they salvage the rest of their anniversary?

At breakfast, Ahmed asked, "What would you like to do?"

"I don't mind," she replied.

"We'll do whatever you want," he said.

If only that were true.

• • •

At Pike Place Market, the sight of the fishmongers tossing salmon to each other served as an agreeable distraction. It had been a long time since Margaret had walked among the bustling stalls offering fish and flowers, produce and crafts. The scene was vibrant but overcrowded with mid-summer tourists.

"Here, take my picture." She handed her camera to Ahmed.

He held it up. "Next to a statue of a pig?"

"It's a landmark. It's not like we are going to eat it." She posed next to the market's iconic large brass piggy bank. Margaret told herself to smile—back to living the lie yet again.

They moved through the crowds, admiring the buckets of flashy dahlias and boxes of plump blueberries. "You don't have to go to the Middle East to shop in a *souk*," Margaret said as she swept her arm toward an artful display of vegetables.

Ahmed smiled weakly but said nothing. She vowed silently not to mention the Middle East for the rest of the day.

Across the street, they walked along the crowded sidewalk, glancing in the smoked salmon shop and pausing at the original Starbucks, a narrow coffee shop with no seating. Ahmed entered the little Middle Eastern grocery store, and Margaret followed him in. It was small and dusty and devoid of customers. The place, which normally interested her, now seemed unnecessary and irrelevant. They continued walking until they reached Sur La Table, the gourmet cooking store they both enjoyed perusing. They entered and surveyed the floor-to-ceiling selection of specialty pots and pans.

"We could spend all day in here," Ahmed said.

She moved past the colorful table linens to the display of glossy hardback cookbooks. One book called out to her: *Cooking of the Arabian Gulf.* She read its subtitle: *Recipes from Oman, Qatar, Saudi Arabia, and the United Arab Emirates.* The sight of the book was profoundly irritating. She turned away and looked for Ahmed. He was handling a large *couscoussière* from North Africa.

"Nice, but expensive," he said.

"I'm done here. I'll be outside," she said, leaving before he could answer. She waited alone on the sidewalk, in view of the retro-neon Public Market sign and the Puget Sound beyond. The Arabian Gulf was a world away and had nothing to do with her. In her mind arose a vision of an Arab souk, crowded with people in traditional dress. Would she have to cover her hair over there? She didn't miss wearing hijab. In fact, she had finally accepted herself without it.

Ahmed joined her on the street. "Usually I have to drag you out of there."

Margaret shrugged. "I want to keep going."

For lunch, they had more northwestern fare—

halibut in a broth of tomatoes—at a sidewalk café in Pioneer Square. The clouds from the day before had surrendered to a brilliant, unbroken blue sky. Margaret looked up and down the tree-lined street, taking in the old brick buildings, flower baskets, and art galleries. "Let's come down here more often."

Ahmed nodded thoughtfully. "Okay, sure."

Did that mean that he agreed to stay in Seattle?

They crossed the street, and Ahmed suggested they enter a map shop. Margaret took only two steps inside, and there it was. In the center rack, amongst dozens of folded maps, she noticed the title of only one: *The United Arab Emirates*. She had never given a thought to this country, and here it was in front of her again. She stood frozen, averting her eyes.

"You okay?" Ahmed asked.

She steadied herself. "I'm fine. Just a little tired." How had he missed the map right in front of them? "I'm not really into maps. I'm going to the bookstore." She left the shop and breathed in the fresh air outside. The bricks and flowers of Pioneer Square were picturesque, but Margaret could scarcely appreciate the scenery through which she was walking. She crossed the street again, heading toward Elliott Bay Books on the corner. A car whizzed past her.

She felt Ahmed take her arm. "Are you okay?"

"Not really."

They entered the well-worn bookstore, which was filled with room after room of wooden bookshelves. Margaret proceeded cautiously. The floorboards creaked as she stepped forward, orienting herself so as to avoid the travel section. She thumbed through a stack of novels, searching for a book to read in Jordan. But could she get away with reading amidst the endless tea drinking and chatter at Fatma's house? *Torture by tea,* as her friend Liz called it.

Ahmed appeared next to her. "You should look at this book." He held it up. *Guide to the United Arab Emirates.*

Margaret recoiled and waved it away. "I'm not interested in that."

"Maybe it has some information you need."

"Not interested." She picked up a novel and pretended to study the back cover.

"Just try to open your mind. Please."

She blinked and turned away.

As they drove back home, the Seattle skyline sliding away behind them, Margaret imagined their messy house, cranky children, and the unending list of complaints that would need tending. The mother would monopolize Ahmed the moment they walked in.

They pulled off the freeway and passed Margaret's favorite park, her library, her super-market—all of which looked exactly the same but had taken on a new significance. These were her places, the sites of her memories, her life, and her future.

Ahmed pulled into the cul-de-sac. A neighbor waved at Margaret. She was home.

Then she saw it. The driveway was filled with cars. There was Khalid's car and Mona's and Ibrahim's. *Damn.*

Ahmed parked. "Looks like everyone's visiting my mom."

"She can't go one day without seeing someone?"

"Why should she?"

Margaret opened the front door, and Tariq and Leena rushed down the steps to hug her. She squeezed them tightly, inhaled their scents, and told herself to smile as she entered the living room, which was littered with tea glasses. "*Salaam*," she said with a nod.

Khalid, Mona, the mother, and the cousins looked up from their conversation and acknowledged her. Nearby, Alison and Jenin were deep in discussion. As usual, Alison was talking politics. This time, she was explaining why Yasser Arafat had been confined to his headquarters in Ramallah.

"How was the anniversary, Mom?" Jenin asked.

Before she could answer, Mona spoke, a sneaky smile on her lips. "So, you're moving to the Emirates?"

Margaret stood in shock. She stared at Ahmed, who looked away.

Then the mother was saying something. Khalid translated. "She says in the UAE, you can live in a compound with foreigners."

Once again, Margaret's chest squeezed in on her. "Everyone knows about this?" She looked at Ahmed, and the room became quiet. "Am I the last to know your plans?"

He moved toward her, took her by the elbow, and led her down the hallway. "I only talked to my mother," he whispered. "She must have told them. I'm sorry."

"You already discussed this with her?"

"So what? I talk to my mother." He shrugged and left her standing in the hallway.

Margaret, trying to compose herself, put on a brave face and went back to the living room, where everyone acted as though nothing had happened. Alison was explaining to Jenin the difference between Fatah and Hamas. Why couldn't Alison give it a rest?

Margaret sat next to the mother. "How was everything?" Margaret asked in Arabic, her voice strangely high-pitched.

"*Alhamdulillah,*" the mother replied. *Praise be to God.*

Alison leaned forward and caught Margaret's eye. "I'd move there in a heartbeat."

Margaret inhaled slowly. Alison was giving

her advice. How could she know anything about moving overseas? Leaving a home? Uprooting a family?

Margaret felt a sudden urge to get out of there. Not to just go hide out in the bedroom—but to get out of the house altogether, far away. She thought of going to see her friend Liz but remembered her husband's parents were visiting from Lebanon.

"Ahmed," Margaret said. "I'm going to my *Qur'an* study group tonight."

"That's good." He looked pleased. "You haven't been for a while."

It was true. Margaret's involvement in the Muslim community had been on a downward spiral since she had stopped covering her head. At the mosque, some women had pestered her about dropping the hijab, so Margaret rarely went there anymore. However, her *Qur'an* study group was still a bit of a safe haven.

On the couch, Alison and Khalid talked softly to each other, then he turned to Margaret. "What time is the study group?"

"Seven."

Alison's eyes lit up. "Do you mind if I come?" Before Margaret could reply, Alison said, "We'll go home, and I'll come back tonight. She stood up. "If that's all right?"

"It's fine." Margaret said.

Of course, it wasn't fine.

✺ Chapter 9 ✺

As they drove home, Alison asked Khalid, "So if I go to this *Qur'an* study, you'll stop bothering me about my clothes?"

Would he really let up? His new habit—to evaluate each of her outfits, checking to see if a garment was too tight, too short, or too see-through—was making her nuts. He used to like the way she dressed, but now Alison had gotten rid of some of her favorite tops and skirts for him. Not only was it exasperating figuring out what to wear, but his requests were so silly and unfair.

"Study the real Islam." He took his eyes off the road and looked at her. "Not the one taught at university. Those classes aren't even taught by Muslims," he said. "They're taught by Jews."

"That was just one Jewish professor." She wished she'd never told him.

He took the exit to Capitol Hill. "It's their strategy, having Jews teach Islam."

"It was just one." She rolled her eyes. "It's not a conspiracy!"

Alison knew better. All sorts of people were drawn to Near Eastern studies and for different reasons. She had never told anyone about the mix of danger and fascination that drew her to the conflicted region—the same region that her own

Syrian-American parents had rejected. How could she explain? Since her first visit there, she had felt an adrenaline rush, a magnetic pull toward all things Middle Eastern. She daydreamed about traveling there again—only now Khalid would be her guide.

He drove down Broadway and took the turn to their apartment. They passed a Dumpster overflowing with garbage. Nausea fluttered inside her. Fortunately, they would be off Capitol Hill by the end of the month, away from the stench and the litter.

She said, "We should do some packing when we get home."

He glanced at her. "Maybe you shouldn't push yourself so much."

"I could get more done if . . ." Nearly four months along, she blamed her pregnancy for slowing her down. That's why she had given in to that Pine View complex in the suburbs. The new place was clean and sterile, the only apartment that didn't make her ill. Besides, they couldn't afford to live in the city anymore, now that they needed two bedrooms. As soon as Khalid got a job, though, they would save up and move back to Seattle.

They packed two boxes together before Alison's thoughts turned to food. In the kitchen, however, nothing looked good. She flipped through her cookbook of Middle Eastern cuisine and decided on *ful*, the food she had subsisted on while studying in Cairo, the food of Egyptian laborers and unemployed Arab-Americans. Khalid made tea and warmed bread while she smashed the fava beans with lemon and garlic. The dish was usually a favorite, but when it was finished, it looked unappealing. She suffered a fresh wave of queasiness as she added chopped tomatoes, a drizzle of olive oil, and fresh parsley. On their tiny table, they arranged the simple meal.

"Bless your hands," Khalid said in Arabic.

"And your hands, too."

They sipped their tea and ate in silence while Alison thought ahead to the *Qur'an* study group that evening. Khalid probably expected her to convert right away—if so, he would be disappointed. If anything, the study group would improve her classical Arabic.

Meanwhile, the graduate school printouts remained set aside, no longer on the table, but placed out of sight. Her intention to apply gnawed at her, yet there was always something to do: write a cover letter for Khalid, prepare a meal, go to work, or wait for the nausea to pass.

After a few bites, the sight of the *ful* swimming in oil sickened her. She pushed the plate away. "I can't eat any more."

He touched her arm. "I'm sorry."

"It's not your fault." She turned away until the *ful* was out of her vision.

Khalid stroked her belly, which was just starting to swell. He was clearly pleased with the pregnancy, showing no worries or doubt. In the beginning, when Alison had first expressed her concerns over finances, he had said with an earnest look, "God will provide for this baby."

At the time, Alison stared at him. *God will provide?* She had never heard Khalid say anything like that before. She hoped he would hurry up and get a job. He would need more than blind faith to support a family.

They cleared the table, and she went to change. She put a tunic on over an ankle-length skirt. Long over long, that's what she called her new look, overdressed for July but perhaps under-dressed for *Qur'an* study group. As she removed her *Qur'an* from the shelf, her anticipation switched to unease. Would she have to wear a scarf? Would they pressure her to convert?

Alison slipped the *Qur'an* in her bag and kissed Khalid good-bye. He would soon be off to play *tarneeb* with Ibrahim and Salim and another friend. The card game, Khalid's escape of choice, lasted for hours.

When Alison arrived, Margaret was ready for *Qur'an* study, already wearing a green headscarf which concealed her red hair, making her look like a different person.

As they drove out of the cul-de-sac, Margaret told her, "We're going to Aisha's."

"Where's she from?" Alison asked.

"From Seattle. She changed her name when she converted."

"Why didn't you change yours?"

Margaret cleared her throat. "I've changed enough things."

They pulled up to Aisha's, a modest single-story home. She answered the door and welcomed them in. Her Islamic greetings were long and formal, as was her floor-length *jilbab*.

Margaret gestured to Alison. "This is my new sister-in-law, Alison."

Aisha looked her up and down. "*Masha'Allah*." She led them into the small living room, where she introduced Alison to the other women: an Iraqi, a Turkish-American, and a woman from Spokane. The Iraqi woman immediately pressed Alison on her personal details—where her husband was from, what he did for a living, and how long they had been married. As Alison provided brief answers, she crossed and uncrossed her legs.

Then Margaret spoke up. "By the way, Alison's family is originally from Syria."

"Christian or Muslim?" Aisha asked.

"Greek Orthodox."

At this, the woman nodded sympathetically at Alison, as though converting to Islam was the next logical step for someone like her.

"We're still waiting for two more people."

Aisha patted her scarf. "Lateefa is bringing a new sister, *inshallah*. So, we'll have two new converts tonight." She smiled at Alison.

"Actually, I'm not Muslim."

"There's no compulsion in religion." Aisha's smile turned into a tight line. "Let me tell you about our group. *Inshallah*, God willing, we'll start by studying *hadith*. Do you know what that is?" She didn't wait for an answer. "It's a saying or tradition of the prophet. Peace be upon him. Then we'll study a *surah* from the *Qur'an*. Then we'll pray." Aisha gestured to the *Qur'an* on the coffee table. "The *Qur'an* is very important. You get blessings for each chapter you memorize, each word you read."

The doorbell rang, and she jumped up. Two women entered—one in a flowing black *abaya*, the other in jeans and a modest blouse. Aisha and the woman in the abaya engaged in a complex set of Arabic greetings. The other woman, the new convert no doubt, stood by, looking ill at ease.

The woman in black sat and arranged her abaya around her. "Lateefa is my Muslim name," she told Alison. "Lynn is my real name. You can call me whichever." She explained why they were late. Her husband, from whom she was separated, had been late picking up their boys.

Lateefa went on talking—complaining actually —about her estranged husband, who was useless when it came to taking care of their two boys. She was clearly bitter yet seemed to take pleasure in recounting this. She spoke with an accent, an inflated version of an Arab immigrant, punctuating every sentence with her fingertips. Her mimicry was not complete, however. Lateefa's manner would be Arab one moment; then she would slip back into Lynn, the American girl she really was.

Alison had known other converts in her classes, but none as flamboyant as this one. It was like looking at the glaring sun when you knew you shouldn't. Was her Arab impersonation deliberate or some subconscious attempt to fit in? Alison knew she shouldn't stare, but she couldn't pull her gaze away from Lateefa and her layers of sequined abaya. Alison wondered if, deep down, that was how Khalid wanted her to dress. Was that why he insisted she change her clothing?

Aisha clapped. "Sisters, let's get started." The women, all wearing headscarves except Alison and the new convert, brought their attention to the book of hadith in Aisha's hand.

After discussing hadith on charity and cleanliness, it was time to study *Qur'an*. Aisha, a model of Islamic behavior and modesty, explained that the *Qur'an* was like no other book. It was the word of God; they couldn't just throw it in their purse along with their wallet and car keys.

Alison shifted in her seat and glanced down at her bag, bulging with the thick *Qur'an*.

The woman from Spokane asked if it was okay to read the *Qur'an* if she were menstruating. Aisha replied that it was okay as long as the *Qur'an* contained an English translation and she didn't touch the pages with her fingers.

Alison blinked as Aisha announced the *surah* they would be studying. Everyone flipped to the page. The menstruating woman used the eraser end of a pencil to turn her pages. The *surah* was one of the little ones from the back of the book. Alison was familiar with it from her *Qur'an* and its Interpretation class, where she had felt so smug. Her classmates didn't know Khalid had been helping her. She had just started dating him—when the relationship had been fresh and thrilling.

For Alison, the *Qur'an* was like a puzzle. Unlocking the roots of unknown Arabic words was as rewarding as any crossword or Sudoku game. But the *Qur'an* wasn't a puzzle or an academic subject to these women. They believed it.

At last, it was time to pray. Alison remained seated while the other women arranged the prayer carpets and lined up. As Aisha led the prayer, Alison and the woman with her period both sat observing. The other women prayed with concentration, their eyes cast down. Only the new convert peeked up and looked around.

Finally, the women relaxed, sipping Lipton tea

and eating brownies. They posed a series of questions to the new convert, focusing primarily on her marriage to a Moroccan man. Alison waited for them to cross-examine her again, but the conversation moved to Margaret.

Aisha asked, "Why haven't we seen you for so long?"

"Sorry about that." Margaret's face tensed. "I've been held captive by my in-laws." She told the women how she was nearly driven crazy from having Ahmed's mother living with them.

While the group offered comforting words, Alison stayed quiet. She hadn't realized the situation was so unbearable. It was a relief that Khalid was not the oldest son like Ahmed, who assumed the main duties of taking care of their mother.

"Something else is going on." Margaret furrowed her brow. "Ahmed has this insane idea about moving to the Gulf."

"Where?" someone asked.

"The UAE. He wants to manage coffee shops there."

The women buzzed. "You'll hear the call to prayer every day," one said.

"Your children could learn Arabic," Lateefa added, and the others nodded.

"I have a lot of concerns." Margaret rubbed her forehead. "The kids are settled here. What would we do with the house? And the restaurants?"

"You have to trust in Allah," Aisha said from her throne, the largest armchair in the room. "Maybe it's a chance to move to a Muslim country." She tilted her head. "Allah is the best of planners."

"You must make *du'a*," the Iraqi said. "There's a *du'a* for making decisions—do you know it?"

"I've already made my decision," Margaret said.

Aisha asked, "What about your mother-in-law?"

Margaret shook her head slowly. "If we moved there, I imagine her taking over the house."

Aisha reached over and patted Margaret's hand. "I'm sure it wouldn't be that bad. You'd get lots of rewards for taking care of your husband's mother."

A long silence settled onto the room. Without thinking, Alison leaned forward. "I think the UAE could be a good move—if you consider the alternatives."

Annoyance rippled across Margaret's face. Then she said in a voice full of false cheer, "Did you know Alison's pregnant?"

"*Masha'Allah*!" The women's faces lit up. "*Mabruuk*!" They beamed, so easily accepting that Alison could be a mother.

"You are how many months?" Lateefa asked.

Alison's face grew warm. She summoned a firm voice in which she said, "Two and a half months." Her response was based on calculations according to the date of their marriage at the mosque, as instructed by Khalid. Originally, she had laughed at this. Why was he so worried about what others thought? Now she went along.

"*Inshallah*, your husband will get a job soon," the Iraqi said.

"He has another interview coming up," Alison said, remembering that the wedding money was almost gone.

Aisha asked, "Have you thought about names?"

"If it's a boy, he wants Abed." Alison twisted her wedding ring. "After his father."

"The name is very important." Aisha spoke in a no-nonsense tone. "It's not just about sounding good, it must have the right meaning."

The meaning behind Abed made no difference to Alison. The name sounded flat and hideous, fitting for an old man maybe but not a baby. There were so many better-sounding Arabic names. Surely they could find one they both liked.

Margaret stood and gathered her things, and Alison felt a rush of relief. They said their salaams and moved toward the door.

Aisha kissed them both on the cheek. "You'll come next week, won't you?"

"*Inshallah*," Margaret said.

Alison stole one last look at Lateefa and slipped out the door.

On the car ride home, Alison asked, "What's up with Lateefa?"

"Lynn?" Margaret glanced at Alison. "She thinks she's Arab."

Alison nodded grimly.

Margaret continued, "She and her husband are separated."

"Why did she leave him?"

"Actually, he left her."

Alison's eyes widened. "But she's so Arab. She completely transformed herself."

Margaret shrugged. "Maybe that was part of the problem." She pulled off her scarf and shook her red hair free. "I came tonight just to get out of the house."

Alison wanted to say that she came so Khalid would stop bothering her about her clothing. She wanted to say he went out to play cards almost every night. She was really almost four months pregnant, not two and a half. She wasn't pleased to be pregnant and couldn't imagine herself with a baby.

Alison sighed and looked out the window.

❧ Chapter 10 ❧

One of the trees in the cul-de-sac made Zainab think of the old lemon tree. She sat in her son's yard and stared across the road at it. There was something about the tree's shape and the cinder blocks arranged around it that called up memories of the old tree. It had stood behind Zainab's childhood home, a house that was only a blur now, like a dream. There was nothing but her fading memory to remind her of that home in the village. Some families had keys to the old stone houses they had left behind, an actual key they could hold and grieve over. The key to Zainab's family home had been lost along with so many other things— the olive trees, her mother's hand-embroidered *thobs*, and the deed to the land. Not that it would have made one stitch of a difference anyway.

In the refugee camp, Zainab's mother had bemoaned the loss of her lemon tree and the fresh juice it had provided for their salads. Of all the things they had lost, Zainab wondered, why did her mother focus on that? *Allahu alim. Only God knew.*

Eventually, the United Nations turned the sea of tents into a permanent camp of small boxy cement houses. There, at their refugee home, her father planted a new lemon tree, one much smaller. Truth be told, Zainab's memories were fragmented. She didn't know which lemon tree she remembered, the original or the replacement.

Her brother, Waleed, bless him, still lived in that house in the camp, as he had stayed on and raised his family there. Maybe he was picking lemons from the tree at that moment. No, he would be sleeping. The time was upside down in America.

Clouds moved across the sky, and Zainab closed her eyes. If she were in Palestine, she would walk down the narrow alley that led to her brother's home and have morning coffee with him and their mother, *Hajja* Zarifa, who also still lived in that house. Zainab would pass through the gate, into the modest courtyard, and past the lemon tree. Her brother's face, round and wide like their sister Anysa's, would greet her. In the house, Zainab would smell mint and hear the neighbors' chickens. Waleed would usher her to a cushion, next to their mother.

"*Yama*," Zainab would say and kiss her mother's hand. Waleed would pour the coffee, releasing its cardamom scent, and pass her a tiny cup resting in its saucer. "Bless your hands," she would reply.

Zainab opened her eyes. She scanned the cul-de-sac, devoid of people, devoid of movement. The sky remained gray, and the only sounds came from the cars on the main road. She looked at her watch: two hours until *asr* prayer. How would she fill her time? In Palestine, there was always someone to visit. She could have tea with her daughter Huda or go to Dheisheh Camp to visit Yasmine.

Yes, when Zainab thought of home, what came to mind was Palestine. Embroidered upon those memories were Anysa, so overbearing but always pleased to see her. They would be tied

144

even closer now that Nadia would marry Anysa's son. It was just like Zainab's own marriage. Abed was the son of her mother's sister. A perfect arrangement. So many benefits: security, ease, familiarity, and predictability.

Zainab continued to stare at the tree across the street. Was it too early to start dinner? Would Margaret be pleased? Zainab was unsure. Margaret didn't ever start dinner until the very end of the day, when the meal should have been finished and the dishes done. Sometimes Margaret would smile and put a hand on Zainab's shoulder. Other times she moved stiffly around the kitchen, closing cupboards too loudly.

When Ahmed returned from his work, Zainab would ask him how many more days until they traveled. She was impatient to get to Jordan, where Nadia was waiting to become engaged. The days would go by slowly at this rate, sitting and waiting for someone to visit or walking the cul-de-sac, eyeing the greenery for a bit of fresh chamomile. Margaret had gone shopping and taken the young children, and Mona was busy with her boys. Where was Jenin? Couldn't she stay with her grandmother?

A raindrop landed on Zainab's cardboard mat. With a dull ache in her heart, she got up and went inside. In the living room, she paced and thought of Khalid and his wife. "*Alhamdulillah*," she said out loud at the thought of Khalid's new job. *Praise be to God.* Now she would have real news to tell her sister. "His position is high!" Zainab would tell Anysa. "He had many opportunities. He was waiting for the best."

That wasn't the only news. The doctor had said their baby would be a girl. Inshallah. How could the doctors find this out so soon from looking at the belly of Khalid's skinny wife? Would this baby arrive only seven or eight months after the wedding? Zainab had seen this before—a first baby born too early, but at the right weight. Everyone exclaimed, *"Masha'Allah!"* What else was there to say? Why stir up trouble for the family? Allah was merciful and compassionate.

Zainab sat on the couch and crossed her arms. Maybe she wouldn't tell her sister the baby was a girl. Anysa was smart. She might say, "You found out already? It's no wonder they had a sudden wedding." Her words might bring the evil eye upon Khalid's daughter.

Fingering her prayer beads, Zainab asked for forgiveness. Her own sister bringing the evil eye to her family! How could she have such a thought?

The good news Zainab would dole out slowly, *shway, shway,* like *Eid* pastries. This week she would announce the new job. Later, in Jordan, she would share the news about the baby. She tapped her prayer beads together. Zainab was always waiting for something: the next prayer, for

Mona to visit, for Ahmed to come home. And now she counted the days until she traveled.

From outside came the sound of the car in the driveway. Then the front door opened; Margaret called out something in English and came up the stairs, carrying a large box full of purchases. Tariq and Leena followed behind, each with a box in their arms.

Margaret nodded to Zainab. "*Salaam alaikum.*"

In the kitchen, there were new items on the counter: bags of pasta, socks, books, a box of frozen something. Margaret must have gone to that warehouse store where large containers of food were sold next to furniture. In front of Zainab sat a box of blueberries. But what was there to make for dinner? She didn't recognize most of the items Margaret was shoving into the freezer. Zainab clicked her tongue and looked up, a small gesture of protest.

Tariq entered the kitchen in a white karate jacket. The boy struggled with the belt. Margaret turned to Zainab and said in her impossible Arabic that they would be back soon. They left as quickly as they had arrived. Zainab stared at the food items left out. Everyone was in a rush in this house. What kind of life was this? Didn't anyone have an hour for tea?

Zainab squeezed her prayer beads and paced the house. Of course, Margaret wouldn't have tea with her. Margaret rarely had tea with her own mother. The woman lived in a nearby city, but how often did Margaret see her? Two times a month? What a shame!

The phone rang and snapped Zainab from her thoughts.

It was Khalid. "I'm calling to check on you, *Yama*. My job starts tomorrow."

"So, you're visiting me today?"

"What about Saturday afternoon? Or Thursday evening?"

"What's this? You're making an appointment with your mother?"

"I'm busy these days, *Yama*. I don't have time to sit around."

Sit around? Was that how he thought of visiting his mother? Khalid said he needed to go. Zainab said salaam, the issue of his visit still unresolved. Her sons were becoming Americans. She came to this country to be near them, yet her youngest son didn't have time for her. She shook her head, having no words for her feelings.

She lived in a strange household, full of tension and arguing. She heard voices late at night, harsh words between Ahmed and Margaret. Zainab couldn't understand them, but she recognized the emotions. The couple barely spoke during the day, but at night, the hushed exchanges would start. They thought she couldn't hear, that she was unaware. Maybe the evil eye had already descended upon the family. So many people back home were jealous of Ahmed, his restaurants, his success.

Finally, *asr* prayer. Standing in the living room, in her white prayer covering, Zainab began. "*Allahu Akbar.*" Arms crossed, head bowed down, she had much to pray for. She pressed her forehead to the carpet and asked for forgiveness. She needed it for the thoughts she had been having lately—the result of having too much time to think.

"I seek refuge with You from the suggestions of the evil ones," she began. "I seek refuge from the mischief of the envious." She recited *surahs* of protection until her head hurt. The words moved about in her mind, giving her a shiver.

Sitting back, Zainab held her palms open and closed her eyes. She asked God for special protection over Khalid's house and Ahmed's house, *dar* Mansour. "Whatever blessings I or my sons have, it is from You. All grace and thanks are to You."

The usual bundle of worries appeared before her. "Allah, help Margaret agree to move. Help her to see what's best for her family." Her supplications moved to Nadia. Zainab prayed for her to be married, settled, and taken care of. At last, Zainab made a request in the name of Abed's soul and got up from her carpet, her legs stiff and heavy.

Another prayer was complete.

Chapter 11

Nearly a month after her anniversary, Margaret made a mental inventory of her choices over the years as she knelt down in the hallway bathroom to mop up the floor yet again. The mother, splashing water about, had turned the bathroom into an Arab *hammam*. Perhaps she hadn't noticed the floor was covered in cheap linoleum and not ceramic tile, nor was there a drain like in an Arab-style bathroom. As she worked, Margaret noticed that the wooden baseboards were now discolored. She lifted up a corner of linoleum to confirm the beginnings of rot underneath.

While she wiped the floor, she reviewed why she couldn't move to an Arab country with Ahmed. Ever since their nasty anniversary argument, Margaret had gone over the same internal monologue every day. She composed long speeches in her head, with all the reasons to stay in her home at the end of the cul-de-sac. Compromises flared up in her mind, a record from the past two decades. This latest request, presented as nearly a done deal, eclipsed them all.

Noise traveled to her from the living room; voices talking over the sound of the television. Who was visiting the mother now? Margaret would have to go out there and make the necessary greetings. Getting up from the floor, she became dizzy from rising too quickly. She closed the toilet lid and sat down, recalling her last exchange with Ahmed—how he had left the house that morning without saying good-bye. They had not spoken to each other in any meaningful way since their anniversary. They had fallen into a shared code of silence, a pattern of mutual avoidance, punctuated only by mealtimes and matters regarding the mother or how to manage the children during the summer break. Despite Margaret's stance, she was beginning to miss him, their talks, and his stories about the goings-on at the restaurant.

How much longer could she hold herself in suspension like this? Waiting for something to happen, for the tension to end. Her heart raced. She tried to calm herself, but it was pointless. She brought her hands to her face, her tears wet in her palms. Oh, to rewind to an earlier time, to when she and Ahmed were still speaking, when her place in the world was secure.

With a damp washcloth, Margaret blotted her eyes. She needed to talk to someone. Her scrap-book group was meeting that evening. The three J's would cover their mouths in alarm at the idea of her moving to the Middle East. There would be talk of terrorism and the mistreatment of women. "You're not thinking of going, are you?" they would ask.

No, Margaret wouldn't bring up the issue with them.

Meanwhile, the women in the *Qur'an* group hadn't grasped the situation at all. The move wasn't about learning Arabic or hearing the call to prayer. An image had formed in Margaret's mind—which she let develop, adding detail and texture. In that frame, she and her family lived somewhere in the Gulf where the weather was hot and dust blew in the air. Their home was an apartment, with its air conditioner buzzing and the smell of cooking wafting in from the neighbors'. The children were miserable, the mother ran the kitchen—the scenario went on and on.

Margaret was not a quasi-Arab wife, like Aisha or Lateefa. Yes, Margaret had visited that avenue briefly at an earlier time, seeking approval through Arabic meals, Islamic sayings, and a closetful of modest clothing. It had all culminated with her covering her head. But it had been an impossible mission, fitting in. Margaret knew that now—and where had it gotten her? It certainly had not helped Lateefa, who had transformed herself, even changing her name. Lateefa was alone now, left by her husband, raising her boys on her own.

Yes, Margaret might have moved to the Middle East ten years before, full of trust, not wanting to say no. But at age forty-one, she was no longer that woman, no longer the wife who spent long hours rolling grape leaves and going along with her husband's every plan.

Liz would understand. Margaret slipped out of the bathroom and went to her bedroom. Voices from the living room followed her down the hallway. She closed the door and reached for the phone.

Liz answered. "Oh my God, I was just thinking of you. Your mother-in-law still there?"

"Oh yeah."

"You poor thing. Mine just left. Finally."

Margaret leaned back and allowed her friend's voice to envelop her.

"I'm now in recovery." Liz said, then shouted something to one of her children in the background. "And what about you?"

Margaret opened her mouth, and tears welled up in her eyes. "Things aren't good." She took a deep breath. "I've got to get out of this house."

"Tomorrow morning, my place? We have lots to catch up on."

"You've no idea."

Margaret said good-bye and walked down the hallway. Sounds were coming from the kitchen. Were they cooking already? It was still morning. Sure enough, in the kitchen was the mother and Mona, who was scooping out the insides of a zucchini to stuff later. The mother was cleaning whole chickens in the kitchen sink, using her preferred method, scrubbing the uncooked birds with salt.

Margaret told herself to smile. "Bless your hands," she said in Arabic.

"And your hands, too," Mona and the mother said in unison.

Mona fixed her eyes on Margaret. "You look tired."

"I *am* tired." It was true, it had been another night of strained sleep, trying to stay on her side of the bed, twisting away from Ahmed.

Leena ran from the living room and hugged Margaret's legs. "Hey sweetie," Margaret said just as Tariq dashed in. "Please don't chase your sister," she told him. Margaret took Leena's hand and went to the living room, where Mona's boys were milling about and Jenin was serving tea to Khalid and Alison.

Margaret turned to Khalid. "The new job going well?"

"*Alhamdulillah*," Khalid said matter-of-factly. "I worked only one week. It's orientation."

She gave him a nod of approval and sat next to Alison. "How's your pregnancy?"

"I need to ask you something," Alison whispered. "Can we talk somewhere else?"

Margaret got up and signaled for Alison to take her tea and follow her to the bedroom. Margaret sat on the bed. "What's up?"

"Baby names." Alison lowered herself into the

armchair. "Of course, he wants Khalid as her middle name."

"That's how they do it. The second name is the father's name."

"I know." Alison touched her belly. "Even my grandparents did it that way, but it's so old-fashioned."

Margaret sighed as though she, too, were a victim of this naming practice, when, in fact, at the time it hadn't bothered her at all. What she regretted most was the choice of the name Jenin. Ahmed had thought it nationalistic to name his first born after a Palestinian village. When the attack on that village occurred, Jenin was thirteen. Ahmed told her the details, the actions of the Israeli soldiers, the bulldozed homes, and the death count. Jenin had been at just the right age to not only be shocked but horrified that such a thing could happen. From that father-daughter exchange, Jenin became forever fixated on the conflict that her father had escaped. She was so much like him, not only outwardly with the same eyes and dark wavy hair, but inwardly, as well, with her fierce identification with Palestine.

Margaret said, "We named our kids Jenin Ahmed—"

"I'm fine with an Arabic first name, even Khalid's last name." Her voice had grown impatient. "But the middle name, too?"

Alison's face was pouty and naïve. She had no idea what was ahead of her. No clue! The baby's name would be just one issue, one compromise in a long string of them.

Margaret shook her head. "Whatever you do, it's never enough." She ran a hand through her hair. "I probably shouldn't be saying this . . ."

Alison leaned in. "Say it."

"My advice? Don't give up anything you can't live without."

The next morning, Margaret dropped off Tariq at summer day camp and headed to Liz's. Her friend's home was also a split-level in a cul-de-sac, but Liz's front yard was cluttered with children's bikes and toys, cast about wherever her children had left them. Margaret let Leena ring the bell. Liz answered and gave Margaret a hug.

"So what've your in-laws done now?" Liz asked.

"Oh, the usual torture."

Liz gave a knowing smile and led them to the breakfast nook where Margaret sat at the table by the window. Outside, Liz's children played on the swing set, and Liz opened the back door for Leena to join them. At the kitchen counter, Liz filled the coffee grinder with beans.

Above the grinding noise, Margaret said, "I bet you're happy now."

Liz silenced the grinder and put her hands on

her hips. "I'm rethinking the whole cross-cultural marriage thing."

"I'm afraid it's too late now, my dear."

"You can't imagine what I went through with Nezar's mother." Liz flicked on her coffee machine and came to the table. "She took my silver serving tray." She widened her eyes. "I found it in her suitcase."

"What did you do?"

"I took it back, of course. Then guess what. It's in her suitcase again." Liz paused until Margaret registered the right amount of shock on her face. "That was a wedding gift! You know what Nezar said?" Liz imitated her husband, his accent and dismissive wave. "It's just a tray. We'll get another one." Liz, with a look of true pain on her face, brought both hands to her chest. "When do my feelings count?" Her voice was shrill. "Never!" Her face flushed, and she went on, ranting about her mother-in-law and her husband in a way that was neither healthy nor helpful, but there was something intoxicating about listening to her.

Liz jumped up and returned with the coffee pot. She filled each mug and described how her mother-in-law had criticized her parenting and about the suitcase of obligatory gifts they were required to send. Margaret stirred cream in her coffee and allowed Liz to carry on.

"I'm so glad they're gone," she said. "I cannot tell you. Two months. It ruined our summer." Liz reached over and touched Margaret's hand. "Your time will come, too, *inshallah*."

Margaret smiled faintly but said nothing.

"At this point, I can hardly stand to be in the same room with Nezar." Liz's cup of coffee sat untouched. "It's always like this, every time, such a strain on our marriage." She lowered her voice. "If I had a way to support myself, I'd be out of here so fast."

Margaret glanced out the window to the children in the backyard. "Yeah, but that's a whole new set of problems."

"Do you ever think of old boyfriends?" Liz asked. "Have you ever wondered how your life could be different?"

"I might be thinking about that soon."

Liz, too wound up, didn't seem to register Margaret's words. "Hey," Liz said, "How's your new sister-in-law?"

"Alison?" Margaret sighed. "For someone so intelligent, she's not very smart."

"Kids these days."

Margaret tried to steer the conversation to her own troubles. "The family's taken over the house. And the mother! She shows no signs of leaving."

"You know what?" Liz's face assumed a look of mock seriousness. "You should get a grant."

"What do you mean?"

"You know . . . for helping refugees." Liz smiled, her eyes shining with mischief.

"Palestinian refugees. All the work that you do."

Margaret chuckled softly. "You're wicked."

"Think about it," Liz said. "Everything you do for that family." She raised her eyebrows playfully. "You've sponsored the brother. You've sheltered the mother."

"You're bad."

Liz kept on. "You've funded God-knows-who in the West Bank."

Margaret's laugh grew deeper, and Liz joined in. They carried on like this, laughing until Liz's eyes had narrowed to slits and the tears were pouring down.

Liz caught her breath. "We had no clue what we were getting into. We didn't marry the man, we married the clan!"

Margaret wiped her eye. "Just when I thought things couldn't get any worse." The words finally began to spill out while Liz stared past her into the backyard where the children played. "I don't know how I'm going to get out of this one," Margaret said. "Things are a mess. Ahmed wants to move to the Middle East."

"Don't they all?"

"He's serious. He sprang it on me during our anniversary dinner."

Liz slapped her own forehead, her version of the Arabic gesture. "What a jerk."

Unthinking, yes. A jerk? No.

"What did you tell him?"

"Well, no, of course."

"Of course."

The next day, Margaret knew what she had to do. After leaving Leena in Jenin's care and dropping Tariq at day camp, she drove into the city, leaving the suburbs behind, heading toward Capitol Hill. With all the family members constantly coming and going from her house, the restaurant was the only place to talk in private.

Ahmed was at the kitchen's back door, inspecting a produce delivery, when she arrived. He looked up from his clipboard to see her standing there.

"We need to talk," she said. It was before noon, the pause between the morning prep and the lunch rush.

"Meet me in the office," he said.

She walked amongst the empty tables, carefully set and ready for customers. The smells of the restaurant were familiar: a mixture of coffee grounds, Windex, and almond extract. The refrigerated glass case displayed the layer cakes, garnished with fresh berries, flower petals, and chopped nuts—Ahmed's showcase. Margaret descended the stairs to the office and flipped on the lamp. On the desk were stacks of invoices and used order tickets, waiting to be processed.

Ahmed came in, closed the door, and sat across from her, the stacks of papers between them. His hair was ruffled, and he looked tired but still attractive in the soft lighting. She felt an unexpected surge of love for him, but that love was so tangled with bitterness, she couldn't separate the two.

"Honey," she said. "Can you forgive me for not wanting to move over there?"

"Yeah, I can forgive you." His voice was composed. Perhaps he finally understood. From upstairs came the faint sound of the bell at the front door. Lunch customers were coming in.

Ahmed crossed his arms. "It doesn't change the fact that I want to move."

Margaret sat silently, aware of the walls in the tiny space confining her.

He caught her eye. "I don't belong here anymore."

"I know you keep saying that, but this is your home. You've made a life here."

"Yes, but it's not me."

"How can you say that? You've done so well for yourself."

"This is not my homeland. I don't want to die in this country." His words were firm, as if he had been waiting to say them.

"And the UAE is? You've never even been there."

"If I could make a life in Palestine, I would. Trust me. Who knows? I still have my residency ID."

Margaret blinked back a tear.

Ahmed continued, "I want my children to have Arab culture."

"We have Arab culture *here*." She felt exasperated at the thought of explaining it all over again. She saw everything clearly. Why couldn't he?

"It's diluted here," he said. "It's not real Arab culture."

She wanted to remind him they had taken many trips to the Middle East, and they would take another very soon. But instead she said, "Well, I don't want to die in an Arab country."

"There's more to the world than this place." He paused and took a breath, his eyes moist. "What am I doing here? My life is passing by." He let his hand fall on a stack of papers. "The restaurants were good for me at first. It's not enough anymore." With that, he swept his hand across the desk, sending a stack of invoices cascading to the floor.

Margaret stared at the papers. She knew she shouldn't say it, but she couldn't stop. The words came tumbling out, fulfilling a pattern of marital arguments they had assumed years ago. "Was this your mother's idea?"

"Leave my mother out of it!" He didn't seem to care if anyone upstairs heard him.

Margaret cringed. "What about my family? My mother would have a fit if we moved."

"How often do you see your parents? Once a month?"

"I see my mother more than that."

"You remember my friend Rashid? He's done so well over there."

Rashid had been Ahmed's first mentor at the university. According to Ahmed, Rashid and his American wife Cynthia formed the ideal mixed couple. They'd moved to the Middle East before Margaret had a chance to meet them. Rashid had a thriving business and Cynthia spoke Arabic—as did their children. They were the benchmark to which Ahmed compared all of his successes and failures.

"I don't want to hear about your friend in Abu Dhabi," Margaret said.

"They're in Amman now."

"Whatever." She glared at him. "They don't concern us."

"He thinks we could have a good life over there."

Margaret shook her head.

Ahmed opened his mouth to say more but changed his mind. Finally, he said, "I might have an interview in the UAE next month."

Margaret sucked in a breath of air. "When were you planning to tell me?"

"I was planning to tell you today." His words turned soft. "I want to check it out, that's all." He shrugged. "See what they offer."

Margaret searched his face. In the glow of the lamp, the light flickered in Ahmed's eyes. His expression was thoughtful and he was more handsome than ever. There were parts of him that were so easy to love—the way he was obsessed with layer cakes, telling stories, and helping others. When she thought about it, it was no surprise he wanted to move out of the country. Lately, that was all he and his friends talked about—where to go and how to get there.

She detected a faint twitching under Ahmed's eye, the delicate skin throbbing. He was clearly under a lot of stress. Perhaps his mother living with them wasn't easy on him, either.

Margaret continued to look at him, and he back at her. It was a long silence, yet another moment for her to review their past, their twenty years together—the compromises, the giving in, with neither one ever completely happy. Something somewhere had gone wrong.

Margaret stood. "I'm sorry. But I'm not moving anywhere." Her words were purposeful and deliberate. "If you take this job, you'll be moving there alone."

With that, she walked out.

❧ Chapter 12 ❧

Alison skimmed the Saturday newspaper. The events came alive on the page: *Clashes in the West Bank Kill Four*; *Israel Announces Withdrawal from Gaza*; *Bombing in Tel Aviv Injures*

Two. She moved to the opinion page: Yasser Arafat was unfit, Israeli settlements broke agreements, the Israeli security wall was illegal.

She leaned back, sipped her cappuccino, and ran a hand over her small pregnant belly. Khalid had just purchased their tickets to Jordan for Nadia's wedding. Soon Alison would be back in the region. It was what she had wanted since graduation, time to travel and see the Middle East before hunkering down in graduate school. Her real life was finally starting.

Alison crossed the living room of their new apartment and pulled out the stack of graduate school printouts, which had been tucked away for weeks now. On the couch, she sat next to Khalid, laptop on his knees, his brow furrowed. After just two weeks as an applications developer at a local investment company, his computer had become his constant fixation.

Turning her attention to the papers, Alison read the name of each university, then began to read the contents. MA in Middle East studies. She skimmed lists of requirements. Her eyes widened at the deadline—the same week as her due date! It was too much for her brain to process.

Khalid looked up. "As soon as I'm done with this, we'll go see my mother. Okay?"

She shoved the papers back in their place. "Sure, babe."

Later, at Ahmed and Margaret's house, Khalid's

mother served them a steaming mound of stuffed grape leaves. The family sat around the dining room picking up the hot rolled leaves filled with rice and meat. Khalid and Ahmed ate hungrily while their mother glanced around, monitoring. Alison rearranged the food on her plate, hoping no one would notice how little she ate. Even in her second trimester, some food aversions lingered.

"How's the new job?" Margaret asked Khalid.

He chatted about his cubicle, his colleagues, and the spreadsheets he managed.

Khalid's mother nudged Alison. *"Kuli, kuli."* *Eat, eat*.

Alison brought a hand to her heart. *"Alhamdulillah." Praise be to God*—the code phrase that stopped her mother-in-law from pushing food on her.

The conversation switched to the trip to Jordan, the topic on Alison's mind. She was grateful to be going, considering her pregnancy and their lack of money. Ahmed reviewed the itinerary. Alison, Khalid, and his mother would fly to Amman in two weeks. Ahmed, Margaret, and their children would fly out a few days later.

Margaret touched Alison's shoulder. "You get to go to Jordan."

"I've been there before."

Margaret raised her eyebrows and said in a sing-song voice, "Not with the family."

Alison smiled back and turned to Khalid. "Can we go now? I'm starting to feel sick."

On the way home, he took Highway 99, the route she despised. She took in the urban sprawl around her: a casino, a strip mall, and a gas station. "Now that you're working, hopefully we can move out of here."

"*Inshallah*," he said. "First we'll pay the credit card. The airline tickets added a lot."

"It'll be worth it." She stroked the back of his head and imagined their first trip as a married couple. Of course, she hadn't envisioned Khalid's mother traveling with them. Not at all. Yet Alison hadn't said a word; she sensed it was not the issue to argue over. She caressed his dark hair. "Have you thought about going to the West Bank?"

"I just started this job. I can't take off that much time."

"It'd be a shame not to go to Jerusalem." She waited for him to respond. When he didn't, she tried a different tactic. "I want to meet Huda and Yasmine."

"They might come to Jordan, *inshallah*."

"You said they probably wouldn't." She paused and proceeded carefully. "I want to see where you grew up."

"Ibrahim got stuck there last time. The Israelis detained him at the border."

"Yes, but he eventually got in."

Khalid glanced at her. "It's not exactly safe for me."

"I can go on my own. I can stay with your sisters; they can show me around."

"They can't go anywhere. Too many restrictions."

"I can get by. I've been there before."

"What about the baby?"

"The baby?" she echoed. "I'm only four months. The midwife said it's the best time to travel." She couldn't believe it. The baby was barely six inches long and already interfering.

He kept his eyes on the road. "I'll think about it."

They stopped at an intersection and sat in silence under the glare of the August sun. Ahead was a billboard advertisement for a glistening slice of pepperoni pizza. A month before, the image would have made Alison turn away in disgust. This time, her eyes remained on the billboard.

"Now that I have a job," Khalid said, "I'm going to send some money back home."

Alison looked over at Khalid, whose jaw had tightened. "Babe, how much money are we talking?"

"I want to send five hundred dollars to my sisters."

She opened her mouth. She'd known this was coming, but did he mean sending that amount every month or only once? She didn't ask.

Instead, she hugged her purse to her chest. "We're behind on our bills. Plus, I'm quitting my job." Alison continued on, listing reasons to delay sending money. They needed so much themselves: maternity clothes, baby things, items for the house, plus there was the trip coming up. When they reached the Pine View sign and entered the parking lot, Khalid stopped in front of Building F.

"You're just dropping me off?"

He nodded. "I've got some things to do."

"You're playing cards with the guys, aren't you? She stepped out of the car. "How much *tarneeb* can you play?" She slammed the door, grudgingly took the stairs, and entered the apartment. She reached for the phone. Her order: a medium pepperoni pizza. Once, Khalid had told her that in Palestine a man would venture all over in search of the exotic fruit that his expectant wife craved. This was her exotic fruit.

Alison stretched out on the couch and waited. For an instant, she wondered if the pepperoni made from pork was a good idea; Khalid always stayed away from the stuff. Then the concern vanished, and her mind turned to the texture of the crust and the melted cheese on her tongue. Her mouth filled with a deep craving for the gooeyness of it.

She went to the window and peeked through the blinds. Finally, a man holding a pizza box appeared, walking across the parking lot. He stopped to allow a car to pass. A black Honda Accord—Khalid's car. He parked, got out, and walked briskly past the delivery man.

"Shit," Alison said.

Within seconds, Khalid entered the front door.

"What are you doing here?" she asked.

"I forgot my cell phone."

There was a knock. The delivery man handed the box to Khalid while Alison fished in her wallet for the cash. She closed the door and slowly turned around.

Khalid stood at the table, holding the lid open. "Is this pork?"

"Babe, I had a craving." By then, the pizza's scent had reached Alison's nose.

He shook his head and smiled. For a moment, she thought it would be okay. Then he picked up the box and went out the front door. From the window, she watched as he crossed the parking lot, balancing the box on his fingertips as though it were contaminated. He threw the pizza, box and all, into the Dumpster and then returned.

"You know we don't have pork in the house," he said.

Alison recoiled to the couch and clutched a throw pillow. "If you hadn't come home, you wouldn't have known."

He paced back and forth. "You should respect the fact that—"

"You didn't need to throw it away!" With her eyes, she followed Khalid, his face glowing with anger.

He glared at her. "Of all people, you should understand. You should know better!"

She glared back. "You're not being fair."

"There's no use talking to you." He reached for his cell phone and was gone.

She stared at the door, tears welling up behind her eyelids. After a moment, she collected herself, went to the kitchen, and stood at the refrigerator. Was he going to start making her eat only halal food now? She opened a cupboard and took in the row of cans. A raw hunger gnawed deep inside her, but nothing appealed.

Aggravated and restless, Alison started unpacking a box of her university papers and textbooks. On top was a senior essay, its topic the British rule of Palestine. She set it aside and lifted out the books, one by one: *The Venture of Islam*, *The Arab Awakening*, and several books by Nawal El Saadawi. Alison paused at *Orientalism* by Edward Said and flipped through its pages, filled with faded yellow highlights and notes in the margins. She thought back to her life as a student and realized that since graduation, her intelli-gence had begun to slip away—her confidence and smarts, her knowledge and understanding—all of it. Alison remembered Khalid and wondered if he had overreacted. Or maybe she was the one who had been wrong? He didn't eat pork, of course—fine—but did that mean she couldn't, either?

As she placed the books on the shelf, a rush of memories rose up: studying intensive Arabic in Cairo, roaming its congested streets with her classmates, eating *ful* and falafel, and struggling over Arabic newspaper headlines in her dorm room in Zamalek. Had all that really happened?

After arranging the textbooks on the shelf, she picked up an Egyptian novel translated into English and went to the couch to read. For a bookmark, she used the dollar Khalid had given her that day at the mosque. After reading a chapter, she picked up the dollar, already creased and worn. She held it in her hand and thought about the money Khalid wanted to send his sisters. Alison turned the dollar over and recalled their silly wedding ceremony at the mosque. One dollar! What on earth made her agree to that? She smoothed the bill repeatedly, trying to press out the wrinkles and make it look new again.

Alison was lying on the couch when Khalid returned just after midnight. He sat next to her, and a calm smile spread over his handsome face, suggesting a private joke between them. It was hard to stay bitter when he looked at her like that.

"How was your card game?" she asked.

He said that Ibrahim kept winning and Salim

was a sore loser. He commented on the well-organized bookshelf and asked about the book she was reading. She said it was *Palace Walk*, which she was reading for a second time.

"I know the story," he said. "I saw the miniseries."

They laughed and she looked at him. "Why did you have to throw it away?"

He shrugged and smiled sheepishly.

"I was dying for that pizza," she said.

"You should've seen your face."

She pointed at him in a mock reprimand. "Don't do that again."

"Don't bring pork home."

"Don't leave every time you're pissed off."

Khalid took her face in his hands and kissed her gently. He tasted of cigarettes and coffee. She felt her body respond and didn't refuse when he led her to the bedroom. Their love-making was greedy, more urgent than tender, fueled by the energy of their earlier argument.

Two weeks later, the day before their departure, Alison and Khalid shopped for gifts to bring to his family overseas. They walked through the department store and Alison made suggestions.

"What about this picture frame?"

"Too cheap-looking."

"How about this tablecloth?"

"What would she do with that?"

There were four sisters to shop for—one of them requiring an engagement gift. Plus, there were communal gifts to buy—bags of chocolates and nuts.

Khalid's cell phone rang; he answered in Arabic. She could tell he was talking to his family by the way he substituted *ch* for *k*, switching to the family dialect. He continued talking loudly in Arabic as he walked around, self-absorbed. When he spoke to his family, he shifted not only his language, but his personality, as well.

Alison pretended to be looking at leather goods while concentrating on what Khalid was saying. He was talking to his brother, and the topic seemed to be about moving to the Emirates. Alison casually picked up a wallet and strained to listen. Khalid was expressing shock, something about Margaret. He gave a dismissive wave and spoke as though he were advising Ahmed to go ahead with his plans, regardless of his wife's wishes. Alison opened her mouth to speak up, to interrupt him, but remembered their task at hand and their trip ahead.

Finally, Khalid said salaam and slipped his phone in his pocket. Soon they settled on sale-priced leather wallets as gifts for all his sisters. For Nadia's engagement, they bought designer perfume, also on sale. As they drove back to their apartment, Khalid appeared to be in a good mood, telling Alison about the four sisters she

174

hadn't met yet. "Fatma's the oldest. She takes care of everyone, and Huda, she and her kids are always joking around. Nadia, she's the most modern, maybe because she's the youngest."

"What about Yasmine?"

"She lives in Dheisheh Camp. She has four kids—maybe five."

"Do you think I'll get to go to the West Bank to meet her?" Alison asked.

"Let's get to Jordan, wait, and see how it goes."

"Wait all you want." She gave him a nudge. "But I'm planning to go there."

That evening they went to see Khalid's mother. It was light out as they drove, and Khalid was still talkative, describing the pleasure of staying at Fatma's house in summer—all those relatives staying up late and sleeping in the courtyard. "Like camping!" he said.

For Alison, it was that point in time just before travel when the hours seemed to slow under the anticipation of it all. Their luggage was neatly packed, waiting back at their apartment. She had traveled to the Middle East before with only one bag. This time, she had managed to fit all her things into a single suitcase and a backpack—including the gifts, purposefully compact.

Everyone had gathered in Margaret and Ahmed's living room, the mood lively. Ibrahim was telling a story about a past trip to Palestine.

Mona was laughing loudly, although she and her family weren't going on the trip. According to Khalid, they couldn't afford it, as they had traveled to Jordan in the winter for the funeral of Khalid's father. In the middle of everyone sat Khalid's mother, smiling and nodding. Meanwhile, Margaret circulated around the room, serving tea.

Khalid's mother asked Alison about the baby's name. Khalid jumped in and told his mother something Alison couldn't catch. She was about to ask for a translation when Margaret appeared with a thick scrapbook in her arms.

She set it in Alison's lap and caressed its cover. "Our last trip there."

Alison opened it to the first page. *Mansour Trip to Jordan.*

Margaret sat down next to her. "We didn't go to the West Bank that time. Too many problems."

Alison nodded and flipped the page. The first photo was of Khalid's parents, his mother looking well-rested and happy, his father with a hand around her waist.

The next page was labeled *Lunch at Fatma's.* The photos showed family members sitting on the floor, crowded around an enormous platter of rice and meat. Alison poured over the album, searching for clues of what was to come. Page after page showed more of the same: mealtime, teatime, or family members sitting around.

When it was time to go, Khalid asked Alison, "Can you help me carry these bags?" He gestured toward some large plastic shopping bags piled by the front door.

Alison reached for one. "What's in them?"

"Some stuff to take with us tomorrow."

She set the bag down. "But we're already packed."

He turned toward her, his face flushed with impatience. "These are gifts from Mona, and these are from Ibrahim and Salim. They're for their families."

Alison straightened, her head dizzy. She lowered her voice. "Maybe Ahmed and Margaret can take some of this stuff? Or your mom?"

He frowned but said nothing and carried the bags to the curb. The sky was dark by then, and as he unlocked the trunk and arranged the sacks inside, Alison said, "I'm not carrying that stuff. It'll have to go in your suitcase. Why did your family wait until the last minute?" Her voice was high and shaky. "I thought we were done packing."

He closed the trunk and spun around. "What's wrong with you?"

She flinched. "Me? Nothing's wrong with *me*."

Khalid shook his head, muttering to himself in Arabic as he got in the car.

She said nothing more. It was a hopeless argument. They would have to drag that junk with them whether she liked it or not. As they drove home, Alison bit her lip, pointedly not speaking while Khalid brought up another subject.

"We need a name for the baby."

"Does her middle name have to be Khalid?" Alison allowed her displeasure to show.

"It's not a middle name, it's the father's name."

"I know the system."

"Then you know it's how it's done."

"We don't have to do it that way anymore."

"At least we have a system," he said, "Not like you—your grandfather changed his name to whatever, Taylor, like he was ashamed of his own family."

She gasped. "He had reasons for doing that—and you know it!"

"Our system is logical," he said. "Anyone can look at someone's name and know their entire family."

"They only know the male side of the family. What about the women?"

"You can choose her first name," Khalid said. "Why not one of my sisters' names?"

A lump rose in Alison's throat. "What?"

"There are five to choose from." He rattled them off. "Fatma, Mona, Huda, Yasmine, and Nadia."

A feeling of dread squeezed her breath. Would she have to fight him on this, too?

"All beautiful names." He drove past the Pine

View sign and parked. They walked toward Building F. Alison glanced at the plastic bags in his hands, bursting full of God-knew-what. The thought of having to squeeze that stuff into their bags sent her adrenaline soaring.

They entered the apartment and she waited until Khalid closed the door behind him. "Your mother got to name her children," she said a bit too loudly. "Let me name mine!"

He set the bags by the door. "But she's my daughter, too."

"Yeah, and she's getting your first name *and* last name."

"What about Yasmine? You can call her Jasmine in English."

"Oh, please."

"It's the name of a flower. Yasmine Khalid Mansour."

"Would you stop!" She stood in the middle of the living room, her hands raised to the ceiling. She had never yelled at him like that.

"What's wrong with Yasmine?"

"Why do we always have to do things your way?" Khalid covered his ears.

"We're not naming her Yasmine!" Her throat was raw. "Or any of your sisters' names!"

At that moment a tap came from the ceiling, a warning from the neighbors above. Alison looked up, horrified, and then back to Khalid. "I hate this place!"

"You're crazy!"

They stood staring at each other.

He went to the door and turned back to her. "Totally crazy." He slammed the door; the blinds rattled in the window.

She ran outside. "Where are you going?" she screamed across the parking lot.

He strode toward the car without looking back.

She withdrew herself from the doorway and kicked the bags by the door. Some of the contents spilled out: a bulky acrylic sweater and an oversized box of cheap candy. She paced the living room. Where was he going? Their flight to Jordan was the next morning.

Her book lay on the coffee table. She picked it up and the dollar bill slid out. A vision of the mosque came back to her. Tears in her eyes, she wondered why they had been in such a hurry. Soon after Khalid had started sleeping over, he'd asked her to marry him. They'd gotten the marriage license two months later. Why had she allowed their relationship to advance so quickly?

Another memory emerged: an exchange from their early days, when their relationship was mostly sex and sleepovers. Khalid had mentioned his mother's matchmaking attempts—the inventory of eligible girls, the pocket full of photos. Had Alison agreed to marry him out of fear? Fear he'd end up with a girl back home?

Alison stared at the dollar, trying to find an answer.

She went to the kitchen, and from the drying rack, she selected a plate, an old chipped one this time. She picked it up and threw it as hard as she could against the kitchen floor. It didn't break but bounced against the linoleum. The plate spun like crazy and came to a stop.

❧ Chapter 13 ❧

From the moment Zainab stepped out of the Amman airport, she walked into a world of memories. The crowded neighborhood in which Fatma lived overflowed with familiar sights and smells—the falafel stand, the spice seller, and the *dukan* stocked with canned goods. Visions of Abed came flooding back at every corner. The flavor of Fatma's *maqluba* and the scent of the coffee each awakened recollections from an earlier time, a life lost. Abed's image reappeared so vivid and complete, it made Zainab shudder.

There were distractions, too, *alhamdulillah*, which left no time to dwell. Upon arriving at Fatma's house, there was a flurry of courtesy visits from all branches of the family. Relations came bearing news and well-wishing—and to steal long looks at Khalid's new wife.

After several days of such visits, Zainab was finally left to her own thoughts as she sat on the floor in Fatma's sitting room, recutting the tomatoes for the salad. Anysa had arrived from the West Bank the day before and was coming to lunch. Zainab could predict what her sister would say. *Were you in a hurry when you made the salad? Do you need a sharper knife?* Zainab slid the newly cut, tiny tomato pieces into the bowl.

Still, Zainab looked forward to embracing her older sister at the door. They had much to discuss and finalize. The engagement was less than a week away.

Zainab finished the tomatoes and began to re-cut the cucumber. It was unbelievable. Fatma was forty years old and had five children. The signs of age were already showing on her face and around her middle, but, truth be told, she still couldn't make a proper salad.

Nadia walked into the sitting room. "*Yama*, what are you doing?"

There was still time for Nadia, though—Zainab had a plan. Of course, she would need certain family members on her side to help carry it out. Appointments would have to be made, documents gathered; God knew what else.

"I'm fixing this salad," Zainab replied. "Fatma was in such a rush."

Nadia shook her head. "*Yama*, you're silly. The salad's fine."

Zainab smiled. Nadia was truly a vision of loveliness. Nineteen years old, beautiful and slim, *masha'Allah*, with glowing skin and bright eyes. Zainab needed her daughter with her in America. Besides, Nadia had stayed at Fatma's since the coldest months of winter, and the arrangement had gone on long enough. Now it was time for Zainab to plant a seed in Ahmed's brain. She would need his help to get a visitor's visa for Nadia to travel to America. It was best for everyone if Nadia waited out the engagement period at her mother's side.

The bell sounded. Zainab rushed to the front gate. "*Ahlan wasahlan!*" *Welcome!*

"*Alhamdulillah asalaama*," Anysa replied. *Thank God for your safe return.* She planted three firm kisses on Zainab's cheek.

Anysa, whose large white scarf reached past her waist, pulled herself away from Zainab and looked into her eyes. "You're back where you belong, my sister." She spoke close to Zainab's face. "What's your news? What gift did you bring me from America?" Anysa threw her head back and laughed as she waddled through the courtyard.

Fatma welcomed her aunt into her home; her children did the same, lining up for kisses. Then Nadia stepped forward to greet the woman who would be her mother-in-law. Nadia cast her eyes down, her movements hesitant—so unlike her usual self-assured manner.

Zainab directed Anysa to the small sittingroom off the kitchen. "Come this way. The food's almost ready." The two sisters settled onto the floor cushions. They sat cross-legged, close together, thighs touching. Anysa arranged a stack of embroidered pillows to lean against and launched into news of the family. Anysa spoke seriously, punctuating each detail with a tap on Zainab's thigh. After every tap, Anysa sat back and raised her eyebrows, waiting for Zainab's reaction. Oh, how Zainab had missed her sister's company. No one else alive knew her as her sister did.

Anysa began with the health of their mother, *Hajja* Zarifa, back in the West Bank. "She's tired but, *alhamdulillah*, not sick." Anysa reported on Zainab's daughters Huda and Yasmine: both well, as were their families. Next was the topic of their brother Waleed, who could not attend the engagement party because he was heartsick over his son in political prison. Anysa suggested in a confidential tone: "I don't think he can afford the Israeli travel tax."

The conversation shifted to Anysa's trip from the West Bank into Jordan. She had traveled with her son Mohammed through the checkpoints and the bridge. Anysa put her hand on her chest, closed her eyes, and spoke about the long wait, the heat, the dirty bus, and the soldiers.

"The soldiers are getting younger and younger. They are giving guns to children!"

Zainab gave her a pat of sympathy. "Curse their fathers."

"Curse their fathers," Anysa repeated and rearranged her pillows. Then she asked, "How are Khalid and his bride?"

For a moment, Zainab couldn't think of her daughter-in-law's name. It was such a tricky one, on her tongue one minute and gone the next. "Khalid and his bride are fine."

Anysa clucked her tongue, which Zainab chose to ignore.

"What's she like?" Anysa asked. "Like Margaret? She's good, *masha'Allah*."

Apparently, Anysa was still unaware that Margaret had stopped wearing hijab. Well, she would know soon enough. In another day, God willing, Ahmed, Margaret, and their children would arrive in Amman.

"*Masha'Allah*, she's good like Margaret." Zainab said, hoping the topic would end there and not turn toward the baby or its due date. It was a relief that Khalid and his wife were off to the souk to get a long, modest *jallabeyah*—a caftan suitable for her to wear in Jordan.

Nadia came into the room and spread a thin plastic covering on the floor. Zainab eased herself up and helped Fatma with the platter of *mensef*—rice and chunks of boiled lamb, garnished with fried almonds and nutmeg.

Anysa's eyes widened. "What's this? *Mensef*? You think the wedding is today?"

Zainab took in the yogurt smell of *jameed*

185

wafting up from the rice. "We need to celebrate the joining of our children." She looked at Nadia, kneeling with her head down, setting out small bowls of the re-cut salad. Then Nadia and Fatma took their places on the floor, and the four women ate, each scooping their spoon into the same mound of rice and lamb.

At last, the two older women leaned back. "*Alhamdulillah*," they muttered as Zainab's daughters gathered up the soiled plastic and removed the leftovers for the children to finish off.

The two older women strained to get up and reach the sink in the hallway, where they rinsed their mouths and washed up. Refreshed, they moved to the formal salon where they sat in armchairs, leaning back, sighing, and touching their bellies.

They discussed the dishes to be served at the engagement party: one lamb slaughtered, five platters of *mensef* with *jameed* sauce and the head of the lamb on the side, followed up by *baklawa* from Anysa's favorite pastry shop.

Nadia entered with a tray of tea. Her hands trembled and the glasses rattled together. Without looking up, she presented the tea to Anysa. "*Tafadhali.*" *Help yourself.*

Zainab's heart swelled with sympathy. It was a stressful time for a girl, just before the signing of the papers. Of course, Anysa would be a demanding mother-in-law, impossible to please. If Nadia gave her an apple she would want the whole fruit basket.

Zainab took her tea and waited for Nadia to leave the room. She turned to her sister. "How's your son Mohammed?"

"*Alhamdulillah, alhamdulillah.*" Anysa looked down at her glass.

Zainab also looked down, dreading the matter she was about to bring up. Yet she had to. Certain things needed to be confirmed before moving forward. "Mohammed, his divorce papers are filed and finished—right?"

Zainab knew the answer, but she needed to ask anyway. Anysa had already assured her Mohammed's divorce would be settled well before the engagement party. Of course, Anysa had to understand the delicacy of the matter. If Mohammed's divorce was not complete, that would make Nadia a second wife, something Zainab would never accept. They were a respectable family, not so desperate to allow a daughter to be in such a miserable position. Besides, what man could afford two wives, two houses, two families? What man could afford the headache?

Anysa didn't answer. Zainab continued, "He's divorced from Suhad—right?"

"That's what I wanted to talk to you about." Anysa pressed her hand on Zainab's thigh.

Zainab's insides fluttered as she waited for Anysa to explain. "The divorce papers," Anysa said. "They're not completely finished *exactly*."

"What?" Zainab sat upright and set her tea aside.

"It's been difficult," Anysa said. "You know, with all the closures and roadblocks in the West Bank. You know how it is, my sister."

"But Mohammed had *months* to finish this. You agreed!" Zainab was standing up now. "You promised!"

"Sit down." Anysa gestured to Zainab's empty chair. "Of course, he'll divorce Suhad. That is not a question. We'll do the engagement and they'll divorce. *Khalas*!"

Zainab's courage began to slip away. She felt Abed's absence more than ever. It was an acute loss, as if she had lost a limb. What would Abed have done? Would he have called it off? Her eyes wet, Zainab pointed a finger at Anysa. "You wouldn't have done this if Abed were alive." Tears ran down Zainab's cheeks.

"Oh, calm yourself. You're exaggerating. Nadia won't be a second wife. As I told you, it's the damned occupation. We can't accomplish anything. It's not our fault. They'll divorce and it'll be over."

"What if Mohammed changes his mind?" Zainab eased herself back into her chair. "He may decide to stay with Suhad. They have a son together. Where would Nadia be then?"

"The two can't stand each other." Anysa rolled her eyes. "Trust me. They'll never get back together."

"How can I believe you?"

"You need to have faith, my sister."

Zainab considered this. Then a wave of sadness moved over her; she drooped forward. She didn't have the strength to call off the engagement or stand up to her sister or even to wait for a new match for Nadia. Zainab had brought this problem upon herself. She had been in such a hurry to see Nadia married. That's why they had settled on a divorced man with a child. Zainab reminded herself—he wasn't divorced yet. She should have had patience for a more suitable man, one closer to Nadia's age. No other wife. No child. No history.

The door to the salon opened, and Nadia stepped into the room, carrying a generous platter of fruit. In her nervousness, she took slow steps and kept her eyes on the platter. The grapes and figs had been artistically arranged—she was clearly trying her best to impress her future mother-in-law. Nadia left and returned with dessert plates and peeling knives. Hands trembling, she placed them in front of the two women. The silence and tension in the room were bearing down on Zainab. The tea had turned cold. She turned to her daughter. "Clear the tea, my love. Bring some water."

After Nadia left, Anysa said to Zainab, "You know, Nadia is lucky to have Mohammed." Anysa poked Zainab's thigh. "He's a good man, *masha'Allah*."

Zainab wanted to speak up, but the words wouldn't come.

"Let's be honest," Anysa continued. "Nadia's an orphan now. With her father gone, who's going to take care of her?"

Zainab sat up. Nadia was not an orphan. *Look at me,* she wanted to shout. *I am her mother, and I am here!* But Zainab's throat was dry; she said nothing.

Anysa picked up a fresh fig and examined it as she spoke. "She's blessed that Mohammed decided to take her. I doubt she could do better. We both know Nadia is the lucky one here."

Zainab's hands trembled and droplets of sweat formed on her legs. Fury brewed inside her. She sat, heart racing, until at last she summoned the courage and jumped out of her seat.

"*Khalas*! That's enough!" Decades of swallowed feelings gave way to a new decisiveness. "It's over!" Zainab shouted. "The engagement is over!" Her gestures were big and sharp. "This was a bad idea from the start. We don't need your pity! My daughter wouldn't take your son if he were the last man in Palestine." Zainab didn't stop there. She marched around the room and ranted, grabbing at her clothing and slapping her own forehead. She told her sister she had had enough of her attitude, enough of her insults. "You think you're so much better!"

Zainab stopped for a moment. Her sister stood before her, a look of utter shock on her face. It seemed Anysa was speechless for the first time. Zainab looked down. At her feet was Nadia, crying, holding onto Zainab's *thob*. There were others in the room—Fatma and her children, all staring at the scene before them.

Then Zainab dealt the worst insult possible to Anysa. "Get out of this house! Get out!"

Fatma and Nadia insisted their aunt stay. They begged Zainab to change her mind.

Equally possessed, Anysa snatched up her purse and waddled toward the door. She turned and pointed a chubby finger. "Yes, it's over! My son is too good for your spoiled daughter." Then she was gone.

"May God forgive me." Zainab collapsed into an armchair. The room felt so much lighter now that Anysa had departed. A wave of relief settled over Zainab until her daughters engulfed her, suffocating her with their questions.

"What happened?" Fatma stood facing her mother, with her hands on her hips.

At Zainab's feet, Nadia, hunched over, choked back tears. "Why did you do that, *Yama*?"

Zainab patted Nadia's head. "Don't worry, my love. It's the best thing. That marriage would've been trouble. Can you imagine Anysa as your mother-in-law? Now stop crying."

Nadia's hysteria became more intense, and Zainab shouted, "*Khalas*! You can do better, *inshallah*. May God give you a better husband."

"But *Yama*." Nadia looked up. "I don't want another husband." She spoke in a whisper. "I want Mohammed. I love him."

Zainab straightened. "How is this possible? You've only seen him a few times. Before that, you were a child." She caressed Nadia's cheek. "How can you love him?"

Nadia wiped tears from her eyes. "We've been writing letters."

"Letters?" Zainab's tone became impatient. "Who delivers these letters?"

"*Yama*, it's email. You know, the computer, the Internet."

Zainab put her hands over her ears to block out these revelations. "No daughter of mine writes letters to a man."

"*Yama*, we're engaged."

"No, you're not. You were never engaged. No papers were signed." Zainab stood and gestured briskly. "It's over!" She moved to the door. Nadia trailed behind, pleading with her.

"*Khalas*! I have decided." Zainab left the room, went to the bedroom, and locked the door. She spread out a prayer carpet and began to pray, even though it was between prayer times.

Outside the door, she heard Nadia crying and Fatma trying to pull her away.

Zainab pushed herself through her prayers. Her hands open, she sat asking for forgiveness. Nadia needed forgiveness for corresponding with Mohammed. Zainab needed forgiveness for mistreating her sister. And more, she needed forgiveness for performing her prayers without *wudu*.

By the grace of God, she hoped her prayers would be accepted anyway.

❧ Chapter 14 ❧

Rumpled and weary from two flights and one long layover, Margaret, Ahmed, and the children arrived in the reception area of the dingy Amman airport. As per their custom, the entire extended family had shown up to greet them— every last niece, nephew, and cousin. With one exception: where was Nadia?

The family members surrounded Margaret. As she submitted to their kisses and handshakes, she shifted Leena, still half-asleep, from one hip to the other. Unlike Tariq, who glued himself to Margaret's side, Jenin immediately mingled with her same-age cousins. Meanwhile, the mother glided toward Ahmed and initiated a private talk, hushed and guarded.

Fatma came at Margaret with a handshake. "*Alhamdulillah asalaama!*" *Thank God for your safe return.* She gave Margaret the Jordanian triple kiss and peered into her face. "You look older."

"I *am* older," Margaret said.

Fatma touched Margaret's hair. "No *hijab*?" She clicked her tongue.

Margaret smiled faintly. On her last three visits to Jordan she had worn a headscarf—to the praises of the family. She was finally one of them! Or so they had thought.

"*Inshallah*, you'll wear *hijab* again," Fatma said. "And Jenin, too."

"*Inshallah*," Margaret replied as the nephews whisked away the luggage. The family herded themselves out of the airport and into the oppressive August heat. Margaret took in the smells of Jordan: dust, body odor, and something decaying. It was already midday, but nighttime back in Seattle. Leena squirmed in her arms and Margaret asked Ahmed, "Where's this hotel we're staying in?"

He didn't answer; he was still engaged in an intense exchange with his mother. Now Khalid was involved, too. Margaret told herself to stay calm as she searched out their suitcases on the sidewalk and kept an eye on Tariq.

A taxi pulled up, and the mother and Fatma immediately got in. Khalid whispered something to Ahmed, who listened with arms crossed.

"*Yalla*, let's go." Margaret said.

Again, Ahmed ignored her. Margaret dropped her shoulders in resignation and looked around. *Welcome to Jordan,* she thought, *the land of not knowing what's going on.*

An old Mercedes appeared at the curb. Fatma's husband Abu Ra'id jumped out and loaded the luggage.

Ahmed pointed to the Mercedes. "Kids, get in the car."

Margaret waved a hand to get his attention. "Not unless it has seat belts!"

Ahmed shot her a look. "Now is not the time for this."

She bit her lip and squeezed into the back of the Mercedes with the children while Ahmed slipped in front next to Abu Ra'id. Seeing that there were, in fact, no seat belts, Margaret held Leena tightly on her lap and braced herself. Abu Ra'id pulled away and sped toward Amman, smoking and talking in a serious tone to Ahmed. The wind blew through the open windows and tossed Margaret's hair about. Under the glare of the later summer sun, the view outside formed a bleak portrait of barren hillsides and swirling dust. Abu Ra'id repeatedly took his eyes off the desert highway to talk to Ahmed. Margaret looked skyward and made a silent prayer to arrive safely.

Ahmed twisted around with a look of pain on his face. "Honey, there's a problem."

She gripped the front seat and pulled herself forward. "I knew something was wrong."

"Nadia's engagement has been called off."

Margaret's eyes widened. "We came all this way and no engagement?"

He explained there had been an argument between his mother and Aunt Anysa. Apparently, Mohammed was still married to his first wife. "I'll deal with it," Ahmed said.

Margaret closed her eyes. There was always a problem in Jordan: bickering over a perceived insult, a sister with marital troubles, or a feud between siblings. But these problems wouldn't be left to fester. Oh no. In Jordan, family quarrels required intervention, and now that his father had died, Ahmed was their man.

They left the dusty hillsides and reached the gritty outskirts of the city, driving through the crowded streets, past blackened buildings and *jilbab*-clad women, through one poor neighborhood after another. It was East Amman, not an area for tourists, but home to the underprivileged and the displaced. Their car joined the throng of traffic—fume-spewing trucks, battered cars, and worn-out taxis, each honking and crowding in front of the others.

Exhausted but wide awake, Margaret sensed they weren't headed to any hotel. Abu Ra'id took a turn, and she recognized the shabby street. *Damn*. The sight of Fatma's modest house sapped Margaret of her last bit of energy.

Standing outside its cement wall was Nadia, who started crying as soon as Ahmed and Margaret got out of the car to greet her. In her broken Arabic, Margaret asked Abu Ra'id to leave their suitcases in the car, as they were going to a hotel. He shrugged and unloaded them at the curb anyway. The nephews scooped up the bags and carried them in.

"I thought we were staying in a hotel," Jenin said.

"Me, too." Margaret tried to keep her voice even. "Your father was supposed to arrange it." She carried Leena and ushered Tariq in through the worn-out front gate. The courtyard was small but pleasant, with a few trees and an area to sit.

Fatma met them at the front door. "*Ahlan wasahlan.*" *Welcome*.

Margaret entered and stepped onto the speckled tile. Inside the entryway, a framed photo of the Dome of the Rock hung above the archway. It was all so familiar, as was the feeling of dread that came over her when she peeked into the salon, filled with family members absorbed in discussion. Margaret continued down the hall to the back sitting room, where she found Alison.

In the crush of relatives at the airport, Margaret had forgotten about her. The last thought of her had been on the flight from Amsterdam to Amman, when Margaret had concluded Alison would have an easier time in Jordan than she had. After all, Margaret had paved the way. Now Alison could waltz in and everyone would think her foreign ways were almost normal.

Alison stood. Her *jallabeyah* was too short and hung wrong, and her hug seemed out of place after the handshakes and kisses. Something else was off with her, too.

They sat side by side on the floor cushions. "We made it," Margaret said as she settled Leena next to her. "Where's Khalid?"

"With the family." Alison's eyes grew vacant. "That pretty much sums it up."

"Are you all right?"

"We've been here almost a week," Alison said, her eyes still glassy. "I haven't left the house—except to mail some postcards and buy this *jallabeyah*." She tugged at her dress. "I haven't even bought a newspaper."

Fatma stepped in with a tray of tea. "*Tafadhalu.*"

Margaret took a glass, hot in her fingertips. "Bless your hands."

Alison shook her head. "*La shukran.*" *No, thank you.*

After Fatma left, Alison said, "Tea, coffee, tea, coffee. That's all they do here. And I thought my Syrian grandparents drank a lot of tea." She wiped a tear with the back of her hand. "I had so many plans for this trip. Khalid doesn't even care."

Margaret gave a nod of sympathy. "I know it's hard." How could she explain? The trip was about family. Period. Especially if there was a problem —and there was always a problem. "But you have to set aside your feelings while you're here," Margaret said, surprised by her own words.

Alison blinked. "I can't do that."

"Just go with the flow."

"Why do I have to make all the compromises?"

Margaret leaned her head against the hard wall and sighed. "Unfortunately, that's usually how it goes."

Alison continued to sulk. "This house is so crowded. I have no privacy. And there's only one bathroom."

Everything she was saying was true, but Margaret, worn down from her countless trips to Jordan, couldn't bear to hear another word. She stood. "Please excuse me. I need to talk to Ahmed." She went to the salon, where a dozen faces turned toward her standing in the doorway. Her eyes fell on the mother, whose frown was severe, and finally on Ahmed, his face full of worry. Margaret gestured for him.

He came to her and said, "We're staying here tonight. We'll find a hotel in the morning."

But he had promised, and she had left the

matter up to him. After all, it was he who was familiar with the city and its hotels. It was just so typical—waiting until the last minute, not planning ahead. *Damn*. Margaret wished she had made arrangements herself. Then her own flip advice came bouncing back at her: *Just go with the flow*.

Margaret woke to the morning call to prayer. The mosque loudspeaker was directed right into the room where she and her family lay on floor mats. Outside, a rooster crowed, and from inside came the faint noises of family members rising for prayers. Margaret, eyes closed, sensed her children sleeping nearby, and Ahmed's soft breathing next to her.

He hadn't said another word about moving to the Middle East, not since Margaret's visit to the restaurant. Maybe his plans were just a phase, a case of midlife crisis. The three J's had mentioned this before. One husband grew a goatee, another took up mountain climbing, and another bought a motorcycle. Maybe this was something like that.

She drifted back to sleep until Ahmed woke her. "*Sabah al-khair*," he said. *Morning of goodness*.

"*Sabah al-noor*," she replied. *Morning of light*. The flowery expressions, so out of place back home, felt natural at that moment with the sunlight streaming through the curtains.

They got up, roused the children, and gathered with the family for Turkish coffee in the courtyard, where the morning air was fresh. They sat on cushions at low tables under the trees. Tariq and Leena played with their cousins while Ahmed spoke in English on his cell phone. Margaret wondered if there was a problem at the restaurant.

"Is everything okay?" she asked when he got off the phone.

"Just fine," he replied.

Meanwhile, Fatma oversaw breakfast. Her daughters set out small dishes of cheese, marmalade, and creamy, white *lebneh*. Entering the gate were two of Fatma's sons, still in pajamas, returning with a plates of hummus and falafel and armloads of round bread.

Nadia served the tea. It was the first time Margaret had gotten a good look at her since her tear-filled greeting the day before. She wore a bright fuchsia caftan that skimmed the ground. Her hair, wavy and dark, swayed across her back as she moved around the courtyard, graceful yet solemn. She had a natural beauty that her older sisters lacked.

When the meal was over, two of Fatma's daughters remained in the courtyard, talking to Ahmed. They glanced toward Margaret.

"What are they saying?" she asked him.

He shrugged and looked away. The girls got up and went in the house.

"Tell me."

"They're praying for you. The whole family . . ."

"For me?"

"That you'll wear *hijab* again."

Margaret ran a hand through her red hair. No matter what she did in her life, it was never enough for the family. She would always fall short.

❧ Chapter 15 ❧

At midday, Margaret and Ahmed were in a borrowed car, driving toward Jabal Amman, the main hill of the city. The car had no air conditioning; the windows were down, creating a swirling wind tunnel. Still, Margaret was alone with Ahmed, and for that she was thankful. It was only their second day in Jordan, when normally they would be swept up in the throes of family reconnection.

She had hesitated to leave Leena behind at Fatma's, where dangers lurked everywhere: hard surfaces, stairs with no railings, and a roof where the children played. Margaret told herself Leena was older now and Jenin would keep an eye on her. Margaret brought her attention back to Ahmed, who was listing hotels they might stay at.

"Honey," she said. "You told me you made reservations."

"I meant to." Ahmed honked at a driver trying to squeeze in front of him.

She exhaled. It seemed each time they came to Jordan, Ahmed reverted back to some disorganized version of himself.

They entered the first traffic circle and his phone rang. He answered in Arabic and chattered away as he negotiated the curves with taxis and SUVs jostling for control, disregarding all concepts of lanes and turn-taking. When Ahmed put his phone down, Margaret remembered something she wanted to do. "While we're here, I want to go to the *ballad*, that downtown *souk* area, I'd like to get a few things." She began counting on her fingers. "Embroidery, pottery—"

"There's been a change in plans." Ahmed stuck his arm out the window to signal. "My mom is on her way to Aunt Anysa's. I need to be there."

Margaret groaned. "Oh, just take me back to Fatma's then."

"Sorry, honey. There's no time. They're heading there now."

"Oh, God." Margaret slunk down in her seat.

Ahmed made a U-turn at the next traffic circle. As he navigated the cars merging from both sides, he talked about Nadia and how determined she was to marry Mohammed.

"What caused this whole problem anyway?" Margaret asked.

Ahmed explained. It came down to Mohammed's

breach of agreement. There was no choice but to call it off. How could Nadia marry a man still married to his first wife?

All of this made sense. For once, Margaret agreed with the mother. "So why's the family going to see Aunt Anysa?"

"So my mother can say she's sorry."

"I thought there was no choice but to end the engagement?"

"We have to finish this problem."

"Your mother's doing what's best for her daughter."

Ahmed didn't reply; he simply drove on. At last, they entered a tidy street, far from the bustle and grime of Fatma's neighborhood. Here, the villas were larger—no worn out gates or patched cement walls.

"This is it." Ahmed parked.

Margaret stepped out and looked through the wrought iron gate at the classic stone villa. "Whose house is this exactly?"

"Mohammed's uncle." Ahmed pressed the bell.

Inside the formal salon, the mother, Abu Ra'id, and Khalid were already there with unease on their faces. Margaret and Ahmed took seats in the circle of armchairs pushed against the wall. She greeted the mother, who was pale and fidgeting.

A polished-looking Arab woman in a pastel

suit and headscarf entered with a tray of juice glasses. Margaret glanced down at her own cotton blouse and jeans. *Dressed wrong again.*

Margaret reached for her glass and Ahmed touched her arm. "No," he whispered. "We don't drink anything until we reach an agreement."

Margaret looked around. The juice glasses sat untouched. The oversized armchairs, which seemed inviting at first, now appeared garish—designed to impress, not for comfort. As beads of moisture formed on her juice glass, she waited for some-thing to happen.

An older, heavyset man entered, his face stern. Everyone stood, and he shook hands with the men. His beard was long and thick and had to be for religious purposes. Passing through his plump fingers were a set of enormous prayer beads, their tassel dangling toward the floor. Then Margaret realized: he was the brother of Aunt Anysa's late husband, Mohammed's uncle.

Everyone sat, and the debate started. Even though Margaret could get by with Arabic small talk, she was lost in a group discussion—always two topics behind and unable to tell where one word ended and the next began. She restrained herself from asking Ahmed what was going on, as he, like everyone else, was gripped by the words of the bearded man.

On the walls were the standard *Qur'anic* passages, hung so high that any reader would strain his neck trying to read them. Crystal ashtrays were scattered about, but there wasn't much else to look at. The juice glasses remained untouched, and the stress level rose. The mother didn't speak but sat with her arms crossed, looking away, clearly pained by it all.

The woman in the suit reappeared, this time with Turkish coffee. Without asking who wanted any, she placed a cup in front of each person. Margaret's coffee had a frothy swirl and a delicate cardamom aroma. Without thinking, she reached for the cup. Ahmed, who must have seen her from the corner of his eye, gently swatted her arm. She pulled back and glanced around the room. No one was drinking.

The bearded man got up to leave. As soon as he was gone, frantic whispering started between the mother, Khalid, and Ahmed.

Margaret turned to her husband. "What's going on?"

He waved his hand impatiently. "Not now."

He was a different person in Jordan, utterly fixated on everyone else's troubles yet oblivious to his own wife. Being in Jordan was an instructive glimpse into who Ahmed really was—a man obsessed with taking care of his relatives. So insistent and tiresome.

Margaret retreated into thoughts of their life in Seattle and their home at the end of the cul-de-sac. Jordan was clearly not the place for her. She could barely tolerate the current visit, newly confirming that she wasn't meant to live in an Arab country. How could she maintain her sanity amidst their traditional ways? She could no longer remember what she had loved about the culture. Besides, she felt no more need for exotic adventure, preferring just to stay home. She counted the days until they would fly back.

The bearded man reappeared with a young man. It was Mohammed, tall and well-dressed, youthful and charismatic. It was no wonder Nadia wanted him. He sat, then spoke, and they all listened. His tone was confident and firm, his gestures insistent. Several times he stressed the word *wallahi*, which Margaret understood as *I really mean it*. The bearded man fingered his prayer beads and nodded in agreement.

Mohammed stood, said something further, and left the salon. When he reappeared, his mother Anysa was next to him. She assumed the same expression as her sister: face frowning and chin jutted upward.

Margaret looked over at Ahmed, who was comforting his mother. He talked to her like he was the parent and she the child. It appeared that a similar exchange was occurring between Mohammed and Anysa.

Finally, they spoke directly to each other, the two women, so clearly sisters with their identical expressions and gestures. After just a few words, they were yelling, fighting for the upper hand. Margaret was instantly roused. The mother stood and pointed her finger at her sister. Aunt Anysa, the larger and rounder of the two, also stood. She shouted back, her hands on her hips and beads of sweat popping out on her brow. The family listened with stunned expressions as remarks flew between the sisters, accusations and insults.

Then all at once, they stopped and stared at each other. Silence settled on the room, and Margaret held her breath.

At last, the mother started talking, her voice strained. Aunt Anysa replied, her tone softened. The next moment, the two women were embracing. Everyone smiled and looked relieved. "*Alhamdulillah*," the room murmured.

"What happened?" Margaret asked Ahmed.

"You can drink your juice." He smiled. "The engagement's back on."

"Thank God." Margaret stood up to stretch her legs.

"Where are you going?" Ahmed asked.

"Aren't we leaving now?"

"No, now we're going to visit."

They pulled away from the iron gate, and Ahmed told Margaret they would stop at a few hotels on the way back to Fatma's. What a relief he hadn't forgotten about this matter amidst the family drama. As he drove, he recounted the highlights of the scene in the salon: how his mother said she was sorry for kicking her sister out of the house, how Aunt Anysa apologized for saying her son was too good for Nadia, how Mohammed swore on the soul of his dead father that he would divorce his first wife.

Ahmed said, "Whatever makes my mother happy."

"What about Nadia?"

"This is what she wanted."

Ahmed reached the hotel, and they left the car with the valet. Inside, the lobby was large but modest, with a simple café. "Wait here," he said. "I'll see if they have any rooms."

The place was busy; guests were coming and going. Was it possible they could find two rooms during tourist season? As Margaret waited, she glanced over at Ahmed, who was handing his credit card to the clerk. He smiled at Margaret and gave her a thumbs-up.

She told herself to stop being so impatient with him. He really was trying. Granted, he wanted to make his mother and sister happy, but he wanted to please her, too.

He walked toward her. "We have two adjoining rooms, one for us and one for the kids."

"How'd we get so lucky?"

"Someone canceled." He clicked his tongue. "See, honey? Sometimes it pays to wait until the last minute."

Margaret didn't argue but followed him to the elevator. Their room was basic but more than adequate. She admired the real toilet and touched the fresh white towels.

"Let's go to that lobby café," Ahmed said. "It could be our last chance to be alone."

The café was well-lit and filled with European families and Arab businessmen. Gigantic brass cooking spoons decorated the walls. The waiter, wearing a vest and a red fez, appeared with their drinks: tea for Ahmed and for Margaret, fresh mint lemonade.

"We'll eat breakfast here every day," Ahmed said.

She nodded just as the waiter delivered a large platter of mixed *fatayer*. They ate a few of the savory pastries filled with cheese and spinach.

Ahmed began arranging and rearranging the parsley garnish, then said finally, "I need to tell you something."

Oh no. Why hadn't she seen this coming? Why else would he have brought her to a restaurant, just the two of them, when all the family was back at Fatma's eating green *mulukhiyya* over rice?

"Do you remember that job in the UAE?"

Margaret covered her face with her hands, then let them drop in her lap and gazed sadly at her husband. Why had she been so foolish to think this problem would go away?

Ahmed looked at her expectantly, waiting for her to reply. "Aren't you going to say something?"

"What do you want me to say?" She was surprised by her own calm.

"I have an interview the day after Nadia's party. I'll be gone two days, three at the most."

"When did you make these plans?" This was not the question she wanted to ask.

"I'd almost given up, but they called me today."

Ah, yes, his phone call that morning. "What about me and the children?" Margaret asked.

"You and the kids will stay at the hotel."

She looked away, her eyes restlessly roving the walls. The gigantic brass utensils looked absurd and gave the impression of a bogus Arab-themed décor. She turned back to Ahmed and brought his face into focus. She spoke softly. "I can't believe this is happening."

"Abu Ra'id can pick you up each morning and bring you to Fatma's."

"So everyone knows?"

"Only you. You're the first to know."

Then her question arrived, her tone flat. "Why are you determined to ruin our lives?"

Ahmed leaned across the table. "Just let me see what happens. This is my chance."

"Yes. *Your* chance."

"It's a chance for all of us."

"Don't pretend like you know what you're

asking of me." Her calm gave way to a breathlessness that filled her chest. She had more to say but could not find her voice.

Ahmed stared down and studied his empty tea glass as if it foretold their future. As they sat in silence, Margaret looked at their situation as though from far away, seeing their impasse from a great distance. She knew Ahmed wasn't going to acknowledge any more of what she had said. He opted to ignore her words, just as he ignored the true issue at hand.

After twenty years of marriage, they were moving in opposite directions. And neither one cared to get back on the same path.

❧ Chapter 16 ❧

"You don't think your family will mind?" Alison asked.

She and Khalid were sitting in Fatma's courtyard under the shade of the trees. He had just confirmed her solo trip to the West Bank; she would return home on a later flight, without him.

"My family?" he asked. "It's not their decision where you travel." His tone was reassuring and calmed her. Then he added, "It's my decision. Not theirs."

Alison looked at him but stopped herself from pointing out how backward his comment was.

At least he didn't mention she was four months pregnant. Actually, four and a half.

Instead, she said, "I wish you could come with me."

"I've been away from my job too long already. Plus, it's risky."

"I know, babe." Alison had heard from Margaret that Khalid could be detained at the border. It all depended on the political climate and the mood of the soldiers.

"You love me, don't you?" she asked.

"You know I do." His expression was so earnest that she couldn't help feeling moved. "Thanks for agreeing to travel back with my mother," he said.

"It doesn't make sense for her to fly back to Seattle alone."

For a week of sightseeing in Jerusalem and Bethlehem, Alison was prepared to do almost anything. The trip with Khalid had started out so wrong—the extra gifts they had to lug along, the ugly fight the night before, his mother attached to them like an appendage. Then there were those first dismal days at Fatma's. And crying in front of Margaret. How had Alison lost control like that?

As for the engagement party, the women's gathering, held in a tent on someone's roof, intrigued Alison in the beginning. It was her first time seeing many of the women out of hijab, wearing makeup and strappy gowns. But the event—loud, crowded, and frenzied—dragged on hour after hour into the early morning. When the women rushed in unison to slip on their hijabs and *jilbabs*, Alison assumed with relief that the event was over. But no. The groom and his entourage were arriving for a photo shoot; the party and dancing went on for another two hours.

Going to the West Bank was the one thing turning out in her favor. Baby or no baby, Alison vowed that she would apply for graduate school as soon as she got home. Otherwise, all this experience would go to waste.

On Khalid's last day in Jordan, Alison spent the day at his side. When they finally had a moment alone together in the salon, he explained the plan. Fatma and her husband Abu Ra'id would drive Alison to the Jordanian border. She would then travel over the bridge by bus to the Israeli side.

"You won't have any problems," Khalid said. "You're an American."

"I'd like to stay in the youth hostel where I stayed last time." Details of the place came to Alison's mind: the Persian carpet, the Arab clerk, the backpackers lingering in the lobby.

"You'll stay at my sister's. Why pay for a place to sleep?"

"You're right." Alison had to admit that it would

be a rare opportunity, staying in a refugee camp.

"Then you'll take a taxi to Jerusalem," Khalid said. "From there, find another one to the Bethlehem checkpoint. Aida Camp is close by. It may take time getting through."

"I don't remember that."

"Things have changed since you were there last time." A look of anguish flitted across his face. "My cousin Belal will be waiting on the other side. He speaks English."

"How will I recognize him?"

"Don't worry. He'll find you." Khalid pulled out a small piece of paper. "Here are the numbers for Belal, Uncle Waleed, Huda, and Yasmine." He handed it to her. "Hide it."

Alison shoved the paper in the pocket of her jeans and made a confession. "I'm a little worried about the Israeli border. What if they figure out my background?"

"You're kidding, right?" He stared at her. "You're an American tourist." He brushed away her concerns with a flip of his hand. "Just pretend you don't know any Palestinians."

"What should I say if they ask?"

"Lie."

The next day Khalid left for Seattle. The family, wiping tears from their eyes, lined up at the gate to say good-bye. The following day, they did the same for Alison—minus the tears.

During the dusty car ride to the bridge, she sat in the backseat with Fatma while Abu Ra'id drove. Fatma talked about how she missed Bethlehem, the city of her childhood. She gave Alison letters for her sisters, which Alison slipped into her backpack next to the wallets she planned to give Huda and Yasmine.

At the border, they said their salaams, and Alison walked away and into the hot, oppressive air. She was on her own now—at least until she met Belal.

On the Jordanian side of the border, as she sat on the bus watching it fill with families, Alison remembered she was pregnant. How strange it was she still had trouble remembering this fact. Her morning sickness was nearly over, and in loose-fitting clothing, she barely showed.

The bus filled up at last, then began its short journey, inching over the modest bridge and stopping at a large, single-story white building with an Israeli flag flapping in the wind. Alison exited with the others, and Israeli soldiers directed them forward. She moved along, averting her eyes from their guns. Inside, the travelers fell into two lines. Ahead was a pretty female soldier with long ringlets in her hair. She smiled broadly. "*Shalom*. Welcome to Israel."

Alison's heart beat nervously, and she wished Khalid was by her side. When it was her turn, she approached the window and presented her passport.

The female soldier studied Alison's face. "What's the purpose of your visit to Israel?"

"I'm a tourist."

"Do you know anyone in Israel?"

"No."

"Are you traveling alone?"

"Yes."

The soldier drilled her eyes into Alison. "You're traveling alone, and you don't know anyone in Israel?"

"Yes. I mean no."

"Go wait over there." The soldier pointed to a row of chairs.

Alison sat and fidgeted until a tall male soldier gestured for her to follow him. Inside a bare room with only a table and chair, he pointed to her backpack. "Your bag."

She placed it on the table. Another soldier appeared, holding Alison's passport. He asked the same questions as before. As Alison answered, perspiration spread under her blouse. Meanwhile, the tall soldier unzipped her backpack. His clumsy hands ran across her belongings until he reached something of interest: her address book. He flipped through it, said something in Hebrew, and left the room, taking the book with him. The remaining soldier spilled out the contents of her backpack and rummaged through it. She bit her lip as she remembered the letters.

The tall soldier reappeared with her address book. "Who is Waleed?"

Her face grew warm. How could she have been so stupid to write the names there? She recalled Khalid's instructions—but any lie refused to rise up.

"Waleed is my husband's uncle," she answered.

"Your husband's Palestinian?"

"Yes."

"You said you didn't know anyone in Israel." He stared at her.

"I've never met him before."

"Is this your first time in Israel?"

"I came in 2000 with a study group." The trip flashed through her mind. The students, the youth hostel, the carefree mood.

"Wait outside." He pointed to the door. The other soldier scooped up her backpack and took it away. Alison took a seat outside. By then, nearly all the other travelers had left. Only a few sad-looking individuals remained. They sat together in the row of chairs, but each was alone.

Young Israeli soldiers strode about the open space with their guns and walkie-talkies. The female soldier with the ringlet hair was smoking now and no longer smiling. Alison reached for her backpack that wasn't there. She worried about the letters and wondered what the soldiers were doing with her things. She envied the tourists who had already made it through.

Eventually a new soldier appeared and called her back into the room. "Your husband's Palestinian?" This began a new battery of questions, mostly repeats from before. He then asked her about her plans for staying in Israel. How long would she stay? Where would she sleep?

"I'm staying at the Oasis Youth Hostel in East Jerusalem." The lie rolled easily off her tongue. She believed it when she said it. She wished it were true.

It was midafternoon when Alison finally squeezed into the back of a shared taxi filled with passengers. During the drive to Jerusalem, her hands trembled as she clutched her backpack and repeatedly fingered the letters inside. The soldiers had said nothing about them. Instead, they repeated the same questions over and over until they finally let her go. "Their game," Khalid had said.

The highway cut through the West Bank, past groves of olive trees and Palestinian villages on rocky hillsides. The taxi reached the edge of Jerusalem, and Alison gazed at the old stone villas, arched windows, and iron gates. They rounded a bend, and the ancient stone ramparts of the Old City came into view, just as she remembered—actually more breathtaking than before. A panorama of the Old City emerged, magnificent with the sun reflecting off the gold on the Dome of the Rock. Alison sucked in a breath. Everyone in the car, even the driver, paused to take in the view.

They reached a parking lot full of taxis where Alison found a minivan heading to the Bethlehem checkpoint. As the van drove off, Alison told herself to relax.

The checkpoint into the West Bank looked more like a border with its high wall and watchtower. Long lines of people wound into a concrete building, and Israeli soldiers swarmed all around. She didn't remember this scene from her student trip to Bethlehem. Khalid's words came back: *Things have changed since you were there.*

Up ahead, a soldier questioned a man in line in front of her. When it was Alison's turn, her stomach quivered, she held up her passport, and the soldier waved her through. She was herded down a metal corridor, and through the infamous security wall, formidable and unnerving. She followed the others, all walking solemnly single-file.

With the wall behind her, Alison continued forward into the bright sun. She shielded her eyes and passed a long row of taxis, their drivers calling out to her. Alison gripped her backpack, which dug into her shoulder. She searched the nearby faces for one that could be Khalid's cousin.

From behind her someone called, "Alison?" The voice had a heavy accent. She turned and locked eyes with a man puffing on a cigarette, dark circles under his eyes. He left the cigarette in his mouth and extended his hand. "I am Belal."

As they shook hands, she avoided staring at his gaunt, unshaven face, not at all how she had imagined him.

Belal's gaze shifted from her face to something behind her. "*Yalla*, let's go."

She followed, hoping he would offer to carry her bag.

He looked nervously over his shoulder. "I have to stay away from the checkpoint," he said in English. "If the soldiers ask to see my ID . . ." He clicked his tongue.

"This is the wall." He gestured with his head.

Alison picked up her pace to hear what he was saying.

Against the blue sky, the concrete wall stood shockingly tall and ugly, more appalling than Alison had imagined. Covered in a bizarre range of angry graffiti, it prompted Alison to stop and stare. Then she had to jog to catch up.

"Like we're living in a tomb," Belal said. "We can't breathe anymore." He threw the end of his cigarette on the ground and climbed into a taxi. Alison slid in next to him, and he continued to speak. "If any foreigner comes here, sees our life, he will know who is the victim."

Alison nodded but didn't know what to say.

She glanced at the watchtower and then back at Belal. He offered her a cigarette.

She shook her head. "No, thanks."

He turned to stare out the taxi window. "If the soldiers stop me, that's it," he said. "It is my mother who will be crazy. I am not afraid of prison. I was there before." Once the taxi let them out, he said, "With my brother there, it will be too much for my mother—two sons in the prison."

Alison remembered, yes, Khalid had spoken of a cousin in prison.

Ahead was the refugee camp, a crowded mass of crude concrete homes. She felt dizzy with the sight of the camp, the wall looming beyond, and Belal's voice in her ears.

Belal turned down a narrow alleyway that snaked into the camp. Alison followed him, still hoping he would offer to carry her bag. Covering the rough cement walls of the alley was a patchwork of Arabic graffiti—slogans of the intifada, no doubt. All around were crowded makeshift homes in deep decline, built by the UN soon after the 1948 exodus of Palestinian refugees and never meant to last this long, decade after decade, refugees living in a hopeless cycle of dislocation. Alison's eyes skimmed the dwellings; some had two or three stories added onto the original structures, slapdash construction built for the ever-growing families.

Barefoot children waved at her. "Hello! Hello!"

Alison smiled back while trying to keep up. Belal turned down another alley, then another. A gutter ran down its center, and she had to watch her feet to avoid tripping.

"Here," Belal said. They stopped at a rusty blue metal door, embellished with a battered arabesque pattern. "This is my brother's house."

"Wait." Alison caught her breath. "I thought we were going to Huda's?"

"My brother is married to Huda."

While Alison considered this, the door opened a crack, and a boy's face appeared—one of the children from the alley. "*Yama!*" he called.

The door swung open into a small courtyard, and a woman appeared. She adjusted her scarf as children clustered around. She was Huda, with the same deep-set eyes as her sisters.

"*Marhaba.*" She gave a simple greeting, kissed Alison on each cheek, and welcomed them into the courtyard, which was compact compared to Fatma's.

At first, Belal refused to come in, but Alison realized she wanted him to stay. "Come on."

"As you like," he said with a shrug.

Huda led them to cushions thoughtfully arranged on an old carpet. Alison sat and finally eased her backpack off her shoulder. She looked around, noting every detail: the worn embroidery on the pillows, the threadbare carpet, and the coarse cement walls. The area was tidy and the ground swept; laundry fluttered on a clothesline. The courtyard contained a single patch of green, probably mint. Facing the enclosure was a small house—Khalid's childhood home. The tiny space was now home to another set of children all scattered about.

Huda and Belal sat on either side of Alison. He took out a cigarette, lit it, and savored the first puff. Huda, who seemed disheveled, as if she had just woken up, started with a series of questions about the family in Jordan. What was their news? How was her mother? How was Nadia? And the engagement party? Belal helped translate, as Huda's dialect was that of the village, the same as Khalid's mother, only faster and more run-together. Huda's inquiry continued until she was satisfied her family was fine. Then Alison remembered what she had brought.

"A gift from America." Alison handed her the leather wallet, which now looked small and trivial. Huda admired it for a moment and then set it aside. Alison felt slightly embarrassed about the gift and reached in her backpack for the letter from Fatma. As Huda read, her two teenage daughters appeared, both wearing pink headscarves. They sat at the edge of the carpet and glanced shyly at Alison. Huda snapped at them to make tea, and they jumped up.

Huda looked at Alison and smiled without speaking. Alison smiled back, knowing she was being examined and evaluated, a process she had already endured multiple times since her first visit to Margaret's. Huda seemed pleased that Alison was there, yet there was a melancholy about her that neither Mona nor Fatma had. Even Huda's smile seemed sad. Her eyes mirrored Belal's, with the same dark circles beneath. Her face was lined, and even though she was younger than her sisters Mona and Fatma, Alison would have guessed she was the oldest of the three.

A dented teapot appeared on a scratched-up wooden tray. Belal and the teenage girls watched as Huda filled the glasses and passed them around. They didn't speak as they sipped the hot tea, more minty than any tea Alison had ever tasted. Belal drank his in the same way he smoked his cigarette—as if it were his last.

"Hungry?" Huda asked.

"Yes," Alison said.

Huda nodded, got up, and went into the house with her daughters. Alison was left with Belal, who smoked mindfully.

"You said your brother's in prison?" she asked.

He nodded.

"What happened?"

"Who can know?" Belal exhaled a column of smoke. "Maybe someone gave his name to the Jewish. The soldiers picked him up at the checkpoint. They looked at his ID and took him."

"How awful," Alison said. "I'm so sorry."

"He only did what everyone does in this hell." Belal studied the end of his cigarette. "Maybe writing political words, maybe making demonstrations." He looked at her. "He is fighting the occupation, my brother. We are all fighting in our own way."

Before Alison could respond, Huda returned and told her to go wash up. Alison followed her inside to the bathroom, tiny and primitive but clean, with a flush hole in the ground for a toilet and a ceramic base to stand on. Alison washed her hands in the small sink and looked at herself in the cracked mirror. She was actually in a Palestinian camp—a real refugee camp. She dried her hands on the towel hanging on a nail. Her eyes scanned the room, the bright green tile and barest of toiletries: a single bar of soap, a tube of toothpaste, and a row of toothbrushes.

In the courtyard, Huda brought out a large platter of stuffed vegetables, steam rising from the top. Alison, the only one with a plate of her own, took a small bite of stuffed zucchini. When the hot rice touched her tongue, she realized how hungry she was. She ate silently, focusing on each bite, in the same manner as the family. She sensed this was not an everyday meal, but rather some-thing prepared for her benefit.

Afterward, more tea appeared. Everyone sipped, a practice that seemed to be the main activity for all branches of the family.

Alison asked Huda, "Where's your husband?"

Huda brightened. "He's working."

Belal lit another cigarette. "Today is the first day my brother works in a week."

"How do people live?" Alison asked him.

"The United Nations gives rice, sugar, tea— enough to keep us alive."

"Do you work?"

"What work is there for me?" Belal took a long drag on his cigarette. "I studied electrical engineering. Sometimes I work with my uncle, but we can't go far outside Bethlehem."

"Do you think you can show me around the camp?" Alison asked.

"Tonight you come to my father's," Belal said. "Do you want I take you?"

"That would be good."

"I go now and come back."

Huda led Alison to a small room with mats stacked in the corner. On the floor, Huda placed one of the mats and a pillow. By then, Alison was exhausted but too keyed up to nap. After Huda left, Alison studied the cracks in the ceiling, the bars on the window, and the poster of the Dome of the Rock. She flipped through her guidebook and thought about places to visit. Plus, there was Yasmine, the last sister to meet.

Later, she rejoined the family in the sitting room. She tried to follow the conversation, but failed, always two beats behind. By then, Huda's husband had come home. He was gray-haired and older than Huda. He smiled slightly but had the faraway look of a man who had given up.

It was dark when Belal finally came back for Alison. She was anxious to get out of the small house, crowded with children. "You come with me," he said.

Alison was surprised to see the entire family go out the door with them. The children's chatter filled the alley, full of shadows and uneven textures. Within minutes, they arrived in the courtyard of Belal's house, where his parents were waiting.

"She is my mother, he is my father." He gestured to his weary-looking parents. Belal's mother kissed Alison, and his father, in a white *kufiyah*, simply nodded. Once Alison realized he was the brother of Khalid's mother, the resemblance was unmistakable—they had the same serious mouth and wide forehead.

Dominating the courtyard was a large tree dotted with lemons, a single sliver of beauty in a sea of concrete. Through a door, Belal's mother ushered Alison, Huda, and her daughters. In the salon, Alison faced bright florescent lights and a circle of women, all standing up. Hands were shaken, cheeks kissed, and tea served. For the first time, Alison appreciated the ritual of tea, as it broke up the monotony of socializing. On the wall were the typical Islamic plaques and a framed photo of Jerusalem, as well as a portrait of a young man: Belal's brother—the one in prison. No wonder the mood was somber.

An old woman entered the crowded room, and everyone stood up again. Alison fumbled with her tea.

Huda whispered to her, "It's *Hajja* Zarifa."

The name was familiar, a relative of Khalid's— *Hajja* Zarifa. Khalid's grandmother. Her face and hands were old and leathery; she wore an embroidered *thob* with a thin leather belt around her fat middle. Bright-orange hennaed hair slipped out from under her wispy white scarf. On her wrinkled face were strange blue tattooed markings.

Instead of greeting her in the usual manner, the women bowed their heads and kissed her hand. Alison waited her turn, and as *Hajja* Zarifa came closer, she thought the woman looked a hundred years old.

Huda shouted in her ear, "This is the wife of Khalid! The Syrian!"

Alison wondered what this elderly woman could understand. *Hajja* Zarifa gave Alison a toothless smile and a kiss on each check. She pulled back and looked at Alison with her milky gray eyes. "*Habibti*!" She touched Alison's belly with a bony hand. "How's the baby?"

Alison blinked. "*Alhamdulillah.*"

Time passed slowly in the crowded salon as Alison struggled to understand their dialect. She had exhausted her own Arabic when, at last, coffee appeared, signaling the gathering was about to end. After drinking, the guests set the tiny cups down and said *m'a salama*, leaving only Huda's family and Belal's family. Alison moved to the door, but Huda told her to stay. It was nearly midnight when Belal's sister served more tea and a tiny meal of bread, olive oil, and *zataar*.

Afterward, Alison walked with Huda's family back to their house. The air was chilly and the alley dimly lit, almost serene at that late hour. The family walked heads down, huddled together, quiet for once. Huda carried her youngest child.

Out of nowhere came a sound—a voice over a loudspeaker. The group's walk turned brisk. One of Huda's teenage daughters touched Alison's sleeve. "It's the soldiers. They say the people must be in the house."

The family was jogging by then, jerking the small children along. They rounded the final turn and stopped abruptly. The youngest girl let out a scream. In front of them were four Israeli soldiers in full army gear and helmets—machine guns pointing every which way. One soldier shouted in crude Arabic. Huda's husband quietly explained that they were on their way home.

"*Yalla! Imshi!*" A soldier yelled. *Hurry! Be off!* As the family hustled down the alley, Alison's heart hammered wildly. When she touched the handle of the blue metal door, her fingers shook. She entered the courtyard, sat on the carpet, and caught her breath. Huda's husband took out a white handkerchief and wiped his brow. The girls gestured theatrically to show how afraid they had been, and Huda chided her husband for allowing them to stay out so long.

When Alison finally lay down on her mat, her heart was still pounding. She had the small room to herself, while the floor of the sitting room was covered with sleeping children. The sounds of the refugee camp seeped into her room. From some-where in the distance a vehicle roared and voices blared from a loudspeaker. She tried to conjure up other images from the day: Belal's chain-smoking, Huda's teenage daughters, and the tattoos on *Hajja* Zarifa's face. But Alison's mind couldn't shake the incident with the soldiers.

The concrete floor was hard beneath her thin mat. She opened her eyes to the moonlight filtering into the room and regretted drinking so much tea. As the caffeine coursed through her, she longed for Khalid and wondered what he was doing back in Seattle.

When Alison finally fell asleep, she dreamt one of the soldiers was chasing her through the camp. She was enormously pregnant and held her belly as she ran down one alley and up another, looking over her shoulder at the soldier and his gun. She stopped at every blue door, pounded on it, and yelled for someone to let her in.

Disoriented, Alison sat up. Her skin was covered in sweat, and her heart raced. She lay awake for what seemed like hours, then fell back asleep after the morning call to prayer.

After breakfast, Belal appeared in the court-yard as Huda's daughters were clearing away the dishes. The circles under his eyes were more pronounced than before. He asked Alison her plans for the day. She said she wanted to go into Bethlehem.

"Will you go with me?" she asked.

He pulled out a cigarette. "As you like."

It put Alison at ease to know she wouldn't face her excursions alone. This trip was so different from her last one, where the Holy Land itinerary had been preplanned and she merely had to follow along with a group. It had been a light-hearted trip during a peaceful time. There was no second intifada or death of Rachel Corrie, no September 11th or war in Iraq. Alison had been a carefree student, a freshman, for God's sake. Now she was pregnant and married to a Palestinian man. During her last trip, she hadn't fully under-stood what it meant to be Palestinian. Not really.

The sky was bright blue when Alison and Belal left Huda's house. As they walked he asked, "You met the soldiers last night in the camp, right?"

"Yes—they scared me."

"But they did nothing."

"No, but it caught me off guard," she said. "I even had a dream about it. A soldier was chasing me through the camp."

"You are here one night and you have this dream?" Belal asked. "Everyone here has this dream."

Neither of them spoke as they walked to the main road. Behind them towered the wall, imposing and ominous. For the first time, Alison noticed the surrounding hillsides swallowed by settlements—Israeli colonies of identical houses arranged in monotonous grids.

They passed an ornate building with a grand entrance. Alison asked what it was.

Belal expelled a ream of smoke. "It's a hotel."

"Next to a refugee camp?"

"Yes." Belal turned his head to the building. "An empty hotel." He went on to describe Bethlehem when he was a boy: how the city had been full of tourists; how he would go to Jerusalem with his brother, so easy, no problem. Now it had been years since he had been to Jerusalem.

They arrived in Manger Square: an open space with a handful of benches, a few trees, a row of souvenir shops, and the Church of the Nativity. They ducked into the church's small doorway and walked inside. They passed a long row of columns and into a grotto, where they stood before the gold star on the floor. The experience was so different from Alison's last visit with rowdy students and born-again Christians all angling to view the spot where Jesus had been born.

Normally, Alison would have been moved to be in such a church, filled with meaning, the site of so much significance—historical and recent. But now she felt numb and empty. Something was missing.

They stepped out of the dark space and into the sunlight, where they shielded their eyes.

"What else you want to see?" he asked.

Alison pointed to the row of shops. They walked across the square, and Belal took out his lighter. He nodded toward the shops, a signal that she would go in alone. After she bought a few dusty postcards, they walked the winding cobblestone streets of Bethlehem, which were nearly empty. She told him the city was so different from the last time she was there.

"When you came?" He flicked the ashes of his cigarette to the ground.

"Spring of 2000." The city had been cleaned up then for the Pope's millennium visit. Doors and shutters had been freshly painted. Flowers spilled out of window boxes. Now the streets were dirty and neglected. Shop doors were covered with political posters in various stages of deterioration, forming a layer of lace across the city.

They continued past more shops and stone churches, ending up at the fruit and vegetable souk she had visited on her last trip. The weather had turned hot and still. There was only one person buying produce. Others were sitting and staring off at nothing. One man sat on the ground rocking back and forth. A Bedouin woman in a raggedy black covering sat nearby with her hand out. No, Alison thought, this was not how she remembered it.

She turned to Belal. "Let's get out of here."

✿ Chapter 17 ✿

Zainab sat in Fatma's courtyard next to the jasmine vines. The low table in front of her held a pan of meat filling and a lopsided pile of dough. Next to her was Nadia, humming and smiling as the two of them worked together, Nadia rolling out balls of dough, and Zainab filling them. As she folded and pinched the dough, her thoughts floated to the events of the past week.

What a relief, *alhamdulillah*, she forgave her sister in the salon of the show-off villa in Jabal Amman. Zainab's resentment had been visible to everyone. Ahmed had told her, "You must forgive her, *Yama*." He said it in front of Anysa. Right in front of her! Then a strange thing had happened. As soon as Zainab mumbled the words, Anysa embraced her and Zainab's heart filled with mercy. The rage had drained out of her body and she'd cried.

Zainab cried again a few days later at the engagement party, held on the roof of that villa. She had danced with Anysa, the two of them swaying, waving white handkerchiefs, and admiring their children as music boomed across the rooftop. Nadia sat next to Mohammed, each perched under the colorful tent canopy. Zainab could see the effort that had gone into her daughter's hair and eye makeup, which was now smudged with tears across her childlike expression. It was then that Zainab's own tears began to fall. Her daughter, her last child, would marry. Soon Zainab would be an old woman on her own. So much to cry over!

Meanwhile, Anysa had started crying, too. Surrounded by family members, the two women looked at each other. After all that had happened between them, they were still able to celebrate together over the joining of their children and over future grandchildren, inshallah.

Anysa gestured for Zainab to come closer. She leaned in. Anysa shouted over the music, "I hope Nadia's grateful for this party!"

At this, Zainab's face contorted. "And your son should be grateful for Nadia!" She pushed past her sister and made her way to the edge of the tent.

Anysa was immediately by her side. "Nadia's lucky to get such a party!" Her face was so close, Zainab could smell her breath.

"It's nice," she yelled back, "but it could be better!"

Anysa threw her head back in disdain, put a hand on her hip, and waddled away. How dare she walk away like that!

This sequence of events from the engagement party now ran through Zainab's mind as she furrowed her brow and wiped her hand on the dishtowel slung over her shoulder. Her mind was clogged with bitter thoughts, stuck with nowhere to go. She would allow herself three more *sambusik* pies to think about Anysa. Zainab moved her hands unconsciously: a spoonful of filling, fold, pinch, and place. The nerve of Anysa to keep bringing up this favor for Nadia. Oh, how Zainab wished their mother and Waleed had been there to keep Anysa in her place.

When the third *sambusik* was set in the pan, Zainab tucked away her last thought of her sister. There were other matters that needed her attention. Fatma's cooking, for example. When Zainab had insisted on *sambusik* for the day's meal, Fatma said, "*Yama*, it's too much work."

Zainab had tried to explain that cooking was a time to slow down and think about life. Now, as she pinched closed another pastry, she glanced at Nadia. Here was another problem, a girl who had to be pulled by force from her cross-stitch embroidery to help with the cooking.

Nadia smiled wistfully and caressed the

dough. "I wonder what he's doing right now."

"Who?"

"Mohammed, silly!"

"You need to focus. I'd like to get this finished before *dhuhr* prayer."

Nadia touched the charm on her necklace. "I wonder if he's at his uncle's." Her hands became still; a distracted look moved across her face.

Was she blushing? Zainab studied Nadia, staring skyward, clearly oblivious to everything but her own daydream.

Ya Allah. These love matches were always doomed. Too many expectations. It never lasted. There was nowhere for the marriage to go except down. Sometimes these couples didn't even make it to the wedding. One misunderstanding and the whole engagement was off.

Zainab took the dishtowel from her shoulder and flicked it at Nadia. "Get back to work."

Nadia jumped in her seat and laughed.

"Don't fret about Mohammed. You'll see him tomorrow."

Zainab caught the scent of the jasmine, and for a moment she was sitting by Abed's side in front of the sheikh of their village; she was a young bride sitting with her groom. As Zainab's dim memories stirred, the images grew sharper. She was barely a woman, and they were performing the *katb el-kitab*, the marriage contract to make their engagement official. Abed was near her, but the space between them was wide. Yes, they had seen each other many times. They were cousins after all. But Zainab had lowered her gaze around him, covered her hair, and behaved modestly, just as her parents had instructed. As she recited a *surah* after the sheikh, she had few expectations of the man she was about to marry, only a fear of the wedding night. Therefore, she wasn't disappointed when they were awkward strangers together—an unease that continued for years. It was only when the last of their children started school that Zainab truly enjoyed her husband's company and took pleasure in his touch. It was then they became companions.

Zainab raised her eyebrows and shrugged. She cradled a *sambusik* in her hand. That last decade with Abed had been the happiest time in her marriage.

Then he died. *Allah yarhamhu.* Her chest tightened and she dabbed her eyes with the ends of her headscarf.

"*Yama?*"

Zainab coughed. "What, my love?"

"Are you all right?"

Zainab glanced at the nearly-noon sun. "It's almost *dhuhr* prayer."

There was hope for Nadia, though. Zainab still had time to make an impression on her. But only if Nadia's visa came through. Zainab might never have pursued the visa if she had understood the work involved: photographs, documents, letters to write. That was nearly all behind them now, as Nadia's appointment at the American embassy was the following day.

"Are you ready for tomorrow?" Zainab took another ball of dough, her swollen hands brushing against her daughter's graceful fingers.

"Mohammed's writing a letter, and I'm putting together my own file."

"Really?" A file of what, Zainab could not imagine. It was Ahmed who had made all the arrangements, completed the application, written a letter of support, and paid the fee. But under one condition: no one was to mention it to Margaret. Zainab had agreed to the condition, but she found it pretty foolish.

Ahmed had insisted. "I'll tell her if the visa goes through."

If the visa goes through. Why did her son have no faith? Her sister Anysa didn't have faith, either. She told Zainab to save the money. No one was getting visas to the US these days.

Zainab had faith. At each prayer, she made a special *du'a* for Nadia's visa. If it were God's will, Nadia would pass the months of her engagement in America at her mother's side learning the necessary skills to be a wife.

After pinching the final *sambusik*, Zainab eased herself up from the ground and went into the house to make *wudu*. After she finished at the sink, she sat at the tub to wash her feet.

Nadia entered and turned on the faucet. "Any news from Alison?"

Zainab washed between her toes. "She's at Huda's but will visit Yasmine, *inshallah*."

Nadia splashed water on her face. "I can't imagine her there. In the refugee camp."

Zainab tried to picture Alison in Huda's salon or in Waleed's courtyard next to the lemon tree, but her mind drew a blank. It was all so unexpected, Alison's trip to the West Bank, traveling by herself to meet Khalid's sisters. Still, truth be told, Alison was a foreigner, barely Arab, and not a Muslim. Here was an area where it was hard to have faith.

Zainab reached for a towel, dried her feet, and reflected on her surprise when Khalid had told her Alison would accompany her back to America. He said that Alison would never allow her mother-in-law to travel alone.

Zainab passed the towel to Nadia. "May God keep her safe."

In the bedroom, Nadia spread out the prayer carpets, and they began their silent prayer. As Zainab knelt, her mind wandered back to Anysa, but she stopped herself. She would not get swept up with spiteful thoughts. It would be a shame to spend her *du'a* asking for forgiveness.

Zainab tried to refocus, but *Surah Al-Kafirun* became muddled in her mind. She had recited

241

this *surah* about the disbelievers thousands of times. Yet now she mixed it up and forgot whole *ayat*, as her mind flitted between Alison, Nadia, and Anysa. Out of the corner of her eye, Zainab saw that Nadia had already left the room.

Palms held open, Zainab prayed hard for Ahmed to pass his job interview. How peculiar. Years ago, Zainab had made *du'a* for Ahmed to go to America. Now she made *du'a* for him to leave. In her mind's eye, she held a picture of him living in the Gulf. He had a large villa where Zainab lived, too.

She snapped herself out of her reverie and squeezed her eyes shut in intense concentration. This time she prayed for Margaret to agree.

❧ Chapter 18 ❧

The day after the engagement party, Margaret accompanied Ahmed to the airport for his flight from Amman to Abu Dhabi. In front of Fatma's house, Ahmed gave good-bye kisses to their children while Margaret looked on. She squeezed into the back of Abu Ra'id's car, wedged between the mother and Fatma, who both reeked of the fried *kibbe* they had prepared for lunch. Nadia sat next to the window, cheerfully jabbering, her mood dramatically lifted since her engagement had been secured. In the front seat, Ahmed spoke intently with Abu Ra'id, their conversation peppered with the words *Abu Dhabi* and *Dubai*.

Several days before, Margaret had brought up the topic of his interview. They were lying side by side in their hotel bed, the children sleeping in the next room.

"Let me go and see," Ahmed kept repeating. "It's just an option." And then finally, "Let's not spoil our trip by fighting."

What was there to say? The discussion had ended before it even started. Margaret hadn't brought up the matter again, foolishly adopting a strategy of avoidance and denial that she now regretted as she rode with the family to the airport. It was if she were going through the motions of someone else's life, dragged along with no free will of her own. That inexpressible anger that had consumed Margaret now gave way to a dull feeling, a slow suffocation.

At the airport, Ahmed strode through the glass doors into the departure terminal, his family following behind, the feeling among them celebratory. Perhaps it was a spillover from the engagement party or maybe it was the thrill of going to the airport—they seemed to go every chance they could.

While Ahmed was changing money, he chatted with the female teller who took his dollars and laughed at something he had said. Ahmed gathered the Emirati *dirhams*, nodded to the woman, and rejoined his family. He tapped his watch and said he needed to check in. Instinctively, the family formed a line, ready to give their farewells. The mother performed her ceremonial send-off—multiple kisses and a mini speech. Fatma and Nadia did the same, invoking God's name and reciting blessings, behaving as though he were never coming back. *For God's sake, the trip's only two days.* Abu Ra'id's oration was delivered more like advice. He gently poked Ahmed's chest and patted his shoulder, like a coach giving a pep talk.

Of course. They were all wishing him well on the job interview. He was pursuing his dream, and his family was cheering him on. Where did Margaret fit into all this?

It was her turn. She stepped forward. Her choices rushed over her: accept, ignore, pretend, or protest. Any confrontation would result in embarrassment. After all, plans had been made, a ticket booked.

Ahmed smiled at her, and the eyes of the family were on them. He leaned in and she inhaled the scent of his cologne. He took her hand and squeezed it. "If I don't do this, I'll always wonder." He then pulled back and said, "I won't make any decisions without you." His look was pleading, and for a moment, she had the urge to tell him she loved him.

"Have a safe trip." Her voice was flat, and her

eyes betrayed her. She bit her lip, fighting the tears.

He said good-bye, let go of her hand, and walked away. Her head filled with new questions. Where was he staying? Did he know anyone there? Did he pack enough clothes?

Travelers rushed past, documents in hand. Margaret momentarily lost sight of Ahmed, but then he reappeared, his eyes meeting her gaze. He nodded, perhaps his way of saying he sympathized somehow. Margaret waved back and stood there with an unexpected feeling of being left behind. She turned away from the family, not able to stop her tears this time, not knowing if they were for Ahmed or for herself.

The first day without Ahmed, Margaret sat in the shade of Fatma's courtyard. It was late morning and the temperature was rising. With the festivities now over, the house was returning to its regular routine. Fatma hung wet laundry while the children tossed a rubber ball around. The mother was showing Nadia how to chop a salad into teeny-tiny pieces.

Margaret massaged the ache in her shoulders. She couldn't help but think of Ahmed, who had called the night before to say that he had arrived safely. Now she wondered about his interview. Maybe the next time she saw him, he would announce he wanted the job. A shiver ran through her, and she longed for a private place to cry.

Then a familiar sound—the *muezzin*'s call to prayer—beamed in from the minaret across the street. The sound had been there all along, but this time Margaret stopped to listen.

Allahu Akbar. Ash hadu an la ilaha ill Allah.

God is great. I bear witness there's no god but Allah.

The words rang on.

Hayya 'alas-salah.

Rush to prayer.

Fatma hung the last of the laundry; the children scurried after the ball. The muezzin's voice played in Margaret's ears. It had been a long time—a year?—since she had performed the prescribed prayer regularly. But now when the call to prayer ended, a force pulled her up. She stood and walked purposefully into the house. She performed her *wudu* and gathered a prayer carpet from the sitting room, but then hesitated. Her prayer covering was back in Seattle. She turned to Fatma's oldest daughter and asked for something to wear. The girl went down the hallway and returned with a white garment.

As soon as it was in Margaret's hands, she saw the white lace trim. "Oh no," she said, handing it back. "That's your grandmother's."

The girl gestured as if to say *no matter* and walked off.

Slowly, over her jeans, Margaret slid on the

prayer skirt, which was clearly too short. The scarf was tight around her face, and Margaret had an urge to snatch it off. Instead, she stepped to the edge of the prayer carpet. She moved through the *surah*, the words coming easily. It felt good to bring her forehead to the ground.

Her thoughts segregated; one mentally reciting the prayer, the other considering why she had stopped praying regularly. The first prayer to go had been the morning *fajr* prayer, followed by the afternoon prayers. The downward slide began just after Margaret stopped wearing hijab. With her head covered, it had been easy to pray; she had been dressed for it.

Margaret finished the prayer in Arabic and remained sitting on the floor. She held up her palms. Now something in her own language, something from the heart. Looking at her open hands, her *du'a* became a series of false starts.

First, she asked for Ahmed to fail his interview. That didn't sound right, so she backtracked and asked for him to return safely. Next she asked for whatever was best for their family. But that wasn't sincere, as she only wished for one thing: to stay in Seattle. That was a selfish prayer. Still, she prayed vigorously for it. Everything in the room —the cold tile floor, the stack of mats in the corner, the plastic sandals scattered about—these and a thousand other details told Margaret that her place was back home.

• • •

Two days later, in the airport arrivals area, Ahmed appeared in front of Margaret.

"Don't worry," he told her. "Nothing happened. We just have to wait." His expression was resigned, even depressed. Perhaps the interview hadn't turned out as he'd hoped. He told her nothing more, but in the car he talked with his family. For once, Margaret felt an acute need to understand every word of their Arabic.

That night, when they were back at the hotel and the children were sleeping, she watched Ahmed get ready for bed. "Tell me about the interview."

"Nothing to tell." He pulled on his pajamas. "They asked me about my style of management, how I motivate workers, deal with conflict, questions like that." He sat on the bed, looking clearly exhausted.

"Well, how did it go?"

"I don't know." He shrugged and slipped into the bed. "Honey, we just have to wait." He pulled the covers around himself and closed his eyes. Any details of the interview stayed shut inside him.

Next to him, Margaret remained wide awake, incensed at the sound of Ahmed's soft snoring. *Damn.* How did she end up married to such a man? He withheld information from her. He made outlandish plans on his own. He left her sitting in the dark as he plotted their lives. Each bit of information he withheld was another stone in the wall between them. He was finally going to drive her insane, she was sure of it.

The next morning in the hotel restaurant, they all filled their plates at the breakfast buffet while Ahmed spoke cheerfully in Arabic on his cell phone. They sat down with their breakfast, and he set his phone aside.

"Honey, there's someone I want to visit."

Margaret looked up from slicing cantaloupe on Leena's plate.

"Remember my friend Rashid? He and his wife, Cynthia, are expecting us this afternoon."

"It's our last day. Aren't you going to spend it with your family?"

Tariq spoke up. "Are we going, *Baba*?"

"No, just your mom and me." He turned to Margaret. "It's only for tea." He studied her, as though gauging her reaction. "You know, they used to live in the Emirates. I thought maybe she could answer some of your questions."

Margaret decided to disregard that comment. "Do we have to go?"

"It's been a long time since I've seen Rashid. Too long."

So that afternoon, they left the kids at Fatma's and drove again through the chaotic traffic circles of Amman. In the car Ahmed recounted details about Rashid—how he had moved to Saudi

Arabia with his American wife, Cynthia, and how they had raised their family abroad. Ahmed had always spoken highly of these choices. Now Margaret would meet them at last.

They drove down a tree-lined boulevard with trendy cafés and upscale boutiques. On the sidewalk were Arab women in stylish hijab walking alongside others in short skirts and sleeveless tops. What a world away from the crowded and conservative side of town where Ahmed's relatives lived.

They found the correct street, where the villas were set wide apart, each protected by imposing walls. The sun bore down on Ahmed and Margaret as they stood at the gate. He rang the bell while she wiped sweat from her brow. They heard footsteps, and then a tall, well-groomed middle-aged man opened the gate.

"*Ya zelamah!*" His casual greeting matched his broad smile as he held his arms open. He was fit and wore a smart polo shirt. They stepped inside, and the men greeted each other with kisses to the cheek.

Rashid shook Margaret's hand. "Nice to finally meet you." He pointed to Ahmed. "I haven't seen this guy in years."

They walked across the courtyard toward the large stone villa. To one side, the blue tiles of a swimming pool sparkled. Rashid led them up the stairs and into the formal entrance, flanked by large pots, flowers spilling out of them. Inside the large entryway, a formal staircase rose up to meet the high ceiling. The house had a different feeling than Fatma's, cool and fresh. It was air conditioned, of course. Margaret stepped over a red tribal rug and passed a framed antique mirror.

They entered a formal sitting room, its floor covered with more red carpets, thick and lush. "Please sit." Rashid gestured toward an over-stuffed cream-colored sofa, arranged with red embroidered pillows.

Margaret sank into the sofa. As the men exchanged the usual questions, her eyes scanned the room. The wide glass-topped coffee table displayed antique Bedouin jewelry beneath its glass, and on top were hefty books on Middle Eastern art and architecture. The walls were decorated with a *kilim* rug, an old Arabic door, and framed maps of the region.

A woman walked in. "Sorry to keep you waiting." She smiled and extended her hand to both Margaret and Ahmed. "I'm Cynthia." Her look was chic and polished, with stylish blond hair and a pale linen dress. "I'm going to go make some tea." She turned to Margaret. "Would you like to come with me?" Her American accent was familiar, but her manner seemed foreign.

Margaret followed Cynthia down a hallway, past various paintings of Arab scenes. Margaret had only a moment to admire them before she entered a spacious kitchen. Hung on its yellow walls were colorful pottery and a plate with the word *Jerusalem*.

"Have a seat." Cynthia gestured toward the kitchen table.

Margaret sat, and Cynthia poured hot water from a kettle into a teapot. The kitchen was spotless and clutter-free; the marble countertops gleamed with a just-polished look. A young Asian woman entered, approached Cynthia, and reached for the kettle.

"It's okay, I've got it." Cynthia pointed to a plate of nuts. "Why don't you bring that to the men?"

"Yes, Madame." The woman took the plate and left.

"I'm still training her," Cynthia said. "She doesn't understand I want to do a few things for myself."

"Oh." Margaret was unable to say more; she knew nothing on the subject of maids.

On an oversized tray, Cynthia arranged a tea set and plates of small cakes and chocolate-covered dates. "Let's take our tea in the sunroom." She picked up the tray and again Margaret followed her. This time they walked down a different hall-way, one featuring framed Chinese-brushstroke paintings.

They entered the sunroom, full of greenery and arranged like a photograph in a home décor magazine—so completely different from Fatma's house or even Margaret's back in Seattle. Outside was a garden lavishly planted with grass, shrubbery, and bougainvillea.

Cynthia poured the tea. The cups were of the fancy sort, fragile and delicately patterned.

Cynthia took the first sip. "I heard you might be moving to the Emirates. I hope it works out."

Margaret raised her eyebrows. "Did my husband tell you to say that?"

Cynthia set her cup down. "I've never met your husband before today."

Margaret wanted to say something to repair her misstep, but Cynthia kept talking.

"The UAE is a good posting, but it depends on which emirate. Do you know?"

Margaret shook her head. "It's not likely we'll move."

"We lived in Abu Dhabi for years." As Cynthia gestured, her gold bracelets slid back and forth on her wrist. "Abu Dhabi is more conservative. Dubai is growing like crazy. It's very international but feels like a construction site. It is the regional travel hub." She ticked off the places they had visited. "Cairo, Marrakesh, Malaysia, Phuket, Kenya, Oman. Even Yemen!"

Margaret smiled weakly. This was just the sort of bragging she disliked. She thought of Liz back in Seattle, how uncomplicated it was to share a cup of coffee with her, so down-to-earth and without pretension. As soon as she got back,

Margaret would tell her all about Cynthia, and they would have a good chuckle.

"Of course, it's getting outrageously expensive." Cynthia crossed her legs. "That's one of the reasons we left. Plus, the expat lifestyle there is a bit over-the-top. They're building man-made islands in the shape of palm trees. I mean, really, is that necessary?"

Margaret listened absently, distracted by a general longing for Seattle. She heard Cynthia's words, but somehow they didn't register. It was hard to make small talk about something Margaret didn't know anything about.

"We wouldn't mind moving back," Cynthia said. "We still visit sometimes." Her eyes lit up. "Hey, maybe we'll see you there."

"I doubt that."

"You sound less than thrilled. How do you feel about moving?"

It was the first time anyone had asked Margaret how she felt. Ahmed and his family had just expected she would go along. Liz had assumed it was out of the question. The women from her *Qur'an* study believed she should follow her husband, whatever his plans.

"We're happy in Seattle. There's no reason to move."

"I understand," Cynthia said with genuine sympathy. "Our first posting was in Saudi. We had just settled in, and Rashid had an opportunity in Istanbul. I told him no way. I didn't want to learn Turkish." Then she spoke wistfully. "I still regret that. I mean, Istanbul. Can you imagine?" She sighed. "I guess I was afraid. I didn't want to start over or have the kids change schools."

"I don't want my kids to change schools, either. And I can't imagine leaving my parents."

"It's hard at first. I was so homesick." She shook her head. "But it gets better. We fly back to Boulder every summer. That helps."

"It's just so far away."

"We did a stint in Singapore. I ended up loving it."

Margaret's eyes took in the room, and when Cynthia wasn't looking, she took her in, too. Cynthia clearly had a different life. For one thing, she had money.

"My advice?" Cynthia leaned in. "Just keep an open heart."

Margaret nodded but couldn't find a word to say in reply.

"Especially if your husband gets a good package."

Margaret nodded again but was unmoved. What was fine for Cynthia wouldn't work for her. How could a desert country possibly compare to their life in Seattle? How could they leave their home, their friends, and the life they had spent twenty years building? The restaurants were doing well, and their children were in good schools. There was no reason to traipse off to the other side of the world. Jenin was already obsessed with the political problems of Palestine. Moving to the region would only make it worse. Who was Cynthia to give advice? Besides, she knew nothing of Ahmed's family.

"My husband has relatives in the region." Margaret finally said. "I'm worried they'd be too much for me."

"Don't worry about that. It'd be easier than you think."

Margaret wanted to mention that Ahmed's mother would be living with them. Instead, she said, "My husband wants to *Arabize* our children." She pronounced the word with more disdain than she had intended.

"They're half-Arab, aren't they?"

"They're American, too," Margaret said a bit defensively. "They get plenty of Arab culture in Seattle." She felt a sudden vulnerability in front of this woman she had just met. Margaret crossed her arms and hated with disgust the blouse and denim skirt she was wearing—so drab compared to Cynthia's clothing. Margaret said in a low voice, "My mother-in-law is living with us." She sat back and waited for that to sink in.

"I know all about Arab relatives," Cynthia said. "It's a package deal with an Arab husband. No way around it. Honestly, the family is easier to handle in an Arab country where they're not so dependent on you. And the villas here are meant for big families. Plus, you can get a maid. Let her wait on the family. Know what I mean?"

A set of images flashed in Margaret's mind: she and Ahmed were in a grand Arab villa—a pool, a maid, and a lush garden with blooming jasmine. The images expanded. Margaret drank tea from fine china and decorated her home with large framed photographs from their travels. The maid performed the household drudgery and tended to Ahmed's mother.

Nearly fooled, Margaret came to her senses. How could she have a strange maid underfoot in her house? How could they ever have a normal life in the Middle East? Besides, she doubted Ahmed could get a "good package," as Cynthia called it. People didn't live like that from running coffee shops. It didn't work that way.

Margaret finished her tea and refused a second cup. She chided herself for nearly falling under the spell of Cynthia's house, her musings, and her bragging. It was all part of Ahmed's plan to entice and persuade. Margaret made a vow. She would put an end to his scheming. She was always the one who compromised. Now he was asking her to make the ultimate compromise: to leave her home, her friends, her parents, and the life they had worked so hard to build. And for what? To satisfy his spontaneous whim. She wondered how she had allowed things to get this far.

Chapter 19

On her way to Dheisheh Camp, Alison rode in a taxi with her backpack at her feet. Next to her was Belal, who had turned out to be the ideal travel guide: readily available, willing to take her anywhere, and silent when she was too tired to talk. She thought ahead to meeting Yasmine, the last of Khalid's sisters. Alison had already been through the ritual four times and could predict the scene: kisses, greetings, and questions: *Do you love Palestine? How many children do you want? Was your grandfather really Muslim? Are* you *going to be Muslim?*

She mentally rehearsed her Arabic responses as Fairuz played on the radio and Belal blew smoke out the window. It was he who had suggested they call Yasmine before heading off to Dheisheh. When Huda made the call, Yasmine was adamant that Alison spend the night and the next day, as well. Alison had replied that she would stay the night but leave after breakfast.

Belal sucked the last bit of life out of his cigarette and flicked it out the window. He turned to her and explained that there were rarely any Israeli soldiers in Dheisheh, so she didn't have to worry about running into any. The soldiers she had seen in Aida Camp were there to guard the checkpoint and protect the Tomb of Rachel. Dheisheh Camp was bigger but quieter, with few clashes.

When they stepped out of the taxi, Alison lifted her backpack to her shoulder and looked up at the sloping hill before her, filled with a network of alleys and concrete structures.

"Before, this camp had a big fence around it," Belal said. "Now no more."

"Maybe things are getting better?" Alison asked.

"No, they are not."

The alley heaved with people passing in both directions, children shouting, and women hovering in doorways. Like the first refugee camp, each cement home had mismatched upper floors, or a room added on. Some additions were only half-complete, with cinder blocks still showing and metal rebar jutting out—perpetually unfinished, as though the builder had simply given up. Dheisheh was even more crowded, with some houses four stories high, sprawling upward, piling four generations of refugees on top of one another.

Belal seemed to know what Alison was thinking. "This place is so crowded, if you sneeze, your neighbor will hear you." He pointed to a simple one-story building. "That place is for *dabke* dancing."

"How do you know about this camp?"

Belal lit a new cigarette. "I have a friend. He lives in Dheisheh."

When they reached Yasmine's house, a boy of about eleven opened the gate into the courtyard. Alison was taken aback by how different it was from Huda's. There was no patch of green or welcoming corner of cushions. The space was scattered with a jumbled mess of plastic tubs and two upturned seats removed from a car.

"*Tafadhalu.*" The boy opened the door for them. Alison entered with her backpack and noticed that Belal was staying behind.

"What time you want me to come tomorrow?" he asked.

"Ten."

Belal nodded and blew smoke into the air. "As you like." He disappeared, leaving Alison with the boy, who had to be Yasmine's son. As she followed him around the corner, Alison realized Yasmine lived in an add-on apartment.

Alison instantly recognized Yasmine at the doorway. She had the same face as her sisters—deep-set eyes and dark circles underneath. Her dark hair spilled down her housedress, which dragged on the floor. She balanced a curly-haired baby on her hip and reached to embrace Alison.

"*Ahlan wasahlan.*" *Welcome.* Yasmine guided her into a small room, sparse of furniture but crowded with four children standing around, including the boy who had let her in—the eldest.

Alison sat on the floor cushions amongst the children. With only one small window, the room was stifling.

Yasmine sat across from her. "I'm glad you are here. I wanted to meet you since my mother told me about you. *Inshallah* your trip is going well."

At least, that's what Alison thought she heard. She understood only random phrases of the local dialect, so different from the Modern Standard Arabic she had studied at university. She missed having Khalid nearby to explain. There was so much she still didn't know.

Before Alison could reply, Yasmine passed the baby to one of her daughters and excused herself, perhaps to make tea. Unlike Huda's daughters, Yasmine's children were all too young to be preparing and serving tea. In fact, the little girl holding the baby on her hip looked about five.

Yasmine returned with two tall glasses filled with an orange drink. She held the tray in front of Alison. "*Tafadhali.*" Alison took the cool glass in her hand. Yasmine sat cross-legged on the floor mat. She shooed her children away and began her questions. How was her mother? Her grandmother? Her sisters? Alison responded, "*Alhamdulillah.*" It was now a familiar give-and-take for Alison, though she searched for the Arabic vocabulary to describe the engagement party, the dancing, and Nadia's dress. When Yasmine was satisfied with the answers, she asked about her brothers. Alison reported in detail about Ahmed and his family.

Yasmine moved on to Khalid. It was a series of questions, one logically leading to the next. How was Khalid? How was his health? Was he working? What kind of job did he have? Was he making money? And then an unexpected question came up, an awkward question. Had Khalid forgotten his sister Yasmine? It was difficult to answer because maybe he *had* forgotten Yasmine. He rarely mentioned her.

"No," Alison said. "Khalid didn't forget you." Then she remembered the gift that she and Khalid had chosen together. She unzipped her backpack and presented Yasmine with the wallet.

Her face lit up. "*Shukran.*" *Thank you.* Yasmine turned the wallet over, opened it, and stared at the space where the bills were supposed to go. Her shoulders dropped slightly. She looked away for a moment and then said, "I know he has forgotten. He never calls. He never asks about me." According to Yasmine, Khalid had been closer to her than to any other sister. Then he moved to America.

As she spoke, tears sprang from her eyes. Her oldest son sat next to her, stroking her hand and glaring at Alison as though she were the cause of all of his mother's suffering.

Yasmine explained the details of her life. Her husband couldn't get to work because the wall and roadblocks made that impossible. There was no work in Bethlehem. This meant no money, except the little bit handed out by the United Nations. Yes, they got some rice, flour, tea, and one hundred and fifty shekels per month. This was for a family of seven. "Seven people!" she shouted. As she spoke, her expressionless children milled about the room.

"I know it's not Khalid's fault." Yasmine wiped a tear. "But why can't he ask about us?" Her tone turned angry. "Can't he take our bad news?" Alison leaned back, inching away. It occurred to her that she would be sleeping in the tiny house and staying through breakfast.

Yasmine looked up at the small window. "I know he has a family now. I know that." She turned back to Alison and finally came to her point. "I can't even buy pencils for my children. Not even a pencil! Would it harm Khalid to help the children? He's their uncle."

Alison, drained by the exchange, was painfully aware that her Arabic was hopeless for what she wished to say. She uttered phrases as they came to her. "Don't worry, we'll send some money. No problem. I'll tell Khalid. He doesn't know."

At once, the expression on Yasmine's face changed. "Don't tell Khalid! It's my mistake." Then came crying. Yasmine looked up and whispered something, maybe a word to God.

"We'll send you money," Alison repeated.

The words made Yasmine cry harder. "I never should've said anything. Forgive me."

"No problem." Alison regretted her feeble Arabic vocabulary. It was clear Yasmine was under enormous stress managing her family under these circumstances.

"I'm sorry." Yasmine pressed her hand to her chest and continued to cry. Alison wanted the topic to change. She wanted Yasmine to pat her belly and ask how many children she hoped to have. Anything but this crying.

"You are a guest and I've put my problems in front of you." Yasmine straightened and began pulling herself together. "Please forget everything I said." She wiped away a tear. "My husband will be home soon, he'll be angry if he knows what I've told you."

"I won't tell him. I won't tell anyone, not even Khalid." Alison searched Yasmine's face. "Unless you want me to tell him?"

"He needs you to tell him?" Her voice turned angry again.

Alison made a mental note to tell Khalid to call his sister.

The rest of the day crawled by. Yasmine didn't mention again the issue of Khalid or her situation, yet an unease hung over dinner as they ate a small meal of hummus, bread, and sliced tomatoes. The children crowded around and finished every scrap of bread. Yasmine's husband ate with them, eyes downcast, fatigue on his face.

That night, Alison lay on the floor mat in the small sitting room. She rolled over, half-expecting Khalid to be there but remembering with a slight shock that he was back in Seattle. Dead tired, she expected to fall asleep immediately. Yet she lay awake, her mind reeling with thoughts of Yasmine, her distraught face and all the children by her knees. So many children! Couldn't she see it was too many? And why did Yasmine have to marry so young? Alison wished Khalid were there to explain it.

An image of Alison's new white apartment hovered in her mind. Their simple life now seemed extravagant. She recalled Khalid announcing he wanted to send money to his sisters in the West Bank. Alison vaguely remembered that both her grandfathers had at one time sent money back to Syria. Her father had told her this proudly, an act to admire—taking care of your kin—never framing it as a burden.

Alison opened her eyes to a streak of moonlight making its way through the window. She was pregnant. What was she doing lying on this uncomfortable mat? Why had she come?

In the morning, these questions remained in Alison's mind. She busied herself packing and repacking her things. Yasmine prepared breakfast, a repeat of the meal the night before. The family gathered around their shared plates, and Alison ran out of things to say.

At ten o'clock, Alison waited with her backpack in the cluttered courtyard. Through the open door, Yasmine was visible doing laundry in an ancient washing machine. Her method, only one step up from hand washing, required adding and draining water with a hose and transferring wet laundry between compartments.

Yasmine hung the laundry on a wire outside while her children hovered around her. She invited Alison to stay longer. "Why are you going? Sleep here another night."

It was easy to say no. Alison had seen enough of their despair and crowded poverty. She looked at her watch and imagined Belal in a taxi. Meanwhile, Yasmine washed another load of laundry and hung it up to dry. Alison studied the shadows on the concrete walls until, finally, Belal showed up just before noon.

As she said salaam, Alison handed forty dollars to Yasmine. "It's from Khalid."

They both knew this was a lie. Yasmine stared at the folded bills for a moment, then reached for them. She kissed Alison forcefully on each cheek, and at last, Alison left with Belal, who was wearing the same clothes from the day before.

"Did you sleep here in Dheisheh last night?" she asked.

"I told you, I have a friend, he lives here."

"But why are you so late?"

Belal looked at her. "We stayed up late playing cards."

"Why do you guys do that? Always playing cards."

"What else is there to do?"

As they rode in a taxi back to Aida Camp, Belal lit a cigarette and sucked it hard. Alison told him about Yasmine being so angry at Khalid.

"It's the occupation," Belal said. "It makes everyone a little crazy."

"I can imagine," Alison said even though, despite her all her studies, she couldn't grasp how it would feel to live there. She tried to picture Khalid as a boy growing up in the camp. Had he run barefoot in the alleyway? Had his family been poor like Yasmine's?

Then Alison's insides sank as she remembered the letter from Fatma. She had forgotten to give it to Yasmine—one small thing that might have made her happy.

Meanwhile, Belal talked on about life there. Alison wanted to ask him how often he worked, if he planned to marry, and how he paid for all those cigarettes. Instead, she let him vent his frustrations until he finally said, "The occupation is in every cell of my body."

The next morning, Belal arrived at Huda's, cigarette in hand. "Where you want that I take you?"

Alison, who had been waiting in the courtyard studying her map of Jerusalem, stood up and announced her destination. She would go with Belal to shop in the Old City. Together, they would visit Damascus Gate, Via Dolorosa, and the Dome of the Rock. They would have lunch at a particular café in the Christian Quarter.

Without looking at her, he flicked his cigarette onto the ground. "I cannot go to Jerusalem. Impossible."

Alison stared at him for a moment; then her brain clicked back to what he had said about checkpoints and restrictions. "Oh yeah." She bit her lip. "I forgot how difficult it is."

"Difficult? It is impossible. First, I need to get permission. It takes months. They would never give it to me."

"Have you tried?" Alison sat back down.

"They don't give permission to men like me."

"But it's only ten minutes away!"

He looked at her and shook his head. "If I go to the checkpoint and show my ID, the soldiers will take me. I told you this." Belal reminded her of his brother in prison and how upset his mother would be if both her sons were arrested.

"Stop." Alison held up a hand. "I don't want you to go to prison."

"Sometimes people walk through the hills between the olive trees. My mother does this to see her sister. But it's dangerous. The soldiers will shoot at me."

Alison pressed a hand to her temple. "It's not worth it."

He took out a fresh cigarette. His lighter refused to light. He flicked it frantically and then threw it on the ground. "A person has to think a thousand times before going to Jerusalem."

All at once, a numbness swept over Alison's body. "I can go alone," she said.

In a minivan headed to Jerusalem, Alison stared out the window at an olive orchard and imagined Belal's mother striding through the trees. This thought stuck with Alison until the minivan stopped at Salah e-Din Street. She got out and walked toward Damascus Gate; the sight of it sent a shiver through her. It was by far the most impressive of the entrances to Jerusalem's Old City, its archway a patchwork of stones reaching high up the ramparts. Pouring in and out of the gate were dual streams of people. Old Arab women sat on the ground outside the gate selling herbs. Lurking about were a dozen or so Israeli soldiers, several poised above on the ancient wall walk, inspecting the scene below.

Alison took the stairs down toward the gate. Inside was a bustling souk. She looked down at the timeworn stones beneath her feet. Once again, she was in the Old City of Jerusalem. She relished an emotional rush as she followed the cobbled alley deeper into the labyrinth of the Muslim Quarter past stacks of pottery, barrels of spices, and endless brass baubles. As she walked, Alison wondered if the medieval souks of Old Damascus had been similar, and she tried to imagine her Teytey Miriam walking in alley-ways like these, shopping for her Arab foodstuff.

With renewed vigor, Alison took in the narrow shops selling flat loaves of bread, hand-painted plates, and rough woolen kilims. She noted the arched doorways and cavernous alleys. But it was the mix of people that interested her most. Most fascinating were the older Palestinians in their traditional dress. The elderly women wore long black *thobs* with red cross-stitch, just like Khalid's mother.

In the Christian Quarter, Alison passed by carved heads of Jesus and bought olive wood rosaries for her mother and Grandma Helen. After walking up and down the Via Dolorosa, she found her way to the Church of the Holy Sepulchre. Christian pilgrims from all corners of the globe were lining up to see the tomb monument. Out of a sense of duty, Alison lit a candle, made a small donation, and said a short prayer for her parents and Grandma Helen—the ones who would most appreciate the gesture—as well as a special prayer for her Teytey Miriam.

By the time she reached the Jewish Quarter,

Alison had meandered through the Old City for several hours. Around her were signs in Hebrew and boys in yarmulkes. She entered a small English-language bookshop and bought the *Jerusalem Post* and the *International Herald Tribune*.

She walked aimlessly until she found herself looking down on the expanse of the Western Wall. She descended the stairs and entered the large open space full of Jewish worshippers and onlookers. It was hard to believe that this large area fit inside the walls of the Old City. She took in the scene from all sides, including the Dome of the Rock, visible beyond.

Exhausted, she dragged herself back up the stairs, pressing on until she found a small café where Arab men were smoking *shisha* and drinking tea. The cook nodded to her and pointed at the *shawarma* meat rotating in front of a flame.

"No thank you," Alison said in Arabic. "A menu, please?"

The cook recited the food on offer. She ordered falafel, sat alone, and turned to her newspapers. In the *Jerusalem Post* was news of unrest: rockets launched from Gaza, the demolition of Palestinian homes, and Arab youth killed in clashes.

In the *International Herald Tribune* was an article about Israel's "Separation Barrier" and how it violated a World Court ruling. She turned the page to an editorial about Yasser Arafat. Despite his government's troubles and his confinement in Ramallah, he endured as a symbol and leader of his people.

Alison ate her falafel without tasting it and then turned to the man slicing the shawarma. She asked how to get to the Dome of the Rock. His directions led her straight to a little gate to the mosque. Her stomach twisted at the sight of a cluster of Israeli soldiers standing by.

The soldier next to the gate gripped his gun. "You want to visit the mosque?"

She nodded, and through the small entrance, she caught sight of the blue-tiled mosque.

He tapped his wristwatch. "They're praying now. They'll finish soon." His English was clear and native-like. "Your bag." He nodded toward her backpack, which she opened. "Your passport please." Alison fumbled for it and felt the eyes of the other soldiers on her.

The soldier removed his sunglasses and flipped through her passport, looking for a long time at her photo. "Where are you from?"

"Seattle," she said. "Washington State."

He handed back the passport. "I was born in California."

Curly blond hair poked out from his helmet. He was about the same age as Alison, and he continued on about how the climates in Israel and California were the same. It was a profound relief to hear a West Coast accent after spending days grappling over Arabic.

She skimmed the faces of the other soldiers, their guns strapped across their bodies. Alison turned back to the curly-haired soldier, and her eyes fell on his vest and the way he casually held his gun against himself. She glanced down at his boots.

"Is this your first time in Jerusalem?" he asked.

She said no. He asked about her last trip, and she told him a few of the highlights. He was looking at her closely, and Alison immediately regretted the conversation. Here she was chatting with her husband's enemy. His enemy! She gave one-word answers, trying to wrap up their conversation.

"You can go in now," he said finally.

Alison nodded and stepped through the gate and into the vast courtyard. The mosque stood directly in front of her; she walked toward it, her eyes on the gold dome.

In the minivan on the way back to Huda's house, Alison leaned against the window, reviewing her day. She had seen all four quarters of the Old City and bought gifts for her family. For herself, she'd bought a beaded silver bracelet and a small woven kilim to hang on her wall back home. She had visited both the Church of the Holy Sepulchre and the Dome of the Rock, where she wandered around and studied the *Qur'anic* calligraphy on the tiles. She had accomplished what she'd intended. So why did she feel so depressed?

She dozed off and awoke to someone nudging her. At the checkpoint line, Alison clutched her passport and glanced at the tired faces. When it was her turn, she held up her passport and remembered the curly-haired soldier who had been so talkative. She decided Khalid would never know about that soldier.

On the other side of the wall, the graffiti depressed her further. She got in the nearest taxi and was soon walking toward Aida Camp. Alison entered the main alley where a smell invaded the air. It was an odd odor, scorched and ominous. People hurried past, pulling their small children along. A young woman ran by, shouting. There was a popping sound from the other side of the camp.

To the left was the nameless alley to Huda's house. But instead of turning, Alison continued on. Except for a few teenage boys, everyone else was going in the opposite direction. People hurried past, their faces contorted with panic. With a shot of adrenaline racing through her, Alison pushed forward, aware of the smell in the air and of another popping sound. Were those gunshots? As Alison moved on, strangely drawn to the sounds and the smoke, the noise level became more intense, with shouts and a voice over a loudspeaker.

The wall loomed overhead, dwarfing her and the camp. The sounds were coming from around the corner. Propelled by some unknown force, she stepped forward, turned down an alley, and stopped at the scene before her: burning tires, a mass of teenage boys, and a cluster of Israeli soldiers beyond. Smoke clung to the air and stung her eyes. The boys yelled and threw stones, taunting the soldiers.

It was the sort of clash she had read about. The soldiers were in riot gear, and some of the boys covered their faces with checked *kufiyahs* to hide their identity. Flames from the tires rose up between the two sides. One boy pelted a stone at the soldiers, who merely stepped back, well protected by their shields and helmets. A soldier shouted over a loudspeaker, which seemed to further agitate the boys, who yelled slogans and threw more stones.

Alison stood, riveted. One soldier held up his gun, aimed it at the demonstrators, and fired. She flinched and snapped her eyes shut. Her body trembling, she took several steps back and cowered in a doorway. She held her breath and stared at the soldier, who aimed and shot again. Alison turned. A boy was on the ground clutching his leg.

She opened her mouth, her voice a scream: "You're shooting at children!"

The soldier lowered his gun and shouted back in English, "You don't have to live here!"

Alison became aware of a new sound, a hissing. The soldiers swiftly retreated, and the boys scattered. Even the boy on the ground was no longer there. Alison turned back as the white smoke expanded and filled the air. Disoriented, she didn't know which way to turn.

Then it hit her: a burning sensation in her eyes. She squeezed them shut, but they began watering uncontrollably. Her throat was inflamed, and when she tried to open her eyes again, she couldn't. Blinded, she stumbled back the way she had come, grasping the alley wall for support. Someone took hold of Alison's elbow and spoke to her—a child. He led her back down the alley, through several turns. As she staggered along, the pain in her throat and eyes intensified.

They stopped. A doorbell sounded, and the gate squeaked open. Huda's voice came next—a shriek—then rushing around. Alison found herself sitting in the courtyard with a wet washcloth on her face. Someone put a cold drink in her hand, and she finally opened her eyes, blinking repeatedly.

Belal was next to her. Ashes fell from his cigarette onto the cement. "Why you go to the demonstration?" He drew on his cigarette until it glowed very bright.

"I don't know." Alison's eyes burned. "I wanted

to see what was going on." Her heart raced in a delayed reaction of anxiety, her mind finally processing the danger. With a sickening feeling, she remembered she was pregnant.

"When you see people or soldiers in groups, you should run away. Just leave."

"But the soldiers were shooting at children. They shot one!"

"Those were rubber bullets." He put his cigarette out, grinding it into the cement floor of the courtyard. He looked at her. "What can you do? You think you're going to stop the shooting?"

❧ Chapter 20 ❧

Zainab shuddered when she saw what Nadia was wearing. Granted, her tunic was loose and fell to her thighs, but her jeans had strange rips up the sides.

"Put on a *jilbab*."

"I'll wear my *jilbab* over this." Nadia looked at her watch. "Where is he?"

As they waited in the salon for Mohammed to take them to the US Embassy, Zainab fiddled with her prayer beads. She hated to see a girl with raggedy jeans under her *jilbab*. So vulgar and cheap-looking. She was engaged to be married, and everything she wore was a reflection upon her and the family.

"You cannot wear those jeans," she insisted. There was still time, inshallah, to get Nadia and her clothing back on the straight path.

Zainab withheld comment when Nadia reappeared wearing a pink *jilbab* with sparkly trim. Nadia fussed over her scarf and fixated on herself from all angles in the hall mirror.

Mohammed finally showed up in a borrowed car, half an hour late. As they drove out of the neighborhood, crowded with cars and pedestrians, a rustle of papers came from the front seat; Nadia was flipping through her file. She had explained earlier: "*Yama*, it's my proof that I won't stay in America forever."

Zainab wondered why anyone would choose to do that—stay in America forever.

They parked, and Mohammed and Nadia got out. "Auntie," he said, "wait in the car."

Zainab said nothing. All her energy went into the wad of worry inside her. *Ya Allah*. She reminded herself to have faith, then closed her eyes and made *du'a* for Nadia to get a visa.

The car was hot and she couldn't unroll the window. That fool. Why hadn't he left one open? Zainab opened the back door partway. Alone and perspiring, she tried to get comfortable as her thoughts turned to Abed. How she needed him now. Still, she felt a flicker of anger toward him. He had never bought a house in Jordan but chose to rent an apartment for years, a decision Zainab now nearly cursed. He'd said it wasn't his country. Instead, he had poured his earnings into Ahmed's studies in America. The plan was never for Ahmed to stay there. Not at all. Zainab had always expected she would grow old in her son's house—in Palestine. She hadn't imagined this fractured life, flying from one country to another. She could see now what they had really lost. Her grandchildren by Ahmed were foreign speaking, and Khalid's wife was carrying a child who might turn out the same.

Mohammed returned to the car and got in the front. "Sorry, Auntie. Only people with appointments can go in." He unrolled his window and said, "I wrote a letter for her, too."

"Bless your hands," Zainab said automatically and without sincerity. She stared at the back of his head, the same shape as his mother's. She wondered about the true reason he had divorced his first wife. Then she remembered: they weren't divorced yet. She sighed and fanned herself, no longer sure why she had been in such a hurry for Nadia to marry. She was barely twenty. There were still years before people would talk.

An hour passed. A cool silence had formed in the car. Finally, Nadia appeared on the sidewalk, gliding toward them in her pink *jilbab*. She as smiling, her eyes revealing her shock and joy as she reached the car.

"I got it!"

•••

That evening, the women gathered on cushions in Fatma's courtyard to celebrate Nadia's visa. Anysa attributed the visa to her son Mohammed. "Thank God he wrote that letter. He gave her permission to go."

"*Alhamdulillah*. It's a blessing from God," Zainab corrected, as she offered a tin of *baklawa* pieces arranged in circular rows.

"*Masha'Allah*. His letter worked on the Americans." Anysa selected three pieces.

"All grace and thanks are due to God."

"It was God's will that he wrote that letter." Anysa popped a pastry in her mouth.

Zainab and her sister went back and forth like this while Nadia sat nearby. Anysa's words didn't spoil Zainab's good mood, though. She handed the tin of *baklawa* to Nadia. "Take it to the men."

Nadia got up and crossed the courtyard to where the men were sitting. When she returned and sat once again, Zainab put her arm around her, wishing she could sweep Nadia off to America at that very moment. Unfortunately, it would take time for Nadia's visa to go through security checks, or some such thing.

Zainab squeezed Nadia's shoulder. "*Alhamdulillah*. You'll be with me in America, my love."

Nadia didn't respond. She was distracted, focused on something across the courtyard.

Zainab turned. It was Mohammed. The couple had locked eyes, oblivious to everyone, mouthing words to each other, some secret lovers' language, a display that was completely unacceptable.

"Nadia? Nadia!" Zainab gently shook her.

"*Yama*? What?"

Zainab stared hard at her daughter. Where was the shyness and innocence that Nadia's older sisters had demonstrated during their engagements? This show of affection did not look good. How to explain something so obvious?

Zainab leaned toward Nadia, scrutinizing her. "Are you wearing makeup?"

"*Yama*!" She pushed Zainab's hand away. "Of course I'm wearing makeup."

Zainab stiffened and scanned the other family members to see if anyone had seen Nadia's behavior. Zainab's eyes rested on Anysa who was leaning back, laughing, her round belly jiggling, as though she were intoxicated from the *baklawa*.

Zainab turned back to Nadia. She had neglected her daughter long enough. Truth be told, Zainab had been absent and inattentive ever since Abed had died. Perhaps there was a way to correct the damage. Inshallah.

Two days later, Mohammed and Anysa received their well-wishers before travelling back to the West Bank. The male guests sat in the *majlis* while Zainab joined the women in the salon, that horrible room where she had been humiliated weeks before.

Zainab sat next to Anysa in the ring of armchairs. On Zainab's other side was Nadia, restless and disengaged. Each time the door opened, Nadia twisted around.

"What are you looking for?" Zainab whispered to her.

"Mohammed." Nadia craned her neck. "I want to talk to him."

"You'll say good-bye with the rest of us."

"*Yama*, I'm not going to see him for months."

Zainab put her hand on Nadia's arm. "You can't be alone with him."

Nadia rolled her eyes. "He's already been married."

"It's *you* I'm thinking of," Zainab said. How could she explain? Sometimes it happened: an engagement fell through and a girl's reputation was compromised.

"*Yama*, that's the old way. No one does that anymore."

Zainab's heart pounded. If only Abed were alive! One word from him, one look, and Nadia would listen.

"No one cares," Nadia said, "if I'm alone with my fiancé."

Zainab glared at her daughter. "They notice. They care."

The taxi arrived, and everyone moved to the street. As the driver loaded the luggage, family members bid salaam to Anysa and Mohammed. Zainab kissed Anysa's cheek and said, "God protect you and keep you safe." She squeezed her sister's hand.

"Forgive me for anything I've done wrong," Anysa said with a glint of tears in her eyes.

"And forgive me," Zainab said, then added, "Nadia will be a good wife to Mohammed." The words tumbled out. "She speaks excellent English." She wasn't sure why she added that last point. Zainab didn't even understand English herself.

"*Alhamdulillah* he wrote that letter." Anysa clicked her tongue.

Zainab opened her mouth, but out of the corner of her eye she saw Nadia and Mohammed across the street, holding hands and laughing together, their faces nearly touching. Zainab elbowed her way past the family toward the couple. With one hand she grabbed Nadia's arm a bit too firmly, and with the other, she moved Mohammed away. "Enough!"

On the other side of the street, the visitors turned in unison, and a laugh rose up. Zainab's eyes swept over their faces. Anysa gave Zainab a reassuring look, Fatma nodded knowingly, and the other relatives had similar expressions. Zainab stepped back, crossed her arms, and felt a heat rise up in her cheeks.

Nadia touched her arm. "*Yama*, take it easy."

Later, Zainab sat alone in Fatma's courtyard. The stalks of *meramia* drying in the sun reminded her of Palestine. The red suitcase in her bedroom reminded her of America. Zainab reached for a stalk of *meramia*. Holding it in one hand, she gently pulled off the dried leaves and gathered them on a tray. It would be used to flavor the tea of three households in America: Mona's, Khalid's, and Ahmed's. *Dar Mansour*.

Nadia walked outside and reached for some *meramia*, too. Zainab tried to imagine what she and Nadia would do together in America, and all that Zainab would teach her.

After all the leaves had been gathered, she and Nadia stuffed them into plastic bags, which would travel in Zainab's red suitcase. Zainab got up from the floor, her creaky joints betraying her more than ever. She reached for a prayer carpet and stood at its edge. Her prayer was long and heartfelt. Then she settled herself for supplications that featured all of her longings. Just as Zainab was thanking God for Nadia's visa, there was a disturbance behind her. She tried to concentrate on her *du'a* but became aware of the surprise in Fatma's voice.

Attempting to focus, Zainab held her eyes shut. The gate clanked and there was another voice, the unmistakable accented Arabic that belonged to only one person: Alison.

Zainab turned and stood as quickly as her body would allow.

"*Alhamdulillah as'salaam.* You're back early," she said.

By then, Nadia and Fatma's daughters had come to the door. Fatma took Alison's bag and guided her into the courtyard, where everyone gathered around her. Zainab sat directly across and took a long look at the girl. Her face was gaunt, her eyes tired, and the rosiness drained from her cheeks.

Fatma fluffed the pillow behind her and instructed her daughter to bring tea.

Zainab leaned forward. "Why did you return early?"

Alison closed her eyes for a moment and then explained that she was tired.

"*Ya haraam,*" murmured Fatma and Nadia.

Alison took a breath. Speaking in slow, child-like sentences, she related two encounters with Israeli soldiers. Sorrow appeared on Alison's face as she described how the soldiers had fired at young boys.

Zainab gasped, as did the others. How foolish for a pregnant woman to be roaming around looking for trouble. Why had Khalid let her go? Curse his father! She never should have gone. Zainab then realized she was cursing her own dead husband and tried to take it back. How reckless of Alison to be so bold. Still, the image of her shouting at the soldier gave Zainab a shiver of pride.

"But why did you come back early?" Zainab repeated.

Alison brought a hand to her face. For a second, it seemed she was about to cry, but she held herself together. Each time she tried to speak, she stopped herself.

"Say it in English," Nadia said.

When Alison finally spoke, the tears came. Nadia translated. "She said she hadn't slept for four nights. She was afraid she would never sleep again."

"*Miskeenah*," they murmured. *Poor girl*. Nadia and Fatma patted her arm.

Zainab was overcome with a sudden surge of sympathy. "Take care!" she said, "By the grace of God, take care of yourself and your baby." She reached over and touched Alison's hand.

The tea was served, and everyone was quiet.

Zainab asked, "Did you see Huda? How is Yasmine? And my mother?"

"*Alhamdulillah*," Alison mumbled but had little else to say.

Zainab stared at her and wondered what the girl was holding back. For the first time, she noticed what Alison was wearing: pants and a shirt that looked like a man's. Zainab wondered once again what Khalid saw in this strange, skinny girl.

❦ Chapter 21 ❦

At Sea-Tac Airport, the US immigration official handed the five passports back to Margaret. "Welcome home," he said.

On the drive up I-5, the midday sky was bright blue. Mount Rainier was visible, rising majestically beyond the city. Margaret gazed at the Seattle skyline, Lake Union, and the Space Needle. She ticked off the exits they passed: University of Washington, Green Lake, Greenwood, Northgate, Shoreline, Lake Forest Park. They slipped by like lost archaeological sites until finally the van turned into their cul-de-sac.

Home.

Margaret slid open the van door and breathed in the scent of freshly cut grass coming from the neighbor's yard. She stood in the driveway and looked up at her imperfect house. It needed a paint job, new windows, and an overhaul of the yard. Margaret knew by heart the collection of defects inside: the shabby carpets, broken light fixtures, cracked hearth, and the woefully outmoded kitchen—all things that could be fixed. It was her home, after all, where she was meant to be. Imperfect, yes, but it was familiar and known.

• • •

The next morning, Margaret woke at daybreak after a restless night of jet-lagged sleep. Suitcases cluttered the living room, begging to be unpacked. While the rest of the family slept, she went outside and stepped onto the lawn where dew coated the long blades of grass. Grass invaded the walkway, weeds filled the flower beds, dandelions sprouted everywhere, and the jasmine was nearly dead. Meanwhile, the neighbors' yards were at their peak, a portrait of summer beauty.

Margaret returned to the house and put on some old jeans and a T-shirt before gathering her gardening tools from the garage. First, she started on the dandelions, plucking them out one by one with a tool that released the entire root in one satisfying pop. As she gathered the discarded dandelions in a bucket, she calculated when the mother would be back.

Ten days. Ten splendid days. This thought energized her. She worked rapidly, plucking and gathering the weeds one after another. If she had no control over anything else in her life, damn it, she could at least conquer the dandelions.

Next, she mowed. Margaret jerked the mower back and forth until the front lawn was smooth. At last, she trimmed, working along the edge of the pathway. Her mind drifted back to Jordan and to Cynthia, whose garden Margaret had admired from the sunroom window. Manicured hedges, frangipani, and cascading bougainvillea made up Cynthia's desert garden—so far removed from Margaret's plain suburban plot. It wasn't just her garden that was immaculate, but the villa, too, with its polished tiles and zero clutter. Margaret scooped up a handful of cut grass and tossed it in the bucket. That house of Cynthia's was more like a gallery than a home.

Margaret wiped the sweat from her neck. Across the cul-de-sac her neighbor Jackie waved and walked toward her. "Welcome back!"

Margaret rubbed the dirt off her gloves. "Thanks."

"How was your trip?"

Margaret opened her mouth but stopped herself from launching into a series of complaints. This was her neighbor Jackie she was talking to, not Liz.

"It was good."

"I bet you have a lot of photos." Jackie clasped her hands together. "We're getting together tomorrow night. My house. Can you come?"

Margaret shrugged. "Sure."

The next evening when Margaret arrived, the women had already spread out their albums and photos. Jackie served a sparkling water to Margaret and wine to the others. The topic of discussion was the first day of school. Each woman reeled off which school supplies and clothing she had bought. It was their standard conversational fare—exhaustive reports on their children, tinged with one-upmanship. They itemized what was left on their back-to-school shopping lists. Margaret wondered why these matters needed to be discussed in such detail.

The women didn't ask about Margaret's trip until she spread out her photos. She didn't know how much of the story to spill. Her marital problems had made her more subdued and private. What could she tell them about Nadia, barely twenty, getting engaged to a man—her first cousin—who was already married, and their mothers—sisters, actually—fighting over whether their children should marry or not. This scenario would surely make Ahmed's family—and Margaret —look like lunatics.

She gave the highlights of the trip: how relaxing the hotel was, how fun the engagement party had been, and how wonderful it was to go overseas.

Then Margaret said it: "Ahmed wants to move to the Middle East." She didn't know what made her blurt it out. Her voice was relaxed, like the whole thing was no big deal. She continued to focus her attention on the photos in front of her, those taken during a meal at Fatma's house. Margaret glanced up; her friends were staring back at her.

Jackie's mouth was open. "You mean to Jordan?"

"No," Margaret said. "Have you heard of the United Arab Emirates?"

"In Saudi Arabia?" Josephine asked.

"It's a separate country," Margaret said. Didn't they ever look at a map?

"There's a war going on over there," Jan said, as though privy to some secret information.

Margaret wanted to reply, *Again, separate country*. But that would've been bitchy, and the three J's never used bitchy tones with one another. Instead, she said, "No war in the UAE."

"You're brave," Jan declared.

"What about terrorists?" Jackie asked.

"What about them?" Margaret's tone had turned impatient. "No place is safe. Look at New York!" Her voice was strident and her gestures too exaggerated for this gentle gathering. Perhaps she was being unreasonable. After all, she had the same concerns.

"You're right." Josephine sipped her wine. "I'm sure you'll be fine there."

"I didn't say we're moving." Margaret was allowing her irritation to show. She turned to Josephine. "I'm sorry. I'm a little stressed. Ahmed wants to move, and I don't."

"Ah," the women murmured, relaxing back in their seats now that it all made sense. Margaret could guess their thoughts: *That's what you get when you marry an Arab man.*

The tone shifted back to sympathy, what the three J's excelled at. "I hope you don't have to go," Jan said.

"I hope he doesn't *make* you," Josephine added.

Margaret looked around at the women. They were her friends, yet they understood so little of her life; they couldn't grasp it if they tried. She imagined closing her scrapbook, packing up her photos, and leaving. The image lingered in her mind as the topic reverted back to school supplies and which was better, Walmart or Target. Margaret took a sip of her water and thought how empty the conversation was, how it rarely deepened beyond this mindless chatter. Her pleasure began to dissolve, but the three J's noticed nothing.

Margaret closed her album and began to put her supplies in her bag.

"Are you packing up?" Jackie asked.

"I'm tired."

"But you just got here."

"It's the jet lag. It hits all of a sudden." Margaret zipped up her bag and said good-bye. She walked back across the cul-de-sac to her house.

She wasn't tired at all.

The following week was the first day of school. Margaret dropped Jenin off at the high school, and Tariq at the elementary school. Finally, she drove Leena to preschool for her first day. Her little girl's good-bye was teary, and Margaret's eyes filled as she left the classroom.

Margaret went home, sat at the breakfast bar, and looked out the kitchen window. Outside, the summer weather of the week before had given way to a gray, drizzly sky, the beginning of autumn.

The phone rang. Liz. "Come over," she said. "Tell me about your trip."

"You come here." Margaret glanced at the tin of *baklawa* on the counter. "The mother's gone for the rest of the week. We'll have the house to ourselves."

Liz arrived at the door looking content and well-rested. Her toddler ran past and into the house. Margaret put a movie on for the little boy and led her friend to the kitchen. She served American coffee alongside tiny *baklawa* pastries.

Liz stirred cream in her coffee. "So, your trip. Let's hear it."

Margaret bit into a *baklawa*, which had a slightly rancid taste. "I have photos." They sat side by side, examining the images as Margaret recounted the events. Holding back nothing, she described the feeling of being trapped while Ahmed resolved the conflict between his mother and aunt. She described the spectacle of the engagement party and the distress of Ahmed leaving for the job interview.

As Margaret talked, Liz responded with the right interjections of understanding, empathy, and laughter. Her toddler came to her, and Liz picked him up as Margaret spoke of the boredom of the last few days when everyone had left, including Ahmed.

Liz cradled her sleepy son and looked at Margaret. "But what about the job?"

"He had an interview in Abu Dhabi."

"Yeah, I got that. But what happened?" Her son startled in her arms, and she gently rocked him back to sleep. "*Inshallah*, he'll get a good offer."

Margaret set her coffee down. "You told me I shouldn't move there."

"Well . . . I didn't expect you'd listen."

They sat quietly for a moment until Liz reached out and touched Margaret's arm. "I would miss you. What would I do if you moved away?"

Margaret sighed. Yes, it would be lonely for them both. Plus, rather than just trailing behind her husband, she wanted plans of her own—what those would be, Margaret didn't know.

"I just don't want to leave this house." Margaret's voice cracked.

Liz raised her eyebrows.

"Did you see the work I've done? The yard is looking better than ever." Margaret wanted to go back to the gossip about Nadia and her fiancé. She wanted to laugh a bit more over Alison bumbling her way through Jordan.

Liz tapped her mug. "Why didn't you go with him when he had the interview?"

"I had no interest in that."

"Weren't you curious?"

"It would've just encouraged him. If I'd gone, he would've thought I'm okay with it."

"It might have been fun to take a trip with your husband."

"And leave the kids with the family?" Margaret reached over and stroked Liz's sleeping child. "God knows if they'd be alive when we got back."

Liz smiled down at her son and took a bite of *baklawa*. "This tastes weird."

"I know. Ahmed's family loves it."

The following week, Ahmed and Margaret left Jenin to babysit Tariq and Leena. Ahmed and Margaret drove to Starbucks, the one in University Village that stayed open until midnight. Being so close to the university campus reminded Margaret of the early days when she and Ahmed had met. The sites of their first dates were not far from where they were sitting.

They sat at a tiny table while Ahmed talked about the restaurants. Her mind wandered to the mother, who would return the following morning. As this reality struck, Margaret felt her pleasure slipping away. Meanwhile, Ahmed jabbered on, now talking about Nadia, but Margaret was preoccupied with unresolved issues: the mother resuming her place in their home, the interview that had never been discussed, and finally, the overall state of their marriage.

Yes. Their marriage. What was happening to them? As a husband, Ahmed had been good to her. Hadn't he? He had never tried to change her into some kind of Arab wife. It was Margaret who had done that. He had understood when she stopped wearing hijab. He had always been supportive. The problem was . . . What was the problem?

Family obligations? Cultural differences? Their marriage no longer contained two distinct cultures. They had each changed over the years, assimilating to the other, forming their own culture, neither American nor Arab, a sort of blend of the two.

Yet that balance had been disrupted, and Margaret could pinpoint the exact moment—when Ahmed's father died and his mother had moved in. She sipped her latte and wondered. Perhaps their marital differences went further back. Her thoughts flared with an image, a sharp frame seared into her memory—9/11, the twin towers tumbling down. Within a year, Ahmed's friends began expressing their desire to return to the Middle East. Ahmed had shared their zeal, and each time he mentioned a possible Arab country, Margaret had dismissed it, never allowing any real discussion to develop.

Ahmed said something that brought her attention back to the present.

"I never expected Nadia to get the visa."

Margaret stared at him. She had sensed his secretiveness in Jordan and assumed it had been related to his interview. Had something else been going on?

"Honey, what are you saying?"

"It's a four-month-visit visa. She won't be coming until everything's finalized." He made no attempt to conceal his delight. "When we submitted the application, I never thought she'd get it. That's why I didn't tell you."

Margaret swallowed. "Four months?"

"Like I said, I never thought she'd get it. Nadia put together her own file, proof she'd return to Jordan. She had letters, even photos from her engagement—"

"Four months—at our house?"

"Maybe she'll stay sometimes at Mona's or Khalid's. Honey, I never thought—"

"Stop saying that." Margaret set her latte down, processing this latest betrayal. He had orchestrated this visa for his sister, yet hid the fact from his own wife.

"All this secrecy. What else are you not telling me?"

He looked away.

"What happened with the interview?"

He closed his eyes.

"Tell me." Margaret froze. A chill ran up her middle.

"They called me today. They offered me a job. General Director. It's a chain in the UAE. Sixteen outlets. Café Arabica. It's a good offer."

His voice trailed off as Margaret stopped listening. A clenching anxiety rose inside her. She didn't trust herself this time. She got up, turned, and stumbled out the glass doors.

The evening air was warm for September, and the outside tables were filled with people sipping coffee and laughing, leading carefree lives— no bombs dropping on them. Margaret passed them, turned a corner, and stopped. She covered her mouth and stood that way until she felt a hand on her shoulder.

Then Ahmed's voice. "It'll be okay."

Margaret shook his hand off and continued walking, past a French bakery to her right, a Barnes & Noble on her left, an outdoor café after that. She kept walking until she reached the marketplace's classically shaped fountain, its circular base covered in Mediterranean tiles. The water pouring down shimmered in the dark, a romantic sight—at once beautiful and infuriating.

She spun back around. "Why did you invite Nadia to stay with us?" The water in the fountain surged.

"I'd be a jerk if I didn't help my sister."

Margaret had heard these words before. *I'd be a jerk if I didn't help my mother.*

She glared at him. "Well, you're being a jerk now."

A couple looked up from a nearby table.

"When does it end?" she cried, hating the shrillness of her voice. "What were you thinking? How can you bring your sister here *and* move to the Middle East? You can't do both." She pointed her finger at him. "This move was never part of the plan." Her expression and gestures were severe, definitely out of place for the upscale U Village. "You can't change our lives on some spontaneous whim." Her voice grew louder. "I have plans, too!"

He raised his eyebrows. "Which are?"

She thought for a moment. "Now that Leena's in preschool, I'd like to go back to the university."

"What?" Ahmed looked taken aback. "You've never mentioned this before."

"Actually, it's *my* turn," she said as she pointed to herself. "I have goals. I put them aside for the restaurants, for the children . . . for you."

"And what are you going to study?"

Her mind drew a blank. Finally it came to her. "Photography. I'll study photography."

"Why are you telling me this now?"

She squeezed her eyes shut. When she opened

them, he was looking back at her. "Damn it!" she said. "You just went ahead with your plans. Like you always do."

Passers-by with shopping bags from The Gap glanced at them. Margaret stood still, rooted to the ground. She tried to discern what was going on behind Ahmed's eyes but could tell nothing of his feelings. Meanwhile, the surging fountain had become almost unbearable.

"You married an American. In *this* country!" Her voice cracked, but then she regained control. "You can't change the rules at this point. Your mother, your sister—I think I can handle them. But this! It's not something I'm willing to do." She waited for him to say something. When he didn't, she said, "You're on your own."

He stepped forward. "What do you mean?"

She lowered her voice. "I have skills. I can support myself. I'm not afraid of divorce."

The threat of it seemed to hit him like a stab. His face dropped and drained of color.

She straightened. "I'm not afraid to be alone. I'm still young enough to—"

He cut her off. "Fine."

"Fine what?"

"I won't take the job."

Margaret looked at the fountain and then back at him. "Don't ever mention this topic again. Ever. This topic is dead."

Ahmed held up a hand. "*Wallahi*, it's over." His

shoulders slumped, and the lines of his face grew deeper.

They walked silently back to the car. For a moment Margaret was unsure if she had been fair. She brushed the worry aside and got in. She wasn't going to be plucked from her home, roots and all, like an unwanted dandelion.

As they drove off, she slouched in her seat the way she had seen Jenin do when she was sulking. Margaret held her breath as they pulled onto the freeway. She stared ahead at the rush of taillights, aware of the lump rising in her throat. With a sudden certainty, she knew something had ended for them by that fountain. She looked over at Ahmed, who glanced at her.

"I wish you'd told me sooner about going back to the U."

She exhaled and slunk farther down in her seat. She should have been happy. She had gotten what she wanted. Margaret closed her eyes and waited for a feeling of relief.

❧ Chapter 22 ❧

Alison arrived back at the Sea-Tac Airport to find Khalid waiting by the luggage claim. She beamed when she saw him, but his mother held out her arms, and he went to her first. Finally, Khalid wrapped himself around Alison.

"I missed you," she said, her hands on his shirt, inhaling his familiar scent.

At first, everything looked the same: the view from I-5, the flowers curling up the Pine View sign, and the parking spaces outside Building F. Inside, the bare walls of the apartment shone stark white. Her books stood neatly on the shelves, and her highlighter pen and graduate school printouts lay where she had left them. However, Khalid had been there alone for a week. The bed was unmade, spreadsheets cluttered the table, and dirty dishes were scattered about.

Alison sat on the sofa, not moving to unpack or straighten the room. Khalid sat across from her, tapping out text messages on his cell phone, which reminded her of Belal and his pack of cigarettes. She wished the trip was a remote memory rather than so near in her mind. All she had to do was close her eyes to see the tear gas canister rolling toward her, sending out its thin hiss of white smoke. She had barely noticed it at the time, but now as she replayed the scene, it was the canister that took center stage. Wedged in her mind was an image of that injured boy on the ground and the words of the soldier: *You don't have to live here.*

During the two flights home with Khalid's mother next to her, Alison had tried her best to focus on the in-flight entertainment, avoiding thoughts of soldiers and clashes. Back home, she lay motionless on the sofa, replaying events from her trip. That evening, Khalid listened thoughtfully to her stories about Jerusalem, the refugee camp, and the tear gas.

For days she slept long hours in the afternoon. At night, she walked silently around the apartment, remembering the curly-haired soldier at the gate of the Dome of the Rock. She wondered if he had ever fired shots at children. While Khalid slept soundly in the next room, the desperate face of Yasmine drifted in and out of Alison's mind. Belal was the only person Alison had told about that episode. To Khalid she simply said, "You should call Yasmine."

Just before dawn on her third day back, the newspaper thudded at the front door. She picked it up, glanced at the headlines, and threw it into the recycling bin. Alison had done this the previous mornings, as well. She could already imagine the news from the Occupied Territories —more demonstrations, more missiles, more victims, and more misery.

Alison called her parents and gave them a cheerful account of her trip. Her mother said they had received her postcard from Amman and asked about her pregnancy. Alison said everything was fine. She explained that the trip had been perfectly safe and that they, too, shouldvisit the Via Dolorosa and the Church of the Nativity.

After a week, Alison recovered from her jet lag. Then Khalid announced that his sister Nadia had received her US visitor's visa and would be coming to Seattle.

Alison was unmoved by this news. Actually, nothing moved her, not the *Seattle Times*, not the graduate school applications, not her pregnancy, not the stack of books by her bed. Everything that had been so urgent before the trip now seemed beside the point.

Back at her part-time job in the International Studies office, Alison put on the face of someone who had returned from an exotic adventure. She entertained coworkers with glib comments about her trip. "Want to travel on a dollar a day?" she asked. "Stay in a refugee camp!" She told them she had witnessed rock-throwing, "the national sport of Palestine." Alison didn't know why she made these horrible remarks, and yet her coworkers laughed as though what she was saying were actually funny.

Khalid worked during the day, then spent most evenings with his family at Ahmed's house. After a few days back, Alison decided to go along, if only to be with Khalid. She sat next to his mother, their relationship newly enhanced by the two of them traveling together. Alison was now at ease with her mother-in-law, who reached over occasionally and patted her hand.

As always, Alison went into the kitchen for her

customary chat with Margaret. Alison climbed on a stool, looked around, and noted, "Something's different with your kitchen."

"I painted." Margaret gestured toward the wall, a soft shade of sage green. "How was the West Bank?"

"Great." Alison took in the fresh color and new display of Palestinian pottery.

"Tell me about Aida Camp." Margaret stood next to the stove, a glass of tea in her hand. "What about Dheisheh? How are the people coping there?"

Alison gave a weary sigh. "It's miserable. It's one thing to read about the occupation—"

"And it's another thing to see it. I heard you left early."

"It was eye-opening." Alison put her hand on her bulging belly, now about six months along. Eye-opening wasn't the word; it was more like a switch had been flipped. Something had shifted. Alison was no longer a mere observer of the conflict—yet she wasn't a participant, either.

"Eye-opening," Margaret repeated while nodding. "I can imagine."

"I wish I could do more. I used to think if only people understood what was happening there . . . Now I think no one cares."

Margaret sat next to her. "During the second intifada, Ahmed and I used to attend these demonstrations in Seattle. I stood in front of

305

Westlake Center and handed out flyers. No one wanted them." Margaret shook her head. "Sometimes, it feels hopeless."

"Yeah, hopeless." Alison wanted to say more but couldn't.

By October, the air turned brisk. Alison began wearing maternity tops and jeans with an elastic panel. She resumed the weekly *Qur'an* study sessions to keep up her classical Arabic but spent many evenings home alone, annoyed with Khalid, and falling asleep before he returned from his family or card playing with his friends.

She began to shrink from his touch. His leg wrapped around her body aggravated her. They were unable to rekindle any of the sexual fervor they had before the trip. His pace was too quick; she felt smothered by the weight of his body.

Alison grew more conscious of her pregnancy and worried about the lie they had told regarding the due date. A second ultrasound reconfirmed that the baby was a girl, and as Alison lay back in the darkly lit room, the cool gel sliding over her belly, she had one reassuring thought: she would not have to name the baby Abed.

That evening, Khalid stayed home to watch the news on CNN. Alison was next to him, her eyes following a report from Baghdad, which described the aftermath caused by three suicide bombings. The grim-faced correspondent reported twenty-six deaths, including five children.

"That's awful!" Alison brought a hand to her face. "Absolutely horrible."

The correspondent concluded by saying that more than a thousand American soldiers had died in Iraq since the start of the war.

Khalid turned the volume to mute. "The Iraqis have a right to fight. They're defending themselves."

She pulled away from him. "Don't mix them up with the Palestinians. The Iraqis are divided by tribes and the Sunni Shiite split."

"The US is occupying their country." He turned back to the television, rapidly flicking through the channels.

Alison looked away. Was he sympathizing with suicide bombers? She turned back to him. "The Palestinian terrorists and the Iraqi terrorists are different—"

"Did you say Palestinian terrorists?" Khalid set the remote down.

"That's not what I meant." She tried to refocus. "You have your enemy, Israel. The Iraqis are . . . killing one another." She wasn't making sense, not in the way she used to—before the pregnancy had pulled her IQ down.

He stood and turned the television off.

"You think it's okay," she asked, "to just kill others in the name of a cause?"

He crossed his arms. "We're at war with the Israelis."

She shuddered. "I guess I'm a pacifist. I hate anything to do with killing."

"What are we supposed to do?" He looked at her. "Just roll over and die?"

"It's not like you're doing anything about it." She stood and faced him. "I don't see you helping your sister Yasmine."

"What are you talking about?"

"I saw how she lived in Dheisheh Camp." There was nothing fair about Alison's words, but she couldn't stop herself. "What are you doing to help her?"

"You told me not to send money." He glared at her. "You said we couldn't afford it."

As her thoughts flew back to their vows at the mosque, Alison twisted the wedding ring on her finger, the cheap one they had planned to upgrade as soon as possible. There was no chance of that now.

"Why did you give me only one dollar?" she asked.

"What?"

"When we married. You gave me one dollar."

"You could've asked for more."

"I didn't know that."

"You could've said—"

"You put me on the spot!"

"It was a token—a symbol. Lots of couples do

it that way." He grabbed his car keys. "I'm going out."

As he said good-bye, she closed her eyes. There was no use trying to stop him.

The days turned colder, and when the wind blew, it hissed through the front door. Alison wore thick sweaters and the silver bracelet she had bought in Jerusalem. She hung the kilim on the living room wall, where its deep colors dominated the space.

She entered her third trimester just before Ramadan and realized she should've been thinking about the baby and how to get ready for it. Margaret had called that week and offered to throw a baby shower, asking Alison to make a list of the items she needed.

Sitting at the table, Alison stared at the kilim. The sound of raindrops hit the windowpane, and she turned back to her list: car seat, bedding, sleepers, diapers . . .

Her mind returned to the soldier, calmly lowering his gun. *You don't have to live here.* She couldn't imagine raising a baby in that refugee camp. Nor could she imagine Khalid growing up there. When she tried to conjure up a picture of it, all that came to mind was Yasmine's clingy mass of children.

That evening, when Khalid came home from work, they ate *mjeddera*, the same meal of rice and lentils Huda had prepared in the West Bank and her Teytey Miriam had prepared when she was alive. As they were finishing their last bites, Khalid's phone rang. He spoke in Arabic for a moment and then hung up. "Ramadan's tomorrow," he said.

"*Ramadan Mubarak*," Alison said, then paused. "Did you ever throw rocks at Israeli soldiers?"

"Of course." His eyes widened. "Actually, I did worse."

"Like what?" For a second she felt as if she were with Belal back in Aida Camp.

Khalid opened his mouth to speak and then stopped. "It doesn't matter now."

She looked at him, his white button-down shirt, his clear eyes, and clean-cut look. If he hadn't gotten out when he did, he might've ended up like Belal's brother—in prison.

For the rest of the evening, Khalid watched the news coverage of the war in Iraq. His cell phone continued to beep. "Ramadan messages," he explained.

In the kitchen, as Alison cleaned up the dinner dishes, she had mental flashes of her old life: attending Arabic classes, studying in the coffee shop, and giving her opinion on events in the Middle East. Now she avoided political topics with Khalid, since they often ended up in some uneasy place she didn't want to be. Plus, she had Ramadan to think about. Khalid would be fasting and depending on her to prepare *suhur*, the predawn meal.

The next morning, the first day of Ramadan, she awoke at 4:30 a.m. and prepared a *suhur* of tea, scrambled eggs, nuts, sliced fruit, Arab bread, and sweet sesame *halawa*. Margaret had given her tips on what to serve, and the food looked appealing spread out in small dishes. It was pitch-dark outside as Alison poured Khalid's tea and watched him eat. She wondered if Teytey Miriam had made a similar effort for Grandpa Sam. Had he even observed the holy month? Alison didn't know.

When Khalid finished, she cleared the table while he sat on the sofa. The *Qur'an* open in his lap, he recited from it in an unfamiliar voice. Then he closed the book, left the room, and returned with a prayer carpet. He spread it at an angle across the floor and began to pray. Before that moment, she had only seen him pray with his family.

Later in the evening, the *iftar* meal took place at Ahmed and Margaret's, where everyone had gathered to break their fast, including Mona and her family. They waited in the living room looking at the clock. Alison excused herself to the kitchen, where Margaret was stirring a large pot of soup.

"New tiles?" Alison asked. Above the counter and around the backsplash were rows of new blue tiles, the same shade as in the Palestinian pottery.

"You like it? I installed them myself." Margaret set a plate of dates on the table, and Jenin filled the water glasses. They continued to glance at their watches.

"It's time," Khalid called out. Everyone, except Alison, reached for their water and a date, muttering a *du'a* in Arabic. Margaret dished up the lentil soup. In silence, the family consumed it with concentration.

Next, the prayer carpets appeared. For the second time that day, Alison saw Khalid pray. She had always considered him a secular Muslim, but seeing his recent religious zeal, she wondered.

With sighs of relief, the family returned to the table. The dishes were brought out one by one in ceremonial fashion. During the meal, Ahmed made an announcement. "I just bought Nadia's ticket. She'll arrive in a week, *inshallah*."

The family spoke all at once, a mix of English and Arabic. Alison's thoughts turned to Nadia back in Jordan. Of Khalid's five sisters, the girl was the closest in age to Alison. She was pretty, Alison would admit, but she was also the most modern. Not only had Nadia managed to learn English—the only sister who had, as even Mona, who lived in Seattle, spoke very little English—but Nadia was friendly and funny and the least judgmental. She probably couldn't wait to get on a plane and out of Jordan.

When the meal was over, Alison followed Khalid to the living room. Everyone was there except for Margaret, Jenin, and Mona, who were clearing the table.

Khalid nudged Alison. "Why don't you go help?"

As soon as he said it, the reality of the arrangement became clear—the men relaxed while the women cleaned up. She asked him, "Why don't you?" and he shot her a wide-eyed look of astonishment, signaling an end to any more discussion on the matter.

Alison took a deep breath, heaved herself up from the sofa, and went to the kitchen. "Need any help?"

Margaret, who was wrapping leftovers, gestured to a stack of dirty plates. Alison took her place at the kitchen sink, loading the dishwasher until Khalid appeared in the doorway.

"We're going to *tarawih* prayer," he said. "You take the car. I'll meet you at home."

Alison dried her hands and went to him. "Babe, you already prayed twice today."

"My family always prays *tarawih*."

"I know," she whispered, "but that doesn't mean you have to."

Khalid's mother came down the hallway in her *thob*. Mona put her coat on and began to gather her children. Khalid handed Alison the car keys. "I'll see you at home."

Alison returned to the kitchen, where Margaret,

her sleeves rolled up, was scrubbing a greasy pan. Alison nearly yelled, "How can you stand it?"

Margaret looked up. "Tomorrow we're eating at Mona's," she said, missing the point.

"I mean, all this work and everyone just leaves."

Margaret put the pan in the drying rack. "I like having the house to myself." She slipped some tea glasses in the dishwasher. "This won't take long. Then I can relax with my coffee."

Alison stared at Margaret and wondered how she could be so cheerful with so many dirty pots and pans in front of her.

"The first day of fasting is the hardest," Margaret said. "After *iftar*, it's like I've been let out of prison." Her use of the word *prison* struck Alison. Wasn't Margaret's life already a prison?

The next evening, the family *iftar* was at Mona's apartment, which was in a complex similar to Pine View. Sixteen family members squeezed into the small space, and the routine repeated itself: dates, soup, prayer, and back to the table for the main course.

Then all at once, the gathering ended when Khalid tapped his watch. "*Tarawih*."

The next few *iftars* continued in the same manner, alternating between Margaret's and

Mona's. Meanwhile, the *suhur* meals before the crack of dawn got simpler. When Saturday arrived, Alison served a *suhur* of milk and cold cereal. As they sat at the table, she told Khalid, "I don't think I'm getting up with you anymore."

Khalid clicked his tongue. "It's depressing getting up alone. It's sad."

"Well, it's exhausting me and so are all these family *iftars*."

"You get a break tonight." He explained that Ahmed and Margaret had other plans, and Mona had guests coming to her house.

Alison felt elated at the thought of an evening free of his family. "I have an idea," she said. "I'll make *iftar*, just you and me." He agreed and she added a condition. "You have to skip *tarawih* prayer. Okay?"

He nodded, and they decided on a menu. That afternoon they drove to the supermarket and slowly walked the aisles together, Alison's arm hooked inside his elbow as he pushed the cart. It was Sunday, and the outing reminded her of when they were dating.

Except that Khalid wasn't entirely himself. He insisted that fasting was easy, a mercy from God. However, just like the Muslim students in Alison's university classes, Khalid looked drained and pale when fasting and was sometimes slow to respond.

On the way home, he turned onto Highway 99.

Alison still despised its ugly urban sprawl but said nothing about it. Instead she said, "Soon we'll have a third person with us."

"Who?"

"The baby, dummy." Clearly, his mind was elsewhere. "It's going to be a girl for sure."

"*Inshallah.*"

Alison could hardly imagine this small child, her daughter. "I wonder what she'll be like." She fixed her eyes on Khalid's sturdy hands gripping the steering wheel. When he didn't respond, she said, "Maybe she'll be artistic. Or sporty. I was on the track team in high school."

"When our daughter is in high school, there's no way she's doing that."

Alison stared at him. "She will if she wants."

"She won't be wearing shorts for everyone to see her body."

"You're going to keep her from sports because someone might see her legs?"

"If she wants to do sports, she can go to an all-girls school."

"You're kidding—right?"

He took his eyes off the road and looked at her. "You know the culture."

"Just because I know it doesn't mean I have to follow it."

"It's about respect," he said.

She remained quiet and stared out the window, where gray clouds were forming overhead.

Had Khalid changed because of Ramadan, or had he always held these traditional views? Alison looked down at the door handle and envisioned opening it and jumping out. They missed a yellow light, and Khalid slammed on the brakes.

He turned to her. "I hated your wedding dress. The sleeves, they were too small."

Alison stiffened. The sound of his voice, his accent, which used to be charming, now grated on her ears.

"And the back," he said. "It was too low. Everyone saw your back." The light turned green, and he drove on.

She said nothing for a while and then simply, "Well, I liked my dress." Alison wiped away a tear and inhaled. She was aware of her protruding belly, the grocery bags in the back, and the sprinkle of rain outside. They passed a casino and a pawnshop. Why did he have to come this awful way?

At the next intersection, he screeched to a stop again and she lurched forward. It seemed he was getting his frustrations out by way of the car brake. So childish!

Without warning, she opened the door and bolted from the car. "I'm walking home!" She slammed the door, then hurried to the side of the road without looking back. The cool October air was energizing. Out of the corner of her eye, she saw their car creep next to her.

Khalid unrolled the window. "Get in the car!"

Alison put her head down and walked quickly. He followed her for another moment and then yelled, "You're crazy!" and finally drove on.

Walking briskly, she breathed in the misty air and looked at the road ahead, realizing it would take at least an hour to walk home. She passed a tattoo parlor and another casino. She touched her belly. Now in her seventh month, she was still fit and could keep a quick pace. At the next intersection she turned right, and the landscape shifted to strip malls.

Thirty minutes passed, and the mist turned to sprinkles. Khalid still hadn't come back for her. What would he say about her jumping out of the car and walking home? Alison pushed on. Forty minutes of walking, and she wasn't even tired. She could walk across Seattle. She could do anything she set her mind to. And so could her daughter. That's what Alison would teach her.

The rain was falling harder. She thought of Khalid and how he had never missed an *iftar* with his family. It occurred to her as she twisted the gold band on her swollen finger that his big fear was offending someone, but he didn't mind offending *her*. He didn't mind storming out of the apartment and leaving her alone. He didn't mind letting her walk home on the roadside, in the rain for more than an hour. Why hadn't Khalid come for her? Didn't he love her?

All at once, an Arabic word popped in her mind —*waheeda.* Lonely. They hardly spoke Arabic anymore. She missed its syntax, so orderly and predictable. She tried to summon up other Arabic vocabulary: *anger, sadness,* and *worry,* but her mind couldn't recall any of those words. Somewhere she had lost her reference.

Just a few more turns, she thought, and she would reach the Pine View sign, then their white apartment, the kilim on the wall, her books on the shelf, and the Arab-style teapot on the stove. By then, the wind had picked up and the rain was coming down hard, pelting her like hail. She picked up her pace, and when she saw the sign, she jogged.

By the time she got to the stairs, she was soaked through. Then fatigue hit her. Each step was shaky, her legs heavy. What made her think she could walk so far? She got to the door of their apartment and caught her breath. Inside, she stepped quietly into the bedroom where Khalid was in a deep sleep. Maybe he hadn't known about the rain.

Silently, she changed her clothing and dried off. In the kitchen, the bags of groceries had been left on the counter. After she put them away, she wrapped herself in a blanket and sat on the sofa. Soon she would have to cook.

A few hours later, it was *iftar.* Alison sat at the table across from Khalid and watched him consume his soup. She had cooked for more than an hour, carefully set the table, and arranged the dates in a crystal bowl that had been a wedding gift.

Khalid finished his soup and looked up. "Where's the rest of it?"

"Aren't you going to pray?" She tilted her head to where he prayed *fajr* each morning.

He shook his head. Alison got up, cleared his soup bowl, and went to the kitchen. With care, she placed the dishes on the table: rice pilaf, an Arab salad, tiny stuffed eggplants, and a pan of baked chicken legs rubbed with lemon and *sumac*.

He heaped his plate. His fork sat untouched as he took large bites with his soup spoon.

Alison broke the silence. "So, how is it?"

"Good." He didn't look up. "It's our turn to do *iftar*."

"What do you mean?"

The exasperated expression on his face showed how dumb her question was. "You think we can eat at everyone's house without them coming to ours?"

"We can't fit everyone here."

"Yes, we can."

"I can't cook for that many people."

"I'll help you," he said. "I told them tomorrow's the best day."

"*Tomorrow?* Why didn't you talk to me?"

"You weren't here," he said slowly. "I didn't know where you were." He took a bite from his spoon, and she looked away. Why couldn't he eat with a fork like a normal person?

"I was walking home," she said, "in the rain."

"A crazy thing to do."

"No more crazy than you leaving every time you're angry."

His jaw tightened, and he said nothing. Later, as they were drinking tea in the living room, she wanted to say something to make amends, but couldn't bring herself to speak.

He glanced at his watch. "*Tarawih* is soon."

"You said you weren't going tonight."

"Sorry, but I need to go." He got up and reached for his coat.

"Wait." She touched his sleeve. "What are we cooking tomorrow?"

His face softened. "We'll talk when I get back."

After Alison watched him go out the door, she got up to take care of the dishes. She didn't break any this time. Instead, she channeled her resentment into clearing, rinsing, and washing. When the dishes were done and countertops wiped down, the phone rang.

"Hi, sweetheart." It was her mother.

"Hi, Mom." Alison's eyes welled up with tears.

"Do you have time to chat?"

"Uh-huh."

"Is everything all right?"

"Fine."

"Sweetheart, I can tell something's wrong."

Alison swallowed and squeezed her eyes shut.

"What's wrong?" her mother asked.

Alison hesitated and then said, "It's Khalid."

"What happened?"

"It's no big deal."

"Tell me."

"It's Ramadan. I have to cook for his whole family tomorrow. Everyone. His mom and his cousins. Plus, his brother and sister and their families.

"That's a lot of cooking. Why do *you* have to do it all?"

"We're taking turns." Once Alison started talking, the words came easily. "Khalid and I argued about the baby today. I ended up walking home alone. He doesn't want our daughter to do sports." Now that Alison had said the words it all sounded so silly, so ridiculous and so many years away! Why had she taken him seriously?

"Is he around?" her mother asked.

"He's at the mosque. He went to the prayer."

"I see." Her mother's voice was tight. "Well, I'm at your grandmother's. She wants to talk to you."

Why now? Of all days? Of course, it was Sunday, when her mother visited Grandma Helen and when they were most likely to call. Alison could hear the hushed sounds of her mother's voice as she passed the phone, talking to her grandmother, telling her God-knew-what. Alison gathered herself and tried to make her voice bright.

"Teytey! How are you?"

"Hello, *habibti*. I'm fine," her grandmother said in her gravelly voice. "How's your pregnancy? Are you taking care of yourself?"

"Yes, I'm eating well and sleeping lots. The doctor says everything's great."

"What's this I hear about your husband?"

"Nothing. Everything's fine."

"That's not what your mother tells me."

"We just have some issues. It's normal."

"When you marry someone so different—"

"I know, Teytey."

"With such a different background, you can't expect to look at things the same way."

"I *know,*" Alison said, tears springing up.

"Believe me, I know how these Muslims are. They may *seem*—"

"Teytey!" Alison stood, heat flushing through her body. "Can I talk to Mom?"

Her mother came back on. "Well, Alison, he's the man you chose."

"This is not helping," Alison said as she paced with a hand pressed to her pregnant belly.

"I'm sorry, sweetheart, but I warned you about this."

"Mom!"

"You may think his culture is similar to ours—"

"Please stop!"

"Oh sweetheart, I hate to say it, but if it's that bad, you can get on a plane and come home."

"Why would you say that? We're having a baby!" Alison screamed, her sob-filled voice betraying her. She would never move back to her parents. Never. She would find a way to make things work. She had to.

"It's only going to get worse," her mother replied.

"Look, Mom. I need to go," Alison said and hung up.

❧ Chapter 23 ❧

At the table in Khalid's apartment, Zainab sat, noting the sound of rain outside. She accepted her bowl of soup and said, "Bless your hands," to Alison, who didn't reply but turned to Khalid. Zainab's eyes followed their exchange, riddled with tension.

Khalid said, "We both made the soup, *Yama*."

Zainab lifted the spoon to her mouth. Scorched. "Well, then, bless your hands, too."

That afternoon while fasting, Zainab had tried to imagine the *iftar* at her son's house. In the end, her suspicions were confirmed. Alison couldn't cook. One dish was overcooked, and another wasn't ready on time. Margaret must have known about her lack of skill, as she brought two dishes of her own, foreign foods unfamiliar to Zainab. It didn't seem like Ramadan; the flavors and smells were all wrong.

Of course, Zainab's own daughters could prepare a proper *iftar*, the right combination of dishes, ready on time. She had taught Fatma, Mona, Huda, and Yasmine, just as her own mother had taught her in that tiny kitchen in the refugee camp.

Now it was Nadia's turn. Zainab's thoughts expanded to what she would teach her after she arrived in America—how to cook *bamia*, *freekah* stew, *mahshi*, and *kufta*—so many productive days ahead. She would disclose all of her cooking secrets; she only wished she had started the process earlier.

The rest of Alison's *iftar* was more of the same, bland, overcooked food. Her *fattoush* salad had too much lettuce. Even her tea was bad—weak and overly sweet. Zainab sipped and pretended not to notice that Khalid's voice was tight and Alison had tears in her eyes. A shame, Alison's mother lived far away and was unable to guide her daughter in meal preparation and the proper behavior of a wife.

From Zainab's position at the table, she took in the rest of her family. Her eyes fell on Ahmed. Truth be told, her worries about him outweighed all others. Hunched over his plate, his eyes tired and dark, he ate quietly.

Zainab caught his eye. "How's the food?"

"I need to teach Khalid some things."

She took her last bite and pushed her plate away. It worried her greatly that Ahmed had such a depressed air about him. Since the trip to Jordan, she had pressed him about the job. He told her, "You'll be the first to know, *Yama*."

Zainab wondered if that company in the Gulf was still keeping him waiting. A shiver of dread ran over her as she realized that maybe he hadn't gotten that job and was too humiliated to tell her. With a blank look on his face, Ahmed was quiet, not joining in the conversation. Meanwhile, Margaret sat across the room, occupied with Leena. It had been a long time since Ahmed and Margaret sat together or shared a pot of tea. It seemed a sadness had sunk down and filled the space between them.

Later, at the mosque for *tarawih*, Zainab prayed two *rak'ah* and sat on the carpeted floor opposite the lattice that looked down onto the men's section. The women's area was filling up fast, but she was alone. Mona hadn't arrived yet, and Zainab didn't recognized the faces of the other women.

She fingered her prayer beads until, at last, Mona slipped through the row of women and squeezed in next to Zainab, who would soon have two daughters at prayer, one on each side.

The prayer started. The imam read a new *juz* each night of Ramadan until the entire *Qur'an* was complete. Zainab performed *rak'ah* after *rak'ah*, until she was lightheaded from going up and down. When the prayer ended, she began her supplications by asking for Nadia to arrive safely. When finished, she gripped her prayer beads with one hand and Mona's elbow with the other. Outside, the light rain had turned to heavy showers.

The weather! So gloomy and wet, day after day. How could anyone live like this?

Finally, Ahmed waved to her from across the drenched parking lot. Wearing only a sweater over her *thob*, Zainab shielded herself with it and hurried over to his car, stepping into a deep puddle on the way. As she slipped into the front seat next to him, her prayer beads caught on the door handle. When she gently tugged, the string snapped and the dark beads scattered. Her heart dropped as she watched them disappear into the puddle and under the car. "*Bismillah*," she said. *In the name of God*. She reached down.

"*Yama*, just leave them," Ahmed said. "We'll get you another one."

She stared at the wet ground before getting in and closing the car door. Her *thob* was wet to the skin. She looked down at her feet, also soaked through. A few beads were strewn around the car floor, and she reached down and picked one up.

"Turn on the heat," Khalid said from the back.

As Ahmed drove, the wipers slapped against the windshield and Zainab shivered. Her anxious thoughts turned to Ahmed. Finally, she blurted out the question plaguing her.

"What happened with that job in the Gulf?"

He sighed. "Nothing, *Yama*."

"Are you still waiting? Have they decided?" Her questions spilled out. "They didn't offer you enough money? You changed your mind?" She stared at her son. "You didn't get the job."

"No, I got it."

"So?" She sat up. "You told me I'd be the first to know."

Ahmed fixed his eyes on the road ahead. "I'm not taking it."

"Why not?"

Khalid's voice came from the backseat. "*Yama*, let it be."

Her throat tightened. "Why not?"

"I just didn't take it."

"*Astaghfirullah*! Just tell me."

Ahmed turned to her. "Margaret doesn't want to move. Okay?"

Zainab held up her hands. "But why? You can make money there."

"It's not about money. She doesn't want to go."

"What reason did she give?"

Khalid spoke again. "Let it be, *Yama*."

Ahmed kept his eyes ahead. "She doesn't think she'll be happy there."

Under her breath, Zainab said, "So foolish."

Ahmed shrugged. "What can I do?"

"What can you do? You can make her go."

"I can't force her." He shook his head. "If she's not happy, no one will be happy."

"You are the head of the family, are you not?" Zainab's voice cracked. "*Astaghfirullah*." *Forgive me, God.* She squeezed the single prayer bead between her fingers. Were her sons to live in America forever? Was she to have nowhere to go? Was it for Margaret to decide? Zainab turned to the window. One thing was for certain. She wasn't going to spend the rest of her years in this cold, rain-filled, disbelieving country.

The next morning, Zainab woke up with dull pain in her side. It was an old ache that appeared whenever she was homesick. Still, it would be Nadia's first day in America, and for that, Zainab felt blessed. Nearly everyone in the family drove to the airport to greet her. The moment she saw her youngest child, Zainab's eyes filled with tears. She embraced Nadia and held her hand all the way to the parking garage.

At home, Ahmed, Khalid, Mona, and now Nadia gathered around Zainab, four of her children talking and laughing, all at once. Zainab's worries floated away, and in their place, joy rose up, filling her chest.

Yet the feeling lasted but a moment, as three daughters were missing. Would she ever have all seven children together again? Was her life to continue fractured like this? No real home. Her children scattered about. She considered the days and years ahead. What would they look like?

Zainab trained her attention back to her children in front of her. Her eyes skimmed their faces. Bless them all. This moment together was short-lived, however. Everyone was drained from fasting and needed to get back to their duties.

In the bedroom Zainab would now share with her daughter, she shooed the cat out and looked through the items in Nadia's suitcase. "What? No *jilbabs*?"

Nadia was at the mirror brushing her hair. "No one wears a *jilbab* in America."

"What about an *abaya*?"

Nadia turned and gave Zainab a stern look. "*Yama*. Please."

Zainab dropped the subject and turned back to the suitcase. So many jeans! At least Nadia had the good sense to bring a selection of scarves. Zainab folded them into a neat stack and handed them to Nadia, who pulled open the top drawer of the dresser. As she placed the scarves inside, her hand landed on the rolled-up *kufiyah*.

"What's this?" Nadia asked.

Reluctantly, Zainab took out the bundle, sat on the bed, and unrolled it.

Nadia sat next to her and said softly, "*Baba*'s things." She picked up his string of prayer beads. "Why don't you take these, *Yama*, since yours are broken?" She put them in Zainab's hand. "It'll help you remember him."

Zainab didn't need help remembering. Abed hovered over her every day—a constant shadow over all events. She looked down at the amber-colored beads in her hand and then up at Nadia. Zainab's loneliness swelled and then lessened when Nadia put her arm around her.

Then from nowhere came a beeping sound. Nadia pulled a cell phone from the back pocket of her jeans and flipped it open. "It's Mohammed." She smiled. "He sent me a text." Nadia turned away and took a long moment to read it.

Zainab slipped Abed's prayer beads into her pocket and rolled the remains of his belongings back up.

Nadia snapped her phone shut. "He misses me."

Zainab shook her head. Clearly a love match. When the infatuation was gone, what was left? Zainab felt a slight pain in her side and touched the spot. If only she hadn't rushed Nadia.

Zainab said to her daughter, "Your jeans, they're tight."

"*Yama.* This is not tight."

Zainab shook her head. "Too tight."

"I beg you, *Yama*." Nadia waved toward the door. "Just go and let me unpack."

Zainab closed the door, stunned that she had been kicked out of her own room. She went to the kitchen, where Margaret was preparing the family *iftar*. Actually, she wasn't cooking but instead staring at a cookbook.

Margaret looked up, and Ahmed's words replayed in Zainab's head. *She doesn't think she'll be happy there.* Zainab's eyes narrowed. By the grace of God, it seemed everyone's future was spinning on what would make this woman happy.

Why did Ahmed allow Margaret to dictate? What about his needs? And the children's? And the rest of the family? An image flashed in her head: her own old age spent pacing the cul-de-sac, getting sick, seeing doctors she couldn't understand. Nadia's arrival was supposed to be a blessed day, yet Zainab fought the urge to curse out loud.

In her heavy Arabic, Margaret asked, "Are you happy your daughter's here?"

"Of course I am!" Zainab huffed, then turned and walked down the hall, asking for forgiveness for the relentless dark thoughts in her head.

Just before sunset, the family gathered for *iftar*. Among the many dishes on the table was Zainab's stuffed cabbage. She had rolled each leaf with care and cooked them slowly, allowing the flavors to come together. As she prepared them, she had imagined Nadia's delighted expression as she bit into one of them.

When it came time for the main course, Nadia filled her plate with foreign foods prepared by Margaret. Zainab slipped a handful of the stuffed cabbage onto Nadia's plate only for her to toss them back onto the serving platter.

"*Yama*, I just ate this in Jordan."

Zainab pressed her lips together and stayed silent. Later, the family sat in the living room sipping tea and sampling American brownies, a disgustingly sweet and gooey cake. Zainab leaned toward Nadia, finally by her side, the result of all that planning and praying.

Nadia held up her brownie and said something to Margaret, which made her laugh.

Zainab patted her daughter's hand. "While you're here, I'll teach you to make *ma'amoul*. We'll make them with pistachios and dates." Zainab did a quick calculation of how many stuffed pastries they would need for *Eid al-Fitr*, the holiday fast approaching, marking the end of Ramadan.

Nadia reached for another gooey cake. "I'd rather learn to make brownies."

Zainab repressed a shudder. "Don't be silly." She kept her tone soft. "We'll cook many foods together, my love. *Mensef, mahshi, sambusik—*"

Nadia laughed. "I want Margaret to teach me American food."

At this, Margaret smiled and said something back to Nadia. The two chatted in English while Zainab looked on. "*Ya Allah*," she said under her breath.

"*Yama*, I won't have time for cooking," Nadia said. "I'm taking English classes."

Zainab sat up. "What classes?"

"At the college. Margaret says she'll drive me."

Zainab furrowed her brow.

"They're free classes."

Zainab let out a small grunt.

Nadia and Margaret exchanged a secretive glance—it seemed the two of them were making plans. Margaret talked in an enthusiastic rush. This was a new scene, as she rarely drank tea with the family anymore. Yet here she was, influencing Nadia on her first day.

Zainab crossed her arms over the ache in her side. She stared at Margaret, talking to Nadia and ticking off points on her fingertips. Zainab wished she could understand what was being said. She asked Ahmed, "When's *tarawih* prayer?" Finally, she would be able to pull Nadia away from Margaret.

Before Ahmed could answer, Nadia said, "I'm not going. I'm tired."

"You don't look tired."

"I just got here." Nadia rolled her eyes.

"Besides, I don't have to go to the mosque. I just came from a journey."

"Don't explain *al-Islam* to me, my love." Zainab got up from her seat and walked down the hall. She would definitely take a coat this time.

At the mosque, Zainab was alone again in the women's section. Mona had decided not to come, either. This cruel solitude forced her to concentrate on her prayers.

When she was in the most submissive position with her forehead pressed to the floor, she whispered her private request. *Please let Ahmed be a man. Make him take this job.* After the last *rak'ah*, she held her hands open. *Please make Margaret change her mind. Please guide Nadia down the right path.* She gripped Abed's beads and recited *Allah is great* ninety-nine times.

The next day, Zainab's ache was still there. What's more, the day was gray and heavy with gloom. In the living room, Margaret and Nadia formed a little clique on the couch. Nadia was showing off her latest cross-stitch project, a strip of black fabric covered in red stitches, which would be the belt to match her bridal thob. Nadia and Margaret spoke in a whirl of English, oblivious to Zainab, who paced the room. She tried to insert herself into the exchange; she asked Nadia if she was tired and asked Margaret about *iftar*. Both times she was brushed aside.

After a while, Nadia stood and announced she was going to rest. Finally, the jet lag was taking hold. Margaret went to the kitchen. Zainab followed her and hoisted herself up onto a stool, her feet dangling loose. Margaret moved about the kitchen as though trying to appear busy, turning to her cookbook with her back to Zainab, who wondered if it had been such a good idea to bring Nadia into this house. Margaret was already filling the girl's head with who-knew-what while Nadia showed no interest in learning to prepare the dishes of her mother. She wasn't even interested in talking to her mother! Zainab had spent so much effort getting her daughter to America, yet here she sat with the same feelings of loneliness.

Margaret remained with her back turned, her red hair falling past her shoulders. Even though she had been married to Ahmed for twenty years, she still seemed like a stranger. Zainab could no longer remember what Margaret looked like in hijab. It had been months since she had prayed with the family.

Zainab's side gnawed at her. She said to Margaret's back, "Why don't you move with your husband?"

Margaret turned with a confused look.

Zainab persisted. "Why won't you live in an Arab country?"

Margaret straightened up and crossed her

arms. Her expression swung from confusion to defiance. It was clear that she understood perfectly well what Zainab was asking.

Zainab returned the stare. "What's the problem? Why can't you move?"

Margaret's face reddened and her freckles darkened.

Zainab yelled to another part of the house. "Nadia!"

Footsteps came down the hallway. Zainab continued to stare back at Margaret, whose eyebrows were cinched in an expression of dread. Finally caught.

Nadia entered the kitchen. "*Yama*? What?"

"Translate for me." Zainab leaned forward on the stool. "Tell her it's selfish to refuse to let Ahmed take this job."

"I'm not saying that."

"Tell her."

"No."

"I am your mother and you must do what I say."

Margaret said something to Nadia, and thus began a new secret conversation. Zainab touched her tender side, wincing slightly, and asked Nadia, "What did she say?"

Nadia sealed her lips and stared back.

Zainab tapped the counter. "Tell me what she said."

"She said it's none of your business."

Zainab opened her mouth to speak, but just

then the pain in her ribcage jabbed her like a sharp stick. She jerked upwards and back, and the stool began to tip. Zainab felt her weight shift, and she swiftly reached forward to grab the edge of the counter. But it was too late.

The stool headed toward the floor and the room spun around her. There was nothing Zainab could do but fall backwards. Nadia and Margaret reached toward her—each with the same horror-struck look.

❦ Chapter 24 ❦

A chill hung in the fall air. Margaret stood at the edge of the driveway and shivered. She hugged herself and watched as Ahmed and Nadia settled their mother into the backseat of the car. Ahmed gave a grim wave, and the three of them drove off to the emergency room, where he had insisted his mother must go.

When the car was out of sight, Margaret turned back to the house, as drab as ever with its peeling paint and lifeless yard. Inside, the silence startled her. She sat on the sofa in the spot normally reserved for the mother. Margaret longed for a cup of coffee but reminded herself she was fasting. In that strange silence, her mind filled with regrets. If only she had warned Ahmed earlier. *Your mother's going crazy. And so am I.*

Margaret should have phoned him when the mother had first summoned Nadia. "Never mind her," Nadia had told Margaret. "She's nervous from fasting."

Within minutes of their disagreement, the mother's eyes widened and she jerked backwards. Together, Nadia and Margaret helped her to an upright position. Blood trickled from a gash in her forehead, where her head had hit the table. The mother looked down at Margaret's hand on her arm and pushed her hand away. Margaret pulled back, dumbstruck.

Now, as she replayed this scene while staring at the cracks in her hearth, she considered why the mother had pushed her away like that. Maybe she had been disoriented. Or maybe she truly hated Margaret.

Margaret told herself the mother would be fine. Ahmed had taken her to the emergency room in a show of love and concern, not one of medical necessity. Right?

Yet when she saw the blood, Margaret had said, "*Asfa. Asfa*," *Sorry*. Sorry—so much to be sorry for: the mother's fall, the gash, and the subject the mother had raised just before her spill.

It was the first time anyone had brought up the topic of moving to the Middle East since Ahmed and Margaret's dreadful argument by the fountain. Each time she reviewed that exchange with Ahmed, she obsessed over who had been right and who had been wrong. Where was this self-doubt coming from? She had gotten what she wanted.

Still, Margaret wondered. Ever since Ahmed had first brought up his plan at their anniversary dinner, she had dismissed his idea. Deep down, she knew she should have listened.

But she couldn't undo that now. Her solution had been to turn her attention to the future. In the six weeks since that argument, Margaret had recommitted herself. She performed the role of loving wife, doubling all previous efforts. She made elaborate *iftar* meals and graciously welcomed Nadia into their home. She threw herself into household improvement tasks and took photographs for the restaurant website. She dutifully initiated sex—not euphoric sex, but the best she could muster. Above all, she stopped complaining. She didn't say a word about lengthy family gatherings or exasperating political views.

Over time, she and Ahmed settled into a truce. She released the grip on her anger and now floated along with her husband, who remained true to his word, never again mentioning the idea of moving to the Middle East. Admittedly their interactions were strained. Margaret tried to ignore this, but under the surface she recognized his barely suppressed resentment. On days when she couldn't bear it, she would blurt out, "Are you angry at me?"

His answer was always the same: "No." But his denial only encouraged her more, and she was determined to make him realize that staying in Seattle was the only possible outcome, the sole choice, the best thing for their family.

When the sound of the car came from the driveway a few hours later, Margaret peeked out the window. Ahmed and Nadia were leading the mother from the car, one on each side. Their assistance was more for effect, as the mother seemed to be walking just fine. The only sign of the ordeal was a small square of gauze on the mother's forehead.

They entered, and the mother moaned when she saw Margaret at the top of the entryway stairs. Nadia took her to the bedroom, and Ahmed came to the living room.

"Well? How is she?"

He sat down. "Four stitches. Nothing broken. No head trauma. Vital signs all good."

Margaret raised her eyebrows and looked at him.

"The doctor said she had a cramp and lost her balance. It happens," he said. "I tried to convince her to break her fast, but she wouldn't."

"She must be fine then."

In the days that followed, Nadia and Ahmed hovered over their mother, bringing her tea and listening to her grumbles. Mona and Khalid came to see her every day. The mother recounted her fall to anyone who would listen, each time the story becoming a little more embellished. The mother recovered quickly—perhaps sooner than she would have preferred.

The days moved forward, the air grew colder, and daylight savings ended. Margaret turned back the clocks, and life became abruptly gloomier. In the middle of Ramadan was Halloween, a minor blip on the calendar. She fulfilled the minimum requirements of the holiday—candy, a single pumpkin, store-bought costumes for Leena and Tariq.

In the evenings, Margaret served tea to the family as they followed the news on the deteriorating health of Yasser Arafat, as well as the reelection of George W. Bush. On CNN, Bush outlined his plan for his second term and vowed to continue the war in Iraq. The bad news expanded. *Al-Jazeera* reported 165 Palestinians had been killed by Israelis the month before. A Palestinian suicide bomber killed three in Tel Aviv.

The gloom grew thicker as the family speculated on how soon Arafat would die. They feared a power struggle would break out in the occupied territories and wondered who would take over. Margaret hoped it would lead to something good—a fresh start for the Palestinians.

One evening after *iftar*, the topic shifted to where Arafat's body should be buried. Margaret set out a platter of fruit and sat next to Alison, bloated from her pregnancy.

Alison asked Khalid, "Why do you care so much where he's buried?"

"Arafat's a symbol. Like a flag."

Margaret peeled an orange, and Alison replied, "But you never liked him."

The television screen flashed photos of Arafat. First the black-and-white images: Yasser as a boy, as a young man, in his checked *kufiyah*, and another with dark sunglasses and military fatigues. Then the color photos: Yasser at the UN, as an old man, and, finally, sick.

Khalid said, "He's the father of our country."

Margaret threw her eyes upward and popped a section of orange in her mouth.

Alison's face was turning pink. "You said he was corrupt."

"No one heard of Palestine until him."

At that moment, Jenin, who was gathering tea glasses, spoke. "He did let his people dream of their homeland."

Homeland. It was Ahmed who had taught Jenin that word. As if she were a refugee like him. As if she didn't have a country of her own.

Khalid nodded. "That's right, Jenin."

"Actually," Alison said, "He gave the Palestinians a bad reputation."

With a sharp edge in his voice, Khalid said, "I don't expect you to understand."

At this, Alison glared back, her face fully flushed. "Just because someone's dying doesn't make him suddenly good."

Margaret lowered her voice and said to Alison, "These nationalistic views, they flare up sometimes. It's best to ignore them."

Alison heaved a sigh and crossed her arms atop her massive belly.

Margaret continued, "Khalid's feelings will die down soon." But then she wondered. Had Ahmed's feelings died down? Naturally, he had been passionate about Palestine, but that passion became sidetracked over the years, as he raised a family and grew his business. Now he was just moody and bitter, blaming his unhappiness on his life in Seattle.

Of course, it wasn't the fault of Seattle, which had always been a welcoming place, tolerant and protected, far away from the conflicts of the Middle East. But when 9/11 struck, the country spun on its axis—a tidal wave of patriotism and security, paranoia, and Islamophobia. Even so, had their daily lives really changed?

Margaret had to admit that a vague looming prejudice did exist, casting a shadow over their lives. She hoped it was a temporary condition, one that would dissipate soon. It had to.

During the coming week, it rained daily, and the gutters filled with wet leaves.

Margaret tried to cheer herself with plans for Thanksgiving and made a tentative guest list. Then she took up shopping. She bought a lens for her camera, a pair of lamps, and an over-priced Persian carpet. She waited for some positive feelings to come. Nothing.

Finally, she drove to the U District and collected a copy of the University of Washington course catalogue. She had announced so brashly to Ahmed that going back to school was a reason she wanted to stay in Seattle. Now the catalogue sat on her coffee table, signaling to all who entered their home that Margaret's life was moving forward. Granted, she had yet to open it. The mere idea of applying to university as a forty-something mature student filled her with dread. Besides, after all these years, the university probably wouldn't even accept her back.

Ramadan dragged on. At last, the end of the fasting month was in sight. The final days of Ramadan held increased spiritual significance, and Ahmed's family experienced a second wind. They prayed with fervor, recited *Qur'an*, and attended the nightly *tarawih* prayer.

As for Margaret, she had lost her momentum for the holy month, her enthusiasm gone. During the final week, she picked up the phone and called Liz.

"So," Liz said, "how's the Ramadan-a-thon?"

"Counting the days until *Eid*," Margaret said.

She named the tasks yet to be done: decorations, baking, buying *Eid* gifts and clothes. Simply listing these chores made her tired.

The next day, CNN announced the death of Yasser Arafat. The entire family skipped *tarawih* prayer to gather around the television. Margaret took in the news and felt nothing.

When the holiday *Eid al-Fitr* arrived, Margaret awoke early with one thought: *coffee*.

In the kitchen, Ahmed gave a hesitant kiss to her cheek. "*Eid Mubarak*, honey." They were his usual words, but now their sentiment rang false. Their game of avoidance did not sit well on *Eid*. The holiday was supposed to be light and loving —full of gratitude and fun.

Margaret flipped on the coffee machine and began to push herself through the rituals of the holiday. She set out breakfast—a jumble of American pastries and Arab *fatayer*—and woke the children and wished them a happy *Eid*.

Next was the obligatory visit to Mona and her husband. Mona wore her trademark outfit, a fitted jacket over a long skirt, but on this day, her hair fell in a cascade of curls, freshly highlighted. Their boys, dressed in little suits and ties, streaked wildly around the apartment. Khalid was already there but not Alison. The family gathered in the living room, where a plate of *ma'amoul* had been set out. The men distributed cash to the children while the television news alternated between Arafat and the war in Iraq. Margaret looked at the grim news on the TV screen, and any trace of holiday feeling drained away.

She reminded herself that the highpoint of *Eid*—the community prayer—was yet to come. The family looked at their watches and left hurriedly in three cars. As they neared, Margaret slipped on her scarf and handed one to Jenin. The prayer hall was abuzz with hundreds of worshippers dressed in festive clothing. Normally this sight brightened Margaret's spirits, but this *Eid* was joyless. What was wrong with her?

The family split up into the men's and women's sections; Margaret followed Mona, her curls now hidden under her scarf. As they rolled out their prayer carpets, Margaret glanced across the room and spotted Lateefa entering with her two boys. She wore a gold-trimmed Saudi-style abaya and sparkly scarf, but she looked exhausted. She and Margaret exchanged waves. The last time Margaret had seen her, Lateefa had announced she was leaving her husband for good.

Margaret's mind leapt to her own marriage. Without warning, her head was flooded with thoughts of divorce. It was an increasingly tempting solution—the pressure to relocate overseas would be gone, along with so many other aggravations. Just thinking of it gave

Margaret a profound sense of optimism. But could she pull it off?

She told herself to halt this train of thought. It was not the day to decide the fate of her marriage. Still, the current situation could not continue. Left unchecked, their bitterness would take over their marriage, and they would grow to hate each other.

On her lap, Margaret held Leena, who was lulled by the *Eid* chant rising up within the room: *Allahu Akbar. La ilaha illallah.*

Suddenly Liz appeared behind them. "Happy *Eid*!"

Margaret brightened at the sight of her friend. She set Leena down and embraced Liz, whose scarf was half on and half off. She wore a regular dress, not trying to fool anyone by dressing Arab-style.

Liz tilted her head toward Nadia. "How's it going with the latest addition?"

"She's nice. I like her."

Liz leaned in and whispered, "You should get a grant for working with refugees." She pulled back and laughed.

Margaret smiled weakly. The joke, which had been so funny before, now fell flat. "Actually, Nadia's okay."

Liz raised her eyebrows skeptically. The imam's voice came over the loudspeaker; the prayer was about to begin. Margaret mouthed a good-bye and turned back to her prayer carpet. She gave an affectionate squeeze to Jenin on one side and Leena on the other. Then she closed her eyes and prayed she would be happy again.

After the prayer, the family met up at their Capitol Hill restaurant, where Ahmed's staff had created a special *Eid* spread, featuring roasted lamb over rice.

Last to arrive were Khalid and Alison, who looked hugely pregnant. *"Eid Mubarak,"* she mumbled as she sat down next to Margaret.

Margaret asked, "Is everything okay?"

"Khalid's mad at me because I didn't want to come."

Margaret glanced at Khalid at the opposite end of the table, talking to Ahmed. "It'll be okay," she said lightly. "He'll get over it. Wait till you see the cake."

When it was time, the staff cleared the table and Ahmed brought it out—five layers scented with essence of almond and garnished with lightly roasted almond slices.

Margaret asked. "What kind of cake would you like for the baby shower?"

"This one would be good," Alison said, savoring a forkful.

"When exactly is your due date?"

Alison looked down. "It's actually January."

She leaned in and whispered, "Early January. No one knows."

"Okay." Margaret processed this latest confession. "We'll do the shower earlier." She patted Alison's hand but asked nothing more. Margaret had enough troubles of her own.

The days passed, one after another. After *Eid* came Thanksgiving. That morning, Margaret slid the stuffed turkey into the oven—twenty-two pounds—enough to feed the guest list: Liz's family, Alison and Khalid, and Margaret's parents coming from Whidbey Island.

Liz's family arrived first, then Margaret's parents, Lois and Barry. The sight of her mother, a pecan pie in each hand, brightened Margaret. As she took the green bean casserole from her father, she glanced at the dish.

"They're imitation bacon bits," her mother said.

Last to arrive were Khalid and Alison. By then, Ahmed had taken the turkey out of the oven, and the house filled with its savory scent. Margaret moved cheerfully from the kitchen to the dining room, setting out last-minute utensils. She felt reassured to see her parents and Liz there and was comforted by the sight of Ahmed stirring gravy on the stove.

He announced the meal was ready, and everyone made their way to the table. Spread upon the white tablecloth was the classic

American meal, strictly traditional, without a single Arab dish—not even a Middle Eastern olive. As Margaret lit the candles, everyone sat and waited for Ahmed to bring the turkey.

Lois said, "We should go around the table and say what we're thankful for."

An old family custom. "Okay, Mom," Margaret said. "You start."

Lois glanced toward the kids' table. "I'm thankful to be near my grandchildren."

"Can I be next?" Liz raised her hand. "I'm thankful for Ahmed's apple pie."

Everyone laughed, and Nadia appeared to be listening with great interest. The mother was eyeing the sweet potatoes, and Margaret worried she might take a bite before it was time.

Someone said Alison's name. She rubbed her belly and looked flustered. "I'm thankful for the baby shower Margaret's planning for me."

At last, Ahmed brought out the turkey, garnished with herbs and cherry tomatoes. The guests murmured their approval.

Lois zeroed in on him. "Ahmed, what are you thankful for?"

Still standing, he waved the question away.

Lois pushed on. "It's your turn."

"No, no," he said.

"You must be thankful for something."

He gave a forced smile and returned to the kitchen.

The others, one by one, obediently revealed what they were thankful for. Margaret stared at the browned turkey and wondered about Ahmed's lack of response. She looked toward the kitchen, waiting for him to return. Her mother's voice brought her attention back.

"It's your turn, dear."

Margaret said, "I'm grateful for this home and for—"

"You hate this house." It was Ahmed next to her, his tone flat.

"Ahmed," Liz said. "Let her finish."

Margaret tried again. "I'm grateful for . . ." She paused. "I'm grateful that . . ." She searched for something to say. Anything. "You're all here on my favorite holiday."

Margaret released the breath she had been holding. By her side was Ahmed, slicing the turkey and behaving as though nothing were wrong. Margaret waited for Ahmed to raise his glass and say his customary toast: *Next year, Jerusalem.* But he never did.

Still, the mood was light and festive, just as it should have been. The turkey was moist, the cranberries tart, and the sweet potatoes flavorful. Compliments flowed freely. Ahmed's mother seemed to relish the foods that she had regarded skeptically only minutes before.

For a moment, everything seemed normal, as it was before—before Ahmed's mother moved in, before the pressure to move, before they were always on edge.

Then Margaret's father brought up the topic of George W. Bush.

"I don't understand how he got reelected," he said.

"I feel like moving to Canada," Lois said as she passed the green bean casserole.

Ahmed laughed loudly. It was a bitter laugh that quieted the table.

"Even you, Lois?" he asked. "Even *you* want to move away?" He laughed to himself, leaned toward Lois, and said in a low callous tone, "You're not the only one."

Lois held the green beans suspended above the table. Her smile slowly dropped from her face as she registered what Ahmed had said. "Don't tell me you're moving to the Middle East."

She said it just like that, pulling the topic out of nowhere, the issue that Ahmed and Margaret had backed away from for so long, circling around it, never mentioning it.

No one spoke except Lois, who gave Margaret a perplexed look. "What's going on?"

Liz coughed, and Margaret squeezed the bridge of her nose.

"What?" Lois stared at Ahmed. "You're not moving, are you?"

He didn't answer but turned to Margaret and gave her a blank look, one meant to conceal his feelings yet expose them, as well.

Khalid took the dish from Lois, who looked at Margaret. "Is there something you're not telling me?" Barry put his hand on hers.

"No, Lois," Ahmed said. "Nothing to tell." He looked over at Margaret. "Your daughter's made sure of that."

Margaret stared back at him. "Ahmed, you're not being fair."

"You think you're being fair?" He began to say more but seemed to change his mind.

Margaret turned to her mother. "Mom, we discussed moving but decided against it."

Under his breath, Ahmed said, "*You* decided."

Lois shook her head. "Don't tell me you're moving my grandkids."

A silence came over the table. Ahmed stood, and Margaret gave him a pleading look, imploring to him to sit back down. He strode to the kitchen with his plate, pausing to say, "No worries, Lois. Your grandkids are staying here."

From the kitchen came the sound of his plate dropping into the sink. He disappeared down the hallway, his seat now a glaring gap. The mother, looking bewildered, had a pile of discarded turkey bones next to her plate.

"Uh-oh," Liz said.

Margaret's eyes darted around the table. "Keep eating, everyone. It's nothing." She took a bite of mashed potatoes and told herself to swallow.

"I'll get him." Khalid stood and dropped his

napkin on the table, only to quickly return. "He says he's done eating."

Stunned and unprepared, Margaret had to remind herself to breathe. The most shocking thing was Ahmed violating his own rules: Never do anything to make people uncomfortable. Never make a scene in front of guests. It had been so foolish to put so much energy into this meal, as if she were trying to create a feeling that no longer existed.

Margaret glanced at Alison. Their eyes met, and Alison tilted her head. "Come on, there must be something you like about the Middle East."

Margaret's chest tightened with fresh irritation. "That's not the point." Rising within her was an urge to reach across the table and give Alison a slap.

Liz slipped into Ahmed's empty chair. "It'll be okay." She put her arm around Margaret. "He'll get over it."

They were the same empty words that Margaret had told Alison on *Eid*. Margaret bit her lip in a vain attempt to keep the tears in.

"No, no, don't do that." Liz patted Margaret's shoulder. "It's Thanksgiving."

"I'll be fine." Margaret realized there was work to be done. She stood and began to busy herself with cleaning up. Finally, working briskly, she assembled the final course.

Out of nervousness, Margaret served the pies

too early. Two by two, she laid them out: Lois's pecan pies, her own pumpkin pies, and finally Ahmed's apple pies, garnished with little autumn leaves.

Margaret stared at the leaves, which Ahmed had carefully cut from pastry dough. He was so well-suited for his work, appreciative of both taste and appearance. Why else had the restaurants been successful? It was a surprise even still that he was willing to walk away.

The family sat in the living room taking small bites while Ahmed's absence hung over the room. Margaret asked Jenin to serve coffee while she slipped away to find him sitting in her bedroom armchair, her escape corner. She sat on the bed near him. He looked weary, almost fragile.

Margaret tried to coax some empathy into her heart. "I know you're angry at me."

"I'm not."

"It's time to join our guests," she said.

"Really, they're better off without me." He looked at her, his expression miserable. "I can't take this anymore."

"Take what?"

"I don't want to be here."

Margaret stared back, processing this ever-widening fracture. "You promised me you'd never mention this again."

He didn't reply. What was happening between

them? How would they ever get out of this endless maze of hurt and denial? She got up, took a final look at him, and left.

At the edge of the living room, she stood and stared at her guests, all pretending nothing was wrong. She turned and took the stairs down to the basement playroom. The space, normally a free-for-all of toys and clutter, was now tidy. Of course, Nadia had done it; she had left her positive mark all over the house.

Perhaps because everything was in place, something in the far corner caught Margaret's eye. It was on the map of the world, which she had pinned up years ago. Yet that day something stood out—a black smudge in its center.

She moved closer. Someone—Jenin?—had blackened out the word *Israel*. Whoever had done it had scratched with such zeal that they had put a hole through the map.

Margaret's eyes scanned the map. They landed on a tiny triangle of a country at the bottom of the Persian Gulf, squeezed between Saudi Arabia and Oman. She counted the time zones between it and Seattle. Twelve. Literally on opposite ends of the world.

No way in hell.

Chapter 25

Alison drove out of the Pine View complex, headed to her baby shower. It was a week into the new year, and next to her was her mother, who had flown in from Chicago just to attend the shower. Poised on her knees was a wrapped gift with an oversized ribbon. Later in the spring, both of Alison's parents would fly out after the baby was born and when they both had time off from work.

The baby pressed against Alison's bladder. In the past month, her ankles had swollen, her nipples darkened, her belly button protruded, and her face had grown puffy. She overate and had stopped exercising. Strangest of all, she didn't care.

As they neared the party, Alison's mind filled with worries. How would her mother behave? Would she finally see something good in Khalid's family? Alison hoped the shower wouldn't be like the childbirth classes—something she had looked forward to but turned out to be awful. After dragging Khalid to the first class, it was Alison who grew to dread it. She despised the moments in the dimmed room when the two of them had to lie on the floor alongside other couples practicing relaxation techniques. Somehow the exercises made her mind race, and her heart, too. Alison simply could not relax.

Her mother looked out the car window, commenting on how many homes still had their Christmas lights up. The two of them hadn't shared any meaningful conversation since her mother's arrival. Naturally her mother had asked about Christmas. But what was there to say? A tabletop Christmas tree, a few gifts from her parents. Her mother also posed a few questions about Alison's pregnancy but didn't probe further. Had her mother always been like this? So detached? Couldn't she see something was wrong?

Alison had been waiting for her mother to get there, hoping finally for some understanding, some empathy. Since their telephone conversation during Ramadan, Alison had avoided the topic of her marriage. Now she longed to delve into what was bothering her.

Alison began, "Married life is sort of interesting."

"What do you mean?"

How could she explain? Sometimes she felt connected to Khalid, like when she grabbed his hand and put it on her belly to feel the baby kick. Yet other times their differences cast a shadow, like when he maintained that violence could serve the Palestinian cause, or said he hoped his mother would move in with them, or insisted his future daughter would never date. When he spoke like that, she stared at him, a sudden stranger.

"I've been trying to sort out Khalid from his culture," Alison said. "Some of it's from his religion, some from his family. Some of it's just Khalid."

"Some of what?"

Alison glanced at her mother. "His attitudes, his behavior."

"What behavior?"

"How he wants me to dress more modestly." Alison kept her eyes straight ahead. "How he doesn't want me socializing with his friends. How—"

"Sweetheart," her mother said, "this is what you signed up for."

Alison ignored her mother's words and turned into Margaret's cul-de-sac. Pastel-colored balloons hung on Margaret's front door. Several cars were already there. Alison parked and turned off the engine.

Alison touched her mother's sleeve. "Mom, I need to tell you something." She looked down at her giant belly. "It's about my due date."

"January 12th—right?"

"Yes, right. Well . . . Khalid's mom and sister think it's the end of February."

"Why would you lie about something like this?"

Alison pinched the bridge of her nose. "It was Khalid's idea. Because I got pregnant before we married."

Her mother fluffed the ribbon on the gift. "Not a great reason to marry, if you ask me."

Out of the corner of her eye, Alison glimpsed Margaret in the front window. "That's not why we got married, Mom. I found out after."

"I see. So, what's the point of the lie?"

"Khalid's mother. She's a bit religious. Khalid thinks she'll freak out if she knows."

"Oh, for God's sake." Her mother rolled her eyes. "Are the women going to be wearing that garb on their head today?"

"I don't know, Mom." Alison remembered that Margaret had invited Aisha and Lateefa from the *Qur'an* study group. "Probably some will." Alison hadn't bothered inviting her college friends. After graduation, most everyone scattered off to different cities. Besides, how could she invite friends whom she had practically ignored for the past year?

Her mother got out and smoothed the front of her skirt. They approached the front door, and Margaret welcomed them up to the living room. Khalid's mother and sisters were already there, as well as Margaret's friend Liz.

As they entered the room, Alison's mother mumbled, "*Salaam alaikum.*"

Alison went straight to Khalid's mother and

greeted her warmly—an attempt to show her own mother, *See? They're not so bad.*

After handshakes, the women sat in a circle.

Liz asked, "How are you feeling?"

Alison explained that her fingers were so swollen she had to remove her wedding ring.

Liz looked at her belly. "It won't be long now."

It was true. Alison was huge, larger than she had ever imagined she would be.

Margaret whispered to Alison, "About the due date, I wouldn't worry. The baby will come when she comes."

There was a knock at the door, and Margaret jumped up. Alison recognized the voices, Aisha's murmur of Islamic greetings and that contrived accent of Lateefa's. They reached the living room and made a beeline for Alison.

Aisha embraced her. *"As-salaamu alaikum.* You're looking well, *masha'Allah."* She wore a black abaya, her head wrapped in a matching *shayla;* meanwhile, Lateefa was swathed in glittering fabric.

"Sorry we're late," Lateefa said. "I had to wait for my husband to pick up the boys." She gave a sly smile, lowered her voice, and said, "Soon to be *ex*-husband."

As Aisha and Lateefa added gifts to the pile on the fireplace hearth, Alison's mother stared openly at the two women. It was hard not to.

They were a study in opposites: flamboyant Lateefa, and Aisha, severe in black.

Alison's mother asked them, "How do you know Alison?"

Alison held her breath as Aisha spoke. "Our *Qur'an* study group. *Masha'Allah*, Alison comes regularly."

Alison's mother arched an eyebrow and said nothing.

Margaret invited everyone to help themselves to the food. As the women moved toward the table, Alison whispered to her mother, "Don't worry. I'm not going to convert."

"Then why are you going?"

"Research."

Her mother shot her a look. Apparently this was not acceptable, either. Alison approached the buffet: a spread of finger sandwiches, savory Arab pastries, and in the center, a frosted almond layer cake from Ahmed's restaurant. The cake read BEST WISHES ALISON.

The women ate and chatted politely. Alison steered the conversation away from religion and described her and Khalid's preparations for the baby.

Lateefa complained bitterly that her husband had never helped when her boys were babies. She said to Alison, "You should be happy if your husband helps at all."

Alison nodded but kept it to herself that she

and Khalid spent most of their free time arguing, a new theme each week. Their current disagreement was about whether or not Khalid's mother would babysit. Khalid stipulated that it was the only way for Alison to return to work. After all, his mother had raised seven babies. Alison argued that his mother couldn't read directions or use the telephone.

Margaret stood. "Instead of games, we're doing something different." She picked up a small brown tube. "Henna!"

This part of the shower had slipped Alison's mind. Margaret handed the henna tube to Nadia and said, "Nadia can do your hand, your shoulder, your ankle . . . whatever you want."

Alison could sense her mother next to her shifting in her chair.

Liz pointed at Alison. "You should do your bump."

"I think I'll do my hand."

"Oh no, you have to do your belly," Liz said with mock seriousness. "It's a requirement."

Khalid's mother volunteered to be first. She sat next to Nadia, who squeezed the tube, and just like decorating a cake, she drew a swirly Arab motif on the top of her mother's hand.

Alison whispered to her mother, "You must have done henna before?"

"I think I'll pass."

"Oh come on, Mom."

"It's not my sort of thing."

"Even Khalid's mother did it," Alison said, but her mother shook her head.

Alison was last. She pointed to her hand, but the room broke into a chorus of chanting: "Bel-ly! Bel-ly!"

She wasn't sure why she gave in, perhaps to make up for her mother's refusal to participate. Alison sat and slid her maternity top up, revealing her protruding abdomen.

Nadia knelt in front of Alison's belly. She held up the tube and Alison closed her eyes. There was a cold sensation, and she threw her head back and laughed. "I can't believe I'm doing this!" Out of the corner of her eye, she saw her mother sitting rod-straight, her purse in her lap.

Margaret patted Alison's shoulder. "It's good to have fun now. Your life's going to change soon."

When Nadia finished, Margaret brought out a hand mirror so Alison could properly see the henna swirls radiating off her belly button. Her mother glanced at it and looked away. By then, the other women's henna had dried and was flaking off.

Without warning, Khalid's mother began to clap and sing a traditional chant.

Alison's mother whispered, "What's the song about? The baby?"

Alison paused to listen. "Yes, she's wishing us well. I'm sure you can understand some of the words."

Her mother leaned in. "Their accent is different from ours. It's a village dialect."

By then, everyone was clapping. A drum appeared, and Mona put it under her arm and beat it rhythmically. The others joined in with trills.

Alison's mother said, "I never knew a bunch of Muslim women could be so loud."

Alison looked at her. *There are a lot of things you don't know.*

Margaret pushed back the coffee table. Nadia was up first, her arms raised, flicking her hips. Lateefa was next, dancing as well as any Arab woman. Even Khalid's mother danced to the drumming, and finally, Margaret and Liz, who danced in their own almost-Arab way.

After several rounds of this, they sat, and Alison opened her gifts: minuscule onesies, sleepers and sweaters, and from her mother— little dresses, ridiculously frilly. Alison looked at each piece and tried to picture a baby inside. She couldn't. She simply could not see a baby, nor see herself as a mother.

There were bigger gifts, as well: a swing from Mona, a car seat from Margaret, and a gift certificate from her parents. When the living room was littered with ribbon and paper, Margaret presented one more gift, a large white baby album. Alison turned the pages. *Baby's Bath. Watch Me Grow. Baby's First Steps.* It all seemed so impossibly unreal.

At last, the shower ended. As they were driving away, Alison's mother said, "Such a sensuous dance for such modest women."

"It's a complicated culture, Mom." Alison turned out of the cul-de-sac. "That's why Khalid's so aggravating." She laughed, but her mother did not.

"With this baby," her mother said, "it might get worse." She turned to Alison. "If things get unbearable, you can always come home."

Her mother's words calmed her at first. She could always go home. A vision formed: Alison and her baby, together on an airplane, then back at her parent's home in Chicago. She could start a new life, maybe apply to graduate school out there. Another image: a crib and changing table crammed into Alison's childhood bedroom—and she, a single mother, living like a child back at home. Then came the flush of anger. "Mom, would you stop!"

"I want you to know you can always come home."

"You think you're being helpful, but you're not." Alison gripped the steering wheel and drove home in silence.

The next day, Alison's mother departed. That week, Alison went into labor.

Khalid paced the living room. "Are you sure?"

"The contractions are regular, babe, just like they said."

"It's too soon."

"The midwife said it could be any time now." Another contraction arrived, and Alison closed her eyes and performed her breathing exercises.

Khalid scratched his head. "First babies don't come early."

She waited for the contraction to pass. "Why don't you time it?" She slid the notepad and pencil across the coffee table. He timed the contractions, six minutes apart, then five.

"They're getting stronger," Alison said.

He continued to pace. She could see he was mulling over the situation, perhaps figuring out how to explain it to his family. She bit her lip and wished her mom were still there.

Finally, she said, "Get my bag." She gestured to her small suitcase, ready and waiting.

Outside, Alison clutched Khalid's arm. He opened the car door and helped her in. As they drove to the hospital, he periodically patted her knee. From his cell phone, he called his mother. Alison concentrated on her contractions, marveling at how rock hard her belly became.

At the hospital, Alison was admitted and led to a room. So far, everything was going according to her plan: no complications, a natural birth, and the baby to be delivered by midwife. As Alison's contractions intensified, she focused on the face of the midwife while Khalid faded into the beige walls. The midwife asked Alison if she wanted to sit in the bathtub. Alison agreed, and the midwife led her to the adjoined bathroom and helped her in. As Alison slipped into the water, she glimpsed the henna design on her belly.

The midwife knelt close to Alison and guided her breathing. Between contractions, Alison maintained her zone of focus. She handled each wave of pain and readied herself for the next one. At once, she was seized by a sensation of power. Her body was preparing for childbirth and she was coping, just as she had laid out in her birth plan. With discipline and planning, she could do anything. She could even raise this baby by herself if she had to.

Alison turned to the midwife. "I'm ready to push."

"Are you sure?"

"Yes," Alison said, and they waited through one more contraction. The midwife helped her out of the tub, dried her off, and guided her back to the bed. Khalid was in the room, pacing and chatting breezily in Arabic on his cell phone. Before Alison could arrange herself on the bed, another contraction came. This time, her attention was elsewhere, and the contraction hit her like an ax cleaving through the center of her body. She screamed and thrashed about. The midwife tried to calm her. When the contraction finished, she checked Alison's cervix.

"Oh my. You're ten centimeters. You're ready."

I told you so. The words would not come.

Khalid came to Alison's side and patted her absentmindedly, his phone still at his ear. "It's okay," he said.

Shut up and get off the phone. Again, the words floated in Alison's head.

She was aware of a flurry of activity in the room. At the next contraction, she winced, and the midwife told her to push. Alison tried to follow the directions, but her pushing had none of the precision of her earlier breathing. Her screams were loud and guttural. Each push brought no satisfaction, but rather a sense that her insides were ripping apart.

This went on until the midwife announced that the baby's head was crowning. A renewed surge of strength came over Alison, and finally the baby slid out of her body. Alison opened her eyes. Sunlight filled the room. Was it morning already?

Alison was conscious of only one thing: across the room was her baby, pink and screaming, her arms trembling.

Then the midwife brought her to Alison. "Here's your daughter."

Alison sat up, took the bare infant and held her against her breasts. She drew the baby's face into focus, acquainting herself with the delicate features, so tiny, so striking. The baby was unmistakably Khalid's, the same eyes, chin, and lips. But her coloring was all Alison, shockingly fair with a fuzz of blond hair.

The baby stared back at Alison. They locked eyes until the midwife said, "See if she'll latch on." Alison performed the breast-feeding technique she had learned. The baby gradually began to suckle.

"Excellent," the midwife said.

As the baby nursed, Alison studied her newborn fingers, her nose, the shape of her head. She whispered, "You're the one who's been inside me."

"Have you decided on a name?" the midwife asked.

"Eman," Khalid said from behind Alison's shoulder. The name, which meant *faith,* was the only Arabic name they could agree on from the dozens—hundreds?—of Islamic names they had considered.

"Can I hold her?" Khalid asked.

Alison stroked the baby's head. "She's nursing. Can't you see?"

He leaned in closely. "She looks like my mother."

Annoyed, Alison pulled away. When the baby stopped nursing, he insisted on holding her. The midwife took the baby, bundled her in a receiving blanket, and handed her to Khalid. He looked at her tenderly. Then he raised her head to his and began reciting Arabic in her ear.

He said, "The first words she hears should be

the call to prayer." He shifted the baby to his other arm.

Alison called out, "Be careful!"

"What? She's my daughter."

Later, when Baby Eman was bathed, dressed, and swaddled, Khalid held her in his arms and studied her face. Each time he shifted the baby in his arms, Alison's heart beat faster.

The nurse came in and told Alison it was time for her to take a shower. Alison preferred to keep an eye on Khalid and the baby. "Later," she said.

"Your family's in the waiting room. I think you'll want to clean up now."

Alison closed her eyes. Khalid's family. She yearned to have her Teytey Miriam there to comfort and reassure her. As this was not possible, her focus shifted to her mother, the only other person Alison wanted to see. She allowed the nurse to help her off the bed. Before going into the bathroom, she turned to Khalid. "Put her back in the bassinet." She waited until he did so.

Baby Eman was only six pounds, smaller than average, so Alison planned on a disciplined routine of breastfeeding. But what preoccupied her most was how vulnerable the baby was. Anyone could hold her improperly or drop her. It was utter torture sitting in the hospital bed watching Khalid's relatives pass Eman from one to another. Mona brought her four boys to the hospital and allowed them each to hold the baby, which was agonizing for Alison, who imagined Eman slipping from their arms and onto the tile floor.

The only one who didn't hold the baby was Margaret. Instead, she gave Alison encouraging words: "You're doing a great job nursing" and "I heard you were awesome during labor." Alison wondered why she had been so critical of Margaret before.

By the time the family had left, it was evening. Only Khalid's mother remained, cuddling the baby as if she belonged to her. Alison told Khalid enough was enough; the baby needed to go back in her bassinet. But Khalid shook his head. Eventually Alison convinced him that it was time for another feeding. With the baby back in her arms, she felt a rush of relief. Then Khalid's mother asked to be taken home, and the show was over.

Alone with her baby at last, Alison brought her in close and felt her first moment of peace. The baby latched on—a prickly tingle followed by a pleasing flow. Eman clenched a tiny fist next to her cheek as she nursed.

Chapter 26

The baby's head fell to one side in her car seat. Alison double-checked the straps to make sure they were protecting her undersized body with the right tension. She sat next to Baby Eman in the backseat as Khalid drove up the freeway to their white apartment. Before being discharged from the hospital that morning, Alison had filled out the form for the birth certificate. *Eman Khalid Mansour*. The middle name sounded wrong—too masculine, too weird.

Alison took in the other cars on the freeway and eyed the drivers going about their days. Of course, for Alison there was nothing usual about her day. She looked at her baby and for once in her life felt perfectly blessed. She had a new purpose, one bigger than academics. Alison turned back to the window. The other cars speeding along gave her a panicky feeling. She put a protective hand over her baby, who was wearing a simple sleeper, a practical item that Alison had bought herself. *Newborn,* the tag had read. At the time, the idea of it had been unimaginable.

It was a relief to see the Pine View sign. Khalid carried the suitcase while Alison transferred Eman in the car seat—ever so carefully, so as not to jostle her. Alison and Khalid went up the stairs to their apartment; she stood behind him as he unlocked the door. They had only been gone a day and a half, but it seemed much longer.

Khalid opened the door and greeted some-one—the voice of the reply triggered a sinking feeling inside Alison. She stepped into the apartment and held her breath. To Khalid's mother, she said, "*As'salaam alaikum.*" His mother set down her tea and got up from her place on the couch. Alison attempted a smile as his mother embraced her.

"*Alf mabruuk!*" *A thousand congratulations.* Khalid's mother turned to the baby. "*Masha'Allah.*" She knelt and fiddled with the car seat straps but couldn't figure them out.

Alison unstrapped Eman while Khalid stood by. He took the baby from Alison's arms and handed her to his mother. Alison went to her bedroom and sat on the bed, her coat still on.

Khalid opened the door. "Are you all right?"

"Why's she here?"

"I told you she would come."

"Yes, but so soon?"

"She's my mother. Of course she'll be here."

Tears filled Alison's eyes. She was exhausted and her body was sore. She yearned to crawl in bed and hold Eman. She took off her coat and handed it to Khalid. "Bring me my baby."

Alison undressed and reached for her nursing gown. Her breasts were swollen and her hennaed stomach loose and soft. She got into bed and slid under the covers.

Khalid returned. "I'll bring the baby when my mother's done."

Alison sat up. "What's she doing?"

"Giving the baby a massage."

"What?" Alison strained to get out of bed.

In the living room, Khalid's mother knelt on the floor, leaning over the baby, nude on a towel. She worked her wrinkled hands over Eman's little body, which glistened. His mother looked up, clearly pleased with herself.

Alison pointed. "What's she's using?"

"Olive oil," Khalid said. "She does this for all her grandchildren."

Eman, alert and aware, was not protesting. Yet something seemed wrong with this scene—the baby on the floor, her naked, oily body. Alison's eyes again filled with tears. Without a word, she went to the bedroom and cried quietly into her pillow.

For the next week, Alison breastfed every four hours. As she did so, she stared at Eman's fragile face and couldn't help but envision the various accidents and injuries that could befall a new-born. When Eman slept, Alison checked for her inhale and exhale. At night, she went to the crib and brushed her fingers against the baby, looking for a sign of life. She kept detailed records on diaper changes and feedings. Meanwhile, Khalid had taken the week off; his mother was there, too, sitting on the couch during the day and sleeping in the spare room at night.

The worst interruptions were when Mona and Nadia came. This was a new form of torture. Their visits were always too long, and Mona typically passed the baby to one of her boys, which made Alison cringe.

It was different when Margaret visited. The first time she came, she brought food just for Alison, lasagna and Caesar salad, something familiar and unlike what Khalid's mother prepared. Margaret did not bring her children nor did she sit and drink tea. Instead, she ran a load of laundry and gathered up dirty dishes, all the while chiding Khalid for not doing more. After the place was tidy, the washing machine and dishwasher both running, she sat down and asked to hold the baby. Margaret held her carefully and told Alison what a fantastic job she was doing. Then she handed the baby back and gave Khalid a small lecture.

"Don't let the dishes pile up. You're home to help." Margaret seemed to be enjoying herself. "Do laundry every day. Don't wait until there's nothing for Alison or the baby to wear."

During that first week, Alison and Khalid were able to set aside their differences and focus on Eman. They expressed their love for her in different ways. Khalid was mostly interested in getting the baby's attention through nursery songs in Arabic, while Alison thought about breastfeeding practices and sudden infant death syndrome.

If Alison found herself arguing with Khalid, she stopped. His mother was always nearby. Even when they were alone in their bedroom, their voices carried to the next room. Granted, his mother prepared chicken and mountains of rice, but it seemed unnatural having her there. Besides, seeing his mother every day, every hour made Alison yearn for her grandmother Teytey Miriam, who would have known what Alison needed. She didn't long for Grandma Helen, though, thinking of her latest words: *I know how these Muslims are.*

The next time Margaret came, she asked Khalid to make tea. Then she sat on the couch next to Alison, who was nursing, and inquired about the baby and how Alison was coping. Finally, Margaret asked, "When's Khalid going back to work?"

"In a few days, after the *Eid* holiday."

Margaret sipped her tea. "It's good the mother's here. She can cook and help with the baby."

Alison didn't answer but glanced at Khalid's mother who was praying in the corner.

Margaret kept talking. "You should take a nap when the baby sleeps. Otherwise you'll be exhausted."

When Khalid was in the kitchen, Alison leaned toward Margaret and whispered, "Do you know how long she's staying here?" She eyed his mother.

Margaret laughed. "Just enjoy the help. Soon enough you'll be home all alone."

That was exactly what Alison wanted.

Two days later was *Eid al-Adha*, the second of the Muslim holidays. It seemed the other *Eid* had just occurred, but that had already been two months before. Alison again told Khalid she would skip the *Eid* festivities. She planned on a day alone with her baby while Khalid and his mother attended to family visits and the community *Eid* prayer. But early in the morning of *Eid*, Khalid, freshly showered, woke Alison to tell her that Ahmed and his family were on their way over.

"What?" she asked. "Why?"

"He needs to wish his mother a happy *Eid*."

Alison rolled over. "Can't Ahmed do that in his own house?"

"No." Khalid stood at the closet, selecting a white dress shirt.

Alison sat up. "This is stupid. I just had a baby."

"Get dressed."

"I'm not ready for this."

"I'm sorry." Khalid buttoned his shirt. "They won't stay long."

He left the apartment to buy some pastries. While he was gone, Ahmed and his children came to the door. Alison put on a robe and let them in. Ahmed, who wore a suit and tie, shook her hand and said, *"Eid Mubarak."* His children and Nadia walked in, all dressed up, as well.

Alison stood back as Ahmed approached his mother. Wearing her velvet *thob* reserved for special occasions, she stood formally to receive him. Ahmed leaned over and kissed his mother's hand. Nadia and the children did the same. Alison remembered *Hajja* Zarifa, Khalid's grandmother back in the West Bank, and how the family had greeted her.

Ahmed pressed money into his mother's hand. Then he gave some rolled bills to Alison. "This is for Eman."

"Thank you." Alison took the money. "You didn't need to do that."

The front door opened, and Khalid entered carrying a box from the bakery, which he handed to Alison. "Can you put the water on?" he asked.

She handed Eman to Nadia and went to the kitchen to put the kettle on. Alison returned to see Khalid opening his wallet, full of crisp new money. He handed each child a twenty-dollar bill and two for Jenin and even more to Nadia. Alison's eyes widened. Khalid gave a hundred dollars to his mother, and then the tea kettle whistled. As Alison was measuring the Turkish coffee and thinking about their finances, Khalid came to her and handed her two hundred dollars. She took the new bills and stared at them.

He kissed her cheek. "Happy *Eid*." He pointed to the money. "That's for last *Eid*, too."

"Happy *Eid*," she mumbled, remembering the horrible holiday several months before.

Khalid asked, "Can you help me with these cinnamon rolls?"

"Sure, babe." With care, Alison took out their crystal platter, a wedding gift not yet used. She arranged the rolls on it.

"That looks good." Khalid poured the coffee into tiny cups while Alison assembled them on a tray. It had been a long time since they had been in the kitchen together, speaking kindly to each other. Together they served the coffee and food.

"Bless your hands," Khalid's mother said.

"And your hands, too." Alison sat and took Eman in her lap. Everyone was in good spirits, laughing and talking. Alison relaxed and found herself enjoying the get-together.

Then the men looked at their watches, and everyone stood. Khalid turned to Alison and whispered, "See, I told you they wouldn't stay long."

"What's the rush?" she asked.

"We need to go to Mona's to wish her happy *Eid*. Then we'll all meet up at my brother's— Margaret's expecting us. Then we'll go to the prayer." He kissed her on the cheek.

Alison bit her lip, and her thoughts flashed ahead to the *Eid* prayer. She could wear the beaded *jallabeyah* that Khalid had bought her in Jordan; Eman could wear one of her frilly dresses. Alison was curious to see the community prayer and all the women dressed up for the holiday. Even if she didn't pray, they could at least go as a family. Alison could be with Margaret, Khalid's mother, and his sisters in the women's section.

The family filed out the door, leaving only Khalid. Alison opened her mouth to speak, but Khalid spoke first. "I don't expect you to come."

The baby in her arms, she stepped toward him. "I think I want to go this time."

He frowned. "Don't force yourself to do something you'll complain about later."

"I think I'll go."

"I want to enjoy myself. I don't want you rushing me." Khalid slipped on his jacket and straightened his tie.

She wanted to insist on coming—yet she couldn't bear him to refuse one more time.

"Fine," she said, and a seed of hurt rose up in her.

"I won't get back until tonight." He went to the door. "Probably late."

For all her attempts at self-control, her eyes moistened and she turned away. "If I'm asleep, don't wake me."

●●●

During the next month, Alison gradually regained her energy. She started leaving the house for brief errands, always taking the baby with her, strapped in the car seat. Each week she was able to accomplish more. Between the laundry and dishes, she nursed Eman. As the breast milk flowed in a satisfying surge, Alison would admire her baby's face and pick up something to read. She put aside her books of Arabic literature in favor of manuals on infant care.

Having Khalid's mother in the house turned out to be only mildly annoying, and Nadia helped serve as a buffer. Now that her English classes had ended, Nadia arrived each morning when Ahmed dropped her off on his way to work. She helped her mother prepare meals—but mostly, mother and daughter talked for long periods while passing the baby back and forth. They prayed in the afternoon and watched Arabic television on the satellite channel. They also chatted with Alison, whose colloquial Arabic was improving.

All of this, however, meant Khalid and Alison were rarely alone. When he came home from work, the four of them ate dinner together. As soon as the mint tea was finished, Khalid drove Nadia back. By the time he returned, Alison was in bed, pretending to be asleep.

When Eman was exactly forty days old,

Alison's recovery period was officially over. Khalid's mother packed up her slippers, *thobs*, and prayer carpet. That night after dinner, Khalid drove his mother and Nadia back to Margaret and Ahmed's house. It was Nadia's last week in America before her visa expired and she flew back to Jordan.

The next morning, when Alison woke to the sound of Eman's cries, Khalid's space in the bed was empty—he had already left for work. While she nursed the baby, Alison relished the silence and solitude of the apartment. Khalid's mother had predicted correctly—forty days after giving birth, Alison felt better. She was able to slide into her prepregnancy jeans and a fitted blouse. As the baby slept, she styled her hair and applied makeup. She put her wedding ring back on her finger and looked at herself in the mirror.

That evening, Khalid came home early. "You look good. How do you feel?"

"Like my old self. Well, almost."

They ate a simple dinner of *ful*, salad, and bread while taking turns holding Eman. They cleared the table and did the dishes together. They sat in the living room, alone for the first time since the baby was born. Khalid switched back and forth between CNN and *Al Jazeera*, following Israel's release of Palestinian prisoners, as well as President Bush's push for more US troops in Iraq. No longer transfixed by international news,

Alison turned her attention to Eman, who was starting to smile.

That night, after Alison nursed the baby to sleep and laid her in her crib, she readied herself for bed. As soon as Alison lay down, Khalid was next to her, kissing her neck. She had already put him off several times that week by saying she wasn't ready.

This time, she turned to him and closed her eyes. He kissed her mouth and touched her breasts, tender from nursing. She winced and lay motionless while he was instantly aroused. The smell of baby powder hovered in the air, and her thoughts moved to Eman sleeping a few feet away. Khalid pulled her nightgown over the top of her head and pressed his body against hers. In her mind, she conjured the right image to help herself along. She settled on her usual fantasy, which began with a handsome Arab man in a long, pristine-white *kandura* leading her into a *majlis*, lavishly decorated with floor cushions.

"I've missed you," Khalid said.

She was about to answer, but his cell phone rang. At first, he continued his attempt to rouse her, which was becoming a hopeless endeavor. The ringing kept on, playing a popular Arabic tune. Alison sighed, and he pulled away. "Sorry." He silenced his phone and turned back to her.

Any thread of desire had vanished. Alison reached for her nightgown. "I can't."

He pressed himself against her. "Come on."

She pulled away and slipped her nightgown back on. By then, Khalid had moved to the foot of the bed and was sitting there, sulking. Alison knew by the set of his jaw that he would soon storm out the front door. Finally, he stood, slipped on his jeans and T-shirt, and grabbed his jacket. "You never think about what I want."

He went to the living room. Next came the slam of the front door. The blinds rattled in the window—she was waiting for the sound this time.

At two months of age, Eman's smiles became genuine. For Alison, all else faded into the background, including the housework, her academic aspirations, even Khalid and his family. After Nadia had returned to Jordan, the family visits occurred only on weekends. This suited Alison, as it left the rest of the week to concentrate on Eman, who was growing bigger and more adorable. Alison and Khalid fawned over her, thrilled with each new gesture and expression.

Early on, sex had been the glue that held them together. Now it was Eman who held them in their places, keeping their marriage intact. Alison focused on nursing, diaper changes, and infant safety. As for lovemaking, how could she lie down and relax? There was always a vague mental pressure, a perpetual risk, some unforeseen harm just about to happen.

When Eman was two and a half months old, Alison's own parents came to visit. They stayed at a nearby hotel, and for five days Alison and Khalid wore the happy faces of new parents. Alison's father was a doting grandfather but oblivious to the tension in his daughter's marriage. He and Khalid bonded over news from the Middle East, the two of them gesturing at the television. Meanwhile, the earlier friction between Alison and her mother lingered. Alison longed to confide in her about the growing loneliness in her marriage but knew she could not. She couldn't bear to hear dismissive remarks or more attempts to get her back home.

But on their second day there, when the men were transfixed by *Al Jazeera*, Alison's mother pulled her aside. "How are things? Everything okay?"

Alison smiled. "Everything's fine, Mom. Isn't Eman adorable?"

Another question, about a different marriage, gnawed at her. The following morning when Khalid was at work, she asked her parents about her Teytey Miriam and Grandpa Sam. Alison knew her grandparents' mixed marriage had never been celebrated within the family but eventually accepted. Yet for Alison, the couple always held a certain mystique, these two people who had broken the rules, a Greek Orthodox woman marrying a Muslim man.

"Were they happy?" Alison asked, looking at her father.

"What do you mean?" Her father grimaced at the question. "They were like regular people, like everyone else."

Alison's mother raised her eyebrows, a little smirk playing on her lips.

Alison turned back to her father. "How did they deal with their differences?"

He shrugged. "I don't know. How does anyone deal with differences?"

Her mother interjected, "They bickered constantly."

"Not exactly." Her father glanced at his wife. "Maybe they argued—but they were working it out. They didn't run away from their troubles or sweep them under the carpet."

"But what were they like?" Alison asked. "Together, I mean."

A smile passed over her father's face. "They laughed a lot. They had a good sense of humor— the stories they told."

Alison nodded, mulling this over.

Later, when her mother was settled on the couch, the baby asleep on her lap, her favorite talk show on television, Alison and her father retreated to the back room. He sat on the bed and gestured for Alison to do the same.

"About your grandparents . . ."

Alison sat. "Yes?"

"Don't believe your mother," he said. "Your grandparents were happy. Despite everything, they were good together."

Alison leaned in, soaking up her father's words.

"It's true, they argued," he said, "but they always forgave. Your grandmother sacrificed a lot to be with him—family support, her standing in the community."

"I always imagined they had a big romance."

"They loved each other." Her father looked down, his eyebrows squeezed together. "I don't know if you know this, but before he died, your grandfather started praying again, reading *Qur'an*, that sort of thing. When his eyesight began to go, your grandmother would sit and read his holy book aloud to him." Alison's father looked up, an unfocused gaze in his eyes. "And when he died, she never got over it—the laughter, the bickering, she missed it all."

Alison blinked and wrapped her arms around herself, an unexpected loss filling her chest. If only her Teytey Miriam were there to tell her own stories. If only she could tell Alison what to do.

When May arrived, Alison still had not returned to her work at the International Programs Office. She requested an indefinite leave. That job would barely pay enough for childcare, anyway. What's more, she was not ready to leave Eman in anyone's care.

On the first Saturday, clouds gave way to a bright, spring afternoon. It was Khalid's day off, and his mother was spending the day with them. Alison was at the dining table, writing the week's grocery list. His mother held Eman on her lap and jiggled her until she laughed out loud. Khalid gave his mother an update on Eman's latest milestones: sitting up with support and sleeping through the night.

Alison announced she and Eman were going to the supermarket.

"Why don't you leave her here?" Khalid asked.

Alison looked at the baby in his mother's arms. Eman was staring at her own chubby little hands, having just discovered them. Alison thought for a moment, weighing the risks and the benefits. Granted, it would be faster not to deal with Eman in the store.

"Fine. I just fed her. I won't be gone long."

Outside, the sky was unusually clear and shone a brilliant blue. Alison got in the car and glanced at the empty back seat. It was odd to push the cart through the supermarket alone. When Alison's cart was nearly full, she looked at her watch and thought of Eman. The distant cries of a baby drifted from the other side of the store.

Alison felt the familiar sensation of her breast milk letting down. Because she was unable to nurse, the feeling was sharp, almost painful. She looked down. Two wet patches announced themselves on the front of her shirt. She crossed one arm to hide the wetness and stop the milk flow. With her cart filled with groceries and disposable diapers, she headed for the checkout.

Driving home, she imagined nursing Eman, and her breast milk let down a second time. She arrived, parked, grabbed two bags of groceries and hurried toward Building F, past some neighbors sitting out on the lawn enjoying the warm sun.

She opened the door and sensed at once that no one was there. The apartment was quiet, and Khalid's mother's slippers were by the door. Alison paced the living room and looked out the window at Khalid's parking space—empty. She reached for her cell phone.

"Where are you?"

"At the department store."

"Why?"

"It won't take long."

"Just come home." Alison could hear the faint voice of his mother talking in the background. "Bring Eman home. I need to nurse her." This triggered the beginning of another uncomfortable letdown. "Bring her home now!"

"We're almost done." With that, he hung up.

Alison redialed, and Khalid answered. "Look, I'm almost done."

"Come home now!"

"Stop calling me."

The line clicked, and she tossed the phone on the couch. She sat and crossed her arms. It was an unsettling feeling, being separated from Eman. Alison went to the parking lot to get the rest of the groceries. Arms laden with bags, she kept her eyes on the Pine View sign, expecting to see Khalid pulling in. She passed the sunbathers on the side lawn and carried the bags up the stairs. After she put everything away, she went to the window to check Khalid's parking space. Still empty. She paced and switched the television on and then off. The room appeared cluttered, so she tidied it until the appearance of control was restored. She looked at her watch—only ten minutes had passed. She glanced around the room for something to put away. Anything.

Then she saw it. How had she missed it? Eman's car seat was on the floor behind the dining table. The implication hit her, a renewed rush of anxiety. She picked up her phone. Her fingers were clumsy, and she had trouble dialing. The ringing started and she heard her own breathing. She looked at the car seat, knelt next to it, and touched its strap. The phone rang on and on. Her heart raced. How could he be such an idiot?

He answered.

"That was dumb to take the baby without a car seat!"

Khalid hung up. She hit the redial button again and again.

She dropped the phone. Her thoughts raced, disconnected, jumping from one worry to the next. She frantically twisted her wedding ring on her finger and pictured a slideshow of graphic images: a car crashing, a baby flying toward a windshield, crushed against the dashboard. The images continued until her ring finger was pink and irritated. She left the apartment in her bare feet and ran down the stairs.

The blue sky was vibrant and cloudless. Alison walked back and forth in the parking lot. The air was warm, and sweat formed under her clothing. As she paced, she became aware of her neighbors sitting on the grass. She wondered why Khalid was so careless, so out of touch.

How did she come to be in this situation? Why did she choose him? There was something besides love that had propelled her toward him. From the beginning, he had seduced her with his smooth finesse and his Palestinian saga of suffering. When he had suggested marriage so early on, she had been flattered. *Too* flattered.

Standing there in the parking lot, Alison decided that as soon as the baby was older, she would leave Khalid for good. She would suck it up and move back to her parents. Alison would finally let them help her. She would start her life anew—orderly and predicable and safe. That's what she wanted, what she and her baby needed. None of this craziness!

Khalid's car pulled into the parking lot and drove toward her.

Her eyes narrowed as she looked through the windshield at Khalid and his mother in the front seat. He slowed and parked. Then Alison rushed to the passenger side, where Khalid's mother loosely held Eman on her lap. Alison sucked in her breath and tried to open the door, but it was locked. She looked at Eman and frantically tapped the window. The baby was smiling and wearing a jacket that was all wrong for the weather.

A renewed surge of adrenaline rose in Alison. When the car doors opened, she screamed, "I can't believe this!"

Khalid got out of the car. "She's fine! Nothing happened!"

Alison swung open the passenger door. Her actions were involuntary, driven by panic and anger. She grabbed the baby from Khalid's mother, who looked stunned.

Alison turned to Khalid. "She could've died!" Alison looked at Eman in her arms—crying now, her eyes squeezed shut, tears rolling down her chubby cheeks.

Tears filled Alison's eyes, too. In the back of her mind, she had a dim awareness that her tone was all wrong. She hadn't properly addressed Khalid's mother, from whom she had just snatched the baby.

Khalid moved around the car and came close to Alison's face. He sneered, his upper lip curling. "Stop talking." He led his mother, who seemed to be shaking, toward Building F.

Alison was behind them, Eman in her arms. She shouted at the back of Khalid's head, "Stupid Arab!" The phrase had been preformed, floating in her mind all along. She felt justified.

Khalid and his mother went up the stairs. Alison remained at the curb shouting upward. "You could've killed her!"

Eman was shrieking. Khalid leaned over the railing.

Alison shouted it again. "Stupid Arab!" The phrase hung in the air. She had never called him such a thing before. The shock of it was sharp and disgraceful.

Khalid shot her a look, one she had never seen, a look of pure hate. Then he turned and disappeared with his mother into the apartment.

Alison stumbled toward the grassy patch next to the parking lot. Clutching her screaming baby in both arms, she fell onto her knees into the damp grass. She sat back and cradled the baby. Releasing all self-restraint, Alison cried uncontrollably, giving in to the cocktail of rage and anxiety churning inside her. Meanwhile, the baby was crying, too. Alison unzipped Eman's jacket and pulled it off. With one hand she held Eman. With the other, she wiped her own tears.

In an attempt to soothe herself, she soothed the baby. "It's okay," she whispered. She grew conscious of her neighbors sitting on the grassy slope nearby. They seemed to be whispering to one another. She turned to them and they looked away.

❧ Chapter 27 ❧

The baby's head rested in Zainab's open hand. She admired her face and whispered, "*Masha'Allah.*" *By the grace of God*. Each time she spoke, the baby smiled, kicked, and tensed her arms. Her tiny features evoked memories of Khalid as a baby. They had the same face, but Eman's fair coloring came from her mother.

Khalid was on his phone, his wife was at the supermarket, and the apartment was calm without her there. Zainab's mind wandered to Nadia's upcoming wedding, a rare occasion, where, inshallah, Zainab would have all seven of her children and twenty-six grandchildren around her. She gave a silent thanks to God but felt a deep ache knowing Abed would be absent. She glanced at Khalid, still on the phone.

"What do you think I should give Nadia for a wedding gift?"

He didn't answer. Zainab's thoughts drifted back to Nadia. Her four months in America had gone by quickly. After Ramadan, her daughter had become swept up in her English lessons. Zainab had accomplished so little of what she had planned to teach her. The girl's heart wasn't in it. She was more interested in learning pizza over *zataar* bread, brownies over *ma'amoul*, and roasted turkey rather than *mensef*.

"What about a jewelry box?" Zainab spoke louder this time. "I saw some at that store."

When Khalid finally set the phone down, she repeated her idea.

"The department store isn't far." He looked at his watch. "We can go now."

"What about your wife?" Zainab asked.

"Let's get the gift and be done with it."

"And the baby?"

"Alison just fed her. She'll be fine, *inshallah*."

Zainab slipped on her sandals and grabbed a jacket for the baby.

In the parking lot, Khalid looked in the car. "The car seat." He tapped his foot.

"Give me the baby," Zainab said. "You go back."

He opened the door. "The store's not far."

As they drove away, Zainab held the baby in her lap. "*Bismillah*," she said. The sky was a dazzling blue and the trees, a vivid green. At the store, Khalid pushed the stroller, and Zainab looked for the jewelry boxes. His phone rang, and he spoke in English. He hung up and said, "We have to hurry, *Yama*."

At last, they found them, exactly as Zainab remembered. She picked a wooden box, spacious with velvet lining and pull-out drawers. She imagined it filled with gold jewelry.

"*Yalla*, choose one," Khalid said.

At the cashier, they waited in line and Khalid fidgeted. His phone rang and he abruptly ended the call. In the parking lot, he struggled with the stroller while Zainab held Eman. He cursed and finally folded it. He slipped it in the trunk, and Zainab put the jewelry box in the back seat. She was still closing the door when he pulled out of the parking space. They were halfway home when she remembered to say *bismillah*. She held Eman tightly, as Khalid was driving faster than before.

They turned into the apartment complex, and Zainab exhaled in relief. Khalid parked, and she moved to get out but was stunned to see someone at the car window.

Alison—her face twisted in distress.

Zainab asked Khalid, "What's wrong?"

He ignored her, jumped out of the car, and yelled back and forth with his wife. Zainab could not understand the furious overlap of words, but the tone was hateful. The baby startled, and Alison seized her from Zainab's arms once she pulled the car door open. Her hands, now empty, openly trembled. Alison continued to shout as Zainab got out of the car, and Khalid took Zainab's elbow and led her away. Relieved, she leaned against him as they walked to the building. All the while, Khalid twisted his head around, screaming at his wife, the two of them creating a scene for the neighbors.

On the stairs Zainab told him, "*Khalas*! Don't argue here."

Inside the apartment, Zainab collapsed on the couch and brought a hand to her pounding heart. Khalid paced the room, rattling his car keys and talking to himself.

"What's happening?" she asked.

He didn't answer, only clenched his fists and flared his nostrils. Zainab clicked her tongue, stood, and put a hand on his shoulder. He flinched and pulled away.

At that moment, the front door opened. Alison entered, disheveled and teary-eyed. Khalid stepped forward and reached for the baby. She ignored him and went to the bedroom. He cursed and left, slamming the door behind him. Zainab eased back onto the couch. *Let him calm down,* she told herself. *Let them both calm down.*

Alison came out and looked around. "Did he go?"

"He left." Zainab raised her arms to take Eman.

Alison handed the baby to Zainab and sat down next to her. Covering her face, Alison sobbed. Zainab patted Alison's leg but this had no effect, so she slid closer and put her arm around Alison, who leaned in and placed her head on Zainab's shoulder. Zainab gently recited verses from the Holy *Qur'an* until finally Alison stopped crying and reached for her baby. Zainab pulled out Abed's prayer beads and looked at the door, expecting Khalid to walk in any moment.

Zainab prayed *asr*. She made long supplications seeking patience and guidance. She put away her prayer carpet and suggested calling Khalid.

"No," Alison said.

Zainab went to the kitchen. In the refrigerator were chicken and cauliflower to make *maqluba* that day, Khalid's day off. It wasn't too late. She rolled up her sleeves. "Call Khalid," she told Alison.

"Please, no." Alison got up and went to the back bedroom.

Zainab washed the chicken pieces, rinsed her hands, and grabbed the phone. She went to Alison's bedroom and gave it to her. "I want to talk to Khalid." Alison dialed and handed the phone back. It rang and rang. Khalid didn't pick up.

Zainab prepared the meal and set the table the way Alison did: three plates, a glass for each, spoons, and one fork for Alison. When the food was ready, they ate in silence. Zainab gave the phone to Alison. "One more time." Still, no answer.

It began to turn dark. Zainab prayed *maghrib*. She sat on the couch and stared at the front door.

Eman slept and Alison moved around nervously, rearranging things, making Zainab feel nervous, too. With a sudden realization, she remembered the jewelry box in the back of Khalid's car. If only she hadn't asked about that box.

Zainab turned to Alison. "Call Ahmed."

It was late and Zainab was in her nightgown. She had just completed her final prayer for the day. Now she sat on the couch next to Alison, who was in a daze with the baby on her lap.

There was a knock at the door, and they both jumped. It was Ahmed, his face grim. "*Salaam.*" He entered, sat next to Alison, and patted her shoulder.

"You talked to Khalid?" Zainab asked.

A flicker of unease passed across Ahmed's face.

"What did he say?" Zainab squeezed Abed's prayer beads. "When's he coming home?"

Ahmed's shoulders slumped. "It's not good."

Zainab glanced at Alison, who seemed to be taking it all in. Then Alison spoke, her voice choked up. "He's not coming back, is he?"

Ahmed looked at her. "Not tonight."

Her lower lip trembled. She handed Eman to Ahmed and went to her bedroom.

Ahmed asked, "What happened?"

"It's my fault." Zainab's eyes became teary. "I wanted to get a gift for Nadia—"

"*Yama*, nothing's your fault." He touched her knee. "Start from the beginning."

She told him the story: the jewelry box, the yelling, the neighbors watching.

Ahmed shook his head. "He says he'll never go back to her."

"How is this possible? Just because he took his own baby to the store?"

"You know their problems are deeper than that."

She knew this. And she knew Ahmed's problems with Margaret were deep, too. But did he slam the door and leave when he was upset? No, he didn't.

"You have to talk to him," she said.

"He asked me to pick up his things."

Abed's string of beads was laced between Zainab's fingers. She brought her hand to her cheeks. The beads were cold against her skin. She yearned for Abed.

Ahmed slid next to her and put his arm around her. "It's not your fault."

"I brought the evil eye to this family."

"Don't say that."

"I thought she wasn't right for him."

Ahmed tilted his head. "Well, we all thought that."

That night, Zainab turned back and forth on the mattress. She wondered about the punishment for breaking up the marriage of her own son. From the next room, she heard the baby stir and Alison's sobs starting up again. Zainab lay flat on her back, held Abed's prayer beads, and silently recited a *du'a* for forgiveness. She wanted to pray for Khalid to come back but hesitated. Was her son really meant to be with Alison?

She whispered under her breath, "Allah has decided and whatever He willed, He did."

But was this the will of God? Zainab rolled over, wide awake. Or was this what *she* wanted? Did she know what was best for her son? She had always thought she held the answers for all her children. But look at what happened with Nadia. Mohammed was clearly not the best match. Yet Nadia was to marry him at the end of the summer.

The phone rang and nearly jolted her off the bed. It wasn't even *fajr* yet. Her heart pounded, and she moved through the dark apartment. She bumped into Alison, also reaching for the phone. She handed it to Zainab. "It's for you."

"*Allo?*" When Zainab heard the voice of her brother Waleed calling from Palestine, her throat tightened.

"*Salaam*, Zainab," Waleed said.

"What's wrong?"

"It's Belal." His voice cracked on the name of his son.

Belal. The thin one, who smoked, the same age as Khalid. "What happened?"

"The soldiers took him. They came in the night."

Pressure swelled in Zainab's chest. *"Bismillah."* She brought a hand to her heart.

"And it's my wife." Waleed's words came out in a rush. "Now two of our sons are in prison. She cries all day. She can't sleep. She doesn't cook."

Zainab moved to the couch. *"Miskeenah."* *Poor thing.* "Have you read *Qur'an* over her?"

"Many times."

"Have you taken her to the doctor?"

"We took her to the hospital when she fainted."

Zainab tapped her chin. She thought of Abed. He would know what to say. Her hands reached for his prayer beads. She searched in the pocket of her nightgown. She patted the couch and slid her hand behind the cushions. Panic and dread rushed over her.

"I'm sorry, Waleed." Zainab wiped her eyes. "This is a big problem. It's in God's hands."

The next morning, Zainab awoke sick and heavy-headed. She hadn't slept until after the morning prayer, when she had resolved to put everything into God's hands, just as she had advised her brother. She looked at the time. Almost noon. Her temples pounded, and she strained to get up. Her eyes moved around the apartment, searching for a sign that Khalid had returned. The crumpled tissues from the night before had been cleared, the coffee table tidied, the furniture arranged neatly. And all signs of Khalid—his jacket, shoes, car keys, phone—were gone.

Eman was in her swing, cooing and kicking her feet. Alison was in the kitchen.

"Good morning. Would you like tea?" she asked.

"Thank you." Zainab sat at the table and observed Alison. Her hair was styled and smooth. She wore a fresh, crisp blouse and her eyes were clear and bright, with no sign that she had spent the night crying.

Zainab reached into her pocket for Abed's prayer beads. Still not there.

Alison brought the breakfast to the table. She poured two glasses of tea, exactly the right shade, sweetened precisely and with the correct amount of mint. She had finally learned.

Zainab cradled her glass. "Did Khalid call?"

"No."

That afternoon, Alison was a bundle of energy, moving about, cleaning things that were already clean. Meanwhile, Zainab's stuffy head grew worse. Her thoughts moved between Khalid and her nephew Belal. Her mind jumped to Waleed's wife, who had to be suffering from shock and grief. Zainab combed the apartment for the missing prayer beads, her one small comfort. She paced the house, her symptoms undeniable: headache, sore throat, and body aches.

Zainab knew what she needed—chamomile, like what she'd seen on the side of the road in the cul-de-sac. She got up, slipped on her *thob* and shoes, and announced that she was going for a walk. Lost in her own thoughts, Alison didn't look up. Zainab's knees ached as she descended the stairs. The late afternoon weather was chilly and windy, unlike the sunny warmth of the day before.

She reached the bottom of the stairs and looked around. This was not the cul-de-sac but the parking lot of Khalid's apartment. Being sick must have shaken something loose in her head.

"*Bismillah*," she muttered.

Perhaps she could still find some chamomile. She circled the edge of the parking lot, imagining the infusion she would prepare. In her mind's eye was the perfect sprig of chamomile, its compact yellow flowers and tiny petals. In Ahmed's cul-de-sac, it grew at the side of the road next to mailboxes. But nothing wild grew around Khalid's building, which was surrounded by tree bark and useless shrubs. No chamomile to pluck and set in a teapot.

Zainab walked to the main road, flanked by natural greenery. She turned right, the gravel crunching under her feet. Grasses, dandelions, and bramble grew next to the road. Still no chamomile. Cars whizzed in front of her. She was at an intersection, so she turned and kept walking. Various wildflowers dotted the brush. At the next intersection, a car stopped and waved her across.

At last, she found her chamomile growing in

the gravel. When she knelt to pick it, she noticed it was dirty. A car had driven over it. She kept walking, looking so intently at the side of the road that she accidently bumped into a parked car. At the next intersection, another car slowed and waved her across. It was funny, all these months with the fear of crossing the street. If only she had known the drivers would stop for her.

Then she saw it. A fresh cluster of the healing flower. She knelt, and the herb filled her hand— the scent familiar and reassuring. She inhaled deeply and turned to go back. On each side were houses she didn't remember. After crossing a street, she noticed a gas station, which certainly wasn't there before. She wondered how many intersections she had crossed. Two or three? Cars zipped past. At the next turn, she hurried along, sensing her illness getting worse. Zainab gripped the chamomile with one hand and reached for Abed's absent prayer beads with the other. She circled back to the intersection. Left or right? Nothing looked familiar. She needed to sit, but where?

Finally, she came to a bench and collapsed upon it. Traffic passed in front of her. Tall evergreens rose up all around, towering over her. In one hand she held the chamomile, in the other, her imaginary prayer beads. She felt Abed's presence, and his image flickered in front of her. She looked up the street. Where were her sons? How long would it take them to find her?

A bus pulled up to the curb directly in front of Zainab. It stopped and spewed black fumes. The driver opened the door and looked at her. She shook her head, and the bus drove on.

She glanced at the time, already past *asr* prayer, and carefully laid the chamomile next to her on the bench. She straightened, closed her eyes, and began her prayer in a seated position. Before she knew it, she had completed the prayer and four extra *rak'ah*.

For the next hour, her eyes followed the cars passing in front of her while her mind churned with thoughts. Memories flashed through her head. She recalled falling off the stool, the air forced out of her lungs, and the dizziness afterward. Then came the hospital and the foreign doctor who prodded her abdomen, flashed a light in her eyes, and stitched up her head.

Yes, Margaret had shown guilt. Well, she should have—saying it was none of Zainab's business where her son moved. None of her business! These foreign wives had no sense of reality. Not only Margaret, but Alison, as well. Zainab supposed that Alison had had some kind of nervous collapse the day before. It was no surprise seeing that she had no family around to advise her, to keep her on a straight path.

Zainab sighed, and her mind filled with renewed images from Palestine: Belal, now in prison, and his mother, broken. The poor woman!

Zainab would have a breakdown, too, if her two sons were put in an Israeli prison. She would go to the prison every day and wail at the gates until the soldiers dragged her away or put her in prison, too.

Another bus stopped in front of her. She again shook her head and thought how odd it was that Khalid or Ahmed had not found her yet. Surely they would have noticed her missing by now. If Abed were alive, he would have missed her right away.

No one missed her now. She furrowed her brow and squeezed her imaginary prayer beads. The gap that Abed had left was growing. Each new event, each new conflict, announced that her life was incomplete and would never be right again. Her days were dictated by loneliness and a constant desire to coordinate the future.

Had Abed already been gone and buried for more than a year? It didn't seem possible. And yet Zainab no longer looked for him upon waking, nor did she tremble when she prayed for his soul. The weight that had once been unbearable had now lightened. Of course, the grief would always be there, but—thanks be to God—it was now compact enough to tuck away when needed.

A flurry of wind sent a chill through her body. The trees swayed and rustled. She shivered. Where was Ahmed? He was such a good son, devoted but so unhappy. And where was Khalid?

He was well-meaning but had much to learn.

Another gust swept in, scattering Zainab's chamomile off the bench. She considered getting up and gathering what was left of the herb, but her body would not move. Zainab inhaled and looked up at the outline of trees; she cursed the wind rattling their branches. The sky began to darken, and the wind shot another chill through her. Zainab's lips trembled, and her hands turned cold and clammy. She fidgeted and worried about what would happen to her. Was this a glimpse into her future self—cold, alone, and forgotten?

Zainab had piously followed the pillars of Islam. Yet she was plagued by loneliness, doubts, and a destiny not of her choosing.

By then, the sky was pitch black and the road empty. It was past *maghrib* prayer. She had been gone nearly three hours. She crossed her arms, but without a sweater, her entire body shook. Soon it would be even colder. An icy panic gripped her body—was she to die right there on that bench? She raised her eyes heavenward.

Only God knew her future. She would leave it in His hands. Wasn't that true faith—what she had professed to have all along?

"Allah suffices us and He is the best guardian," Zainab said aloud.

She told herself not to worry. God had protected her so far. He had always been there to hear her prayers. He had kept her healthy and free from disease. He saw everything and understood everything. If she walked to Him, He came running.

Another gust of wind, stronger this time. Zainab closed her eyes and prayed fiercely for patience and perseverance—for herself and her brother's family. She thanked God for her health and that of her children and grandchildren. She did indeed have much to be thankful for.

Next she prayed for Nadia, her marriage, and her future. This prayer sent Zainab again reeling with worry—so much could go wrong. Then Zainab realized: there was no point in dwelling. Nadia's future was in God's hands. As was Khalid's. And Ahmed's. And Baby Eman's. It was all meant to be. She wondered if her life's purpose had been that—orchestrating the lives of her children. And in the end, what did her children do? They grew up and moved away. And now Nadia would do the same.

In that moment, Zainab decided if she were to survive this test, she would have faith. She would stop fighting the future. She vowed not to direct her sons' lives anymore. Or the lives of her daughters. There was no sense going against what was written.

Finally, she said, *"Subhan'Allah." Glory be to God.*

A tap at her shoulder. Which son had finally come to her, Khalid or Ahmed? She drew a breath, gathered herself, and opened her eyes.

Alison.

"*Alhamdulillah*," Alison said and put her arm around Zainab. "I've been driving down every street looking for you."

"*Allahu Akbar*." *God is great.* Zainab stood, and Alison guided her to the car.

Inside, Alison looked at Zainab and repeated, "*Alhamdulillah*."

As they drove, Zainab glanced behind her. The baby, bless her, was strapped into her seat, kicking her feet.

"I have something of yours," Alison said as she reached into her purse and pulled out Abed's string of beads. "I found these." She handed them to Zainab, whose heart quickened as she took the beads into her hands. By the grace of God, she stared down at them, those reassuring amber-colored beads, their tassel long gone.

They had passed through Abed's hands for years, and now they were Zainab's.

❧ Chapter 28 ❧

Margaret drove the minivan to the end of the cul-de-sac. She groaned at the sight of the cars parked in front of her house. The driveway was already occupied by Mona's and Khalid's cars.

"What's wrong, Mommy?" Leena asked from the backseat.

Margaret parked in the street and looked up at her house. "Everything's fine, sweetheart."

The spring weather was bright, luminous, and achingly beautiful. Yet for Margaret, their home remained gloomy. Ahmed was slowly fading from her. Their argument by the fountain still haunted her—her threat, her demand that he never again mention moving overseas.

The week before, Margaret had googled Abu Dhabi out of curiosity. But as soon as images of the city popped up, she recoiled from the screen and snapped the laptop closed.

Now the idea of a separation seeped into Margaret's thoughts. Sometimes, just before drifting off to sleep with Ahmed by her side, Margaret visualized a conversation. She would tell him how sorry she was, sorry she had lied about wanting to go back to university, sorry she had threatened divorce. She would tell him they could now discuss a possible move overseas. No promises. Just a discussion. Each time she rehearsed this scene in her mind, her breathing grew short. She had to switch her thoughts away, only then could she breathe normally again.

It wasn't simply her and Ahmed's marital troubles that cast a dark shadow over their home. There was also the problem of Khalid and Alison. The family had hashed and rehashed this issue, but found no way out of the couple's rift. Yet the latest news eclipsed all of that. In the West Bank, Ahmed's cousin Belal had been arrested and imprisoned; Belal's mother was inconsolable.

"Mommy, come on!"

"Just a minute, Leena." Margaret sat for another moment and stared at the house. It had been a week since Khalid had left Alison. Now, like a dog who had chewed up the furniture, he was finally showing his face again. Margaret still didn't grasp what had happened.

After the incident, Alison had said simply, "I lost it." When she started to explain more, Alison had stopped herself, squeezed her eyes shut, and waved a hand to avert tears.

At the time, Margaret told her, "*Inshallah*, you two will work it out."

She got out of the van and helped Leena down. "Come on, sweetie."

Margaret walked toward the house. Floating in her head was a clear idea of what was going on inside. The mother and Mona were praising Khalid for finally coming to his senses. The mother would have her matchmaking photographs out—those girls from Jordan and Palestine. She would be flashing their too-young faces at Khalid. *Don't lose any more time, my son.*

With these thoughts, Margaret felt a fresh wave of annoyance. She opened the front door and let Leena in. In the entry was Jenin, her arms crossed, irritation stamped on her face. She whispered, "They've been here forever."

"Why don't you take Leena downstairs?" Margaret went up to the kitchen, past the Arabic conversation in the living room. "*Salaam alaikum*," she mumbled. As she passed, she glimpsed the mother and Mona standing over Khalid, who was sitting in the armchair.

Mona was shaking a finger at him. "This is no good."

In the kitchen sat a tray of dirty tea glasses and an Arab coffee pot full of wet grounds. It seemed they had been at it for a while. The mother was talking now, her grating Arabic stretching all the way to the kitchen. Margaret took a seat on a stool and strained to understand.

"What's wrong with you? She's the mother of your daughter! When are you going to wake up?"

The words were coming from the mother. For a change, Margaret understood their Arabic, rather than just random phrases.

"How can you be such a fool?" The mother went on. "I didn't teach you like this."

Next came Mona's voice. "Yes, you are a fool."

Tariq came into the kitchen, and Margaret put a finger on her lips. He began rummaging in the pantry. She grabbed a package of cookies for him. "Take it downstairs."

His eyes lit up. "Really?"

Margaret shooed him away and flipped her attention back to the exchange.

"When are you going to stop acting like a child?" It was Mona's voice, loud and sharp.

Then the mother: "You must go back to her. You must."

Margaret got off the stool, walked to the edge of the dining room, and peeked around the doorway. Khalid sat in the corner cowering like a trapped animal. Mona was next to him, arms crossed, face pinched. Meanwhile, the mother paced, gesturing at Khalid with one hand, prayer beads swinging from the other.

"You left your wife and your baby. *Haraam*!" The mother practically shouted the last word. *Sinful!* "It's been a week. *Khalas*!" *Enough!*

Khalid stared at the cell phone in his hand.

"Leave the phone and listen to me!" the mother yelled.

He set the device on the coffee table and slouched in his chair.

"Yes, your wife made a mistake," the mother said. "She said she was sorry."

He looked up.

"Yes, I know. She told me. It's time to go back."

Khalid said nothing and the mother resumed her pacing. She turned, and at that instant, her eyes caught sight of Margaret, who jerked her head out of sight.

"Margaret!" the mother shouted.

Margaret winced at the sound of her name. She stepped out of the kitchen to find the mother standing there. Her eyes revealed a deep sadness, and Margaret felt bad all over again.

"You!" the mother said. "Talk to him. Maybe he'll listen to you."

Margaret touched her chest and mouthed the word, *"Ana?" Me?* Taking a deep breath, she walked cautiously to the living room. The mother settled herself on the couch, content to be a spectator during this round. Margaret sat across from Khalid and tried to make eye contact.

"I can see you're upset," she said.

He crossed his legs and shook his foot furiously.

"I'm sure what Alison did made you angry," Margaret said. "When is it time to forgive?"

The question hung in the air. Khalid began to play with his cell phone on the table, spinning it to the right, spinning it to the left. He probably drove Alison insane with this.

"It's been a week," Margaret said. "Don't you think you've made your point?"

Refusing to look her in the eye, he said, "I can never go back to her."

"You chose Alison." Margaret picked her words carefully. "You two fell in love. You wanted her to be your wife."

Khalid began to spin his cell phone again. Margaret put her hand over his. "Stop." She gathered herself and said, "She didn't cheat on you, didn't spend all the family money, didn't—"

"She's crazy." Khalid had his own crazed look in the eyes.

"She's stressed out. It happens to new mothers."

"I can never be with someone like that."

"Let's say she's crazy." Margaret gave a shrug. "You wouldn't leave her if she were sick, would you?"

"I can't be with her." He pressed his fingers to both temples to show his pain.

"You're angry." She looked at his face. "You need to calm down so you can think clearly." She waited for him to speak. Then something came to her. "Your anniversary. It's this month."

"So?"

"You love her, don't you?"

He remained silent, his dull expression registering nothing.

"You remember when you first brought Alison here? You two were glued together—totally in love. You need to find that connection again."

He crossed his arms, rolled his eyes, and looked away, suggesting that Margaret was probably crazy herself to say such a stupid thing.

"She's the mother of your daughter," she said, but he remained unmoved. She needed to dig deeper. "Look at Ahmed and me."

He rolled his eyes again, and Margaret had an urge to shove him off his chair. She felt a renewed appreciation for Ahmed, who, in their entire marriage, had never behaved like this.

"You think I don't drive Ahmed crazy sometimes?" There was a crack in her voice. "The point is we accept each other." She searched Khalid's face for some hint of understanding. When she found none, she continued, "There are good times in marriage and there are times that . . ." Her throat was dry, and she couldn't say more.

Mona and the mother remained quiet while Khalid held himself stiffly, refusing to look at Margaret, who said finally, "Don't be so afraid."

He snapped his face toward her, anger flaring in his eyes. "Afraid of what?"

"Admitting you made a mistake?"

At this, Khalid stood up. Mona jumped up and pushed him back in his seat.

Margaret looked at him closely. His expression confirmed both his pride and vulnerability. She searched for something more to say.

"Just keep an open heart," she said.

The phrase was familiar. It was strange that the words came back to her now, almost a year after she heard them in that sunroom in Amman, Jordan, sitting across from Cynthia.

"Khalid, you can't always get your way." How could Margaret make him understand? Marriage was about negotiations, deals, concessions. It was about give and take, meeting halfway, even giving in. But most of all, it was one generous leap into the unknown.

Margaret inhaled and said, "In marriage, you need to compromise for the one you love." She noticed Khalid's face softening, which encouraged her. Maybe her guidance was having an effect. She choked out one last piece of advice. "Sometimes you even have to make sacrifices."

Khalid looked at her strangely. "Why are you crying?"

Margaret waved away his question. She wanted to say more but had run out of words.

He stood. "Some things can't be fixed," he said and headed for the stairs. Mona tried to stop him, but he jerked himself away and disappeared out the front door. His sister and the mother went to the window. As they watched him drive away, they shook their heads and clucked their tongues. They gave Margaret a look of sympathy, then shrugged and retreated down the hallway to the mother's bedroom.

Margaret was left alone. Sighing deeply, she ran a hand through her long hair and wiped the tears from her cheeks. She stared at a sunbeam lying across the new Persian carpet. She didn't know why she had cried.

She got up and stood in the center of the room, which in that moment felt like an alien place. Margaret fixed her eyes on the mother's spot on the couch, then on the coffee cups scattered about, and on the mother's prayer beads. A stale smell of cardamom hung in the air and merged with the cross-stitch pillows, the Palestinian pottery, and the photos of Jerusalem. The items all seemed strangely unfamiliar, even though Margaret had placed them there herself.

In the kitchen, she gazed with new eyes at the walls she had painted and the tiles she had installed. She returned to the living room and looked long and hard at the Persian carpet—too fancy for their home—the pair of lamps she had bought and bricks she had replaced in the hearth. She thought about the years they had spent in that house, her marriage to Ahmed, and the time that had passed.

For the first time Margaret saw the house for what it was—a hodgepodge of isolated attempts at improvement. Each project had been a superficial patch, covering up the multiple defects but ignoring the bigger problems that lay beneath.

❦ Chapter 29 ❧

Alison exited I-5, drove along 45th Street, and crossed University Way, past the Burke Museum of Natural History and Culture on her right and the fraternities and sororities on her left. Her destination was beyond the U Village Shopping Center, the far corner of campus.

The December before, Alison had, without telling anyone—not even Khalid—submitted her application for the University of Washington Middle Eastern Studies Program. A fantasy, a lark, totally pointless—she had thought at the time. Still, she had done it.

But now she had an appointment with family student housing to see a two-bedroom apartment. Alison parked, got out, and approached the office. Inside, Alison told an older woman working there who she was. After checking the files, the woman grabbed a chain rattling with keys. "Please come."

Alison followed her out of the office, down a tree-lined path toward a housing cluster. The three-story apartment buildings ahead were not that different from the suburban Pine View apartments where Alison had lived for more than a year. Still, a tingle rose up her back, a little thrill at the idea of what lie ahead.

Three months earlier, her graduate school acceptance letter had arrived—the week after Khalid had bolted from her life. Like a gift, the letter appeared—a promise of a new life. Alison immediately accepted the offer and, the same day, applied for family housing and on-campus childcare.

"The playground is over there." The woman pointed through trees to a grouping of play-ground equipment. "Do you have kids?"

"A daughter," Alison said. "Almost eight months."

The woman turned to Alison. "Sweet."

"She's at a fun age," Alison said. Then a spark of panic shot up, and she blurted, "I don't know how I'm going to do graduate school with a toddler!"

"People do it all the time." The woman stopped at a building and walked up the stairs. "I'll show you a two-bedroom model. It's already furnished to give an idea of the place." The woman pulled out her keys and stopped before one of the front doors. "Remind me. How many people will be living in the unit?"

"Just me and my daughter."

"You'll have plenty of space then." She unlocked the door and gestured Alison in. "In this model you've got two bedrooms, kitchen, living area, one bath, and a utility closet."

Alison stepped into the center of the living room and slowly turned around. The generic yet cheery display furniture filled the space. She imagined herself studying at the dining room table at night, under the beam of the light fixture, books on Ottoman history and the Arab-Israeli conflict spread out before her, the baby monitor next to her, and Eman sleeping in her room nearby.

Then another image: Eman awake and needing attention, Eman awake and crying. Being a single mother had proven more grueling than expected.

Alison dreaded the long stretch of the week, taking Eman to the doctor alone, making decisions by herself, and the worst part—having no one with whom to experience Eman's milestones, like crawling and sitting up for the first time.

And yet Alison had managed so far. What other choice did she have? She and Eman were plodding along. But this was the easy part. No work or study. What would the next two years look like? Alison still couldn't quite picture how she would shoulder both classes and parenting. Of course, she still had time to change her mind.

After the walk-through, the woman gave Alison information on move-in dates and the children's center, which would provide full-day care for Eman. Alison thanked her, and before driving home, she decided to walk to the hall where her classes would be held.

The walk was invigorating, past sports fields, over a bridge, and into the university grounds. The late summer day was mild, the air fresh. She inhaled and took in the familiar brick buildings washed in warm sunlight. The campus glittered with possibility, and her thoughts raced with images of her future: academia, research, a life of scholarly studies. Somehow this excited her more than anything else had, including travel, marriage, having a child, and even falling in love.

Whenever she looked back, Alison remembered

their fights first. Khalid refusing to listen, she hoarse from yelling, he storming out of the house, and she home alone. Occasionally, a happy time came to mind, and finally those qualities that had drawn her to Khalid: his good looks, his family background, his seductive manner. She had not merely been attracted to him. She had been possessed by him.

Alison reached the hall where she would spend most of her time over the next two years. She looked up at its arches, bricks, and engravings, and she felt suddenly small. How was she going to pull this off?

Later, as Alison drove northward back home, her thoughts turned to the past months, all that had happened, and how people had surprised her. Some of Alison's old college friends, abandoned for Khalid, were now back in her life. Khalid's mother, whom Alison sometimes saw with Khalid, was still surprisingly kind to her, calling Alison *habibti* and patting her hand.

Her own mother had seemed genuinely relieved when Alison announced she would be working on a master's degree in Middle Eastern studies.

"Of course," her mother had replied. "It's meant to be."

Her parents had offered to pay her tuition. Even Grandma Helen offered a financial gift. And with a few student loans and support from Khalid, Alison and Eman would be set for the next two years. Khalid continued to surprise her in small ways, too.

She neared home, and her thoughts jumped ahead to him and the trajectory of their marriage, how they couldn't sustain what they had started. For months after he left, Alison had tried to unravel the question of where things had gone wrong.

Beyond the Pine View sign, the rows of apartment buildings spread before her.

She pulled into her parking space, ascended the stairs, and opened the front door. On the floor sat Khalid, who had left work early that day to cover for Alison. Eman sat across from him, toys spread out between them. Eman was laughing hysterically at some voice Khalid was making. When Alison entered, the two of them looked up.

"Hi," Khalid said. "She's really sitting up by herself now."

"I know." Alison reached down and caressed Eman's chubby cheek. "Did you have fun with *Baba*?"

"She said *baba* so many times," Khalid said, "and she knows her own name."

"How did she do?" Alison asked.

"She was crawling around; I had to watch her every second. She ate half a banana and a bit of rice with yogurt."

Alison collapsed onto the couch.

"How was the apartment?" he asked as he got up from the floor.

"A bit old, but I like the children's center—Montessori."

Khalid sat down next to her. "That's supposed to be good, right?"

"Very good. But it's going to be so hard to leave her there."

"She'll be fine," he said with firm confidence.

She folded her arms across her chest. "Honestly, I'm starting to feel freaked out by the whole thing."

"You'll do it," he said. A calm smile spread over Khalid's handsome face, and Alison experienced a splintering of pain and affection for him. They had never talked about Alison's ugly meltdown outside the apartment building—or any of their past fights. No discussion, no apologies. What brought Khalid around was Ahmed, who served as mediator. And then Eman; he couldn't stay away from his daughter for long. With Ahmed's help, they had agreed upon a parenting schedule and financial arrangements.

"When exactly do you move?" he asked.

"Supposed to be middle of next month. Before fall quarter begins." She spoke in a detached manner despite her burst of tenderness for him. She looked away and then down at Eman, babbling to herself.

Alison blinked. She had a beautiful daughter,

masha'Allah, and she had learned something about herself: her passion for the Middle East was best sated through study and travel—not love. But what about Khalid? What had drawn him to her? Had it been love?

Alison now understood what drove Khalid. Over the past months, the signs from their early relationship shifted into focus: Khalid sleeping over, his sudden proposal, and the lies about Eman's due date. It all pointed to guilt. Guilt over premarital sex.

And what about her? Yes, there had been love, but fear had pushed her headlong into marriage—fear he'd choose another, maybe a Palestinian girl his mother had picked.

Khalid picked up Eman and bounced her on his knee, causing a cascade of giggles. "Are your parents still planning to come out?" he asked.

"I wouldn't be able to move without them."

"As soon as you get your stuff cleared out," he said. "I'll move back in the following weekend. I'm sure Ibrahim and Salim will be happy to be rid of me."

"I don't blame them." She tilted her head. "It'll be better this way—easier when we each have space for Eman."

"*Inshallah*," he answered.

"When are you leaving for Jordan?" she asked.

"In two weeks."

"Your mother must be thrilled."

"She's happy," he said. "But I really want to bring Eman with me. Everyone wants to meet her. There's still time to add her to my ticket."

"I already told you—she's never been away from me for that long." Alison's shoulders dropped. "It will be too hard on her—and you, too. Besides, Jordan's not exactly the safest country for small children."

"I'll keep her safe."

"How?" Alison asked. "I saw Fatma's house, and most cars don't even have seat belts."

"I think I've proven myself," Khalid said. "I can keep her safe."

Alison brought a hand to her forehead. "Have you forgotten I'm still breast-feeding?"

"Maybe you can use that pump thing?"

"You're kidding, right? Pumping for ten days while she's passed around Jordan, exposed to God-knows-what. We've already discussed this!"

"But they really want to see her."

"I don't care!" Alison threw up her hands, exasperated once again. "It's not the time!" She shook her head, freshly confirming to herself that she was never meant to be with Khalid, that she would never go back to him. "Look, maybe one day I'll travel there," she said, "and bring her along. Then everyone can meet her."

Khalid rolled his eyes. "That's crazy."

"Why? Why is that crazy?" When he didn't reply, she said, "I think you'd better go."

"Fine." He got up from the couch and gave Eman one last hug. "See you this weekend, *habibti*." He passed her to Alison and walked to the door. "If she needs anything, let me know."

"Thanks," Alison said without looking up.

With that, he was gone.

❧ Chapter 30 ❧

The rocky hillside was dotted with old Jordanian villas, boxy and randomly placed. A lone minaret rose up to the sky. Margaret was next to Ahmed in the rental car, their children restless in the backseat. They had just arrived at the Amman airport, where no family members had been there to receive them. Ahmed had told them not to come. He said they would meet up at Fatma's, and just like that, he changed the ritual of the Amman airport welcome.

They were headed to the same hotel where they had stayed the summer before. Ahmed had made reservations early this time and had shown Margaret the confirmation in advance. They checked in and made their way through the lobby. She glimpsed the restaurant, the site of their argument about Ahmed's job interview in the UAE. With a shudder, she recalled the disbelief and pain that had stung her that day, almost one year before.

She glanced at Ahmed, who strode by her side. He looked at her and smiled, his mood upbeat, practically exuberant. It had been months—years—since she had seen him this happy—the effects of being around his family, no doubt, and knowing Nadia was finally getting married.

After dropping off the luggage in their room, they drove to Fatma's. Nadia, the cheerful bride-to-be, greeted them at the door. She embraced Margaret. "Auntie Margaret! Welcome!"

Next were formal greetings in the salon, overflowing with visiting family members. Huda and Yasmine had travelled from the West Bank. Mona and her family had arrived earlier from Seattle along with the mother. Fatma circled the room offering tea while Nadia, lovely and talkative, seemed to relish being the focal point of the family's attention. For Margaret, it was strangely pleasing to see all five of Ahmed's sisters in one room.

Then there was Khalid—restless, stubborn, not-knowing-what-to-do-with-himself Khalid. The family had given up advising him and had resigned themselves to his separation from Alison. Now in Fatma's salon, Margaret looked at Khalid and felt a stab of sympathy.

Meanwhile, the mother was finally together with all of her children. She seemed pleased, yet she had a wistful, longing look in her eyes. Perhaps this was because her brother Waleed would not be coming to the wedding. Apparently, he and his wife were unable to celebrate with both of their sons in prison.

Nadia took Margaret's arm and guided her to the back room, where they sat on the floor and talked about the celebrations ahead; first the henna party, then the wedding. Nadia seemed more mature and self-assured than she had just the summer before. She slipped an envelope into Margaret's hand. "Open it."

Margaret took out a card embellished in Arabic script and motifs of Palestinian cross-stitch embroidery. "What is it?"

"My wedding invitation." Nadia explained there would be a surprise at the wedding.

"What is it?" Margaret asked.

"I can't tell you." Nadia laughed, and her expression was that of a young girl again.

The morning of the henna party, the women in the family arranged an outing to the local hair salon. A car was borrowed, a taxi called. The vehicles waited outside for the women to cover them-selves in abayas, *jilbabs*, and scarves. Then the ten of them, from older women to teenaged girls, all squeezed into the two cars. Each had her head covered except Margaret and Jenin.

Margaret braced for one of them to comment on her lack of hijab. Yet none of the women mentioned it. Margaret's bare head was simply no longer the issue that it once was. They did make comments to each other, though. Wedged in the backseat, Mona nudged Huda with her hips and told her she was getting fat.

"It's true," Huda replied. "But I'm not as big as Fatma."

At this, Fatma feigned shock from the front seat and gave Huda an affectionate swat.

When they arrived, Nadia was the recipient of the full bridal treatment—hair plucking, makeup, hairstyling, and henna designs on her hands and feet. She basked in her role, the focus of so much admiring attention. As Margaret waited her turn with the stylist, Fatma approached Yasmine, inspected the crown of her head, and announced that Yasmine's hair was turning white.

With a deadpan expression, Yasmine said, "The occupation is turning it white."

Fatma then pointed to Yasmine's crow's feet. "Is the occupation causing your wrinkles, too?"

"*Khalas*!" Huda said. "Leave Yasmine alone." Huda poked Fatma and reminded her that she was the oldest and most wrinkled among them.

At this, Fatma threw her head back with a howl and winked at Yasmine.

A realization struck Margaret: Ahmed's sisters didn't make brutally blunt comments only to her. They made them to one another. It was their own direct way of interacting.

When it was Margaret's turn, she sat in the chair and stared at herself in the mirror. Under the harsh lighting, she looked older, and her hair— her hair! Totally neglected. And she had worn it the same way for years: long and shapeless.

The stylist asked in English, "How style?"

Margaret took a deep inhale. "Can you cut it?"

The stylist ran her hand through Margaret's long red hair. "How much cut?"

Margaret touched her neck to indicate the desired length. "And add some layers."

It was time for a change.

That evening, Margaret led Jenin and Leena up to Fatma's roof, where the henna party was under-way. The rooftop was fully enclosed within a festive tent, where some women were already dancing. Margaret scanned the scene, and her eyes fell on Nadia sitting on an elevated seat. She wore a glittery gown that revealed her neck and bare shoulders. Margaret approached and complimented her dress and her beauty.

Nadia beamed back. "You look beautiful, too."

Margaret touched her new shorter hair and smiled. Her daughters had joined their cousins, and Margaret settled herself in the corner, content to observe. The young women on the dance floor sported revealing backless and strapless dresses with plunging necklines. With scarves tied around their hips, they danced in front of Nadia to the loud Arabic pop music. It was a women-only celebration and their chance to show off.

After Anysa arrived with her entourage, the celebration began in earnest. Nadia's mother started the time-honored dance for the bride. Clapping and swaying as she danced, she gazed lovingly at Nadia, still seated. Margaret couldn't help but feel an unexpected tug of affection for the mother, who, at long last, seemed to accept this marriage. Granted, it helped that the groom was finally divorced from his first wife.

The first to join the mother was *Hajja* Zarifa—the grandmother to both the bride and the groom. Then, one by one, Nadia's sisters joined them, creating a rotating circle of female joy.

From the dance floor, Mona noticed Margaret and rushed over. "*Yallah!*"

"No, no," Margaret said as Mona tried to pull her into the circle. The trills increased, a call for her to join in, but Margaret held firm. She preferred to watch rather than make a spectacle of herself. Mona finally let go and slithered off in her purple dress and matching heels.

Finally the chants began. Mona played a drum, and the rest of the women sang while looking adoringly at the radiant bride. It seemed every-one—except Margaret—knew the words to these traditional Arabic songs of love and loss, marriage and joy. Naturally the crying started. First, Nadia, then her sisters and mother, and finally all the women were overcome with tears. Margaret viewed this show of emotion and longed to experience the same release.

But she simply didn't feel it. She found herself bringing a finger to her eye, making a display of wiping away a tear that wasn't there.

The next day was the wedding—no vows, which had been completed months before, but a celebration and ritual sendoff.

Margaret, Ahmed, and their children set out in early evening through the congested streets of Amman. The prelude to the festivities was to begin at Fatma's. Ahmed wore a suit and Margaret, a Palestinian *thob*, as instructed by Fatma, who had loaned her the dress. It was the traditional black floor-length caftan with red cross-stitching across the front and down the sides. In the back seat, Jenin also wore a borrowed *thob*, hers a soft beige with red embroidery. It suited her.

Margaret ran a hand over the stitching on her *thob* and touched the three gold bangles on her wrist, the gift from Ahmed's mother so many years ago when Margaret had been newly married herself. She stared at the bangles, and images came flooding back: her first trip to Jordan, the crowded house of Ahmed's family, the eager faces of his sisters, and that moment, so long ago, when the mother gently slid the gold pieces onto Margaret's wrist.

They reached Fatma's house. Inside, male relatives milled about, filling the courtyard. Margaret, Jenin, and Leena were ushered into the salon, where the furniture had been pushed back. The mother, sisters, and nieces swayed slowly as they advanced in a circle around the center of the room. The women, striking a different tone from the night before, wore cheerless faces and traditional *thobs*. They chanted and swayed to the stark sound of a drum.

Amidst this sober ambiance sat Nadia in her classic white gown. She sat poised in an armchair against the wall, her expression stoic. A bride, at last. It wouldn't be long before the groom arrived to bring her to the wedding. These were Nadia's final private moments with her family before she would leave their home for good.

The door opened. Ahmed and Khalid entered, looking striking in their black suits. They approached their sister, now standing, her face newly brightened. The mood lifted as everyone clapped, and someone shrieked a bridal trill.

Khalid took Nadia's hand. The two of them danced, and it was the first time Margaret had seen him happy since his falling out with Alison. It occurred to her how much Alison would have appreciated this trip and this wedding, and how unfortunate it was that she and Eman weren't there.

As Margaret mulled this over, Ahmed stepped in and took Khalid's place. Nadia looked up at her eldest brother with a teary expression of love and gratitude. They danced gracefully while soaking up the approval of those around them. Pride radiated from Ahmed's face, and he looked at Nadia as if she were his own daughter. He said something to her, and she laughed, visibly pleased to have him there.

Family rituals of this sort usually left Margaret feeling detached. But this time she was moved, and she understood why Ahmed's presence at the wedding was so crucial. He really was standing in for their father. In the weeks leading up to this day, Ahmed had spoken with renewed purpose of the importance of representing his late father. Now surrounded by his family, he was finally fulfilling that role.

Without warning, Fatma shouted, "He's here!" In her hand was a white, silky cape, which she slipped over Nadia's head. Through the crowd, Ahmed and Khalid guided the bride out of the room. Margaret rushed out with the others, but by the time she reached the street, the couple's car was pulling away.

At the curb was a bus, its windshield decorated with a fringe of colorful tassels. Ahmed and the children were climbing aboard. He turned and extended his hand to Margaret.

"Come on. It'll be fun."

Margaret took Ahmed's hand and stepped onto the bus, where the rest of the family was already seated and Mona's boys ran up and down the aisle. Margaret wanted to sit with her own kids, but they were with their cousins. Since their arrival in Jordan, her children had gravitated to their Palestinian relatives, interacting easily with them, trying out their Arabic, and enjoying the doting attention of their aunts.

Ahmed had moved to the back of the bus with the men, so Margaret sat alone. She turned to the window, caught her reflection and touched her hair. With her new cut, she looked better—even younger. Why hadn't she made this change sooner?

The bus pulled away, and someone brought out two drums. The atmosphere quickly turned rowdy as Ahmed's mother and sisters danced down the aisle, clapping their hands over their heads. Warming to the celebration, Margaret's own enthusiasm began to grow. For once, the family and all of their commotion didn't overwhelm her. She glanced back and caught Ahmed's eye. He gave her a tender smile, got up, and sat next to her.

For months, she had tried to block out the argument by the fountain, but a vision of it came to her again with Ahmed now seated next to her—the defeated look on his face that night as she blurted out words she never should have said.

Ahmed put his arm around Margaret, squeezed her shoulder, and pulled her closer. His affection didn't lessen her guilt, though. Instead, it stirred a host of regrets—namely, those concerning her rigid decisions and attitude. How did she come to behave in this way? Margaret, not wanting to ruin such a happy moment, pushed away these thoughts and concentrated on the singing and clapping around her.

The wedding was segregated into two ballrooms. The women's party spread out into a mass of guests greeting one another with kisses. Of course, anyone remotely related or vaguely acquainted would be there. At the edge of the dance floor was a small band of musicians playing lutes, drums, and a flute. The party buzzed as wave after wave of women spilled in; just when it seemed it had reached its capacity, a new surge arrived.

Then the room quieted as the music stopped and the lights went out. Everyone turned to the back of the room and stared at the double doors, where a spotlight shone brightly. With all the drama of a stage show, Mohammed and Nadia stepped through—he, elegant in his tuxedo and she, luminous in her white gown. She held his arm and beamed as they strode onto the dance floor.

As the couple twirled under the spotlight, Margaret sat captivated, conjuring up visions of

Alison and Khalid dancing at their wedding the year before. That memory seemed so recent, yet the couple had already had a baby and were separated.

Her eyes followed Nadia and Mohammed, but her thoughts turned to her own marriage, which unlocked new questions: Where would she and Ahmed end up? Would they stay together, their marriage one sad compromise? Or would they finally give in and release each other?

The dance ended, and an absurdly tall layer cake was wheeled in. The eight layers towered over the bride, who brandished a long, curved sword. She slashed at the ceremonial decoy cake, and the guests shrieked. After this show, the couple moved to their raised love seat next to the dance floor, and Aunt Anysa took her place standing before them. The band began playing, and the drumming started up again. Aunt Anysa bellowed out a wedding song, rocking her large body from side to side, her mouth wide open, her song more like a sad wail.

Then the mother stood. The room grew silent, and Margaret's heart quickened. The mother turned to the couple, straightened herself, and began. Her voice, haunting and sorrowful, carried across the room. She gestured gently toward Nadia, then Mohammed, and finally brought her hand to her heart as she sang her wishes to the couple. The act was so direct, so poignant, even

Margaret felt the bittersweet angst in the mother's voice. How painful for her! Her last child was marrying. For the mother, her children were everything. What else did she have?

A flash of insight hit Margaret. It was one of those moments when life's shroud was peeled away, when Margaret could see the truth—the mother lived her life the only way she knew how. For the past year and a half, Margaret had been oblivious to what the older woman had been going through. From the day Ahmed's mother had moved in, Margaret had been overly judgmental, engulfed in her own self-pity.

The mother appeared noticeably older than when her husband had died—as though she had aged ten years. Margaret's eyes scanned the other women, all gripped by the theater of this singing ritual. She hated the segregated arrangement and wished Ahmed were next to her. He had been so happy lately—all because of this trip. She realized, despite the flaws in their marriage, that at least she had someone to share her life with, someone who loved her. The mother had no one; she was alone. Belated compassion filled Margaret's heart as she watched the mother, who, with red-rimmed eyes, reached out to her daughter, symbolically embracing Nadia and Mohammed.

It was then that Margaret's own eyes began to fill until the tears poured down. She cried over the mother—a widow!—while thinking of Nadia and Mohammed, Khalid and Alison, and most of all, Ahmed. Her tears flowed in a great gush, an amazing letting-go, a release of the bitterness that had churned inside her for so long. She wiped her tears and sat stunned.

The meal followed—a simple buffet that looked splendid in Margaret's still-misty eyes. It had been an enormous relief to cry, and she felt refreshed. She was sure that she could now find a way to set things right with Ahmed, to correct her past mistakes, and fix their marriage.

The first moist bite of rice gave Margaret immediate pleasure. She savored it all: the lamb, the *fattoush* salad, the rice pilaf soaking up the yogurt. It was all oddly and amazingly delicious. Beyond the spread of food, placed strategically out of reach, was the actual edible wedding cake, another multitiered creation, covered in real flower blossoms, just as Ahmed liked to do. Was this Nadia's surprise?

After the meal, a row of young women entered the room, their arms linked over one another's shoulders as they made their way to the dance floor. They were Nadia's cousins, all dressed in intricately stitched *thobs*, forming a chain of *dabke* dancers. The dancer in front twirled a white handkerchief high in the air. They reached the dance floor and turned to the guests, who clapped and trilled.

Margaret glanced at the love seat, now empty. Where were the bride and groom?

When the music kicked in, the girls jumped in unison and stomped their feet. They raised their arms and twirled around. The guests were out of their seats and shrieking wildly. What was once simply a folk dance for weddings, the *dabke* had become a defiant show of Palestinian identity.

As the dance went on, it generated a rush of boisterous pride, which rose up in a swell of zeal, so infectious that Margaret's skin tingled.

Suddenly, the attention shifted to the back of the room. Nadia and Mohammed were making a second entrance, dancing and twirling handkerchiefs. Nadia had changed out of her white gown and was wearing a *thob* so completely covered in red cross-stitch, it looked more red than black. At her waist was the embroidered belt that she had stitched in Seattle. She wore a headpiece, too, a sheer scarf with an embroidered headband and a row of silver coins flickering across her forehead, the style of a Palestinian bride of an earlier time. Mohammed wore a black vest, white shirt, and red sash around his middle. They performed a clever choreography of gentle *dabke* steps, moving together and apart and back together, keeping their eyes on each other.

Mohammed gave a loud stomp, and Nadia

sashayed forward and back. As Margaret watched the couple, she opened her mind to the scene around her, the rosy cheeks of her own daughters, the faces of Ahmed's sisters, and the tears in the mother's eyes. How had Margaret, all this time, failed to see the love among these women? She had been clinging to the wrong things, searching for some kind of normalcy that she could never find, nor would ever make her happy.

All at once, the women of the family swarmed up to the couple and created one enormous *dabke* line that snaked around the floor with Nadia leading the way, waving her handkerchief.

And their dance—so exhilarating! As Margaret stood clapping at the edge of the dance floor, the women's faces became illuminated, and the colors of their *thobs* turned vibrant. Margaret trembled with a sudden jolt of tribal pride. She did indeed love this dynamic, over-extended family and all of their generous, emotional ways.

The dancers moved by Margaret, their *thobs* brushing past her. Jenin was dancing, too, her arm locked around her grandmother's shoulders. As the mother danced by, she gave Margaret a gentle smile. In that instant, Margaret found herself slipping into the dance line, wrapping her arms around the mother and Mona, and allowing herself to become swept up in the joy.

Chapter 31

The dance floor pulsed with drumbeats. Near the end of the *dabke* line, Zainab linked arms with her daughters and granddaughters. She breathed in their warmth and glanced at her daughters alongside her, as well as Jenin, and even Margaret. Seized by awe at the sight of their beautiful faces and vibrant *thobs*, Zainab felt a happiness so profound, she felt her body might levitate off the ground.

Then the drumming ended and the *dabke* line fell away, all of the women smiling and out of breath. Her heart beating wildly from the dance, Zainab swayed from side to side and brought a hand to her chest.

The musicians stepped back from their instruments, and everyone drifted off the dance floor, leaving Zainab standing alone, admiring the backs of the women as they moved away. The sight of those embroidered kaftans made her think of Palestine. And then: a flicker of homesickness.

Zainab signed and wandered to a chair off to the side of the room, where she took a seat. As she sat alone, all at once she thought of Abed, then of her future. With her last daughter married, where would she live?

A place in her chest ached, and there in the midst of this delight and festivity, the wound inside awakened. The sorrows of her life trickled up.

Visions of Palestine appeared in her mind—Bethlehem and Jerusalem and her home in the refugee camp. She wondered about the years ahead. Where would she go? Zainab had lived in Jordan and America, but no matter where she was, she couldn't shake Palestine. Lodged in her memory were its curving hillsides and stone walls, its lemon trees and grape leaves, stone homes and ancient mosques. So much had been lost! But most of all, Abed was gone from this world, save for Zainab's lingering memories.

She had no home in Palestine, no son with whom to stay, only daughters living in their husbands' homes and a brother, already caring for their mother. Zainab could visit, of course, but not stay. Stabbed by an unexpected grief, she felt herself close to tears.

From across the room, Nadia smiled at her. But the act of smiling back was impossible. In her red-stitched *thob*, Nadia glided toward her.

"What's wrong, *Yama*?" Her daughter's cheeks glowed pink from dancing.

Zainab's shoulders dropped. "Just feeling happy for you."

Nadia looked back at her from behind the row of coins on her bridal headdress. She squeezed her mother's hand. "Tell me what's wrong."

447

Zainab squeezed back. "I'm missing your father."

"Oh, *Yama*. Me, too. Me, too." Nadia sat down next to Zainab and they remained silent, lost in their own longings until Nadia said, "May God have mercy on his soul. Oh, how I wish he were here." Then she brightened. "But so many people came. It's hard to stay sad with so much family around."

It was true. Everyone was there: Zainab's two sons, her five daughters, twenty-five grand-children—not counting little Eman, of course, back in America with her mother. Even Zainab's brother Waleed had come, along with their mother.

"You're right, *habibti*." Zainab patted Nadia's knee. "You're smart. *Masha'Allah*, and a beautiful bride, too. *Alf mabruuk*." *A thousand congratulations*. "Go enjoy yourself."

"Are you sure?" Nadia asked.

"Yes, *alhamdulillah*. I'm fine."

Nadia floated off, leaving Zainab with the questions that plagued her: Would she ever live in the one place she truly belonged? Or would she only be a visitor, a traveler carrying her homeland around in her heart? She feared she would end up in a substitute country, like so many others—in Jordan or somewhere in the Gulf or—God help her—America.

Through Zainab's mind passed the story of her life, her childhood, her marriage, her seven children, and the places where she had lived. Only then did the meaning of it unfold inside her. The answer was there—dangling like a lemon on a tree. She had never been alone. Despite her woes, God had never abandoned her. He was always at Zainab's side.

Not only God, but her family surrounded her, too, an everlasting constant in her life. She had been hurt in this life, yes, had suffered through loss. Truth be told, she would forever yearn for Palestine and for Abed. Yet she didn't want to live her remaining days wallowing in this ache.

Her life would march forward, but she would never lose her capacity for the love of her family. Zainab thought of Nadia's words, and she decided: no matter where she lived, if her family were near, she would try her best to be content and remember her blessings.

"*Allahu Akbar*," she said to herself. *God is great*.

Zainab became aware of the music rising up and renewed movement on the dance floor. Waddling toward her was Anysa, beads of sweat on her brow.

"*Masha'Allah*, what a beautiful couple," she said. "Our children are joined at last, my sister!" Anysa sat down next to her.

Zainab gave her a nudge. "*Inshallah*, we'll be grandmothers together next year!"

❦ Chapter 32 ❧

By the time Margaret and her family took the wedding bus back to the hotel, it was the early hours of the morning. Margaret's eyes followed Ahmed as he made his way down the aisle, taking care to have a word with each family member. Finally, a touch on Margaret's shoulder, and Ahmed slid into the seat next to her. She opened her mouth and felt a rush of affection so distracting that she forgot what she was going to say.

"Honey," he said. "I have an idea." He took her hand and held it between his, just as he used to. "You know how I'm always saying, 'Next year, Jerusalem'?" His eyes gleamed. "While we're here, I want to go to Palestine and see Jerusalem. Just us and the kids."

She blinked. "Isn't it a bit risky?"

"How long am I supposed to wait?" Ahmed squeezed her hand. "It's been ten years."

A sudden thrill pounded inside her, a sensation she hadn't felt in a long time.

"We can push our flight back a week." He spoke excitedly. "We'll pack tomorrow and leave for the bridge the next morning. We'll stay in a hotel in Bethlehem." As he talked, he transformed into his old spontaneous self, the man Margaret had missed.

She thought for a moment. "And the restaurants? Don't you need to get back?"

He clicked his tongue and flicked his head back.

"Honey, what if they don't let you in?" she asked.

"They'll let me in. I'm traveling with my family. I'm not a young man anymore, not like Khalid." He put an arm around her. "They'll ask me a hundred questions, then let me in."

Margaret's chest filled with an old love for him, a love of more than twenty-one years. How could she possibly say no?

"Okay," she said, "Let's do it."

The next morning in their hotel room, Margaret sat by while Ahmed spoke on the phone making new travel arrangements. They would leave for the border into the West Bank the following day. As Margaret sorted through what to bring, the children became keyed up.

"Do we take an airplane to Palestine?" Leena asked.

"Taxis and buses," Ahmed said.

"Can I go to my village?" Jenin was referring to the village that she was named after.

Margaret looked at Ahmed and back at Jenin. "I don't think we'll have time, sweetheart."

"Will we see the wall?" Jenin asked.

"Can't avoid it," Ahmed said.

Later, they drove to Fatma's to tell the family their plans. Would they tell Ahmed it was a foolish idea? Would the mother expect to come along?

Everyone talked at once. Margaret held her breath. Someone said, "*Fikra kwaisa.*" *Good idea*. Huda, who was traveling that afternoon, said she'd serve them lunch when they arrived in Bethlehem the next day.

Fatma's husband, Abu Ra'id, turned to Margaret. "Ahmed, he's lucky. He still has his ID." Abu Ra'id shook his head. "I tried thirteen times to visit Palestine. The Israelis said no." His eyes became moist. "Thirteen times!"

All that Margaret could say was, "I'm so sorry."

That night after the children had fallen asleep, Margaret lay next to Ahmed and wrapped herself around him. "You're traveling on your American passport, right?"

"I haven't decided yet." He caressed her arm. "If I use my passport and they discover I have residency, I could get into trouble. I don't want to risk losing my ID."

Ahmed had always emphasized that his ID card —his residency in the West Bank—was something to hold on to. He clung to it like he clung to his dream of one day returning to Palestine.

They were quiet for a moment until at last he said, "I'll decide at the border."

They began the winding descent toward the bridge with Abu Ra'id at the wheel and Ahmed next to him drumming the dashboard nervously.

From the backseat, Margaret glanced out the window and squinted at the sweeping view of the valley and the switchbacks etched in the hillsides.

At the Jordanian border, they waited for their passports to be stamped. Then Ahmed ushered them onto a bus, where they sat silently as the seats filled with other passengers. What a contrast to the jubilant ride to the wedding two days before. Finally, the bus lurched forward, and the first Israeli flag appeared. Then another. At last, the bus stopped at a building. Inside, long lines of travelers filled the space. Young soldiers strode by, talking loudly to one another in Hebrew.

Tariq asked, "Are those the Israelis?"

"Yes," Margaret said. "*Shh*."

When it was their turn, she handed four blue passports to the female soldier. Meanwhile, beads of sweat appeared on Ahmed's forehead. "I have a residency ID," he said and handed over the small identification card in an orange plastic cover.

Margaret blinked but kept her face neutral.

The soldier flipped open the cover, revealing an outdated photo of Ahmed. After reviewing their documents, she gestured toward some chairs. "Go wait over there."

The children sat, and Margaret whispered to Ahmed, "What are they doing?"

"Checking my background."

Margaret groaned softly.

After an hour, a male soldier approached and asked for Ahmed. They walked away, and Margaret stared at the empty seat next to her. Regrets began to pile up inside her. Why had they come to Palestine?

She repeatedly ordered Tariq and Leena to sit still until finally Ahmed walked back toward her and sat down. He sighed wearily. "They're almost done."

"What did they ask?"

"The usual questions," he said. " 'What's your purpose in Israel? Where are you staying? Who do you know?' Over and over."

By the time Ahmed and Margaret were called back to the window, they had waited three hours. A female soldier gave Margaret and the children two-week visas, stamped on a separate sheet of paper. To Ahmed she returned his identification card, still in its worn plastic cover.

Soon they were in a taxi, the Israeli border behind them. Driving through the Palestinian countryside, they passed olive groves sloping gently toward them. Arabic music played on the radio, and tassels swayed in the windshield. Squeezed in the backseat with the children, Margaret declared, "We made it!"

Ahmed turned to her and smiled. "I knew we would. Kids, we'll be in Bethlehem shortly."

Margaret leaned forward. "What about Jerusalem? Can we go to Jerusalem?"

"That's the tricky part," he said. "You and the kids can, but I don't have permission to go there on my ID. Maybe we can try, though."

"How? Planning to scale the wall?"

"I can try showing them my passport. Hopefully they won't look inside."

They arrived in Bethlehem. The taxi took them to an old palace that had been converted into a hotel. Most important, it was in walking distance to Aida refugee camp. After they settled into their two rooms, they left on foot for Huda's house. Ahmed hurried down the hill and into the camp, and the children had to run to keep up. They followed him through the narrow winding alleys, past graffiti-covered walls.

"How do you know where you're going?" Tariq asked.

"I grew up here," Ahmed said. "This is my home."

"This is where you lived?" Leena's voice was full of disbelief.

"You'll see my home soon, *habibti*. Aunt Huda lives there now."

Ahmed paused in front of a rusty blue door. "Here it is."

Before they could ring the bell, the door opened. Huda stood there, a smile on her face. She welcomed them into the courtyard, and her children gathered around. Hands were shaken, cheeks kissed. Ahmed's sister Yasmine and her small children were there, too, having traveled from their home in Dheisheh Camp. Yasmine's eyes filled with tears as she embraced her brother.

Seated on cushions in the crowded courtyard, Ahmed laughed and talked with his sisters, who hung on his every word. Margaret realized that this was filling a gap for him, a void that had grown bigger every year he'd lived away from his home. Could he ever be satisfied with a life in Seattle? And yet—could a job in the Gulf fill the empty spaces for him? That wouldn't be his home, either.

Cooking smells wafted to the courtyard from the tiny house. Huda brought out the meal, a steaming platter of rice, fried cauliflower, and chicken—*maqluba*, Ahmed's favorite. After the meal, they drank tea, and the sun crept down until it was no longer visible. Huda sat next to Margaret and gave her an affectionate squeeze.

The next morning over breakfast, Ahmed talked intently with Huda's husband about plans for the day.

Margaret asked, "So, we're not going to Jerusalem?"

"Honey, I have to go." His tone was high-pitched. "What's the point of coming here if we can't go to the Old City?"

"But what about your ID?"

"We'll just try to use our passports at the checkpoint." He shrugged. "I have to try."

"And if they look inside? They'll see you don't have a visa."

"Each year it's worse. Maybe next time we won't be able to see Jerusalem at all."

At that, Huda smiled sadly. "Go see Jerusalem for me."

Margaret exchanged a look with Huda, who explained that she had not been to Jerusalem for years. A fresh wave of compassion arose in Margaret, as she thought of Ahmed's family living in the refugee camp. They lived a harsh life, unable to move from city to city, coping with checkpoints, restrictions, living with so much uncertainty.

Ahmed and Margaret agreed they would go. With their children, they left hurriedly for the hotel, where they caught a taxi to the massive wall covered in graffiti.

As they approached, Ahmed said, "*Bismillah.*"

They walked through a caged metal corridor, across an open space, and into a building, where they took their places in line. Through a high-security turnstile they passed, then a metal detector, and they turned a corner to find more lines.

"The passports," Ahmed said.

Margaret reached into her backpack. Ahead of

them were long lines of Palestinians waiting, documents in hand. When it was their turn, she held them up for the soldier. She spread them out in a fan, five blue passports. She held her breath as the soldier slowly passed his eyes over their family.

He waved them through.

Outside, Margaret sighed deeply, but there was no time to pause. They slipped onto a minibus heading to East Jerusalem, the Arab side of the city. They sat, and Ahmed brought a hand to his chest. "Thank God. What a relief."

The ride was short. When they got out, they walked briskly toward Damascus Gate. Ahmed pointed to the ancient stone wall. "That's the Old City," he said to the children.

"Wait!" Margaret called out. "I need a photo!"

Ahmed and the children turned and posed. She lined up the massive gate inside the view-finder, her family in the foreground. As soon as she snapped the photo, they rushed down the steps and into the gate. They followed Ahmed through the labyrinth of the Old City, admiring the pottery and barrels of spices, and buying trinkets for the children.

At each stop, Ahmed told the vendor the high-points of his life story. It went like this: He was from Aida Camp and studied in America, where he got married. At that point, he would gesture to Margaret, who smiled and nodded. Ahmed explained he had lived in *amrikia* for twenty-four years. He announced it as though it were the most extraordinary of facts.

It occurred to Margaret that Ahmed had been in Seattle for more than half his life. She had secretly admitted to herself months ago that a move to the Middle East had actually been a reasonable suggestion. In truth, Ahmed was part of a larger trend: Arab immigrants who, since 9/11, were disillusioned with the States and hoped to return to the Middle East. But Margaret had been so dead set against it, so sure of herself. This self-righteousness, where had it come from? And yet, over time, Ahmed had dropped his plan just as she had demanded.

In the Muslim Quarter, Ahmed tapped his watch. "It's time to pray." They followed him down a covered alley, past shops selling *Qur'an*s, prayer beads, and plastic *adhan* clocks. The gate leading to the Dome of the Rock was ahead of them, the entrance for believers.

They passed through the gate, stepped into the courtyard, and shielded their eyes from the sun. As they walked down the tree-lined path toward the mosque, Ahmed reached for Margaret's hand and held it. They examined the intricate blue tiles of the mosque and its gold dome from all sides. Margaret snapped photos while Ahmed and the children walked around, heads tilted up, gazing at the calligraphy.

Outside the mosque entrance, older Palestinian women gathered in their traditional *thobs* and white scarves. Margaret couldn't help but think of Ahmed's mother and how she had spoken so fondly of attending Friday prayers in this mosque. That was when she had lived in Bethlehem, when she had gone regularly to Jerusalem— before the wall, before the restrictions.

What a different world this was compared to their life in the cul-de-sac. It was no wonder Ahmed's mother was miserable back there. Homesick and tragically displaced, the mother could never adjust to life in that cul-de-sac, so lifeless and foreign. Of course, the mother knew of no way to live other than her own.

The sun beat down on the worn stones. Ahmed guided Margaret and the children off to a grassy area, where they sat under the shade of a tree. Ahmed, his dark curly hair graying handsomely, reclined on his elbow, picking tufts of grass. "This spot," he said, "is where I used to meet my mother after prayer."

Margaret had always seen their marriage through the prism of their tiny world: the cul-de-sac, the restaurants, their children. But now, sitting near the Dome of the Rock with the walls of the Old City in view, she could envision her and Ahmed's life as part of something bigger.

And she could also envision the country where Ahmed hoped to move. She had finally done her research—in earnest this time. While researching for their current trip to Jordan, a switch had flipped in Margaret's head, and she found herself googling the UAE and reading up on the county. The place wasn't perfect—what country was?—but now she had a visual. When she thought of the UAE, she saw skyscrapers and highways. She saw beaches and deserts and palm trees. She saw luxury hotels and malls. And international schools and villas, too.

Keep an open heart. The words played in her mind. She longed to tell Ahmed what had been on her mind for months. Margaret searched Ahmed's face and started to speak.

At that instant, the *adhan*, the call to prayer, rose from the loudspeakers. Margaret sighed and closed her eyes. The melodic voice of the muezzin floated in the air, alerting worshippers that the prayer was about to begin. Ahmed announced that he and Tariq would pray in the adjacent mosque with the men while Margaret would take the girls into the Dome of the Rock.

Inside, the mosque was cool and cavernous, with tall marble pillars reaching upward. Amidst the hushed calm, they took their place in line, Margaret in the center with Leena and Jenin at her sides.

It was a comfort to pray inside the ancient mosque, embellished with elaborate mosaics and carpets, the third holiest mosque in Islam. With this thought, the turmoil inside Margaret subsided, and when the communal prayer began, she listened to the familiar phrases and murmured her responses. And as she knelt in *sujud*, a renewed sense of faith swept over her. Everything would work out. God willing, she would set things right with Ahmed.

At the end of the prayer, she whispered to the girls, "Make *du'a*." Shifting to English, Margaret held up her palms and made her silent prayer. *Please guide and protect me and my family. Forgive me, God, for all my mistakes.* She opened her eyes to see the other women rising and Leena tugging on her sleeve. Margaret closed her eyes again. *Fill my heart with love and faith. Help me overcome my fear.*

Later, they walked among the alleyways again.

"I know where I want to go now," Ahmed announced. "Come with me." They followed him down one long straight alley, until he said, "This is it."

He stopped at a small dessert shop; its sign read AL JAFFER PASTRIES. They filed into the shop and eyed enormous trays of sticky sweet *kanafe*, *basbousa*, and *baklawa*. They sat at one of the marble tables, and Ahmed said, "Now you get to taste my childhood."

He ordered tea and five servings of *kanafe*. The waiter served them each a flat slab of the bright orange pastry filled with soft cheese, garnished with chopped pistachios and drenched in sweet sticky syrup. They had all eaten a variation of it back in Seattle prepared by Ahmed.

"This," he declared, "is the real thing." He put a bite in his mouth, closed his eyes, and chewed. His face became flushed with the taste of the *kanafe* and nostalgia embedded together.

Margaret gazed at her husband as the gooey sweet cheese rolled over her tongue. Leena climbed up onto Ahmed's lap, and Tariq put his arm around his father.

"This is the best, *Baba*."

Ahmed nodded. "I can never get mine to taste like this back home."

Back home.

It was in this perfect atmosphere of warmth and nostalgia that Margaret felt her pleasure recede. She glanced at the tender faces of her family, and her eyes landed on Ahmed, who was smiling at something Jenin had said. Margaret's spirit flooded with both love and angst. She looked down at her plate of half-eaten *kanafe* and pushed it away. All of the distress she had endured for the sake of staying in Seattle— clinging to her sad house in the cul-de-sac—was now reduced to a realization, a sudden click in her head: she had made a mistake.

A knot formed in her chest, and she had an abrupt urge to escape the pastry shop. She needed to breathe. "We haven't gotten anything for your mother," she told Ahmed. "Why don't you finish up here and I'll find a gift for her."

"Good idea," he said, and they agreed to meet up on the steps outside Damascus Gate.

"See you then." Margaret said good-bye to the kids and turned down the alley. Wandering aimlessly, her mind spun a web of regrets. She drifted through the souk until a shopkeeper enticed her into his pottery shop by asking, "You want something authentic?"

She entered the narrow shop and picked up a stack of hand-painted plates.

"You're my first customer today," the shop-keeper said. "My first! Things are getting worse and worse. Few tourists come to Jerusalem any-more."

Margaret, in a private turmoil of her own, looked down at the plates in her hand without really seeing them.

He went on. "So many problems."

Margaret sighed. "Yes, I know." She selected a decorative plate for the mother. It had a scene of the Old City and the word *Jerusalem* in English. "My husband's Palestinian. I know about the problems here."

He asked where her husband was from, and Margaret told him. She handed him the shekels and wished he would stop talking. As soon as she paid the man and accepted the plastic bag containing the plate, she realized it was a silly gift. Ahmed's mother couldn't read the word *Jerusalem*, and she didn't have a wall of her own on which to hang it.

He said, "Your husband, he is a lucky man."

Margaret looked at him and then away. "He's not."

The shopkeeper rocked back and forth on his heels. "He's a lucky man." He smiled and tilted his head at her. "I can tell these things." His face was that of a friendly uncle, but his words made Margaret angry.

No, she wanted to say. Her husband wasn't lucky—he had a wife who was self-centered and hard-headed. Totally stubborn. Margaret turned to leave but then paused and stood there. Like an image in her viewfinder suddenly brought into focus, the reality of her choices became clear. In that cramped pottery shop, Margaret knew what she needed to tell Ahmed.

She turned out of the shop and hurried toward Damascus Gate. The alley was crowded at that time of the day, and it was already past the appointed meeting time. When the sight of the gate finally came within view, she hurried toward it.

After passing through, she took an enormous breath. The heat of the day had lifted, and the golden light of the late afternoon sun shone on the steps where Ahmed and the children were supposed to be. She climbed halfway up the stairs and turned back to Damascus Gate, scattered with passersby and vegetable sellers. She scanned the faces of the people streaming out of the Old City. Where was her family?

Margaret sat on the one of the steps and stared at the gate. She thought about Ahmed, her life partner—who he was, and who he wasn't. He would never turn away a family member who needed help. He would never opt for a quiet evening when he could have a loud one with his family. He would never spend a weekend on yard work or home repairs. He would never be satisfied with their cul-de-sac life. What had she expected?

Margaret's thoughts jumped to worries. With mounting impatience, she stood up and began to pace. The bag holding the plate, loosely wrapped in newspaper, slipped from her fingers, fell to the steps. The plate shattered.

She had held herself together so far, but now her eyes smarted with tears. What if a soldier had asked to see Ahmed's identification? An ache spread through her body. The sky darkened, and she told herself to breathe.

What if? her mind kept asking. Her thoughts ran ahead, jumping from one fear to the next, finally landing on Ahmed and the children being detained by Israeli soldiers.

Her worries expanded into a physical pain in her heart. Margaret knew that in the past several years, she had not appreciated Ahmed. She had lost sight of his fundamental goodness and had spent too much time imagining a life without him. Now Margaret was sure of one thing: she wanted to be with Ahmed for another twenty years. Another forty, God willing.

The *maghrib* call to prayer sounded, and Margaret found herself trembling. There on the steps she prayed. *Bring Ahmed and the children back safely.* She didn't make her usual weary promises to be a better wife or mother but simply prayed for their return. She continued to wait until the sky was completely dark.

Then Ahmed and the children appeared.

She stood, and he walked toward her, their three exhausted children dragging behind. He raised his handsome eyes and fixed them on her. She felt so much love for him that her eyes filled. At first, there were no words. They just looked at each other. She was struck by his familiar face, the face she had seen every day for twenty-one years.

"I was so worried about you!"

Ahmed explained, "Sorry. I ran into an old friend in the pastry shop. We chatted awhile. Then I took a wrong turn. I don't believe it—I can't find my way around the Old City anymore."

"Let's sit and catch our breath," Margaret said. They all sat and stared at the gate, now flooded with lights. Leena snuggled against her while

Jenin and Tariq talked over each other, explaining to Margaret what they had seen. She decided it was time. Ahmed had taken a leap by making his life in a foreign country. Now she would do the same.

When everyone quieted, she put her hand on his. For a moment, her mouth was dry, and her thoughts were blocked. At last, she said, "I've decided something." She searched his face for some reaction. "Okay, I'll move." When he didn't answer, she added, "I'll move to the Middle East. To the Gulf—wherever you want—well, almost." The words hadn't been so difficult after all, even though it had taken her a year to say them.

Ahmed inhaled, visibly bracing himself. He waited for what seemed like a long time, then shook his head. "Now you decide this?"

"Honey, I've been thinking about it for months—"

"That job?" He stared at her. "Someone took that job last year."

"Maybe there's another job." Unplanned words tumbled out of her mouth. "It wasn't the right time last year. Your mother had just moved in." Margaret stopped. She hadn't planned to mention the mother. The children, who had been listening, began to speak.

Tariq asked, "What are you talking about?"

"Are we moving?" Jenin asked.

Ahmed and Margaret looked at each other,

waiting for the other to answer. Finally, he turned to the children. "We're just talking. Nothing more."

"There must be other jobs," Margaret said.

"You think it's easy to get a job there?"

She shrugged. "I have no idea."

"Well, it's not. I had my chance, and it's gone," Ahmed sounded far away. Then a silence fell between them, and Margaret felt like she had stepped into the wrong conversation.

"I'm sure there are other opportunities, other restaurants."

"It's about contacts," he said and then finally: "We're all tired. Let's go find the bus."

On the ride home, they were all quiet. Ahmed held his mouth in a tight line. Not another word came from him toward Margaret, who looked out the window without seeing anything.

That evening at Huda's house, Margaret played the part of the cheerful visitor, while Ahmed coolly ignored her, not mentioning their earlier conversation. The family asked about every detail of Jerusalem and insisted on pouring over their purchases.

At last, they returned to the hotel. In their adjoined room, Ahmed collapsed onto the bed. "Good night," he said and flicked off the light.

The next morning, she awoke to find Ahmed awake next to her. The room was still dim, but light entered through a gap in the curtains, illuminating their faces.

He turned toward her. "*Sabah al-khair*," he said. *Morning of goodness.*

"*Sabah al-noor*," she replied. *Morning of light.* "Why won't you speak to me?"

"I'm speaking to you now."

"What do you think about what I said?" she asked.

He rolled over and stared at the ceiling. "I shoved that dream away for so long—just like you asked me. It's hard to know what to think." He shook his head. "I'm not even sure where to look for a job now."

"Do you still want to live over there?" she asked.

"I do."

"Well, the timing is better now," she said. "A year ago your father had died, your mother was in mourning. Nadia was staying with us."

"I know, I know." He twisted his mouth in thought, and she kissed him on his forehead and looked at him. The sight of his face in that moment, mulling things over, filled her with certainty. "I'm sure you'll find a way."

"We'll see." Ahmed threw an arm around her and pulled Margaret close.

She added, "A move like this has to be good for everyone. Even your mother."

At this, he laughed and his face relaxed. "Yes, even my mother."

❧ Chapter 33 ❧

One year later

The container was larger than Margaret had expected. It filled the driveway, stretched into the cul-de-sac, and caused a stir among the neighbors. Each of the three J's came to witness its loading and say farewell. They stood at the end of the driveway, one by one, on that cloudless summer day, asking questions about the move.

Liz dropped by, too, to collect the cat and say good-bye. She opened her arms and hugged Margaret hard. "Don't go," she said.

Ahmed's new employer had sent movers to disassemble their furniture and pack their belongings. As they finished up the last items in the living room, Ahmed asked about the shipping route to the Arabian Gulf. Jenin, her hands on her hips, surveyed the empty space. Margaret recognized the look in her daughter's eyes—a reflection on her life spent there. Margaret had made her own such peace; now her thoughts skipped ahead to the destination.

She walked down the hallway. The house, bare and exposed, already felt like it belonged to someone else. Tariq and Leena were temporarily staying with Margaret's parents, and now the rooms filled with unfamiliar echoes. In her bedroom, Margaret paused in the spot where her armchair had stood. She thought of the hours she had spent withdrawn in that corner. She returned to Ahmed and told him, "I better go now."

"Go," he said. "I'll finish here." He kissed her on the cheek.

Margaret kissed him back. "*Salaam.*"

She got into their rental car—her minivan had already been sold. As the house slipped away behind her, her eyes skimmed the cul-de-sac. She drove slowly toward the city, the sky an incredible blue and the trees a rich green. Margaret marveled at the colors, trying to fix them in her mind. At the exit, she pulled out the directions emailed from Alison, who had insisted they meet at a particular café in the U district.

Alison's directions were precise, and Margaret arrived quickly. She parked and sat in her car, stalling. But why? Perhaps because the two of them hadn't spoken for so long. Although she saw Eman frequently, Margaret had lost contact with Alison when she gave up the Pine View apartment and found her own place on campus. Intending to stay in touch, Margaret had gotten swept up with planning a new life and dismantling an old one.

From the outside, the café looked plain and

uninviting. Margaret entered and glanced around the space: brick walls, colorful art posters, and a barista—tattooed and pierced.

At first, Margaret didn't recognize Alison seated in the last booth. A year had passed. Alison's face had rounded, and her trendy haircut had grown out. She waved, and there was a moment when Margaret didn't know whether to hug or shake hands.

Alison stood. Gone were the fitted clothes. She wore loose jeans, flat sandals, and a T-shirt. She hugged Margaret tightly. "I'm so glad you came."

"Me, too." Then Margaret noticed Eman, a rosy-cheeked toddler, clinging to her mother's leg. Margaret gave her a little wave. "Hi Eman."

They sat and Margaret said, *"Masha'Allah,* she's getting big. The last time Khalid brought her by—" Then she stopped. Without thinking, she added, "My God, she looks like him." She turned to Alison. "Sorry."

"It's true." Alison shrugged. "She's a mini-Khalid."

An awkward pause, then relief when their cappuccinos were ready.

Alison tilted her head. "I cannot believe you're moving."

"We fly out this weekend."

Alison leaned forward. "I remember the advice you gave me. Never give up anything you can't live without."

Margaret winced. "That was terrible advice."

"But it makes sense."

"People change." Margaret ran a hand through her hair. She had kept the short cut from her trip to Jordan the summer before. "Relationships evolve. We're lucky if we just keep up."

"Well, I obviously couldn't keep up." Alison leaned in. "But you sure did. I didn't see it at first, but I do now—how you manage to make everything work."

Margaret blinked. "So, what about you and Khalid?"

"We're talking at least. Whenever he drops off Eman, we usually have a chat. Sometimes even about politics."

"That's great."

"Our divorce is final next month."

"I'm sorry," Margaret said.

Alison's eyes turned misty, and Margaret wondered if she was still in love with him. Then Alison inhaled and gathered herself. "You know, I'm back to the U."

"I know. Graduate school. We're all proud of you."

They ordered sandwiches, and as they waited for the food, Margaret talked about Ahmed's new job in the Gulf, how they had sold two of the restaurants but kept the third, and how Mona and her family would live in their house.

Alison cradled Eman, who had crawled up into

her lap. "That must be hard, letting them live in your house."

"I never liked that house. Besides, they need the space."

Eman had fallen asleep, and Alison gently laid her on the bench next to her and turned back to Margaret. "What are you going to do over there?"

Margaret took a deep breath. "Something with my photography. Take some classes, get better, maybe start a business."

Their food arrived, and Alison asked, "How's Zainab?"

"She's fine. At least the last time I saw her."

"She's in the West Bank, right? That's why you're in such a good mood?"

Margaret feigned a look of shock and explained, "Nadia's about to have her baby."

"Why do they have babies so soon?"

"You should talk."

Alison laughed, and then her expression changed. "What about Cousin Belal?"

"Still in prison."

Alison clicked her tongue and frowned.

They finished their sandwiches and ordered more coffee. For the next hour, they discussed Alison's studies and Margaret's move. She explained her growing excitement—similar to how she felt just before her first baby or opening the restaurant.

Alison said, "Zainab must be happy."

"She'll spend summers in Seattle with Khalid and Mona, a few months with her daughters in Jordan and Palestine, and the rest of the year with us." Margaret took the last sip of coffee from her cup. "Of course, she thinks we're moving because of her prayers."

"You never know."

Their plates were cleared. Alison leaned forward, looking into Margaret's eyes. "We should stay in touch." Then her voice turned gentler, as if she were about to confide something. "I have a question for you."

"Just ask."

"What do you think if . . . This may sound odd. What if I visited you over there? Would that be strange?"

"No, it wouldn't be." Margaret smiled at the thought. "I would love it, actually." She reached out to Alison, this young woman who now somehow felt more like a friend than an ex-sister-in-law, and touched her hand.

"I want you to see our new home." As Margaret said the words, a completely renewed idea of home sprang up in her mind, and a warmth radiated through her—a glow of anticipation so bright, the intensity of it thrilled her.

Acknowledgments

My sincere gratitude to the following:

My Dubai writers group, for their friendship, encouragement, and criticism. Special thanks to: Eileen Bucknall, Kirsten Decker, Susan Dibden, April Hardy, Linda MacConnell, Mary Olson, Tej Rae, Zvezdana Rashkovich, Sharon Shepherd, Carrie Serhan, Sue Tatrallyay, and Karen Young.

Friends and readers along the way: Rima Aburashed and Berna Ramey, for their insightful feedback. Andrea Braun Albalawi, Bharti Kirchner, Christine Mason, and the Marina Book Club of Dubai, for reading early drafts of the novel. Randa Jarrar, for her critique of the opening chapters. Karalynn Ott and Michele Whitehead, for their astute edits.

My writing instructor, Russell Rowland, for his thoughtful criticism on various drafts.

The Pacific Northwest Writers Association and *The Writer* magazine, for recognizing my work.

Beth Mahmoud Howell and Solimar Miller, \ for their friendship, laughter, and shared stories. My Tuesday Night Book Club, with whom I've been reading, talking, eating, and traveling for the past twelve years.

My agent Priya Doraswamy, for her unwavering

confidence and perseverance. My editor Chelsey Emmelhainz, for her wise edits and passion for my book.

My husband's family, for their hospitality, humor, and grace.

My own family: My father, for his belief in me. My mother, for passing on her profound love of books. Zayd, Leila, and Zak, for their joyful optimism.

And finally Sami, for his feedback, love, and endless support.

Center Point Large Print
600 Brooks Road / PO Box 1
Thorndike, ME 04986-0001 USA

(207) 568-3717

US & Canada:
1 800 929-9108
www.centerpointlargeprint.com